THE HEIR'S BARGAIN

ALSO BY NEENA LASKOWSKI

OF FIRE AND LIES

The Heir's Bargain: Fynn's Story (prequel)

The King's Weapon, book 1

The Crown's Shadow, book 2

The Throne's Undoing, book 3

The Kingdom's Reckoning, book 4

OTHER BOOKS

Between Blades and Vows

First Edition published May 2024

Published by Neena Laskowski

Map Design and internal illustrations © Neena Laskowski

Cover Design © 2024 Moon Press

https://moonpress.co/

Identifiers:

ISBN: 979-8-9876368-4-8 (paperback)

ISBN: 979-8-9876368-5-5 (eBook)

THE HEIR'S BARGAIN

NEENA LASKOWSKI

OF FIRE AND LIES

BOOK 1.5

& to the hopeless romantics and the dreamers.
May you never stop believing that happy endings exist.

THE SEVEN KINGDOMS OF VANERIA
THE MIST
THE WHISPERING SPRINGS
PONTIA
THE RED SEA
BORGANI
TWIN
THE THREE LADIES
TETRIA
THE QUEEN'S CROWN

THE GLACIERS
RIVER OF ICE
RAGOLO
THE FROZEN LAKE
KADIA
THE NORTHERN SEA
LUCIAN R.
ALDERIAN MTNS
HIGH R.
TROJIAN MTNS
LAKE OF TEARS
ARDENTOL

CONTENT WARNINGS

The Heir's Bargain includes elements that may not be suitable for all readers, such as references to alcohol consumption, mature language, explicit sexual content, death of a parent (off-page), grief, and violence.

If any of these topics are harmful to you, please proceed with care.

PRONUNCIATION GUIDE

Please note: these are fictional characters and places. The following pronunciations are simply the way the author pronounces them. However, if you, the reader, have a different way of pronouncing the names, please do so.

<u>*People*</u>
Alysinth - al-I-sinth
Danisinia - *dan-i-sin-EE-uh*
Esmeray - *es-mer-ay*
Fynneares - *FIN-near-is*
Everly - *ev-ER-ly*
Ferrios - *fair-EE-os*
Graeson - *grey-sin*
Jorian - *jor-EE-in*
Kentos - *ken-TOS*
Menides - *men-I-dees*
Moris - *MOR-is*
Lysanthia - *lis-an-THI-uh*
Nadarean - *nuh-dare-EE-in*

Rosalina - *ro-zuh-LEEN-uh*
Sabina - *sa-BEE-na*
Sorinia - *sor-in-EE-uh*
Sylvia - *sil-VEE-uh*
Terin - *TARE-rin*
Theenah - *THEEN-uh*
Pontanius - *pon-TAN-EE-us*
Yelsania - yel-zan-I-uh

<u>*Kingdoms*</u>
Ardentol - *ARE-den-tall*
Borgania - *bor-GAN-EE-uh*
Frenzia - *Frenz-EE-uh*
Kadia - *Cade-EE-uh*
Pontia - *Pont-EE-uh*
Ragolo - *ra-GOL-o*
Tetria - *te-TRI-uh*

Before there was tragedy, there was the bargain. . .

PROLOGUE
DANI

"You're a real sadist, Ferrios, you know that?"

I slowed down and peered over my shoulder, my eyes locking on the boys trailing behind me as we sprinted through the fields of lavender.

Fynn smirked as he and Graeson matched pace, Terin trailing only a few steps behind. As Fynn ran into the wind, his chestnut brown hair was pushed back, revealing a sun-kissed forehead speckled with sweat. Golden brown eyes sparkled in the sun, lit with mischief and delight.

Amusement twisted the right corner of my mouth as I looked from the prince to his twin to Graeson. Their faces were flushed pink with annoyance and exhaustion. Yet, all the same, they bore wide, unfettered smiles that mirrored mine.

Behind my three best friends, the lilacs crawling up the castle walls were a purple stain upon the gray stone, and the guards were mere specks. In our wake, patches of lavender were flattened from our careless footsteps as we traipsed through the fields.

"If you boys can't keep up, that's your fault!" Before I turned around, I added with a wide grin, "And that's Sergeant Ferrios to you!"

Then I was off, my arms pumping faster. The cool spring breeze swept across the lavender and brushed across my cheeks as I bounded forward. My head tipped back as laughter poured from my throat, the sun spilling onto my face and warming my skin.

Sergeant might not have been as prestigious a title as major or general, but it was my first real promotion. Unlike my previous position as team leader, which didn't require a rank change, the rank of sergeant gave me my first sparkling metal to pin on my uniform.

When my battalion's major pinned the new insignia on my lapel, I ignored the pointed stares and skittering murmurs. Unlike Fynn, I didn't need to read my comrades' minds to know what they thought of my promotion. It should have taken two years to reach sergeant, but I had achieved it in one, and I was damn proud of that.

Even if my ears rang as the whispers swam through the crowd.

Perhaps that was why I had opted to celebrate with my best friends rather than my squad. And perhaps it was because the four of us—Terin, Graeson, Fynn, and myself—had seen each other less and less these days. With our growing responsibilities, there was less time to run through the castle halls or the fields like we used to as children. But right now, for one moment, we could all ignore the responsibilities of our kingdom, our positions within it, and the whispers that spread like wildfire.

"Ha! If we're suddenly using titles," Fynn called after me, stirring me from my thoughts, "please address me as Your Highness."

"In your dreams, Fynneares!" I shouted.

"Terin can arrange for that, can't you, Ter?"

Heat flushed my cheeks. If only Fynn knew what consumed my dreams these days.

"Don't bring me into this!" Terin coughed out.

"Only a couple of hours as sergeant, yet it's already gotten to her head," Graeson said, his eye roll almost audible in his tone.

I looked back over my shoulder and imagined throwing daggers at him.

Graeson—as if he knew what I was thinking—cocked a brow as if daring me to try. His ragged black hair shifted as he ran, revealing the jagged scar that ran across the left side of his face.

Scoffing, I rolled my eyes and ran faster.

The top of the hill was quickly approaching, and I could taste the freedom waiting on the other side. My fingers flew over the polished silver buttons of my freshly pressed cotton blouse.

"Can you imagine how she'll act when she gets promoted to captain?" Fynn asked, his voice cutting through the wind. "She'll be absolutely vexing."

I huffed, spinning around on my heel as I jogged backward and up the hill. My shirt hung open, flapping in the air and revealing the black training bodice beneath it. "Captain? Try general."

Before they could respond, I turned around and flew down the hill, their boots pounding the ground behind me. I tugged at the silk ribbon holding my hair and let the wind run through the tight curls.

This was what I had needed, what I had been missing for the past few months after being knee-deep in training.

Freedom, carelessness, reprieve.

At the bottom of the hill, I ripped off the laces and tossed the worn leather shoes that had finally stopped giving me blisters. I unbuttoned my trousers, a smile spreading across my face as I took in the sight before me. Brilliant marigolds and rich violet geraniums surrounded half of the lake. On the closest side, a small dock extended from the shore, its boards worn and bleached by the sun. Small ripples broke up the otherwise smooth surface.

As I stepped out of my trousers, Fynn slid down the hill. He dragged his heels in the wet grass, spraying mud across my bare feet as he stopped in front of me.

My hands froze as his gaze met mine and then dipped down to my legs while I stood in nothing but my undergarments and the unbuttoned shirt.

Indifference soaked Fynn's face as he quickly returned his gaze to mine. Chuckling, he wiped his forehead with the back of his hand.

"Aren't we too old for this?" Terin asked as he joined the rest of us. "The spring equinox only just passed. The water is going to be freezing."

Fynn and Graeson looked out toward the water and then back at each other as if they, too, were questioning this choice.

I propped a hand on my hip and turned my attention to Fynn. "What say you, Fynn? Is the water too cold for the prestigious prince of Pontia?"

Fynn scoffed. "Don't get too cocky just yet, Sergeant Ferrios."

My gaze scanned over him, assessing him. "Is that a challenge?"

"Your Highness," Fynn corrected.

I waved a hand in the air. "No need for such formalities. Sergeant is perfectly fine," I said with a wink.

His lips parted. But before he could respond, I ran straight for the water, sparing only a single glance back.

With quick precision, Fynn unbuttoned his white cotton shirt.

I snapped my attention forward, my breathing quickening.

With each step, I reinforced the mental shields I had spent the past decade perfecting. Fynn might have been one of my closest friends, but even friends kept secrets from each other. And some things were better left unsaid.

The thin layer of ice from the winter had melted a few weeks ago, yet the cold water nipped at my toes as I bounded into the lake. Water splashed up my calves, sending shivers up my body and cooling the unwelcome heat that seared my cheeks as Fynn's shirt fell to the ground with a soft thud behind me.

Feet pounded against the wet sand, but I didn't look back. I didn't give him the chance to catch up to me.

I was faster than him. I always had been.

When the water hit my waist, I inhaled, then dove. The frigid tendrils of water rolled over my body as I swam beneath the waves. The deeper I swam, the warmer the water became, enveloping me as I tried to wash the flush from the silly childhood crush coloring my cheeks.

But before the cool kiss of the water could wipe it away completely, a hand wrapped around my ankle and tugged. I tried to shake it off, but as if I was a fish caught in a net, I was forced to succumb to its pull.

I tried to swim away, but instead of swimming, I flailed. I was dragged up and out of the water.

But not for long.

Before I could escape from his grasp, Fynn threw me further into the lake. When I hit the bottom, I pushed off with my feet and swam up to the surface. I spun around to face him, daggers flashing in my gaze.

Fynn simply smiled, the gold flecks in his chocolate brown irises dancing in the sunlight.

The invisible daggers dulled as my heart thundered in my chest. Because, by the gods, Fynn was beautiful beneath the spring sun. Strands of hair stuck to his sun-kissed forehead, now soaked and dripping. He pushed them back, his fingers digging into his hair, his biceps flexing. Water droplets ran from his cheek, down his neck, and over his bare, bronzed chest. Down, down—

A rush of water smacked me in my face. I screeched, rubbing the water and the previous daze from my eyes.

"You're going to pay for that!" I shouted before jumping and grabbing onto his shoulders. Using my weight, I tried to force Fynn under the water, but he resisted with that godsforsaken smirk nudging at the left corner of his mouth.

The bottom of my core hummed, and my brows twisted together.

For years, I begged for this crush to go away. For years, I reminded myself that we would only be best friends—two people who cared deeply about each other and would do anything for the other. But we would never be more than friends.

For years, I kept the truth buried within the safety of my mind, tucked away so far back even he would not be able to reach it.

Would it have been so wild if I had told him the truth, though?

I blinked, my eyelashes brushing the tops of my cheeks. My lips parted—

"Fynnie!" a bright, feminine voice shouted somewhere behind me.

His smile faltered, and then I was flying through the air.

My vision blurred as I was submerged underwater.

When I resurfaced a few seconds later, Fynn was already heading back to the shore.

His latest girlfriend waited at the edge of the lake, her features twisting in disgust as she looked at the pile of wrinkled clothes on the ground. Rosalina Florentine was the daughter of one of the most prominent and wealthiest families in Pontia. Her mother was close friends with the queen—or at least Rosalina liked to say she was.

Rosalina tugged her shawl tighter around her shoulders as Fynn reached the shore. She wore a silky yellow dress that made her warm brown skin appear golden in the sunlight. Her mousy brown hair was brushed back into a tight bun, and her lips were stained red.

After surveying the four of us, Rosalina scoffed, her eyes rolling back before she returned her attention to Fynn.

"What are you all doing?" Rosalina asked, her sharp brows drawing together.

"Just having some fun, Rosie," Fynn said.

"Fun?" Rosalina asked, her delicate fingers digging into her hip.

Unlike the four of us, the blood of the gods did not run through Rosalina's veins, rendering her giftless. But who needed an ability—or any worthwhile talent or personality—when one had money and beguiling charm? She was wealthy, daft, and gorgeous.

And I absolutely despised her.

"Yeah, Rosie, fun," Graeson said as he and Terin swam over to me. "You should try it sometime."

I tried and failed to swallow my laugh, the noise coming out as a muffled snort.

Rosalina's attention snapped to me, and I arched a brow.

While Rosalina might have been the picturesque choice for a prince, she was also a snob who never toed the line. It didn't matter if she was wealthy. It didn't even matter that she had no ability remotely on par with Fynn's. She was completely and utterly wrong for Fynn.

Yet, when Fynn got out of the water, he reached for her.

I glanced away, but my attention returned to the couple when a shriek sounded.

Rosalina shoved Fynn. "Fynn! You're wet!"

I snickered and mumbled, "Only way to be if you ask me."

Beside me, Terin and Graeson burst into laughter as Rosalina turned into a ripe tomato, her jaw dropping.

Shaking his head, Fynn picked up his clothes from the floor. But as the wind blew his hair away from his face, his lips twitched. He quickly erased the amusement from his countenance as he straightened and looked at Rosalina. "Don't listen to the guys. They're only messing around."

Like a stone in water, my heart sank straight to the bottom of the lake.

Had I honestly expected anything different from Fynn, though?

Fynn shook his head. Water droplets flew from his hair, causing Rosalina to shriek yet again.

"Could you be more careless?" Rosalina asked, stumbling back several steps as she patted her dress with a look of horror splayed across her face. "This is silk!"

Fynn scratched the back of his neck. "Oh, sorry."

Rosalina groaned as she wiped a hand down the length of her dress. "Can we please go now? We're meeting my parents for dinner, remember?"

Without another word, Rosalina turned and strutted away.

Fynn pushed the fallen strands of hair away from his eyes and nodded. Turning to us, he offered a quick wave and an apologetic smile before jogging to catch up with Rosalina.

When he reached her, Fynn tried to put his hand on her back, but she swatted it away, mumbling something unintelligible.

Unwelcome regret rose in my stomach and up my throat. I swallowed it as Fynn's wet handprint faded from Rosalina's silk dress.

It didn't matter if I had liked Fynn since we were little kids who chased after one another through the castle halls. The two of us were never meant to be anything more than what we already were. It didn't matter that my breathing quickened in his presence or that my heart quaked in my chest or that my fingers buzzed with a nervous energy every time he looked at me.

None of that mattered when our fates were clearly misaligned.

So, I dove and swam to the bottom of the lake, letting the cold kiss of the water freeze the thoughts and drown them.

CHAPTER I

FYNN

My mother tapped her thin, delicate fingers along the stiff fabric of the couch, her pale pink lips curving down, not quite sure what to do with me. Because today, I became Fynneares Andros Nadarean, prince and heir to the Pontian throne, and I was completely and utterly hung over.

When my brother and I returned home last night and retreated to our rooms, dawn had come quickly. After having gotten only three hours of sleep before my attendant Jorian woke me for breakfast, I had shouted harmless obscenities at him to get him to go away. Jorian, however, hadn't relented. Apparently, future kings didn't lie in bed all morning. If I did, that would, of course, make me appear "indolent and irresponsible to my future subjects."

How having breakfast with my nagging mother meant the opposite, I wasn't quite sure.

Nevertheless, I was forced to dine with her while Terin was absent, no doubt flying through dreams while trying to find his own.

Even in the early morning hours, my mother was ever the queen. Not a strand of hair stuck out from her taut bun; not a single dusting of lint lingered on her lavender dress. Everything was in its place. Pristine, polished, flawless.

Her prim posture, however, couldn't fool me.

The corner of my lip twitched, and I reached for the invisible string that only I could see and tugged.

"By the gods!" I shouted, squeezing my head between my palms as pain seared through my brain.

My mother scoffed and set the porcelain teacup on its saucer. "Are you still so drunk that you are foolish enough to try and weasel your way into my mind, Fynneares? Didn't you learn your lesson when you were a boy?"

"Apparently not," I mumbled, snatching a pastry from the plate.

Maybe I *was* still drunk after last night's card game with Terin and the Wilton brothers.

However, I would never admit that to my mother.

As a child and teenager, I had tried to slip into her mind one too many times not to know the repercussions now. Her mental shields were well established, forged in steel, and more impenetrable than our kingdom, surrounded by dangerous cliffs and protected by the kraken. Yet, it had never prevented me from trying.

In my twenty-three years, I had only been successful once at slipping through my mother's shields.

I was five years old and had begun to discover my ability to read thoughts. At the time, hearing the thoughts of the grumbling staff and the other surrounding adults was as if a new world had revealed itself. I had learned then that adults were not as open as children. Where children often spoke their minds without concern for any repercussions, adults were closed lip about anything and everything. This only made me more curious. Discovering their secrets was like stealing a sweet treat from the kitchen behind the chef's back.

Despite being told numerous times to tell my parents about

anything odd I experienced, I kept my ability a secret for a couple of days, too set on learning everyone's secrets.

When I had found my mother's thoughts locked away with dozens of bolts and chains lining the walls of her mental fortress, I was determined to break through it.

I had been trying to pry into my mother's mind for days with no luck when my family and I had ventured to the old summer home in northern Pontia. There, I had finally succeeded.

In the safety of her home, with only her children and husband around, her shields were down. An onslaught of thoughts drenched in worry, concern, and responsibility poured out of her mind. The kingdom's secrets, the growing rebellions in the southern kingdoms, the weight of the crown, the fear of the future—it all came rushing out before I could close the door.

The following day, I woke up with a splitting migraine and no recollection of how I got to my bed.

I should have learned my lesson then, but I didn't. I kept trying.

I should have considered it a blessing that my mother's mind wasn't as wide open as so many others around me. It was hard enough to bear the thoughts of everyone else. I didn't need my mother's worries pressing down on my shoulders, too. Yet I never learned my lesson, no matter how many times I was knocked out cold.

Maybe it was because I was a glutton for punishment. Or maybe it was because I wanted to know she was hurting as much as I was behind that small smile.

After all, over the past fifteen years, we had never once discussed that dreadful night that changed our entire world and stripped our kingdom of its king and princess. We had lost two of the people who mattered most to us. All I wanted to know was if the bull king haunted her dreams, too. If she still wept some nights, crying out for my father and sister.

I wanted to know if some days the anger was too painful to bear that she had to drink her nights away, too.

I wanted to see the face beneath the crown.

I knew my mother missed my father. I could see it in her sea-blue eyes. But instead of talking to us about her pain, she locked it away.

Because that's what Nadareans did.

After all, I was the prince with the cocky smile and loud laughter. I was the one who never took himself too seriously. Who stayed up late, who drank too much at parties and gatherings, who danced with little care in the world, who kissed and slept with too many women.

And based on my mother's stare from across the table, I was also the prince-about-to-be-named-heir who was already becoming an even bigger disappointment than he already was. I most certainly didn't need to read her mind to know *that*. It was written in all the small movements—the way her blue eyes had turned stormy, the way the corner of her mouth ticked down, the way she rubbed the ring hanging from her necklace with two fingers.

Gods, I thought as I dropped her gaze.

I should have taken Lukas' offer to sleep in one of his guest rooms instead of coming home last night. But when Terin had given me that Mother-will-be-pissed look, I knew it was time for us to return to the castle. Apparently, Lukas' brother Riley was not enough of a draw to convince my twin to disappoint our mother.

Although, now, I wasn't sure which look from my mother would have been worse.

She folded her hands on her lap and tilted her head an inch. "Fynneares."

I exhaled. "Yes, Mother?"

Porcelain clattered as she set the cup on the table. "Fynneares, you are a king—"

"Ah," I said, interrupting as I waved a piece of bacon in the air and leaned forward on the couch. "*Future* king, Mother."

"Fynneares Andros," she warned.

"Esmeray Ledia." I pointed the bacon at her, my brows bunching together in mockery.

She massaged her temples with two fingers, groaning, her calm demeanor slipping. "Son, can you be serious for one moment, please?"

I snorted and popped the rest of the bacon into my mouth. "I am *always* serious, Mother," I said, my words muffled.

My mother's eyes narrowed as she leaned over the table.

Unflinching, I went to grab another piece from the table, but the room spun. I gripped the edge of the couch, steadying myself.

"You *are* still drunk." She sat back, shaking her head. "And today of all days, Fynneares?"

I rolled my eyes and leaned against the couch, throwing an arm over the back.

"Fynn, you do recall what today is, right?"

"The fourteenth?"

"By the gods." Her head fell into her palms. "To think, we could have chosen Terin instead. He's responsible and considerate. He's—"

"Also drunk," I mumbled, interrupting my mother from diving into one of her needless comparisons and bouts of what-if and if-only.

Even though Terin and I were identical in appearance, we couldn't have been more different. Terin preferred to play it safe. He didn't want to break the rules. Even when he did after following me, he ended up ratting me out more often than not. Each time, we both would get yelled at, but Terin's punishment would always be less severe. When we were fifteen, he told our mother we had broken into the royal liquor cabinets. Yet even though Terin had his fair share of rum that night, he escaped our mother's berating since he had been the one to confess.

While I should have been upset that Terin didn't receive the same treatment, I wasn't. According to my mother, I should have known better since I was older (by a mere ten minutes). But I knew the truth.

Terin lived with his punishment every day and night. While my ability to hear people's thoughts was often an annoyance, I could at least shut them off when I slept. Terin's gift, on the other hand, was a different form of torture. The ability to walk through people's dreams left him a walking corpse most days.

According to the advisors, Terin was, therefore, unfit to rule. A king needed to be at least alert to his surroundings.

Which left me as the only viable option.

While many thought I was too immature to rule, the gift granted to me by the blood that ran in my veins was at least advantageous for a ruler rather than a hindrance.

That was the reason I was chosen to become heir.

Not because I was older.

Or because I was preferred by the people.

Or because I had proven myself more knowledgeable about the politics and the history of Vaneria's seven kingdoms.

Not even because I could wield a sword better (I could, but that was beside the point).

At the end of the day, the reasoning for who was named heir was because of the gift I bore.

Perhaps my mother thought I was self-sabotaging; however, I couldn't care less about being named heir or if the people thought me fit to rule. I would much rather be doing something worthwhile to help my kingdom. Sitting on a throne would do nothing to protect my people from another attack.

My mother shook her hand, mouth hanging open before quickly shutting it. "Funny, Fynneares. You know your brother has issues sleeping. His gift is—"

"*Sensitive,*" I finished for her, rolling my eyes. I pressed my hand against my head where the pressure was building—and not from the hangover. I sighed. "I am well aware of the strain of Terin's gift, but it doesn't mean I do not speak the truth. Last night, he drank just as much as me. If you do not believe me, go find out for yourself." I held out my hand and squeezed my eyes shut as I anticipated the world to fall away and spin around me as she searched my memories.

Her cold touch, however, never came.

Instead, my mother scoffed and picked up her tea. "Do not try to distract me. This is not about Terin." She took a sip of tea, her searing gaze accusatory. "Now, about tonight."

Rolling my eyes at my mother's blatant disregard for the existence of a single flaw in Terin, I licked the bacon grease off the tips of my fingers. "What about tonight?"

My mother pursed her lips with an absurd amount of discontent.

Huffing a laugh, I pushed myself upright on the couch, ignoring the spinning room. "Stop worrying. I know what tonight is, Mother. My suit is already pressed and hanging up in my chambers. My shoes are already shined. I'm prepared to stand as pretty as the statues of the gods in the Whispering Springs in front of the entire kingdom while you place that golden crown on my head." I flicked a dismissive hand in the air. "Afterwards, I will eat my weight in little cakes and dance the night away like the good little prince you've raised me to be."

My mother's jaw flexed. But it wasn't until her face softened that a chill crept up my neck. "And you will find a wife."

Hot tea spurted from my mouth as my throat seized up. "Excuse me?" I asked, wiping the dribble from my mouth. "What did you say?"

Unwavering, my mother raised a single brow. "You can dance and eat all you want, but tonight, you are to find a wife."

Through clenched teeth, I said, "Mother, we talked about this."
"We did."
"We agreed," I said, my hands curling around the edge of the cushion.

Peering over the cup, she said, "No, we did not."

"But you said—"

She held up a hand, silencing me. "Do not test my memory, Fynn. You know better than to do that. *I* said it was time you found a wife; *you* said you would think about it. Thinking time is over."

"Mother, you are still young. There is no need to rush—"

She lifted her chin. "Today, you will be named heir to the Pontian throne. How will the kingdom know you are serious about your title if you do not take your own life seriously? How are they supposed to respect you if you do not even respect yourself?"

I shifted in my seat and glanced around the room.

Jorian stood near the window near my mother's handmaiden, Elyza. Their faces were blank, but their minds were wide open. I latched onto the threads coming from their minds instinctively, following them as if they were a third hand, an extension of myself. I passed their flimsy mental walls with no more than a brush of a hand, and the floodgates to their minds opened.

He is a little. . .immature at times, Jorian thought.

Is something wrong with him? Elyza wondered. *Is that why he is still unmarried?* Then, after a momentary pause, she thought, *My daughter would marry him in a heartbeat. Then again,* he *would have to be pretty desperate to marry her. She is rather unbecoming.*

I scoffed. *Desperate? I am not desperate.*

Despite what my mother said, I didn't *need* a wife. I was still young. Sure, when my mother was my age, she was already engaged to my father. My grandparents were even younger than my parents were when they married.

They all had it easy, though. They found the ones whom their souls sang for, the ones who enhanced not only their gifts but their lives as well.

They found their soul bonds.

I still had yet to find mine.

To be happy, I needed more than a marriage out of convenience and politics. I needed the connection. And with my ability, I didn't see that happening any time soon.

My mother set her teacup down and stood, smoothing out the wrinkles in her dress. "The advisors have agreed. Tonight, you find a wife. You are to wed by the end of the year."

"By the end of the year? But what about—"

My mother shook her head. "It has been decreed. Either you will choose, or we will." She waved a hand in the air, the movement delicate and light. "Rosalina is a nice girl, and the two of you have been off and on for nearly half a decade now."

I blinked. "Rosalina and I are not soul bonds, Mother. You know that."

My mother sighed. "A soul bond can appear at any time. Perhaps it is already there. Maybe that is why you two keep ending up with each other." She rounded the table and placed a hand on my shoulder. "We all wish to find our soul bond, Fynneares, but some are not as lucky as others. View it as a blessing."

My mother brushed her fingers across the worn, golden ring hanging from her necklace. With a sad smile, she tapped my shoulder again before taking her leave, her handmaiden following her.

The ring she wore was forged from a rare metal found beneath the sands of the Mist, a small island off the western coast of Pontia. According to the stories, the god Pontanius blessed the metal in the hopes of enhancing the connection between soul bonds.

However, my mother was right. Not everyone found their soul bond. Some never did, and they were said to live happy lives, nevertheless. Even those who did find their soul bond weren't guaranteed an eternity of happiness.

Soul bonds were once-in-a-lifetime connections, but losing a soul bond was said to be as painful as shedding a piece of one's heart.

Still, I wanted that connection, *craved* it.

When you are gifted with the curse of hearing everyone's thoughts, it is too easy to discover your partner's true motive. I didn't wish to be with someone who wanted me for only my name or crown. I wanted a deeper connection, something unbreakable and overpowering. Something that proved that the relationship wasn't some farce or display of power.

I swallowed. "Jorian?"

My attendant stepped forward, hands folded behind his back. His hair had grayed over the years. He was nearing sixty years old but was as quick as ever and even more persistent than before. "Yes, Your Highness?"

I twirled the remnants of the tea. "Grab me some whiskey, will you?"

"But—"

"Jorian," I said, cutting him off, "I don't need to hear it from you too."

"Very well, Your Highness."

Footsteps disappeared out of the room. I leaned against the couch and threw my arm over my eyes. There was already plenty of pressure on tonight, but now I needed to find a wife, too?

Fuck me.

CHAPTER 2

DANI

"Come on, Moris! Keep your knees up!" Major Kentos shouted from the sidelines, his voice bellowing over the stomping feet and exhausted grunts of the hundreds of soldiers running through the obstacle course.

I chuckled, the sound barely audible. My lungs pounded against my chest as I neared the finish line. After stopping to pick up one of my comrades when they had taken a nosedive into a pool of thick mud, I had fallen behind.

But I wasn't for long.

Now, only a few soldiers were ahead of me.

My feet were swift and light as I jumped from one platform to the next. My legs were nimble; my body energized.

Quick, easy touches.

When I reached the last platform, I didn't hesitate. I dove.

Chest to the ground, I crawled beneath the barbed wire. The rough ground tore through the linen fabric of my training uniform. My knees scratched against the ground, dirt piled beneath my nails, and sweat beaded at the base of my neck. My joints burned and screamed at me, yet I didn't stop.

I wouldn't stop.

I *couldn't*.

This was my chance to prove to the leaders that I had all the skills necessary to rise in the ranks. Not only could I be a team player, but I also had the strength to carry the team. I had the endurance and willpower to keep going and push through the pain.

Since I could crawl, I had been training for this moment.

If a child was blessed with a gift, the child usually showed signs of the gift early on. However, according to my parents, I showed no signs. Their concern was like a blazing siren in my ears whenever they looked at me. Because despite my entire family having been born with a gift, it had looked like I was bound to be giftless. I watched as my older brother Sawyer mastered any weapon he touched, and my younger brother Xander crafted tools before he could form a coherent sentence. I could see the pride in my father's eyes as he watched his sons' gifts flourish. And there I was, giftless.

So, I took to my studies like a moth to a flame, eager to prove that lacking a gift would not hinder me.

Little did I know my gift had already shown itself.

The gods hadn't blessed me with an ability that improved my sword handling like Sawyer. I wasn't given enhanced speed like Gabriel or increased physical strength like Maximus.

I was a huntress, through and through. My ability was not flashy. Most, in fact, didn't even notice it.

Not everything needed to be covered in diamonds or gold to be of use, though.

My ability was an internal sensation that rose in the pit of my stomach and sent warning signals flaring through my body. It was subtle: the twitch of a finger, the click of a heel. It allowed me to assess my opponents' skills and outmaneuver them, to prey on their weaknesses and outsmart them before they even knew who was sneaking up behind them.

I didn't need strength or speed to be the best. While Gabriel's speed might have helped him during the two-mile run, his speed could only help him so much.

Gabriel hissed as the razor of the wire tugged at his skin. As blood bubbled along the fresh wound, his body shook, and his brown skin turned a sickly shade of green. Gabriel's fear of blood was almost paralyzing. Countless times, I had seen him freeze up because someone had nicked another with a blade during training. His speed was rendered useless.

Unwilling to let the opportunity pass me by, I hurried past him.

Clearing the barbed wire, I pushed myself up and off the ground, then sprinted. My arms pumped faster and faster.

Twenty more yards.

I was ahead of everyone now. I wasn't going to lose this. I *needed* this.

Fifteen more yards.

My legs burned, but I didn't stop.

Everything was riding on this moment. I had spent my life training, studying, and shaping my body and mind to be the best.

Ten more yards.

Another pair of feet pounded behind me, but I didn't waste the precious seconds to note the distance between us. I couldn't afford to. Today was the day all my hard work would prove to be worth it.

Today was the day I finally won.

Today was the day I came in first.

Today was the day the leadership saw me for who I was.

Seven more yards.

I could taste the victory on my tongue, the salt dripping into my mouth as beads of sweat rolled down the contours of my face.

Five more yards.

I ran faster. Faster. *Faster.*

Two yards.

My heartbeat echoed the sound of my feet slapping the ground. One yard.

"Nice job, Captain Ferrios."

I skirted to a stop a couple of yards past the finished line. Holding back the need to keel over, I saluted Major Kentos, forcing my body to remain still as I looked at him. My legs trembled, but I wouldn't show any sign of weakness. Not now. Early on in life, I learned that it wasn't merely about your performance on the training course that mattered, but what you did afterward that counted even more. It was about how you carried yourself after you had won and stripped off your uniform. So, I held my head high and prevented the bubbling excitement filling my body from spilling over.

Major Kentos nodded once before returning his attention to the finish line and jotting down Gabriel's time as he crossed it next.

I forced my shoulders back as I headed toward the bench. I grabbed a canteen and took a swig of the cool water. Only when the canteen touched my lips did I let the smile appear.

I had beaten *everyone*. That promotion was mine.

Gabriel joined me as we waited for the next group of soldiers to finish. I passed him the canteen, and he nodded in gratitude before pouring a stream of water into his mouth.

After he wiped his face, he exhaled a small laugh. "By the gods, Captain Ferrios, I never thought I'd see the day someone would beat me on that course."

My lungs throbbed as I chuckled. The air was ice-cold in my lungs despite the early spring heat. "Can't always be first, Lieutenant Celris."

"True, but I never thought a huntress would be the one to beat me."

I snorted.

It was a common misconception that the gift the gods gave me meant that I simply excelled at tracking people and animals. While that was true in part, my abilities expanded beyond my gift. Tracking down game in the woods taught me to be patient and still my body and mind. That skill helped me train and push my body to excel beyond my gift's capabilities.

"My ability has nothing to do with why I just kicked your ass on the course."

Gabriel laughed. "Don't worry, I'll get my title back next time."

"Better get ahold of your fear of blood first," I said, cocking a brow as the mere mention of blood turned Gabriel's skin green.

Shaking my head, I turned my attention to the course. Several other soldiers had finished and were either drinking too much water that would no doubt cause a cramp soon or were heaving behind the bushes. Five of the soldiers in my company crossed the finish line, making it into the top twenty-five. Pride sparkled in my eyes when they saluted Major Kentos with their backs straight before walking over to their canteens on steady feet. Only when they were at the benches drinking water did they let their fatigue show.

I beamed.

There was no way I wouldn't get this promotion.

Gabriel nodded and left to stretch somewhere away from the heaving soldiers. Two familiar faces joined me, canteens in hand.

"Lieutenant Monistare and Captain Torian, took you two long enough," I said.

"Oh, shut it, Ferrios," Moris mumbled as he bent in half, his breathing heavy and his face red.

Quint patted him on the back. "Arms up, Lieutenant."

Moris grunted, but he straightened. He rubbed his fingers across his short, tight black curls before lacing them behind the back of his head as he inhaled.

A smile tugged at the corner of Quint's lips. I bit back my laughter, opting instead to take another sip of water.

Slowly, others filed in around us, heaving and downing water as if it would rejuvenate them and extinguish the pain piercing through their limbs. While my body ached, a charged energy flowed through me. The anticipation of the upcoming announcement had me bouncing on my toes with nerves that even an hour-long obstacle course couldn't smother.

Having joined us, Sylvia, the lieutenant of one of my platoons, leaned forward with a broad smile splitting across their face. "I heard that promotions are happening today." They wiggled their ginger brows at me.

"Oh?" I diverted my gaze to the obstacle course once more, watching the soldiers run across the finish line.

For weeks, I had known promotions were happening today. I supposed there were some perks to having your father as the commander of the military.

Yet, had he told me *who* was being promoted? Of course not. That would have been too easy. If my father taught me anything, it was that when we were in uniform, bloodlines were nonexistent. All that mattered was rank and your squad.

Leaning back on their heels with their hands folding behind their back, Sylvia shoved my shoulder. "Oh, come on, Captain."

I held back my smirk. "What, Lieutenant Larpos?"

"It has to be you. I mean, you were the first to finish the course, and your leadership is unparalleled. Who else could it possibly be?"

Sylvia had a point. Even if I hadn't finished first, the soldiers in the companies under my command ran like a well-oiled ship preparing for a storm. Everyone knew their job and their position. I hadn't dedicated my entire life to learning the proper way to lead, different strategies, and the history of the seven kingdoms to be passed up for a promotion. Winning today's obstacle course was simply sharpening a well-worn blade.

At only forty years old, Major Kentos was retiring, which meant his position would soon be vacant.

Why anyone would retire from such a prestigious position was beyond me. I would rather die in the military than spend the remainder of my life wandering aimlessly. It was how my grandfather died, my great-grandfather died, and the ones before him. And as much as I did not want to think about the day ever coming, it would no doubt be how my father went. It was who the Ferrioses were. The fight was in the blood that ran through our veins. We were born warriors, and we would die as warriors.

I didn't want my name to be another Ferrios in the history books, though. I wanted my legacy to live on for centuries after I traveled to the Beneath.

While I might have been young, I had proven my ability and skill time and time again.

Major was the obvious next step.

And it was within my reach. I could feel it.

We stretched as we waited for the rest of the soldiers to finish the obstacle course. Moris and Sylvia joked together, placing bets to see who would finish last, but I barely heard them. My attention was fixed on the leaders gathering upon the raised platform.

As if he could feel my eyes on the stage, my father turned. For a second, despite our uniforms, he was only my father as he winked, his mouth twitching up.

The moment vanished too quickly, though, for the stern commander returned and gave me his back once more.

When the last soldiers filed in, the commander's secretary whistled.

Canteens were discarded haphazardly across the benches as everyone lined up before the leaders. The only noise that ripped through the silence was the ragged wheezes of those still trying to regain their normal breathing. Several soldiers—more than usual— had been directed to the healer tents to recover.

Nevertheless, my father began. "Great job out there today, soldiers. As you all know, physical fitness is important to any soldier's well-being." His gaze scanned the crowd, and he took his time, looking at each company, each platoon. "You are the ones in the front lines—the ones who are the first to the action. If you cannot carry one of your own off the field in the heat of battle, you are a risk to the rest of your squad and the rest of your platoon—a risk to Pontia. If you are not strong enough to fulfill your duties, that is on you. But the weight does not solely lay on your shoulders. Your leaders—lieutenants, captains, majors, marshals, and generals—have trained you. If you fail, they fail. You will only go as far as they have led you because, at the end of the day, there is more to a well-trained military than their physiques."

"But a good physique does give us something nice to look at," Sylvia mumbled behind me, and Moris snickered beside them.

I wiped the amusement from my lips when the commander glanced at my company.

My father continued, "Strong morals, values, and communication are also a necessity. A company can only go so far without those things." He looked toward Major Kentos, who had joined him. "Major Kentos, you have led your soldiers well—better than most, if I am to be frank. However, you have set yourself a new goal, a new mission to look forward to as you put your own family first."

Behind them, Kentos' wife sniffled on the stage as she pulled out a handkerchief.

My father winked at the major. "Your second family, however, will always be here if you ever get bored in retirement."

Major Kentos laughed but shook his head. "I have given the majority of my life to our kingdom. It is about time I give some to my wife."

"About damn time," his wife said through sniffles, and the crowd of soldiers laughed.

When the noise died down, my father added, "It is with sadness that we must fill your position with another, but I know that you have trained your successor well."

"Indeed, Commander," Major Kentos said with a nod.

Flutters filled my stomach. This was it. This was the moment that would change the rest of my life. After this, I would be one step closer to becoming the youngest general in Pontian history.

My father's gaze fell upon me, and a small smile flashed across his face. As it disappeared, though, my brows quivered, and a cold sweat broke out over my skin.

"Captain Torian, please step forward."

My heart fell to the bottom of my feet as Quint stepped out of line and headed for the stage.

"I—I don't understand," I whispered as Quint shook Major Kentos' hand. Quint's wife stood beside him with a big smile as she rocked a newborn with bright, rosy cheeks on her hip.

I had no complaints about Quint as a person. He was even a good soldier, but his heart was with his family. Everyone knew that.

Which made this decision that much harder to bear.

"Don't understand what, Captain?" my father asked. After the ceremony was finished, he had come down the stage. A black silk ribbon pulled back his long, dark braids. He brushed back a braid that was too short to pull back, which kept falling in front of his face.

My mother, who had been waiting off to the side like she did every pinning ceremony, now stood beside him, her hand wrapped around his arm. Her small round face bunched up, crow's feet forming on the outer corner of her hazel eyes. Next to my father, their height difference was even more dramatic. Despite the elegant heels she wore, my mother was still shorter than him by at least a foot.

"This—" I said, waving a hand in Quint's direction. Then quieter, I added, "The promotion. The *lack* of promotion. I have done everything. I have excelled at everything."

Since the announcement, I had swallowed the frustration, but now it was building, threatening to boil over. I steeled myself, my nails digging into the pad of my palms. "It's because I'm too young, isn't it? For years, you have said that we value the youth, but that's not true, is it?"

My father sighed, but his gaze remained earnest. "It is not your age, Captain."

"Then what is it? You're the commander. You should—" I gasped, eyes widening. "That's the real reason! It's because *you're* my father. I thought we were past this, but I can see that I was wrong."

He rubbed a hand across his face, the skin growing taut. My father said something—a disagreement perhaps—but I wasn't listening anymore. My mind was spiraling as I tried to make sense of the promotion.

I wrung my hands together, my gaze becoming unfocused as I stared out beyond my parents to the sea of bodies. "If I were promoted, the soldiers would believe I had gained the position because of you. That I didn't earn it, that it was simply handed to me." I crossed my arms over my chest as I tapped my foot. "Well, that's utter bullshit. I've worked my ass off. Every day, every night. I have fought harder than anyone. I have trained nonstop since I could walk. The fight is in my blood; the *military* is in my blood. It's who I am. It's what I was born to do. How dare the other leaders think—"

"Captain Ferrios!"

My heels clicked together, my posture straightening at the shift in my father's tone.

"Menides!" my mother chided beside him, her pale cheeks turning pink. She glanced around us at the nearby families who continued their cheerful conversions.

My father sighed. As he exhaled, his eyes briefly closed shut, and his age showed across his face in the deepening wrinkles. "Listen to me, Dani. It's not because of who I am or how old you are."

"Then what—" I snapped my mouth shut as he quirked a brow.

"You have done everything right. None of the leaders question your strength, loyalty, or drive." Reaching out, he squeezed one of my shoulders. "However, there is more to leading than rising in the ranks. Pontia is our home. We fight to protect it. We fight, train, and lead to protect the people within it. But more than that, you and your mother are my *home*. Every day, I do what I do for the two of you. I come home every day for *you*."

My gaze bounced between my parents. My mother looked up longingly at her soul bond, her grip around his arm tightening as a warm smile spread across her face.

"And?" I asked, my eyebrows drawing together.

My father surveyed Quint, who was holding up his baby, giggles spewing from the child's mouth. I tried to recall the child's name, but it was lost on my tongue.

"Captain Torian has a family. He has a goal outside of the military."

"Exactly, so why should—"

My father squeezed my shoulder again, halting me. "The soldiers need to know that their lives outside of the military—outside of their squad—are equally important as their life in uniform. While the military is their family, it is not the only family they must care about. If they do not have strong ties at home, they are bound to lose hope when war comes." His hand fell from my shoulder, yet the weight of it remained. "Because war is coming, my dear. Rebellions are rising throughout the seven kingdoms. It is only a matter of time before it reaches us."

My brows twisted together. "I do have people. I have you and Mother."

"Mhm. And?"

"And?" My gaze flicked between my parents. "What do you mean, *and?*"

"And what happens when we are gone?" he asked, pulling my mother closer. My mother's countenance dripped with pity. "While I like to believe we are still young, time will catch up to us."

I bit down on my tongue, unwilling to think of a time when I wouldn't have my parents beside me. Several of my friends had lost their parents, some younger than others. I saw the pain that loss had caused. I couldn't imagine experiencing it firsthand.

"Who will you have beside you when we are gone?"

My lips parted, but he cut me off as if knowing my response.

"When your friends have found their own families to care for?"

Shaking my head, I stared at the sky. Pain laced my jaw as I bit down, grinding my teeth.

"Look, honey," my mother said, wrapping her hand around mine. "This is a good thing. You cannot go unmarried forever."

Startled, my gaze dropped from the sky. "Unmarried?" I glanced around and lowered my voice when a few heads turned our way. I grimaced, but to my father, I asked, "I didn't get promoted because I am *unmarried?*"

My parents exchanged glances, and my mother shrugged.

"It is more complicated than that, Dani," my father said, sighing—I was so sick of his sighs. "But yes, in layman's terms, your marital status does play a part in why Captain Torian was picked over you."

I threw my hands in the air, aghast. "Unbelievable!"

"Dani, you're a strong leader, and you will be a great major and even general one day."

His hands fell onto my shoulders. It was supposed to be grounding, reassuring, but the once comforting touch only reminded me that I remained in the same place as I started. What once felt within my grasp suddenly felt miles away.

My father's hand tightened around my shoulders. "General Walen is retiring in five months, which means roles will be shifting again. Perhaps if you show the others that you have a life outside of the military, you could sway their decision."

"Oh, that's a fantastic idea, Menides!" My mother clapped, grabbing my arm. "I know of so many young men who would be wonderful partners for you, Danisinia."

"Excuse me?" I spat, almost choking on the words.

"You know, suitors? Potential husbands?"

My expression flattened. "I know what a *partner* is, Mother."

With a soft huff, my mother tossed a hand in the air. "Well, you never know. The only real partners you have had are your squad members. Your father is right. It's time for you to settle down. Make a family like your brothers. Sawyer and his wife, Ambrosia, are on their second child already. Even Xander and Vera are happily married. Soon enough, my next grandson or granddaughter will be on the way soon." My mother grabbed my father's arm, shaking it. "Oh, Menides, wasn't their wedding two summers ago beautiful? And so young, too! Just imagine another wedding! Our final one. It's making me emotional even thinking about it."

I stared at my father with fear in my eyes. "*Father.*"

He scrunched his face, his gaze darting between us. "Sorinia, Dani doesn't need—"

"Nonsense," my mother waved a hand in the air. "I've been meaning to have this conversation with you for a while, Danisinia. It is time we think about your future."

"Mother, I don't think—"

"I know. You haven't had time to think about possible suitors with all this training, but do not fret. Sawyer married Ambrosia only after ten months; Xander, only eight. What is five months? I'll talk to some of my friends tonight at the ball. See if we can find you a nice boy, one with good standing." She tapped my arm. "Don't you worry, dear. I have it handled."

"*Handled?*" My voice went up an octave.

I glanced at my father, pleading for him to help me, but he only gave me an apologetic grimace. We both knew that once Sorinia Ferrios had a plan, there was no changing her mind.

I was downright screwed.

And not in the way I preferred.

CHAPTER 3
FYNN

Women thought getting ready was easy for men, and to some extent, I suppose it was.

The staff didn't have to spend an hour or more on my hair to get it perfectly curled or braided into an intricate design. On the contrary, my hair only took a little over a quarter of an hour to give it that flawlessly rolled out-of-bed tousle that all the women in Pontia fawned after (was that egotistical of me to think? Maybe, but I couldn't help it if it were true). Even if the women didn't say it aloud, I often saw how their eyes flicked to my hair as their heated gazes drank me in. If that wasn't enough confirmation, the thoughts I overheard as I passed them by proved it.

I did not have to don a corset that sucked in my waist and restricted my breathing or mobility. Instead, the staff spent a tedious amount of time polishing every inch of me, from the buttons on the collar to the tops of my shoes—which was a different sort of pain to bear. Because to stand in front of a mirror while someone primed and polished you had a way of dehumanizing you. It was as if they were shaping me into a statue, molding the clay to fit their vision of the ideal prince. Yet no matter how much the buttons sparkled or the creases in the trousers were ironed smooth, I felt like a fraud.

One would think that growing up a prince my entire life would have made this behavior feel normal. However, I don't think I could ever get used to feeling like a human smothered in clay and marble only to be stared at and admired.

No one would be paying attention to the shine of my shoes. Soon enough, the very buttons the staff fretted over would be smeared with some woman's fingerprints—especially if my mother was set on me finding a wife.

I had thought my mother had set aside that wish, but apparently I was wrong. Tonight, my docket would surely be filled with women awaiting their turn to dance with me. When I was younger, I appreciated the attention. But now?

Now, I saw it for what it was: a race for the crown.

Still, when my mother walked in and brushed the lint off my shoulders with a crisp swipe of her hands, I smiled at her.

"You look just like your father," she whispered, the tinge of loss and longing lingering in her voice as it did every time she talked about my father.

Once, Pontia was the safest kingdom in the world. For centuries, no foreign kingdom had been able to infiltrate the land. With the god Pontanius watching over the Red Sea, the waters were treacherous and wild. One had to be a skilled sailor with a seasoned crew and the gods on their side to traverse the sea without incident. If an enemy were able to cross the sea and surpass the torrential storms brought forth by Pontanius, they would have the kraken to face—a creature brought down from the stars by the gods themselves. Very few enemies had managed to cross the waters and navigate the cliffs in Pontia's history. The last time an enemy had managed to step foot on Pontian soil, everything had changed.

Fifteen years ago, our defenses failed us, and our kingdom was infiltrated. That night, we lost so much as our home burned down and my father and sister were taken from us.

My father had been dead for fifteen years. While we did our best to carry on, the pain of his death still marked the castle. Yet many of us—myself included—still wished for revenge upon our enemies. No matter how much we tried, it was hard to put the past behind us.

When we were children, we didn't understand what had happened. We were angry, upset, and scared. But we were only children. What could a bunch of eight-year-olds do?

We were no longer children, though.

Yet now was not that time either.

Now was never the time, according to my mother. Currently, her primary focus was on me and my future rule.

Lucky me.

"You say that every time, Mother."

"And it continues to be true." With an assessing gaze, she nodded. "Any woman would be lucky to win your heart."

I straightened, swallowing the lump in my throat. Changing the topic, I asked, "Is Terin ready?"

My mother chuckled. "He's been ready, darling. It is you whom we have been waiting on."

I couldn't help the eye roll.

Terin was lucky. While being second in line for the throne still meant that my brother had to look his best, he didn't bear the impending weight of the crown.

I forced a smile and faced her. "Were you not the one who said a royal is never late, but rather their guests simply early?"

My mother grinned. "Ah, so you *have* been listening to me."

"When it suits me, I suppose." With a wink, I held my elbow out.

With a wistful sigh, she slipped her arm around mine. "I suppose I will need to cherish these moments at your side, son, for soon—if all goes well—your future wife will be at your side instead."

I knew what the people thought of me: I was a rebellious and flippant prince. Some believed I did not take my role as heir to the throne seriously. But it wasn't the crown that I feared. In truth, I enjoyed visiting the villages and the people of Pontia. When I thought about it, I even looked forward to taking the necessary steps to make this kingdom even better than it already was one day. This kingdom was my world, my life, my home.

However, a king or queen should not need to become some stuffy ruler to be a good one. I wanted my people to know who I was. I wanted them to see that I was human.

My fear of the crown was rather a result of how the title changed my mother when she was in the public eye. Her chin rose an inch higher, her posture straightened and grew more rigid, and the humor left her lips.

When the time came, I knew I would settle down, but now was not that time. Life was fleeting, and our youth even more so.

We only had our youth for so long before it was stripped away from us once our freedom was taken away by age and responsibility.

Finding my soul bond aside, marrying meant I was one step closer to acquiring the full responsibility of the crown. When I was crowned, where would that leave the woman beside me?

The heir or not, the king's crown was not on my head yet, however.

So, I put one foot in front of the other as my mother held onto my arm.

She was right. We would cherish this moment while we still had it.

As I LOOKED out toward the crowd, the sun's rays that poured in from the window warmed my back. The fur-lined robe was too heavy for the early spring heat. But it was tradition, so I kept my chin high and eyes cast on the crowd before me.

Soon, however, my attention flicked to my shadow, large and looming as it stretched down the center of the aisle.

Would I be able to fill the shoes of the kings and queens before me? Of my father? Of my mother? Or would my shadow swallow me whole?

I wasn't sure of the answer.

Neither were the people in the crowd whose thoughts slithered around the edge of my mind.

Since only a select few people were granted clearance about abilities like mine, most of the minds in the room were wide open. While my hangover was long gone, my ability to shut the unwanted thoughts out was dismal at best. Their thoughts came at me like a storm at sea, loud and consuming.

He may look like his father, but he sure doesn't act like it.

A kind boy but a spoiled one.

My choice would have been the other twin. He's quiet and moldable. What was his name again?

Long live the queen.

My fingers twitched at my side as each thought rolled into my mind, each a wave I couldn't prevent from smacking into the shore.

Despite the thoughts, when my mother stepped forward, I kneeled before the subjects of Pontia. Dropping my gaze to the silver runner covering the stone floors, I tried to cut the threads leading to the unwelcome yet persistent thoughts.

With my gaze diverted, the voices quieted.

Marginally.

In this large of a crowd, there was still a rush of noise, as if I was standing behind a waterfall. I slowed my breathing and focused on shutting out the thoughts. The silence of the room was an incessant buzz in my ears and only allowed the thoughts to seep through. I might have been skilled at breaking down the barriers of strangers and leaders, but I had little control over my own mind.

Silence, I found, was not a comfort but a nuisance, only leaving more room for the spiraling thoughts to take over.

It's only a crown, I told myself as my mother lifted the piece of metal over my head.

One breath in; one breath out.

The crown sunk into my hair, the metal digging into my skull as if it meant to stay there.

With one light brush of my shoulder, my mother stepped back.

I rose, my legs heavier and my body stiffer than it had been moments before as I lifted my head.

"Please rise for the Crown Prince of Pontia, Heir to the Throne: Fynneares Andros Nadarean, first of his name, son to Queen Esmeray Ledia Starling Nadarean and the late King Marc Lorin Nadarean."

My gaze swept across the room, and a thousand faces stared back at me, standing, shuffling on their feet. I quickly grabbed for the familiar threads, the ones that were warm and felt like home, before the torrent of thoughts rushed over me again.

As if they felt me reaching for them, my friends' thoughts poured down the invisible threads swimming in the air.

You've got this, brother, Terin whispered down the line. His thoughts were clearer than all the rest as he stood in the front row.

Beside Terin, Graeson, our childhood friend whom my parents had taken under their wing when his mother died, stood. I tugged on the strand leading to his mind, but per usual, Graeson kept his mind locked up. He crossed his arms over his chest and smirked, his silver eyes incandescent in the sunlight.

My smile grew wider. Leave it to Graeson to keep me in my place.

At last, my attention turned to the final member of our quartet. I trusted few people in this world. Terin, Graeson, and Dani were three of them. The four of us had grown up together and spent much of our childhood running around this castle, playing with wooden swords, and wreaking havoc for the staff. While there was less time for such tomfoolery these days, I could always count on the three of them to show up. Even if Dani, who stood beside her parents, grimaced as she fiddled with the lace gloves her mother probably forced her to wear.

As my closest friends and allies, they had all been trained in building mental shields to block out my ability. While it may have put me at a disadvantage when trying to read their minds, their protection was more important than my ability to invade their privacy. Because if there were one person who could read minds, who was to say there wouldn't be another? While we knew our gifts came from the old blood of the gods running through our veins, there was plenty about our gifts that were still unknown. Graeson needed little training, for his abilities countered any interference with his mind lest he willed it. Terin took to it quickly enough since our relatives on our mother's side all had a natural affinity for creating shields due to the nature of our gifts. And Dani? Well, she was able to achieve anything she set her mind to.

A smile blossomed on Dani's face. I knocked on the door of her mental fortress. A single thought, quiet but crisp, escaped her carefully crafted barriers: *I hope the crown doesn't make your head look bigger than it already is.*

I stifled the snort and looked away from my friends.

I could always count on them to support me, even when the rest of the world did not.

Music from the most talented musicians in Pontia filled the ballroom as people danced and chatted the night away.

I smiled down at the current woman in my arms as we flew across the floor with the other couples. The woman was beautiful, but for the life of me, I couldn't remember her name. She was talking, yet I couldn't focus on the words coming out of her mouth. No amount of pleasantries, it seemed, could override the thoughts pouring out of her mind.

By the gods, he's so handsome, she thought. *My mother would die if I became queen.*

It was hard to be interested in someone when you knew what was inside their mind. And while it might have been rude to admit it, my current dance partner had nothing going on in her mind besides superficial thoughts that held little weight.

When the song finally ended, I smiled politely and placed a gentle kiss on the back of her hand. She curtsied, her cheeks bright red, as I tipped my head to her.

As she walked away, I quickly scanned the room for a staff member. Spotting a tall, slim man balancing a tray of glasses in one hand, I made a beeline for him before anyone could pull me into another dance.

"Let me help you out there, Jordan," I said, picking up a glass.

Jordan tipped his head. "Having fun, Your Highness?"

"Immense fun," I mumbled, taking a sip of red wine. The wine was bitter on my tongue, perfect for how I felt as I observed the dancing and chattering guests.

I had lost track of the number of women my mother threw at me.

Blondes.

Brunettes.

Gingers.

How many dances would it take to make my mother happy?

Part of me thought I should simply pick one. Gather all the women my mother had made me dance with into one room and make them stand in a big circle. Then, with a blindfold tied over my eyes, I would spin around until the music stopped, and whomever I pointed to would be deemed my wife.

My mother would be more than happy with that if it meant I would settle down. It would no doubt appease the advisors and make them believe I was finally taking my role seriously.

At least, if I took that route, the search for a wife would be over.

Yet I couldn't even contemplate whether any of the women I had danced with thus far could be a potential wife. They were all beautiful, and many found me attractive. But when they curtsied at the song's start and placed their hand in mine, their thoughts swept through my mind like a windstorm. The women may have differed in height, accents, and backgrounds, but they all had one thing in common: they all sought my attention in the hopes of gaining a crown.

If I could have shut out the thoughts, perhaps then I could have been ignorant of their truths and their reasons for wanting to dance with me. But I couldn't.

I spun the glass of wine between my fingers, the red liquid sloshing around the glass globe.

How many drinks would it take until the thoughts disappeared or until the voices in my head were finally silenced?

I sighed and scanned the crowd.

Across the ballroom, Graeson leaned against one of the pillars, wearing his usual annoyed expression as he listened to Terin, Dani, and a few others discussing something. Perhaps I only needed better company to occupy my mind. As I stepped forward, the tension in my shoulders lessened. But too quickly, it returned as another woman intercepted me.

But not just any woman.

"Rosie," I said with a terse smile. My grip around the glass tightened.

"Fynneares," Rosalina said, dipping into a curtsy. When she

straightened, she brushed back the soft caramel curls that had fallen over her shoulder. She trailed a finger across her bare collarbone, my eyes tracking the movement. "I wanted to give you my personal congratulations on being crowned heir."

"Thank you," I said with a polite smile.

Rosalina and I had a complicated history. Over the past decade, I had courted her off and on. We often fell into our old routine when I needed someone to attend a ball or a charity function one of the advisors or lords was hosting. However, I officially ended our arrangement a year ago when Rosalina finally realized there was no proposal coming any time soon. Apparently, I hadn't been clear enough about my disinterest in marrying *her*.

But then I heard her thoughts.

Mother better be right about the queen's desire for Fynneares to marry.

Of course, my mother was to blame. Lady Florentine was one of the women my mother often had tea with. According to Rosalina's unfiltered thoughts, Mrs. Florentine had weaseled her daughter's way onto my mother's list of possible wives for me.

My gaze darted to Terin. But before I could catch his attention, Rosalina grabbed my hand and snatched my wine glass before discarding it. As she snaked her hand over my shoulder, I saw my mother watching from the corner of my eye.

My mother smiled, wide and bright-eyed.

I held back a grimace and swallowed my pride.

I promised her that tonight, I would be the Crown Prince she wanted me to be.

CHAPTER 4
DANI

"I KIND OF FEEL BAD FOR HIM," I SAID AS I SWIPED THE ORANGE WEDGE along the rim of the glass.

"For Fynn?" Terin asked, snorting. "Why?"

"Look at him," I said, pointing the orange toward Fynn. "He's been dancing all night nonstop. That must get exhausting at some point." I split the orange from its peel and took a bite before dropping the half-eaten wedge back into the glass.

"Let me get this straight: you pity him because he's been bouncing from one woman to another all night?" Graeson asked, leaning against the pillar beside me, his arms crossed over his chest. The tips of his black hair brushed the pale scar running from his brow to below his cheekbone. The scar did little to soothe his features or the irritation plastered across his face. However, that annoyed expression had been a permanent mark on his countenance since we were children. And it had little to do with the scar.

Before the royal family was attacked, so much love, life, and laughter that spilled from the castle. After the attack, however, a fog coated its inhabitants. The queen's laugh lines faded, Terin's under eyes darkened, Graeson's features hardened. Graeson became more solemn than usual, preferring to hide away in the shadows than talk about the darkness lurking inside him. Shadows loomed large over him wherever he went. It was only on the rare occasion when the darkness in Graeson's silver eyes disappeared.

While he still laughed with us, the sound was tainted with a sorrow that wouldn't disappear. He spent most days either training or obsessing over a premonition his mother had before she passed.

Terin was sweet but quiet, often preferring to slip into the background of the action.

And Fynn—well, Fynn welcomed anyone and everyone with open arms. To many, it probably seemed as if the attack didn't change Fynn like it had the rest of the family. But when I was younger, I might have paid too much attention to the prince. After the tragedy, I had seen how a coldness lay beneath the mischief in his deep brown eyes.

Watching Fynn now, I wondered if the coldness had softened.

I hoped so. All three of the men deserved to live and be happy despite the tragedies that had befallen their family.

"Yeah, I feel *terrible* for the guy," Moris said, pointing his glass in Fynn's direction and wavering on his feet slightly.

Turning away from the prince, I rolled my eyes.

One would have never guessed Moris was a military man because of how he carried himself when he wasn't wearing his uniform.

"A dreadful position to be in, truly," Moris stammered.

I huffed. "All right, but if it were me—"

"But it's not," Moris said, interrupting.

I cocked a brow and started again, "If it were me, I would get tired from the small talk after the first two or three partners. How many times can you talk about the weather?"

"If I know my brother," Terin said, raising his glass to his lips, "there's no way they're talking about the weather."

"Then what—" I snapped my mouth shut as mischief lit Terin's brown eyes. I forced myself to nod, ignoring the sour taste in my mouth.

"This is his day. He deserves the attention," Terin said with a shrug.

And for that, I was grateful that the attention wasn't on me and my lack of promotion.

"But did he have to dance with Rosalina? I thought he finally put her in the past?" Graeson asked.

I snorted. Graeson had a point, but I didn't wish to talk about Fynn and Rosalina. Turning to Terin, I asked, "Is it strange for you?"

"Is what strange?"

"The fact that Fynn has officially been named heir?"

"Sometimes being second isn't all that bad. I've never wanted the title or the responsibility. My mother and her advisors might have debated who would be named heir for the past few years, but it was all for show. It was never going to be me."

"You can't mean that."

He quirked a brow. "Come on, Dani. Fynn has always been more outgoing than me."

"But—"

Terin waved me off. "Fynn is the right choice. It might take some people a while to see that, but they will. My brother can be reckless, unserious, and—"

"A complete moron," Graeson added.

Terin chuckled. "*And* a complete moron, but he is a good man and will be a great king one day."

I nodded and took a sip of wine. From the corner of my eyes, I spotted Fynn twirling Rosalina across the dance floor, her olive green dress glittering beneath the flickering lights of the chandelier.

Right now, no one would have questioned whether the heir to the Pontian throne was having the time of his life. Fynneares Andros Nadarean had everything: wealth, power, strength, and the support of an entire island. Not to mention a decent physique. Even though I had put aside my crush years ago, I was not ignorant of what the other women around me saw when they looked at the newly named Crown Prince. A tall, muscular build, tousled hair that suggested he had just rolled out of bed, and arms that could easily lift his dance partner into the air without breaking a sweat. He was, in simple terms—and in that feigned ideal sort of way that women my age gawked at—perfect.

But no one else saw the way he brushed a light hand across his temple when he spun Rosalina outward, the way his brown eyes squinted, or the way his shoulders sagged as the song came to an end. No one else saw who he was without the title upon his head.

No one saw the man. They only saw the prince.

For a second, though, when his gaze met mine across the ballroom, Fynn was just Fynn—a tired man with too many responsibilities thrust upon him.

Only a best friend could see that.

No matter how much had changed or how little we saw each other, that friendship would still exist.

My gaze swept across the room, landing on Queen Esmeray. Fynn's mother beamed at her son as he danced in the center of the room. Beside her, though, my mother stood, her critical gaze locked on me. Even from here, I could see her eyebrows scale her forehead as she tilted her head to the center of the room, as if asking, "What is your excuse for not dancing?"

Refusing to think about our conversation earlier at the ceremony, I turned away from her.

"Want to get some fresh air?" I asked the others.

Graeson pushed himself off the pillar. "I thought you'd never ask," he said, leading the way through the crowd to the patio doors, not bothering to look back to see if we followed.

HAVING FINISHED PERFORMING a ridiculous solo act in the middle of the garden, Moris bowed low, his arms spreading out wide. He leaned forward, and his legs wobbled.

Terin sprung up. But as Terin reached for Moris, the prince froze. His hand was midair, inches away, as Moris came crashing down.

"Fuck. That's not what I meant to do," Moris mumbled, rubbing his head.

He squinted at Terin, and the prince fell, catching himself with his hands before he smacked against the concrete alongside Moris.

"Shit, Moris. Maybe next time, don't paralyze me when I'm trying to help you?"

"Sorry." Moris attempted to push himself up but fell flat on the ground. He groaned. "Maybe I am a little drunk."

"A little?" Terin countered.

Laughter bounced off the castle walls. Even Graeson struggled to keep the grimace on his face.

Because of the temperamental and dampened blood of the gods, we spent our childhood nurturing and caring for our abilities. Yet our gifts were still fragile little things if not properly used or cared for.

When Pontanius came to the moral world, he had fallen in love with a mortal woman, Alysinth. As a result, their children had been born with both mortal and immortal blood, granting them the power of the gods. While the children were not as strong as their immortal father, they were stronger than mortals and had unforeseen abilities. To help his children master their abilities, Pontanius and the goddess Sabina built the Whispering Springs, a waterfall infused with the gods' will, in the center of Pontia. By visiting the springs and speaking with the gods, a child could learn to control their gift.

However, our gifts could sometimes remain volatile years later—especially if someone had one too many glasses of wine.

"Already started without me, huh?" Fynn asked as he hopped down the stone steps, glass in hand and crown crooked on his head.

"Not our fault Mother-dearest was parading you around like a prized cow," I said.

Terin snorted beside me.

Fynn threw himself onto the bench with an exasperated sigh. "Don't even get me started, Ferrios. Do you know how many times I had to smile and nod as one woman after the next chided away about her frivolous accomplishments?"

"Aww, the little prince's life is so hard," I mocked. "He's forced to dance with pretty women."

Those around us chuckled, raising their glasses to cover their amused grins.

Fynn narrowed his eyes and said, "*Forced* is the key word here."

Sylvia scoffed, kicking their feet in the water as they perched on the concrete wall. "*Hot* is the more accurate description." Sylvia wore a simple dark green ensemble that complimented their auburn hair. The green fabric was draped over the concrete wall and dipped into the water like ivy crawling over stone.

"Sylvia's right," I said. "At least *your* mother is trying to set you up with attractive partners."

Fynn's attention flicked to me again, his eyes locking onto mine for a second too long. I scrambled, double-checking that my shields were up.

A smirk slipped upon his face.

Too late.

I slammed the door shut and forced him out of my mind.

"So, both of our mothers are trying to set us up, huh? Are they part of some mothers-seeking-spouses-for-their-reluctant-children club that we need to dismantle?"

I snorted. "Perhaps that should be your first decree as Crown Prince."

Fynn plucked the crown from his head and spun it around his finger. "If only this crown were more than a physical representation of the symbolic chain that will be locking me to this castle in the near future." He gripped the crown within his palm and sat it on his knee.

Moris' brows twisted, confusion spreading across his face.

I clicked my tongue. "If I have any say in the matter, my mother's plans will not work. I'll entertain her options. Let whatever poor suitors she chooses court me, and then get rid of them."

"Get rid of them?" Moris squawked. "Dani, you can't just go around killing people!"

Huffing, I waved a hand in the air. "Oh, calm down. I'm not going to kill them, Moris. I'm simply going to show them that courting me is the exact opposite of what they want to do. I don't care if they think a relationship with me is advantageous. My father might be the commander and one of the queen's advisors, but his position in society will not be worth courting me."

"So, you're going to sabotage *all* the suitors your mother lines up for you?" Sylvia asked.

I smiled over my glass. "That's the plan."

"But what if there's someone you like? What if some of the men your mother chooses are suitable options?"

"Doubtful."

"You're not even going to give them a chance?" Terin asked.

I shrugged. "Pontia isn't *that* big. At least, the area in which she's probably searching. I know my mother. She's going to want to find someone whose family is close by. That's how she picked Sawyer and Xander's wives. Ambrosia and Vera's families are no more than a half of a day's journey away. She will want the same for whomever she plans to set me up with. Someone with strong morals and a good standing in society. Someone who will make a good father and put their family first." I lifted the glass to my lips and mumbled, "Since, according to her, that is not in my nature."

"She's not wrong," Fynn said.

I straightened. "What's that supposed to mean?"

Fynn arched a brow but kept his gaze on the stars. "You're not the most gentle or soft-handed person in the world, Ferrios."

"I'm sorry, but when have soft hands and a gentle voice ever gotten anything done? If I want to become general sooner than later, I need my soldiers to respect me. Gentleness gets me nowhere."

"I disagree. You do not need to be an aggressive warrior to earn someone's respect."

"Fynn's right," Sylvia said. "My mother is terrifying, and she's only a painter."

Fynn waved a hand as if one measly example proved his point. "Second, is it such a bad thing that your mother wants you to be happy?"

With a look of incredulity, I lowered the glass and peered at Fynn. "A man isn't going to make me happy."

"Do men really make *anyone* happy?" Sylvia asked.

"Hey!" the men shouted.

"Oh, shut it," I said. "My point is a *marriage* won't make me happy —a promotion will. However, it seems that is not enough to appease my mother or the leadership. I need to appear more 'family-oriented.' It's bullshit if you ask me."

"Well, we didn't," Graeson mumbled.

"Anyway," I said, ignoring the grouch. "The pool of suitors is not going to be big, nor will it be worth my time. Do you know how many men are viable options that will meet my mother's high standards?"

Moris snorted. "She might as well set you up with Terin or Fynn at that point."

The group burst into laughter.

"Don't even joke about that, Moris," Fynn said, his face contorting with disgust.

I couldn't agree more. Maybe a few years ago, I had dreamed of marrying Fynn or even being viewed as more than just a friend in his eyes, but those days were long gone.

GRAESON WAS the first to head in for the night, muttering about an early training session. Sylvia, Moris, and Terin were quick to follow after him.

It was unfair, I thought as I stared up at the star-speckled sky.

No one blinked an eye at how much time Graeson dedicated to his training. Why, then, was it a problem for me when I focused on my career? When Graeson did it, he was a martyr. When I did it, I was *too* career-focused.

I snorted. *What a ridiculous thing to hold someone back for.*

"Is it, though?" Fynn asked.

Lying on the bench across from him, I propped my head up, turning on my side. "Excuse me?"

With the others gone, Fynn had taken up the entire bench, spreading his limbs across it as he lay on his back and looked at the stars. One hand hung down, his knuckles scraping the edge of the cobblestone patio. The other was draped across the back of the bench beside his jacket. His messy brown curls were spread out along the seat. A slight indentation marked his hair from the crown, which still sat precariously on his knee. The top three buttons of his shirt were undone, and his tie hung loosely around his neck.

Fynn picked up his crown and turned to his side to face me, mimicking my position. "Is it that ridiculous of them to want you to have a connection with someone? To have something and someone to fight for when the time comes?"

I sat up, my fingers curling around the edge of the bench. "How many times have I told you to stay out of my head, Fynneares?"

"Using my formal name now, are we?" He winked.

"Would you prefer *Fynnie?*"

Fynn grimaced. "Never call me that again."

I chuckled. "How about Fynneares Andros Nadarean, Crown Prince of Pontia?"

A cocky smirk appeared on his face, the pleasure of hearing his new title practically illuminating his face in the dark of night.

Smug bastard, I thought.

"I heard that."

"Good."

Fynn huffed and mumbled, "Well, at least get your facts right when you insult me. I am not a bastard, and you know that."

"Oh, is the little prince upset?" I asked, putting on my best mocking smirk.

As much as Fynn tried to play it off that he did not want the title, he cared more about the crown he twirled around his finger haphazardly than he let on. He might have been reckless most of the time, but his heart was always in the right place. He never did anything to harm another person or put his kingdom at risk.

Fynn laid back on his back, dropping an arm over his eyes. "You're just trying to change the topic."

"And what if I am?" I slunk back against the bench, my back hitting the cold metal.

He sighed. "Avoiding the problem isn't going to solve it, Dani."

"Like you're the one to talk. Aren't you avoiding your problems by being out here instead of in there?"

"The ball ended nearly half an hour ago," Fynn said.

I snapped my head toward the castle, and my brows furrowed.

The music and chatter that once poured from the closed doors were now nonexistent. The only people I could see through the grand windows were the staff cleaning up and the musicians packing up their instruments. I hadn't even noticed that the music had stopped or that the crowd's constant chatter had dwindled. Usually, I was more observant of my surroundings.

Deep wrinkles creased the center of my forehead. Perhaps it was for the best that I had not been promoted after all. If I hadn't even realized that the ball had ended and almost everyone had disappeared, was I responsible enough to lead a battalion into battle safely?

"Come on, you know you don't believe that," Fynn said, with a click of his tongue.

The muscles in my jaw tightened. "Get out of my head, Fynn."

"What? It's not my fault your thoughts are so loud right now. They're practically begging me to listen to them."

"That's no excuse. You reading my thoughts is a complete invasion of my privacy."

"You know that I can't help it sometimes. It's not like I can turn it off."

I narrowed my eyes. "You could at least *try* not to listen to them."

Fynn shrugged. "Normally, you're more closed off. Unlike some people, you're usually good at keeping your thoughts to yourself. Except, you know"—he waved a hand in the air—"when you're distracted."

I pursed my lips. I *was* distracted tonight. Usually, I could shake the concerns and worries of the day away easily. Blocking things out and separating them into their designated boxes within the confinements of my mind was not just easy but necessary. Protecting my mind from Fynn's abilities aside, being able to walk away from the stresses of the day was a vital skill for a soldier and leader. While there hadn't been a war in Vaneria for almost one hundred years, political strife was rising across the seven kingdoms. Even though Pontia was separated by a body of water, messengers and spies traveled back and forth, relaying news about the unrest in the kingdoms to the south.

I needed to focus.

My palms pressed into the bench, about to stand, when Fynn called out.

"Wait, Dani," Fynn said, leaning on his side again, making me pause. "Stay. Just for a little longer."

I gave him a cursory glance. "I'm not the only one avoiding my problems. Now am I?"

Fynn rubbed a hand across his face. "I never said I wasn't avoiding them, too."

"You're ridiculous," I said with an eye roll as I settled against the bench.

Fynn grinned. "But also charming and handsome and smart, right?"

I rolled my eyes again but laughed. "Sure. If that's what gets you through the night."

His smile fell. "I am sorry that you didn't get the promotion. You've worked so hard for it over the past year and a half."

I shrugged. "Some things cannot simply be handed down."

Fynn flinched.

My face twisting with guilt, I rushed to apologize. "That's not—that's not what I meant, Fynn."

The corners of his lip turned up, but the smile didn't quite reach his eyes. He shook his head as if he could shake the emotion away. "It's fine. I get it. I was set to become king the moment I was born." He dropped his gaze, focusing on the cobblestone pavement between us.

"Fynn," I said.

My attitude was only a result of my frustrations with my situation, not Fynn acquiring the title of heir. My father was the commander of the entire Pontian military. He oversaw the promotions of the leaders, so I knew that to some soldiers, it would have appeared like a handout if I had received the promotion. But it wasn't. I had spent my entire life training. I had worked hard to build a solid knowledge base of strategy and to build trust among the soldiers in my platoon. My soldiers knew how hard I worked and how much I lived and breathed the military.

Still, it wasn't enough.

No, I corrected, *it was too much.*

I groaned. "I don't get it, Fynn. What more can I do? General Walen is retiring in five months. I have five months to prove to them that I—what? Can have a serious relationship? It's preposterous."

"Let someone court you then."

My jaw fell open. "You have to be joking."

"What?"

"You, of all people, cannot be telling me to listen to my mother when you aren't even listening to your own!"

"I mean—I *attempted*. You saw me dance with several women tonight, did you not?"

"And when the first opportunity to get away arose, you took it."

Fynn shrugged. "When the opportunity presents itself, whom am I to deny it? I am just a measly man."

"The queen isn't going to give this up," I said.

Fynn sat up, his head falling to the side as he looked at me with a narrowed gaze.

I jerked back, but my shields were still intact. Still sound. "If you're trying to read my—"

Shaking his head, Fynn held up a hand. "I'm not. I promise. It's just—"

"What?" I asked, still not trusting the mischievous glint in his brown eyes.

"What if—now hear me out before you say no," Fynn held his hands up, "What if *I* pretend to court *you*?"

If I had been drinking something, I would have choked. Instead, my jaw dropped, my eyes nearly popping out of my head. "Good one, Fynn," I said with a forced laugh.

For years, I had dreamed of Fynn asking to court me. Never in my wildest dreams, however, did I imagine him asking to *pretend* to court me. While my feelings about Fynn might have changed since we were teenagers, it still felt like a slap in the face.

"Hear me out." Fynn stood and began to pace, waving his hands as he spoke. "I pretend to court you. We go to a few public events and make a grand show of it. In the process, we appease *both* of our mothers. Not only that, the military leaders will see that you do have ties to hold you down and that you do, in fact, have a life outside the military. Then, once you get your promotion in five months, we end things."

"Just like that?" I asked, laughter bubbling in my mouth.

Fynn nodded, no hint of amusement marking his features.

His proposition was ridiculous. Outrageous, really.

"That could *never* work," I said, shaking my head as I stood. "Our mothers would see right through that. Plus, I don't want to be courted. I don't want a relationship, Fynn. Even a fake one."

He grabbed my wrist, his fingers cool against my skin. "Think about it, will you?"

I snorted. "Goodnight, Fynn."

CHAPTER 5
DANI

My mother was a terrible matchmaker.

When I returned home after training the following week, my brother, Sawyer, had stopped me at the door. His mere presence immediately revealed what was happening.

Sawyer never came home randomly during the day, especially when Ambrosia had given birth to her second child two months ago. The moment Lia entered this world, Sawyer was so smitten that it was hard enough to pull him away from his little family of four for our monthly dinners.

If my mother thought his presence would help comfort me, she was wrong. I didn't care if Sawyer claimed our mother was a "pretty good matchmaker" based on his and Xander's wives. Based on the group of men before me, I was beginning to think that either my mother had poor taste in men or she was trying to spite me.

At least thirteen men were scattered around the sitting room when I entered. Several men sat on the white leather couches, a few stood by the large windows, and a couple leaned against the bookshelves lining the back wall of the room. And now they were all staring at me, smiling at me, puffing up their chests and straightening their collars and ties. And for what? To impress me?

I could have gagged.

"Danisinia, we've been waiting for you," my mother said, lowering her teacup and grinning triumphantly as she sat between two men. She wore one of her favorite yellow dresses, and her golden brown hair was crafted in an intricate braid that flowed down her back. She blinked up at me, her hazel eyes threatening death if I walked away—which, granted, the thought had passed my mind the moment I stepped foot into the room.

One man leaned against the piano, and his hand slipped. A horrendous combination of notes filled the room, screeching. His brown cheeks reddened as he straightened and chuckled nervously.

My hands rolled into fists at my sides.

My mother's stares be damned, I spun on my heel, rushing out of the room and down the hall.

"Excuse us for a moment, gentlemen," my mother said before the door clicked shut.

Behind me, my mother hissed my name, but I ignored her and quickened my pace. My boots hit the tile floor, echoing throughout the halls.

When I was halfway up the stairs, my father's voice called after me, his tone a mix between comforting and commanding.

Despite myself, I stopped.

Begrudgingly, I turned around, but I didn't descend the steps. Instead, I held my ground. After all, Father had always said that the best position a soldier could take was the high ground. And right now, as a petite woman rounded the corner with a flushed face and angry eyes, I was facing my worst nightmare: my mother.

"Oh, on second thought, dear," my mother said, placing a hand on my father's wrist. "It might be best if Dani changes first."

"Why would I do that?" I asked, propping a hand on my hip.

My mother surveyed me. Her gaze went from the dirt smeared across my training shirt to the worn khaki trousers with scuff marks on my knees.

Little did my mother know that the streaks of dirt were badges of honor. Today's focus was hand-to-hand combat training, and I had wiped the floor with every one of my opponents.

I lifted my chin.

"First impressions are everything, Danisinia. You do want to make a good impression on your future husband, do you not?"

"What?" I sputtered, then looked to my father, pleading.

My father, however, only held up his aged, brown hands in defense as he stepped backward. "Oh no, I am not getting in the middle of this."

My mother waved him off. "Go chat with our guests, Menides. I'm sure some of them would love to talk to you; after all, a few of them are soldiers themselves."

My father grumbled something under his breath. But with one disapproving glance from my mother, he nodded.

"Thank you, Menides," my mother said, her attention returning to me. Behind her, though, my father gave me an apologetic look. Yet instead of heading toward the drawing room where the dozens of men waited, he snuck off down in the opposite direction, toward his office.

"Unbelievable," I said under my breath.

"Did you hear me, Danisinia? I said some of the suitors are soldiers."

"And?" I asked.

"*And*," she took a step forward, "I want you to know that I only wish for you to be happy, dear. You can marry a soldier. By the gods, you can marry a baker for all I care. I only want you to be happy, like your brothers."

I sighed, rubbing a hand across my face, and then descended the steps. Meeting my mother at the bottom of the steps, I grabbed her hands.

Where she was soft and dainty, I was all sharp edges. My mother fit into her role as the commander's wife perfectly. She kept a clean house and raised my brothers and me with a gentle, nurturing hand. She organized charity functions and had afternoon tea with the other leaders' spouses. She taught me how to sew, how to hold my tea cup with grace, and how to dance in heels and uncomfortable, albeit gorgeous, dresses. She modeled how to take care of a household and gave me all the tools needed to be the perfect wife. The perfect mother—but that was never the life I wanted. Especially not after my father would come home, wearing his scratched armor with dirt on his cheek and a smile spread across his face.

While I appreciated everything my mother did for me, I wanted to be able to fight the enemy and then return to the home I purchased and sit with a good book in my hands.

My mother taught me many things. One thing she did not expect to teach me, however, was a sense of determination. When someone told Sorinia Ferrios *no*, my mother found a way around it. When she set her mind to something, she did it. No questions, no hesitation. She was fierce and strong and more stubborn than even my father.

When I told my mother I wanted to join the military, my mother took it in stride. She didn't even miss a step. I was lucky; I knew that. My mother had supported every decision I had made with a smile on her face. My mother had never asked me to be anything less than who I was—had never demanded that I quit and put the military behind me.

Yet despite her support, I saw the disappointment in her gaze when I would brush off her previous attempts at encouraging me to court one of her friends' sons.

Like she was now.

My mother squeezed my hands. "Please try. For me?"

I closed my eyes and swallowed. She was never going to give this up.

"Fine," I whispered. I released my mother's hands and walked past her.

But before I could get too far, my mother called after me.

"Yes?"

My mother stared at me with wide, shocked eyes, waving her hands in exasperation. "Aren't you going to go change?"

I snorted. "Mother, if any of those men are upset by my choice in apparel, they can leave right now. I will never change for any man. You taught me that."

I made a beeline for the sitting room as my mother whispered, "Gods, help me."

When I reached the door, I tipped my chin up and scanned the group of men, quickly analyzing the situation before I attacked. Some men shifted on their feet and in their seats as I surveyed the room. Some seemed to cower as my gaze met theirs. Sleeves were tugged down, jackets straightened, and voices lowered as if they were peacocks fluffing their feathers in the presence of a female.

It was horrendous.

I cocked my head, curious.

If I moved too fast, would they scurry away like a deer in a forest?

I could admit, though, some of them were attractive.

My gaze landed on a man standing in the corner of the room. He wore black slacks and a white cotton button-up shirt with his sleeves rolled up. The stranger looked like he wanted to be there as much as I did.

"You," I commanded, pointing at him. "Let's go."

Shock colored his face. But without seeing if he followed, I left the room and headed for the front door.

My mother's eyes widened as I flew out of the room. "Danisinia, where are you going?"

"Out, Mother," I said over my shoulder without slowing my pace.

"Out? What do you mean—?"

Someone cleared their throat and said, "Mrs. Ferrios, I will bring her home safe."

Gag.

Hurried footsteps sounded behind me, the suitor finally catching up to me.

"Name?" I asked, not turning around.

"Kaleb, my lady," he said.

I snorted. "My Lady?"

"Well, you are a lady. Your father is—"

I stopped at the door and faced him. Kaleb skirted to a stop, snapping his mouth shut and straightening as I surveyed him.

Kaleb was not a soldier. He was tall, a little lanky, but handsome enough. Definitely not a love-at-first-sight type of man, nor a man I would fall head over heels with in the next hour—or however long this affair needed to be. But that wasn't why I picked him.

My mother said try, and try I would.

But that was all I would do.

I would let Kaleb take me for a walk—or whatever frivolous activity people courting one another did. I would let him think he had a chance. Then, I would chase him away the moment I could so that he never came back.

One by one, the suitors would disappear.

"All right, Kaleb, where to?"

"Miss Ferrios?" Kaleb scratched his short blond hair.

Folding my arms over my chest, I arched a brow. "Where are you taking me?"

"Oh, right." Kaleb cleared his throat, straightening. "Uhm, right this way."

Kaleb didn't work out.

Nor did Jasper.

Or Felix.

Or Martin.

They were all so. . .*boring*.

One afternoon, one of them—which one? I couldn't recall—had decided to take me to the kingdom's archery competition. However, when the judge opened the competition to volunteers, I decided to put my name in the hat, needing something to entertain myself. The suitor of the day (Felix perhaps?) had decided to do the same, flexing his biceps in a vain display of masculinity.

To my amazement, his aim wasn't too bad. However, when I won the competition, he ran home in tears.

I ended up taking a small trophy home. And, if I was being honest, it was a better prize than spending the rest of the day with Felix (or was it Lewis?).

I had thought that after the first suitor had run home practically screaming, my mother would have relented, but she was, in fact, relentless.

The suitors kept coming.

It had been almost two weeks of dates. Two weeks of putting on frilly dresses and my best smile.

The spring sun beamed down on me as I walked beside the latest suitor through one of the parks in the southern village off the coast. My gaze kept wandering to the sea as we twisted through the sections of flowers.

". . .that's when I realized the medical field wasn't for me. The—" The man—whose name escaped me—swallowed, his fist over his mouth. "The blood is just too much for me."

I hummed in acknowledgment as we circled the gardens for the third time. For the past half hour, the man had gone on and on about his intent on becoming a doctor. Apparently, during the first day of being an apprentice, he had been brought along to tend to a butcher who had chopped off his finger on accident. After one look, he fainted on the floor, and his dreams of being a healer fell to the wayside. Now, he was a researcher.

Or was trying to be.

Either way, he had no sense of direction. Based on the constant switching of careers—for before he tried to be a doctor, he wanted to be a baker, before that, a metallurgist, and before that, a musician—the current suitor was a wanderer. A dabbler. And if I knew anything, it was that a man without a purpose was no better than a man lost at sea who couldn't read the stars. Hopeless and disappointing.

"So, have you ever wanted to do anything outside the military?" he asked.

"No," I said.

"Never?"

"Nope."

"I see," he said, nodding.

After a painful moment passed between us, I stopped walking and pulled the suitor to a stop.

"I—" I bit down on my lip, my brows drawing together as I stared at the freckle-faced man with blond hair. I sighed. "I'm sorry. What is your name again?"

The man chuckled nervously, tugging the low ponytail at the back of his head. "Torrince, Miss Ferrios."

"Torrince," I said with a soft, polite smile. "Look."

Torrince's shoulders dropped, his head hanging down as he stared at his feet. "You don't need to say it."

I sighed in relief, the knot of tension between my shoulders releasing. "Good. That makes this a lot easier. You seem like a nice man, but—"

He snapped his head up. "I said you don't need to say it, yet you're still going to? Perhaps if you listened—" Torrince stepped forward, but when I leaned away, he tripped and fell into the bed of roses. He screeched.

"Are you—are you all right?" I extended a hand, and he grabbed it with a sneer.

"Do I look like I'm—" Torrince shut his mouth, his eyes growing wide as he stared down at his outstretched arm.

"Torrince?"

His pink face turned green.

Then he vomited on my shoes.

"Not again," I groaned, staring at the clouds floating in the sky.

These men would be the death of me.

CHAPTER 6
FYNN

My arm smacked against the table as gravity was ripped from me, stirring me awake.

The silence was deafening as each advisor around the table turned to face me.

Biting my tongue, I glared at Terin sitting across from me.

It was the only way to wake you up without drawing attention, my twin said through the connection he left open. His mouth was bunched up, twisting together in an apology.

My jaw ticked.

There had to have been a better way for my brother to wake me than forcing me off a cliff in my dream.

I hadn't realized I had fallen asleep. But after only three hours of fitful sleep last night, it was hard enough to stay awake when Rolan, the kingdom's treasurer, was relaying Pontia's current financial status.

"Prince Fynneares, is there something you would like to add?" my mother asked, her blonde eyebrows scaling her pale, smooth forehead.

I cleared my throat, quickly rifling through the minds of the advisors who were ignorant of the details of my ability and finding the highlights of the current conversation. Since the advisors were well-trained, most were adept at creating proper shields. However, some shields were weaker than others. I usually tried my best to drown out their thoughts. How often could one hear that widowed Lord Cunningway thought that the healer, Theenah, was attractive or that her dress accentuated her curves? As valuable as my ability was when deciding whether someone was being truthful or hiding something, it was nauseating to hear the frivolous thoughts of people.

Still, it was fruitful when my attention had wandered elsewhere.

"Yes, there is," I said, smoothing down the front of my shirt, which had since wrinkled in my sleep.

My mother raised a brow. "Well?"

"The Summer Solstice Ball," I said, tapping my fingers on the table. "It needs to be grander this year. Many are worried that the rebellions in the south will filter into our kingdom. While most of our people are happy now, the strife across Vaneria suggests that war is closer than we once thought. We need to show the people that we are strong and that we still value fostering our community. Our enemy must believe that despite the growing concern, our barriers and spirit remain steady."

During the summer solstice, people across the island celebrated with grand festivities. While it might have been the shortest night of the year, it was the night almost everyone looked forward to all year round.

Lord Cunningway hummed. "It's not a bad idea, Your Highness." To himself, I overheard him think, *If I host the Summer Solstice Ball this year, I can show Theenah the latest addition to the manor. She'll love the view from—*

I cut off the connection to Cunningway's mind, holding back an eye roll.

Of course, the lord would try to use the event for his personal gain. He wasn't as conniving as some of the lords and ladies I had come across over the years, but neither was he the most selfless of advisors. He would do anything to parade around his wealth and status.

My mother tapped her fingers along the table, her nails clicking on the pine. "Very well."

The corners of my mouth flicked up, and I sat back in my chair as the advisors debated the details of the Summer Solstice Ball. While they talked, however, I could sense the undercurrent of the uneasiness that plagued our kingdom despite the lively conversation.

Since the rest of Vaneria was in the dark about the gifts many of us bore in Pontia, our people were primarily stuck on the island. With our kingdom having been built on secrets, it was risky to let too many people leave it. There were some, like the sailors, who could travel back and forth to import goods and other resources. The rest of us were primarily stuck on the island.

There was a time when the barriers weren't so strict. My mother once told us stories about the years she spent exploring the kingdoms of Vaneria in her early twenties. Meanwhile, Terin and I had only left Pontia once to visit Tetria, one of our long-standing allies. Even that trip, however, had been heavily guarded and restricted.

My mother's rules regarding limited travel were well-intended. Before Graeson's mother died, Lysanthia had informed my mother about a vision she had seen: *once the sea burns, secrets will unravel, and war will break out.*

According to the vision, blood would saturate the seven kingdoms, fires would destroy homes, and death would plague the streets.

At first, we thought our mother was making up the story to threaten us. But over the years, the air shifted, and the tide turned.

A war was coming.

With the rising rebellions in the south, it was only a matter of time.

I snatched the goblet sitting on the table in front of me. Some nights, Lysanthia's prophecy still haunted my dreams as if it held some piece of vital information that I didn't have the knowledge to comprehend.

Yet my mother's greatest concern was my need to find a wife.

"FINE, I'LL DO IT."

I coughed, my spoon clattering on the table as it fell from my grasp.

Jorian rushed forward, smacking my back, but I shrugged him off, my gaze set on the woman who had barged through the royal dining room.

"Leave us, Jorian," I ordered, my throat raw.

"But, sir—"

"Leave us," I repeated, my voice clearer.

Jorian bowed. As he shuffled out of the room, he stopped twice to look over his shoulder, concern flashing across his countenance.

His concern was useless here.

When the door clicked shut, I asked, "What happened to you?"

"That's beside the point," Dani said, pressing her palms flat against the table. Her brown cheeks were flushed, the green in her hazel eyes wild. A few of her braids had fallen out of the loose bun hanging at the nape of her neck. Her blouse had a tear in it, dirt and grass stains smeared across it.

I lifted a brow. "I believe that is the whole point, actually. Have you seen your reflection lately?"

Dani made a noise that was somewhere between a groan and a

screech. She untangled her hair and let the braids fall behind her shoulders. Her frustration was palpable, sour.

Brows furrowed, I reached out for the strand connecting to Dani's mind. High walls made of stone surrounded her mind. But even the best-built castles had cracks. When Dani was emotional, I found her mind much more accessible. All I had to do was look for the way in.

There.

A fissure in her carefully crafted walls.

Get out of my head, Fynneares.

I slumped back in my chair. "You're no fun."

Dani rolled hers before plopping down into one of the chairs. "Fine. If you must know—"

"I must."

Dani gave me a glare that I was all too familiar with, one that said shut-up-you-cocky-prick.

I smirked.

She rubbed a hand across her face and spoke through her fingers, "My mother set up a meeting with one of her suitors. A *few* meetings, in fact."

"And this"—I waved a hand in her direction—"is the result of a simple *meeting?*"

Dani's hands dropped, revealing an ice-cold gaze that was as sharp as the throwing knives she had hidden somewhere on her person—the guards knew better than to confiscate them. I also didn't need to read her thoughts to know that if she could—and if she wouldn't be marked a traitor for doing so—she would stab me right then and there. Still, I couldn't prevent the smugness from twitching at the corner of my lip.

In a flat, unamused tone, she said, "Two men have thrown up either on or near my shoes, Fynn. *Two* of them."

I didn't know if I should laugh or gag. Either way, the resulting noise from my mouth was some garbled combination of both.

I peered beneath the table. Thankfully, the black riding boots were clean. Or at least somewhat clean. I squinted.

Was that. . .?

I quickly snapped my attention up to Dani.

"It's mud," she clarified.

"And why, pray tell, are your boots covered in mud and your blouse torn?"

Her head slammed against the table. "One of them tried to kiss me," she said into the wood.

"And you what? Flipped him on his back and ran away?"

Dani lifted her head, an incredulous look twisting her features as if I was the one who had said or done something as preposterous as running away from a suitor.

"I didn't run."

I cocked my head, hearing the white lie on her tongue.

She pursed her lips, as if by keeping her lips closed, she could keep the truth bottled up. At last, however, she said, "I rode my horse."

"You're not serious, right?" I blinked. Multiple times. Yet Dani didn't react; she only stared at me. "By the gods, you are serious. You attacked the poor guy and then sprinted away on horseback?"

"Yes." Dani cocked her head. "What was I supposed to do?"

"Not run?"

"You don't understand, Fynn! He smelled absolutely horrid," Dani whined.

"And you are *absolutely* ridiculous." I rubbed my palms across my face.

"So, is that a no, then?" Dani asked.

I poured some cream into my tea and stirred it. "A no to what?"

Dani waved her hand in the air. "To the whole fake courting thing."

I sat back in my seat and smirked, stretching an arm over the chair beside me. "The 'whole fake courting thing'? Do explain." I took a sip, enjoying watching Dani squirm in her seat.

"You know, the proposal you came up with the night of your crowning ceremony?"

"Doesn't ring a bell." When Dani gave me a questioning glance, I shrugged. "What can I say? My memory is a little foggy. Remind me. It's been what—a week? Two weeks? I say so many things to so many people."

After I hadn't heard from Dani the next day, I didn't think she would take me up on the offer. Dani was a stubborn woman. She always had been. If it wasn't her idea, she often didn't want to hear about it. Even as a child, she refused to play some games simply because she hadn't been the first to suggest them.

But now here she was, asking for my help.

And what a splendid sight it was to see her groveling before me.

"You're abhorrent."

I shrugged. "I've been called worse by women begging me to court them."

"I'm not—ugh!" On the table, her fist rolled into a tight ball. "I've had a long week, Fynn. Please, for once, stop playing games. I know you remember the conversation. You may act like a drunken fool at parties, and more often than not, you are one, but I know when you've sobered up. Is the offer still on the table or not?"

"Are you sure you want it to be? From what you've told me so far, it sounds like you're having so much fun with your mother's batch of suitors."

Dani stood. "Forget I even said anything."

"Oh, come on. I'm only joking." I waved a hand at the seat Dani had just vacated. "Sit."

Dani sighed but sat nevertheless, crossing her arms over her chest.

Relenting at last, I sat the porcelain cup on the table, my fingers tapping along its side. "You said that General Walen retires in five months, correct?"

"Well, now it's more like four months and two weeks, but yes." Dani picked up a cluster of grapes and began eating them one by one.

"So, we have five months to convince your father and the rest of the military leaders that you do, indeed, have a soul." Unable to help myself, I lifted a shoulder before dropping it and added, "Although we both know that's a lie."

"Fynn!" Dani shrieked, chucking a grape at me.

Swiftly dodging it, I said, "What? We both know you are soulless."

Dani shrunk back into her chair. "Whether I have a soul or not is beside the point."

"Ah, so you admit it then."

Dani popped a grape into her mouth. Then, the muscles in her face twitched. She swallowed the grape. "You do realize a fake courtship would only delay the inevitable for you, right?"

"Sure, but at least five months will give me some reprieve from my mother's endeavors."

Dani grew quiet, her hand falling away from the grapes and hiding beneath the table. "You're still set on finding your soul bond, aren't you?"

I dropped Dani's gaze, unwilling to see an ounce of the pity lingering there.

"Is that such a foolish thing to want?" I asked, still not meeting her gaze.

Silence sat between us as the memory of the night I had confessed this truth to her resurfaced. When we were teenagers, I drunkenly admitted wanting to find my soul bond. I thought Dani, whose parents were also soul bonds, would understand, but instead, she laughed in my face.

This time, however, Dani remained silent.

"She's out there somewhere. I just need time to find her."

"What if you don't?" Dani asked quietly.

"If I don't find her, then I will let my mother marry me off to whomever she thinks is the most suitable partner. I understand that part of my duty as Crown Prince is to have an heir. But if there's a war coming, I do not wish to bring a child into it anytime soon. There will be time after."

I finally met Dani's gaze.

She offered me a small smile. "Tell me the plan then."

She was throwing me a bone, a way to avoid thinking about the weight of the future and the oncoming war. Although one day we would need to face our fears and talk about the future, I took the opportunity to push that discussion further away.

I waved my hand in the air as the loose plan took shape. "We will attend a few public events. Maybe a dinner or two with our families?"

"Simple enough. Can we at least set some ground rules if we do this?"

I chuckled but nodded, not surprised in the slightest. If I was the king of breaking the rules, Dani was the queen of making them.

Dani stood and paced, one arm hugging her body as she tapped a finger against her cheek. While there might have been nothing we could do about an unpredictable future, we could at least do something about our mothers' current pursuits.

Stopping in place, Dani spun toward me and held up a finger. "Rule number one: nothing can interfere with my training."

"I wouldn't dare interfere with Captain Ferrios' training—soon-to-be Major Ferrios," I said with a wink.

Dani's features, however, only hardened. She pointed a firm finger at me. "Major only *if* we pull this off."

Weaving my hands behind my head, I leaned back in the chair. "All right, fine."

"Rule number two: we tell no one."

"No one?"

"No one," Dani repeated, her gaze flat and unyielding.

It was the first time I questioned this plan. Not because I wasn't good at keeping secrets—I was. With the nature of my gift and my title, I learned early on to keep my mouth shut—when I had to, anyway. Still, there was one person from whom I never kept secrets. One person whom I had always been able to confide in.

"Not even Terin." Dani folded her arms over her chest as she leaned forward. "Is that a deal breaker for you?"

I pursed my lips, thinking it through.

One secret would not kill me. If Terin were in the same position as me, he would do the same thing.

Wouldn't he?

"We tell no one," I agreed.

Dani nodded, satisfied. "Rule number three: no kissing or holding hands or—"

"Anything that would make it appear like we are courting one another?" I asked, raising a brow.

"Correct."

"Dani, you do see the problem with that, don't you?"

"What do you—" her hazel eyes widened, the gold within them shining as the sun touched her face. Her soft, brown cheeks reddened. "Oh."

"Oh."

She cleared her throat and rolled her shoulders back, nodding once. "Only necessary touches, then."

I saluted her and said, "I will do my utmost best only to touch you when necessary, Captain."

"Good. It's a—"

"Wait," I said, interrupting.

"What?" Dani turned around, hands landing on her hips and impatience painting her countenance.

"Don't I get to make a rule?"

"Why? More than three rules would be too many."

I cocked a brow. "Just one? It's important."

Dani rubbed her temples. "Fine."

"All right, last rule." I folded my hands on the table. "By no means, or at any point, may you fall in love with me."

For a moment, Dani stared, unblinking. Then, suddenly, she burst into laughter, bending at the waist. When she looked me over and saw that my expression was even, she asked, "You're serious?"

I nodded. "We're friends, Dani. I would like us to stay that way."

"Trust me, Fynn, I won't fall in love with you."

It might have been pointless to add, but I valued Dani's friendship more than words could explain. Courting someone, whether for pretend or not, was always bound to get complicated at some point. We needed to ensure that we preserved our relationship.

I extended a hand. "Then it's a deal?"

As Dani stared at my outstretched hand, I would give anything to get a closer look at what she was thinking, at what was going on in her mind. But then again, I could barely understand what was happening in mine.

To make this believable, Dani and I would have to put on a great show for not only the leadership, but our friends and family as well.

If Dani was any other woman, I would have never suggested this. At the end of this, we could part ways amicably and maintain that friendship.

As long as we stuck to the rules.

Dani's fingers wrapped around mine, and with one shake, our bargain was sealed.

"Deal."

CHAPTER 7
DANI

Three days had passed since Fynn and I had made our deal, and not a second had gone by when I hadn't questioned my decision.

For this to work, we would need to announce our courtship; however, my schedule had been packed with training for the past few days.

Or at least, I was blaming my training. If I wanted to make time, I probably could have, yet I didn't.

With every passing day, I questioned the deal even more. There was no way it would work, even with our rules. As a trained strategist, I couldn't help but see the long list of flaws in our plan.

Number one—

I gasped as my back smacked into the training mat with a loud thump.

"Ha! Finally!" Sylvia punched the air.

An icy stream of air coated my lungs as I tried to regain my breath. I groaned out in pain and frustration. I couldn't remember the last time Sylvia—or anyone, for that matter—had put me flat on my back during combat training. Sylvia was a good fighter, but not *that* good of a fighter.

I pushed myself onto my elbows. "Don't look so smug, Lieutenant Larpos. I was distracted."

"Nope. Uh-uh." Sylvia waved a finger in my face. "No excuses, Captain. You've always said that if you can catch your opponent distracted on the mat or in the field, you better take the opportunity lest your back hit the mat first."

I rolled my eyes, grimacing as Sylvia repeated the words my father had said to me a thousand times as a child. I looked over to General Walen, who was overseeing the matches.

The general shrugged. "A win is a win, Captain Ferrios."

I struck the mat with my fist. "I want a rematch."

Sylvia laughed as Walen shook his head, amusement tugging at his lips. The other soldiers who watched shifted on their feet, unsure if it was safe to join in the laughter.

It wasn't.

Walen sighed. "Not today, Captain. Let some of the cadets take a turn on the mat."

He surveyed the line of eager young men and women waiting on the side. It was nearing the end of their schooling, and soon, the cadets would join our battalions. During the spring months, battalions across Pontia opened their training sessions to the nearby schools of cadets to give the young pupils a glimpse of life in the battalions.

"Take this as a lesson, cadets. Even the strongest can fall," General Walen said.

A couple of the cadets giggled.

My nails bit into the flesh of my palms. When I had stepped on the mat with Sylvia, the plan wasn't to show the cadets how to get knocked out.

Sylvia extended a hand, a smug grin inching across their face.

At that moment, I didn't know what I wanted more: to slap the lieutenant's smug expression off or yell at Fynn for distracting me. But he wasn't here for me to do that, was he?

I could already hear the snide remark he would make: *Already distracted by courting me, huh? My reputation truly does precede me, doesn't it, Ferrios?*

I scoffed.

"Something to say, *Captain*?"

At the voice, my head dropped against the mat with a thump.

This cannot be happening to me right now.

Nearby, someone cleared their throat as the glow of the sun disappeared behind my eyelids. I didn't need to peel my hands away from my face to see who it was, but I did so anyway.

Dark, shaded brown eyes blinked at me through a halo of chestnut brown hair. And at the bottom of Fynn's face, there it was—that cocky smirk and stubborn dimple shining down at me, as wide and as clear as the blue skies behind him.

"Is this what you look like flat on your back, Ferrios?" Fynn whispered. "I should store it in the back of my mind for safekeeping."

I glared at him. Perhaps, years ago, I would have blushed bright red hearing those words. But if there was any coloring tinting my cheeks now, it was only from anger.

"You know, in case someone ever asks." He winked and offered me a hand.

"As if anyone would ever ask that." I slapped his hand away and pushed myself off the ground, groaning slightly.

"General," Fynn said over his shoulder. "Do you mind if I borrow Captain Ferrios for a moment?"

"Wait, no, I have—"

Fynn arched a brow.

"The rules?" I mouthed. This was not a good sign. This directly interfered with my training, which was rule number one.

But before I could disagree any further, General Walen tipped his head. "Of course not, Your Highness."

I looked back at Sylvia, who was no help as they stared at Fynn with curiosity freckling their cheeks.

"Lead the way, *Your Highness*." I rolled my eyes and followed Fynn off the mat and away from the rest of the soldiers.

We walked for a couple of minutes until there were no prying ears in hearing distance.

Fynn turned to his guards. "Give us a moment, will you?"

The two guards raised a brow in unison as they sent cursory glances in my direction.

I propped a hand on my hip. "Come on, boys. What am I going to do? Stab him?"

Lance, the younger of the two guards, scratched the back of his neck, shrugging. Lance was six or seven years older than me. When I was a private, he had been the captain of my company before he had been tapped to join the prince's royal guard. Several years had passed since then, but I was only marginally less lethal with a blade back then.

With an exasperated sigh, Fynn brushed a hand through his hair, the waves flowing back. "She's not going to hurt me. You saw her get knocked flat on her back a moment ago, didn't you? I can take care of myself."

"Very well, sir," Lance said, holding back a snicker. Then, he and Telis, the quieter and more seasoned guard, nodded and walked out of earshot.

Folding my arms over my chest, I turned my attention to Fynn. "I was distracted."

Fynn chuckled. "Oh, about what?"

My gaze narrowed on his smirk, and I wondered how long he had been watching. However, we were not here to discuss my failures.

"Are you going to tell me what was so important that you needed to interrupt my training?"

Fynn inspected the peonies in the garden beside him, his long fingers brushing over one of the pink petals. "We should make the announcement. We cannot keep delaying this—"

"I'm not delaying anything," I said, quickly interrupting—too quickly, based on Fynn's raised brow. I cleared my throat. "You've been busy."

Instead of pointing out the lie we both knew I spoke, he stared at me.

I chewed on the inside of my cheek and peered at the crowd of soldiers who continued fighting on the mat. "Do we need to do this right now?"

Fynn snorted and shook his head. "Gods, no. We need to do this *right*. I can't just say that I am courting you. It doesn't work like that."

"Why not? When Sylvia started courting Riana, they didn't make a whole show of it."

Tugging at the back of his hair, Fynn sighed. "Dani, I'm the Crown Prince. Nothing is ever simple."

"Of course it isn't." I rubbed a hand across my face, then shoved my hands in my back pockets. "Do you have any ideas, then?"

The smirk that slipped over Fynn's face had my heart beating rapidly against my ribcage. A thin layer of sweat coated my palms. That look never meant anything good.

"I do."

I wanted to scream.

So I did.

Straight into a pillow.

Over the span of an hour, I had nearly emptied my entire closet of clothes. Dresses lay across the back of the vanity chair, over the end of the bed, on the floor. All that remained inside my closet was an abundance of training gear, which was not helpful for tonight's outing with Fynn.

When I finally stopped screaming, the back of my neck prickled.

"Is courting me that bad that you need to suffocate yourself, Ferrios?"

At the sound of Fynn's voice, I screamed again, squeezing the pillow closer to my face.

After seeing me get knocked flat on my ass, apparently him finding me in precarious situations was our new normal.

Eventually, I peeled the pillow away from my face and hugged it close to my chest. "Fynn, what a pleasant surprise," I said with a grimace.

"Surprise?" Fynn leaned against the door frame, his hands stuffed casually in his pockets and his ankles crossed.

He wore a freshly pressed suit, one more extravagant than his earlier ensemble. It was a rich, dark purple with an elegant floral design embroidered on the lapels. It was so *royal*—the opposite of anything lying in my room. The corners of his lip twitched with amusement, the faint mark of his dimple appearing. "I told you I was going to meet you before dusk."

"But it's—" I looked out the window, where golden light streamed inside the room. Dusk had already arrived, yet I still had nothing to wear, even though my entire closet was on the ground, sprawled out around me.

"What happened in here, anyway?" Fynn asked, pushing himself off the doorframe and taking a few steps inside my room. "It looks like someone ransacked the place."

I slammed the pillow down on the bed. "Very astute of you, Fynn," I said, annoyance and frustration coloring my voice.

Fynn snorted.

"It's not funny!" I grabbed the first item of clothing my fingers touched and chucked it at him.

Fynn caught it without even looking.

Stupid mind-reading ability.

"Stupid? Or useful?" he asked, arching a brow. He held up the blouse I had thrown at him, inspecting it.

"I'm serious, Fynn."

He tossed the shirt onto one of the many piles of clothes littering the floor. "Let's go, Ferrios."

"Go? I'm not ready."

"Just follow me, will you?"

"Follow you *where?*"

He hit the door frame with his hand and glanced over his shoulder. His dark eyes sparkled gold in the soft, warm hues of the sun. "Ferrios, I know you better than most. I also know you dislike being late, so I made arrangements."

Before I could respond, he disappeared around the door. Despite the anxiety turning in my stomach, there was nothing else I could do but follow him.

CHAPTER 8
DANI

"MORE WINE, YOUR HIGHNESS?" THE STOREKEEPER'S ASSISTANT, Lorallye, asked as I tugged the slip down my hips behind a thin curtain.

Since arriving at the royal family's preferred boutique, Everly's, I had tried on at least a half dozen dresses. The first was an ivory dress with long billowing sleeves that tangled around my limbs every time I moved. The second was an equally pretty, emerald green dress with a deep dip at the chest. I couldn't quite remember the third one, or the fourth, for that matter. All of them were equally beautiful and elegant as the last, yet none felt right.

I had seen the dresses Fynn's former partners had worn when they had attended functions with him. They were all extravagant and classy and fit them perfectly. Meanwhile, all the dresses I tried on felt like I was putting makeup on an armored soldier. Ridiculous.

Gripping the tulle in my hands, I tugged again, the fabric finally releasing me and pooling at my feet in a heap. I groaned, loud and very *un*-royal.

"Why not?" Fynn said from the waiting room. "We might be here for a while, Lorallye."

I groaned, tossing the frilly gown onto the mountain of tulle, satin, and taffeta in the corner.

"I'll grab another bottle, Your Highness," the woman whispered.

"Thank you, Lorallye," Fynn said, and I could hear the wink in his voice. "Oh, and could you grab some of those little butter cookies? You know, the ones dipped in chocolate that they sell across the street?"

"Of course, Your Highness!" Lorallye said, her voice rising three octaves.

"Of course, Your Highness," I mouthed at the curtain, my eyes rolling to the back of my head.

Since we walked into the boutique, Lorallye had been fawning over Fynn. Her pale pink cheeks grew pinker with every passing interaction between them.

It was both comical and appalling.

As Lorallye's quick steps disappeared in the distance, there was shuffling on the other side of the curtain, followed by slow, approaching footsteps.

"Cookies?" I hissed as I stepped into the next dress. "Really, Fynn?"

"What? I'm hungry."

"You're ridiculous."

"Or I simply wanted some time to talk to you before tonight. It'll take her a minute to grab them from the bakery since Kade fancies her. She'll be busy for at least a few minutes."

I sighed. "You didn't have to take me here."

Something thumped against the adjoining wall as if Fynn had leaned his head against it. "So you've said, but I'm not very good at listening."

"Well, at this rate, we're going to be late," I mumbled, fumbling with the ribbons at the back of the dress.

Fynn hummed. "Which means less time for small talk before the performance starts. You should be overjoyed."

While Fynn might have had a point, being late was not my preference. In my experience, being late only meant more eyes would be on you. Between the dresses and the anxiety spinning in my stomach and up my throat, I was already working up a sweat.

"Perhaps, but"—I stretched, my fingers straining to grab the ribbons—"you know how I feel about being late."

"Oh, I know."

With a frustrated groan, I ripped open the curtain and spun around. "A little help?"

"Huh?"

"The ribbons, Fynn," I hissed, the bottom of my hair dampening from the sweat coating my neck. "I can't reach them, and since you sent Lorallye away. . ."

"Hmm. But the rules state that I can only touch you when necessary."

"Oh, shut it and help me."

"If you say so, Ferrios." Fynn took a small step forward.

The heat from his body pressed against my back. I tried to remain still, thinking about anything else as notes of sea salt and wine surrounded me. The ribbons flew in the air as Fynn laced the corset as if he had plenty of practice tying women into corsets.

"Personally, I prefer untying them," Fynn said, his breath kissing the back of my neck and—

My eyes widened, and I quickly reinforced my mental shields before he dug deeper into my thoughts.

Fynn chuckled. "Is it tight enough?"

I cleared my throat and shifted in the dress, the silk fabric suddenly uncomfortable. Peering down, I rolled my eyes and adjusted the top of the corset. As I held it in place, I said, "Tighter."

He pulled the strings, and the corset tightened around my torso. I turned back around, skirting around Fynn to look in the mirror.

My eyes widened at the sight. I cocked my head to the side and turned, the purple fabric swishing across the floor.

While the others were nice, this one was—

"It's as if this one was made for you, Miss Ferrios," the assistant said, returning and snatching my attention from the dress.

I wished she was lying, but a smile bloomed when I viewed myself in the mirror again.

Chipper Lorallye was right. This dress was perfect. Stained a beautiful, rich purple, the silk fabric flowed down my body as if it were air, floating around me as I twisted side-to-side. When I took a couple of steps forward to see if it would tangle around my ankles, instead of ensnaring me, the fabric spread out and became slightly transparent. My legs peeked beneath it, turning the purple a brilliant, warm shade. The bodice dipped low between my breasts while somehow still providing ample support.

In this dress, I didn't see the little girl who always had mud smeared across her shirts and grass stains on her knees.

I spun in a circle. When I stopped, I faced Fynn and asked, "Does it get the Crown Prince's stamp of approval?"

Fynn took a long swig of his wine. "It's. . ." He paused, and my smile wavered. He wiped his mouth with the back of his hand and shrugged. "Nice," he said at last.

My hands fell to my hips, my nails digging into the fabric. "*Nice?*"

Fynn nodded and then grabbed a cookie from the tray Lorallye had sat down.

Pursing my lips, I nodded and spun toward the mirror, running my hand along the soft fabric.

"Oh, don't listen to him, miss." Lorallye gasped. She spun toward Fynn and fell into an apologetic curtsy. "I say that with the utmost respect, Your Highness."

Fynn shrugged dismissively, brushing the crumbs from his trousers.

Lorallye turned to me again, her voice slightly quieter. "Miss Ferrios, this is one of Madam Everly's favorites."

For good reasons. The dress was splendid—more than splendid, truthfully. It was extraordinary beyond belief.

But maybe Fynn was right.

On me, it was just *nice*. It didn't matter what I wore. I wasn't some lady who wore frivolous dresses and gossiped at afternoon tea parties.

"Let's try the black one," I said after a moment.

"Are you sure?" Lorallye asked, her hands curling beneath her chin, sadness dripping from her bright eyes. "That one is so simple compared to this."

I offered her a soft smile. "Simple sounds perfect, Lorallye."

Her brows twisted together, but when she realized I wasn't going to back down, she nodded with a small sigh. "Very well."

Fynn grabbed his suit jacket from where it was draped over the side of the couch. "I'll be waiting in the carriage."

"Oh, but the accessories! We haven't talked about those," Lorallye said.

Fynn flicked a hand in the air, already nearing the doors. "Get whatever you want, Dani. Just be quick about it. I'll send Jorian in for the payment. I am sure he is getting antsy by now."

With my mouth hanging open, I stared at the back of Fynn's head as he pulled the door open and the nighttime breeze swept inside the small boutique.

"What do you think about this, Miss Ferrios?" Lorrallye asked, calling my attention back to her. She held up a simple silver necklace with a brilliant amethyst hanging from it. Her eyes widened. "Oh, I have just the heels to go with them, too! They are absolutely stunning. They have matching amethysts on the heels!"

"Sounds lovely," I said, my previous smile fading.

It didn't matter how many of Pontia's gemstones embellished the ensemble. A hundred amethysts would not change anything.

Wisps of pink and orange painted the sky as the sun dipped into the sea. My heels snapped against the cobblestone as we made our way up the stairs of the theater hall. The steps to the theater were clear of any other guests, which only meant one thing: we were late.

Panic surged through my body, from the beautiful heels to my brows.

Fynn and I walked silently as Jorian and his two guards strolled several paces behind us. Each step we took up the staircase only raised another question and concern.

No one would believe that we were courting. The entire kingdom knew that we had grown up together. Why would our feelings for each other change now?

Suddenly, it was as if we were about to head into a battle before gathering the necessary intel.

How many people stood on the enemy's side?

What was our plan of attack?

Were we going to use the element of surprise and sneak into the enemy's camp in the middle of the night, or would we dive headfirst into the mezzanine?

When the enemy was your own kingdom, your own family, what was the proper strategy to implement?

My feet hit the platform, and I stared at the doors, the air stuck in my lungs. We had reached the top of the staircase, but we hadn't even gotten our story straight.

I grabbed Fynn's arm and tugged him to the side.

Immediately, he signaled the men behind us to hold on. Turning to me, he gripped my shoulders. "Relax, Dani. There's nothing to worry about."

"Nothing? You mean *everything*," I spat. "We haven't even talked about how this whole *thing* started. Your mother and brother are going to be inside. They know us too well. They're not going to believe it. They're going to see right through our act."

Fynn brushed a hand through his hair, tugging at the strands. "Look, you're right. Everyone will question this; that's to be expected. But have you somehow forgotten that I can read minds? If people start questioning it, I'll do some damage control and fix it." He squeezed my shoulder. "Stop worrying so much."

His words were meant to comfort me, but they only increased my rising anxiety. I didn't go into things without a plan. Yet somehow, I ended up here in front of Fynn without any concrete plan.

I shoved a finger at his chest. "This is not just your reputation on the line here, Fynneares. If your laissez-faire attitude ruins this—"

Fynn grabbed my wrist and tugged it down. "It'll be fine. Just follow my lead."

"Easier said than done," I mumbled.

I was not a follower and never had been. I didn't like relying on others to do the legwork for me. How could my soldiers trust me as a leader if I wasn't willing to run into the fire first? I trusted the soldiers in my company to have my back because I had proven to them over the years that I had theirs.

Fynn though? He was another story.

I had known him since I was three years old, which meant I knew the tricks he often played. During our lessons as children, he would constantly throw crumpled-up paper balls at the back of my head. When we were teenagers, he purposely told the son of a prominent Pontian lord that I had a crush on him to get me to blush and run out of the room. If he had the opportunity to make me appear a fool, he usually took it.

But what other choice did I have?

"Fine, but what's our story? If this is going to work, we need to be on the same page. And unlike you, I can't read your mind."

Fynn released an exasperated sigh. "Our relationship is new. After the crowning ceremony, one drink led to another, and things escalated from—"

"We are *not* telling people that," I said, shoving him.

Fynn chuckled. "Do you have any better ideas?"

I tapped my foot on the ground, running through the possible scenarios. When it came down to it, it was always best to stick to the truth as much as possible when lying. Fewer traps to fall into.

I took a deep breath. "Actually, I do. I've had a crush on you since we were little, but—"

He snapped his fingers, nodding. "But you were too scared to say anything because I made you too nervous."

"What?" I jerked my head back. "That was not what I was going to say! I was going to say that it was nothing serious and quickly went away."

Fynn folded his arms over his chest, a sideways smile appearing on his face. "Nope, I like my version better."

"Fine," I said through clenched teeth. "The night of the crowning ceremony—"

"You were jealous seeing me dance with all those women and finally had enough. After the ball, you finally confessed, but I brushed it off."

My nails bit into my arms, but I added, "Then, when you heard about the suitors my mother was having me see, you grew even more jealous than I was and realized you had secret feelings for me, too."

Fynn snapped his head toward me, aghast. "What? *That's* ridiculous."

Smiling, I shook my head. If one of us was harboring a childhood secret in this fake courtship, both of us were—even if one of us might have been telling the truth.

I poked him in the chest, hoping he couldn't see the truth. "Nope, we're sticking to it."

"Fine." Then Fynn did the unexpected.

He slipped his hand in mine, and my brows twisted together. When I peered at him, he quirked a brow.

"Jorian and the guards might not be able to hear us, but they are watching. Might as well get used to it now."

I bit down on my tongue, and Fynn leaned closer, his scruff brushing against my cheek. "Rekindled feelings, remember?"

"Right," I said as he led us forward.

I wrapped my arm around his and hoped that the fluttering in my stomach was only a fluke and nothing more.

CHAPTER 9
FYNN

Arm in arm with Dani, I tipped my chin up as I strolled into the private suite, a nonchalant grin plastered on my face.

All the patrons within the suite—my mother, Terin, Airos, and various lords and ladies—turned in their seats toward us as the curtains on the stage rolled back. The conductor stepped onto the stage and raised a hand toward the royal box, yet all eyes in the box were on Dani and me.

Terin's thoughts spiraled toward me. *Why is Dani here? And why is she on your arm?*

Ignoring my brother's pressing thoughts, I led Dani past the sitting patrons. The thoughts of the lords and ladies brushed across me, quick and fleeting.

Is that the Ferrios daughter?

What is she doing here?

Are they holding hands?

When we reached my mother, she said, "Fynneares, I'm so happy you decided to join us. For a moment, I thought you weren't going to show."

"And miss one of Lorenza's world-renowned performances?

Never," I said, leaning forward to place a quick peck on my mother's cheek. The gifted singer could pull tears from the audience with a single note. It was truly a sight to behold.

My mother smiled. "And you brought Dani! What a pleasant surprise. It has been too long since I've seen the four of you together. Although I suppose it will be longer yet since Graeson refused to come."

Dani curtsied. "Fynn gave me a bargain I couldn't refuse, Your Majesty," Dani quipped, giving me a sideways glance.

When Dani stood, I tugged her closer, weaving my fingers between hers as I smiled down at her. Dani smiled back, but it was slightly forced, her hand squeezing mine tightly and cracking one of my knuckles.

My mother's gaze dropped to our entwined hands.

Before she could ask the question that I saw on the tip of her tongue, I cleared my throat and signaled to the two empty seats. "Come, Dani. Let us take our seats before Lorenza's performance starts."

As we passed, I squeezed my mother's hand, hoping she would only see what I wanted her to. I kept everything else buried lest she strip the wrong memory away from my palm.

At our seats, Dani squeezed past my brother, whispering a quick greeting.

"Hey Dani," Terin said, the skepticism palpable on his tongue as he observed us.

I signaled for one of the servants and grabbed two glasses of sparkling wine. I handed one to Dani.

"Thank you," she mumbled, then gulped half of it.

"My pleasure," I said, sitting between Dani and Terin.

Terin leaned forward in his chair. "I heard about Quint getting the promotion."

My lips formed a tight line as Dani shifted in her seat. Around us, the spectators clapped as the singer walked onto the stage wearing a beautiful dress with a long train that swept across the stage. When she reached the center of the stage, she curtsied, smiling at the audience.

"Quint's a good guy," Terin said, still leaning forward, "but you deserved the promotion."

Dani's shoulders sagged. "Thanks, Ter." She raised her glass and took a large sip of the sparkling wine.

The tension slowly left her body as she sank into the chair. Terin always had a way of calming her nerves. I supposed it was one of the effects of his gift. My brother was almost always in a dream-like state, his voice melodic and soothing, like a soft lullaby. Many people underestimated Terin because of it. He was the quiet brother, the reserved one, the one who appeared to be fine with staying in my shadow.

In truth, Terin was the one to watch out for. Because asleep, it was nearly impossible to protect one's mind.

"Is that one of Madam Everly's dresses?" Terin asked, nodding to Dani's dress.

Chewing on the inside of her cheek, Dani peered at me from the corner of her eye.

"It is," I said.

Terin hummed. "It looks nice."

Dani's hand froze as she raised her drink. It was only for a second, but it was long enough for me to notice it and for the tension in the air to thicken. Soon, though, she was smiling at Terin. "Thank you, Terin."

Terin nodded.

Then, the theater darkened, and the clapping stopped.

I wrapped an arm around Dani's shoulders, pulling her closer. "Oh, the performance is starting, hon."

Dani almost choked. Terin shifted in his seat awkwardly beside me as I struggled to retain my laughter. Dani glared at me as Lorenza's voice filled the room, a soft, melodic sound.

Hon? When did Dani become hon?

"What?" I mouthed to Dani, ignoring Terin's thoughts pressing down the line.

Having recovered, Dani leaned over and hissed in my ear. "Was that truly the best you could come up with?"

I shifted toward her, my nose brushing against the curls surrounding her face, the scent of cinnamon wafting off them. "Would you have preferred sweetheart or some other cliché?"

Dani snorted. "My name would have sufficed."

"I'll keep that in mind next time." I placed a hand on top of hers and grinned at the way Dani jumped slightly.

Behind us, I could sense the watching eyes.

My lips brushed her ear as I shifted closer. "Pretend to like me, remember?"

Dani scoffed but scooted closer.

"Ter is indeed skeptical," I said. "More shocked than anything, if I'm being honest. Still, we need to give them no reason to doubt us."

"I told you this would happen," she mumbled.

"Nothing we can't handle." I cocked a brow. "Now, lean back and giggle."

"Giggle?" Dani asked, her nose brushing my cheek lightly before she jerked back. "Why in the world would I do that?"

"To give the others the impression that I've been whispering sweet nothings in your ear."

"Why would I *giggle* because of that?"

"Because, Ferrios, when I flirt, a blush usually colors the woman's cheeks. But a blush cannot be seen in the dark, now can it?"

"That's preposterous."

"Or it only seems so because you haven't heard the things I say in private."

At that, Dani laughed. It might not have been a *giggle,* but truth be told, the full sound was even better.

"That a girl," I whispered as Lorenza reached the first chorus of the night.

Perhaps this wouldn't be so bad, I thought as I settled in my seat. Other than the hand-holding, nothing was different. The question, then, was whether we could convince everyone else. After all, the night had barely begun, and Terin was already casting us wary glances.

As Lorenza's first song reached its final note, I leaned over to Dani, raising a brow. "How about princess?"

"Oh, shut it," Dani whispered, smacking me in the chest lightly as the clapping erupted throughout the theater.

I chuckled.

Courting my best friend might be the most fun I've had in a long time.

CHAPTER 10
FYNN

"You and Dani, huh?" Terin asked.

A grunt escaped my lips as I swung the blade. "What about Dani and me?"

Without missing a beat, Terin blocked my attack, metal clashing together. Using his sword as leverage, he pushed against mine.

I spun away, retreating a few steps.

He swiped a hand across his short, buzzed hair.

Once, when we were no older than twelve, Graeson had decided to shave my hair, making Terin and I even more indistinguishable from one another than usual. Never again would I cut my hair that short. I found I liked giving my partners something to tug—even if the soft waves often fell into my eyes.

"It's a simple question, brother," Terin said, his forehead slick with sweat.

Terin and I kept nothing from each other, which only made keeping this secret from him that much harder. But as much as I loved and trusted my brother, I promised Dani I wouldn't tell him.

I couldn't necessarily blame her for adding the rule to the list. If our mother came asking him questions about my courtship with

Dani, he would spill the truth after only a little prodding on our mother's part.

Neither Dani, nor I, could afford the risk.

So, despite how wrong it felt, I wouldn't tell Terin the truth.

Was it hypocritical of me then to go searching for whatever truth he was keeping from me?

Perhaps.

Yet I searched anyway, for reaching for someone's mind was like breathing air, instinctual and compulsory.

I dug beneath the fortress of his shields, finding the holes he had forgotten to fill. Once behind his walls, the task was easy. Because Terin, despite his long list of strengths, was predictable. He always buried the thoughts he didn't wish me to know by trying to distract me with other images—childhood memories or other trivial things that happened in his day-to-day life. I pushed through the thoughts of what he ate that morning, of which dark-haired man currently piqued his interest. Then, finding the dark corner of his mind, I scoured the walls for the lock. Once found, all it took was one quick pull before it snapped. A rolling flood of concerns struck me.

Childhood friends.

Strange.

Mistake.

Mess up our dynamics.

I slammed the door shut with a groan. "My business is my business, brother."

"Then you should not dig for answers you do not wish to hear." Terin struck, his sword coming down hard and fast. "Dani is our oldest friend," he spat.

I drove forward with equal force. "What's your point?" My hands tightened around the hilt.

"You're going to mess this up," Terin said, cementing his feet into the sand.

"I am not."

We may have been evenly matched in physical strength, but I was quicker when it came to fighting and strategy. I could read my opponent's mind and see their next move before they even made it.

Terin tried to block me out, but after an hour of training, he was growing tired, his mind weakening.

I pushed, and Terin's face reddened as he held his ground. Swing after swing, the muscles in his arms began to shake. Soon, his sword was trembling in his hands.

But my brother wasn't a quitter.

Neither was I, though.

"If you hurt her—"

"I won't," I said, cutting him off.

Terin swung, and I pushed my sword and spun. He came barreling forward, barely catching himself before he hit the ground as I dipped out of the way.

Huffing, he raised his sword once again. "I know how you can be."

I narrowed my gaze. "What is that supposed to mean?"

Terin's mental shield cracked open, and a flurry of names fell down the thread connecting his mind to mine.

Marla.

Drisilia.

Marisil.

Selena.

Rosalina.

"Dani is *not* one of them," I said through clenched teeth.

"Are you sure about that?"

"She's different."

"How? You brought her to the concert hall. How many other women have you paraded around there? How many other women did you have sitting in your lap as you whispered promises into their ears —promises you always break?"

"Dani and I are *different*."

We weren't in a real relationship, for starters. She would not fall for me, nor would I fall for her. There were no strings attached, no faulty promises or hopeful gazes. Dani knew my history. But more than that, she knew who I was.

We had a deal. It was that simple.

"I won't hurt her, Ter."

Still, Terin attacked.

I dodged, but Terin saw through it. He snatched my collar and forced me to the ground. My ears wrung as dust flew into the air.

"And what's to say she won't hurt you?"

I laughed, the sound like gravel. "She won't."

Terin's eyes flicked over my face. "You don't know that."

"I do."

"When the two of you break up—"

"Who is to say we will?" I asked, even though I knew we would. The whole purpose of this fake courtship was that it was temporary. But Terin didn't need to know that—he couldn't.

"Look, I care about you both too much." He took a deep breath, his hand loosening. When he looked down at me, pain dripped from his gaze. "We've already lost one sister. I don't want to lose another."

Without thinking, my fist slammed into his jaw.

Terin rolled off me, palm caressing his cheek. "Shit, Fynn. I didn't—"

"Don't you bring our sister into this. This isn't about her."

His words had struck a chord.

Perhaps, it was because I did not wish to think about our sister right now. Or perhaps, it was because he thought so little of me that I would cause Dani to erase us from her life. Either way, I tried to tame the rage. I tried to let the sea of anger wash over me, for the tidal wave to subside, but I couldn't.

"You're right. I—" Terin swallowed, struggling for the right words.

We both knew there weren't any. It might have been fifteen years since we last saw our sister, but we hadn't forgotten her.

One day, however, we would get her back.

Even if it was the last thing I did.

I exhaled, long and hard. "It's fine." I ran my fingers through my hair, pushing back the fallen strands.

"You're serious about this then?" Terin asked.

I bit my cheek as I met my brother's gaze and lied. "Yes."

In truth, it wasn't a complete lie. I cared about Dani, so I was serious about doing whatever I could to make this arrangement work.

"Then you better not fuck it up," Terin said and shoved back against the dirt.

"Come on, Ter," I said, a smirk rising to the surface. "Let's be honest, I'm pretty good at fucking things."

"By the gods, Fynn! She's practically family." Terin groaned, rubbing the palms of his hands over his head, his lip curling in disgust.

"Hey, I never said anything about her and I, but if you're curious—"

"Stop," Terin said, shaking his head and standing, kicking dirt into my hair. "You can never take anything seriously, can you?"

I shrugged, and Terin shook his head.

"If you do—if you have," Terin gagged as he spoke, "I don't want to know *any* details."

Even though Dani and I would never cross that boundary, I forced a coy smirk onto my face because that's what my brother expected of me. How many mornings had I spent relaying details of my escapades with women to him? How many nights had I come home after climbing out of manors and houses after spending it with someone I probably shouldn't have? If I acted as if Dani and I sleeping together wasn't a possibility, he would know something was wrong.

Terin shifted on his feet, his gaze fixed on the ground. After a moment, he peered at me and asked so quietly I almost didn't hear him, "Have you?"

I scratched the back of my head as I looked toward the castle. "We're. . .taking things slow."

Terin snorted. "You? Taking things slow? I didn't know that was even a possibility for you."

I laughed, but it was short-lived because as his words hit me, I finally understood the consequence of this deal.

I would have to be celibate for the next several months.

I stared down at my hand.

Shit.

CHAPTER 11
DANI

"As some of you might have heard, I will be retiring in a little over four months."

Gasps echoed across the lines of soldiers. While I had known this was coming, hearing the words from the general increased the weight pressing down on my shoulders. As excited as I was about the opening Walen's retirement created, it also sent a prickle spiraling down my spine. I couldn't help but think about how we were now losing two of our top generals to retirement within the same year.

Change was often good, but sometimes, it meant something was coming—something the older gentlemen did not wish to be a part of or risk their lives for.

I tilted my chin up.

Whatever it was, I would be prepared.

Walen continued, "I won't get into the sappy nonsense today, but know I will be leaving with a heavy heart." He cleared his throat, then saluted. "That is all for today. You're released."

The soldiers all fell out of formation, relaxing their stances and walking out of their lines. Whispers immediately passed between soldiers as they discussed the general's announcement.

Someone tugged my arm. When I spun around, I found Sylvia staring at me with a raised brow.

"Tell me the rumors are just rumors."

"What do you mean?" I asked. "The general admitted—"

"No, not about the general. Tell me that you and a certain prince are not, you know. . .a *thing*."

"How did—where did—" I tripped on my words.

"So it is true!" Sylvia shouted, causing a few of the soldiers to look our way.

I pulled them to the side, away from the crowd. "Do you have to be so loud about it?"

Sylvia scoffed. "Did the prince really take you to the concert hall?"

"Yes," I said, leaning away from them.

"Wow," Sylvia said. "I'm shocked you let him. That's like his whole thing."

"What whole thing?"

With their arms crossed over their chest, Sylvia gawked at me. "Are you that daft? I thought you two were close or something."

"We are," I said, straightening beneath Sylvia's scrutiny.

"You're not *that* close if you don't know."

I chewed on the inside of my cheek.

I was thirteen when Fynn started loosely courting women and started talking about his dalliances with them. Where they went, who he went with, what they did or talked about—and more often, how they *didn't* talk.

At first, I couldn't help but listen. Perhaps I was curious about what I needed to do to gain his interest. Back then, our two-year age difference felt like a generation splitting us apart. I had made myself believe it was better to be his friend than not be in his life at all—even if that meant he would only ever see me as one of the guys. But then my jealousy grew.

Soon, I found excuses to slip out during those conversations—an extra study session or an early dinner with my grandparents I had forgotten about.

Eventually, leaving when the conversation came up became normal. As we grew older, I found more and more reasons to separate myself from Fynn.

I had thought it was for the best. I had seen how Rosalina or one of his other partners would look at me. I didn't want to face the questions that were bound to follow if I stayed around.

I was still in Fynn's life, but I was no longer an active part of it. He was still one of my best friends, but our relationship was tied to our history rather than our present.

Maybe Sylvia was right.

Maybe I wasn't as close to Fynn as I had thought.

Still, I needed to know what Sylvia was talking about.

I grabbed Sylvia's wrist, dragging them away from the crowd. "Sylvia, what *thing*?"

Sylvia sighed. "Fynn's a nice guy, and I'm sure he'll be a decent king. But he's not like. . . a *good* guy, you know?"

"No, I don't know. Out with it already, Sylv."

Sylvia sighed. They rubbed a hand over their pale, freckle-covered face. "The whole kingdom knows that the prince gets around."

My hand fell from Sylvia's wrist, the tension releasing despite the pang of jealousy sprouting.

This was not news.

Fynn always brought a different woman to events. A couple of times, he ended up leaving with a different woman on his arm than the one whom he came with. But based on Sylvia's concerned gaze and the purse of their lips, I knew there had to be something they weren't saying.

"How does this have to do with me going to the concert hall?"

Sylvia sighed and grabbed one of my shoulders. "I'm telling you this because I care about you as a friend, all right?"

I nodded, my brows furrowing. The creases threatening to become permanent.

"The concert hall is his go-to. He always brings his latest conquests there and parades them around his family. It's like a show on top of a show. There's been stories about what happens there."

I snorted and shoved their hand off me. "You shouldn't believe all the gossip you hear, Sylv."

"I just. . ." Sylvia stared at me, eyes scanning my face. "Be careful with him, all right?"

"You can't be serious."

Sylvia crossed their arms over their chest.

"We're friends—"

"Friends or *friends*, Dani?" Sylvia cocked a brow.

I cleared my throat. "Friends who are seeing where this could go. I'm not jumping into anything. It's. . ."

"Different?" Sylvia supplied.

"Yes," I said, but based on Sylvia's disapproving gaze, that was the wrong answer.

"That's what they all say, Dani. I'm sure he says you're different too." Sylvia cocked their head in the direction of a group of nearby soldiers. "That's what Marisil said a few months ago. Look at her now."

Sure enough, Marisil, one of the soldiers in my company, was sending me metaphorical daggers with watering eyes that burned with flames.

I quickly looked away and leaned closer to Sylvia. "Why is she staring at me like that?"

Sylvia patted me on my arm. "Like I said, word gets around. She's still heartbroken over that boy, and she's not the only one."

A sour taste filled my mouth as I shifted on my feet. My gaze swept across the hundreds of soldiers gathering their belongings and leaving the training yard. Some of the women, however, hesitated as they spotted me, their gazes turning cold.

"He's a prince and one of the most eligible men in Pontia." Sylvia squeezed my arm, but the gesture did little to comfort the rising anxiety in my stomach. "Captain, you might have just earned yourself a few more enemies."

"FYNNEARES ANDROS NADAREAN!"

Fynn snapped his head around, his unbuttoned blouse billowing in the breeze that swept across the castle's training grounds. Sweat glistened on his face. His hair was tousled as if he had been running his hand through it nonstop.

I barreled forward. I slammed my palm into his chest, hitting muscle that I didn't let surprise me.

Fynn stumbled back. "What the fuck, Dani?"

"Don't." I shoved a finger in his face. "Don't play the coy, ignorant prince. It does not suit you, Fynneares."

"You know," he said, swatting my hand away, "this would go more smoothly if you simply explained what you are upset about."

"You know exactly what—" I snapped my lips shut as someone nearby cleared their throat.

My gaze slipped to behind Fynn, where Terin shifted on his feet, appearing as uncomfortable as ever.

"Hey, Dani," Terin said with a half-wave. He scratched the back of his head. "Trouble in paradise already, huh?"

"I—" The blood rushed to my cheeks, and the back of my neck heated. I glanced at Fynn for help. But when I turned to the prince, his back was to his brother, and his arms were crossed over his chest, a cocky half-smirk splayed across his face.

Arrogant asshole.

The corner of his lip tugged upward as I let the words slip beneath my shields.

A little help here? I added.

Fynn rolled his eyes, his shoulders dropping. "Don't worry. Dani's simply mad because I didn't give her a goodnight kiss last night, aren't you, love?"

Fynn's lashes fluttered across his cheeks as he blinked at me.

My nails bit into my palms. I exhaled, slow and steady. "Right, *love.*"

"I think we're done training for the day, Terin. Do you mind?" Fynn asked.

"Sure," Terin said, elongating the word. "Whatever you need. I don't want to be in the middle of whatever is going on between the two of you, anyway. Later, Dani!"

I haphazardly waved at Terin as he strolled away, my gaze never leaving Fynn as he shoved his hands deep into the pockets of his linen trousers. He casually leaned back on his heels as if everything was fine.

Because to Fynn, this was only another one of his games.

After a moment, Fynn smacked his tongue against the roof of his mouth and nodded, pointing in the direction Terin had left. "This has been fun, but I better get going. You know, princely duties await."

Fynn made to step around me, but I cut him off. "Nope. You're not going anywhere," I said, ramming my hand against his chest.

His chest was surprisingly firm for a prince who seemingly would rather spend his time drinking and sleeping around. I, however, refused to think about whatever other muscles might have developed over the past few years.

"If you insist." Fynn brushed his fingers through his hair. He groaned, his hand falling to his side. "What are you so worked up about, anyway? I thought last night went well. Terin seems to—"

I spun on my heel. "Worked up? Fynn, you took me to the *concert* hall."

"And? I thought we had a nice time."

"A nice time? A *nice* time?"

"Yes," he said, taking a few steps back. "Am I wrong? Or is it simply your strange aversion to the word nice?"

"Let me make this clear, Fynneares. Because apparently, it needs to be repeated." I stalked forward. When Fynn swallowed, his smug attitude dropping for a moment, a small part of me was overjoyed that he at least marginally feared me. "I have a reputation to uphold. I am *not* one of the women you can parade around—"

"What in the stars are you talking about?" he asked, interrupting.

I groaned. "Marisil?"

"What about her?"

"You took her to the concert hall, didn't you?"

"Sure, but I've taken a lot of people there. It is a common place for—"

"People or women, Fynn?" I interrupted.

"Well, both." Fynn shrugged nonchalantly. But nothing about this was nonchalant.

That's what I deserved for not having thought this through—for having been distracted by his stupid smirk. Again.

"You're unbelievable!" I spun on my heel, pacing the castle's training grounds. "If the leaders are going to take this seriously, they have to believe it's not another one of your silly little flings! If your mother is going to believe this—"

"All right, all right, I get it. Look, Dani," Fynn said, grabbing a hold of my wrist and forcing me to a stop. "I meant nothing by it. Many people—yes, myself included—take their partners to the concert hall. I thought that Lorenza's performance would provide enough publicity without the need for unnecessary conversations with others. I knew we hadn't had enough time to get our story straight, so a performance would provide the entertainment we needed to prevent those conversations."

Crossing my arms over my chest, I snorted. "Well, it had enough publicity, that's for sure. My soldiers are already talking about it."

"That's a good thing, isn't it? The whole point was for people to know. It's not like my history is a secret."

"Your history is none of my business."

"But you just—"

"I said it's none of my business! I don't care what you did before. I only. . ." I groaned and pressed the heels of my palms against my temples. Once the pressure dwindled, I let my hands fall. "I suppose I hadn't fully thought through the repercussions of courting you."

Fynn's gaze narrowed, and I shifted beneath it. He was only a foot away now, and I could feel his breath touch my forehead. "When have you ever cared about what others thought of you, Dani?"

I blinked. "I don't."

"Then why are you so upset?" He tilted his head, and a single brown wave fell across his forehead. "Because it's not like we are actually courting one another, right?"

I swallowed. Hard. "Right. It's just—it's the principle of the thing."

"The *principle?*"

Unable to do or say anything else as the space between us grew smaller, I nodded.

Fynn cackled. "All right, fine. Next time, I'll—"

I shook my head and interrupted, "No, next time, *I'm* choosing where we go and what we do."

"Fine, if that's what you want," Fynn said.

"It is."

"Then it's settled."

"Good."

"Good," Fynn repeated, crossing his arms over his chest, mocking my stance.

I didn't know why it bothered me. Like Fynn had said, I knew his history. While I might not have known all the details—and quite frankly, I didn't want to know them—Marisil's hurt gaze bothered me. I didn't like my soldiers—or anyone, for that matter—thinking that I was another woman fawning over a charming prince.

His gaze bounced across my face, his brown eyes flicking between mine. "Are you really that upset about this?"

Sighing, I rubbed my face with my palms. "I don't know, Fynn. It's just. . ." My words melted into the air.

But Fynn wasn't going to let this go.

"Just what?"

I tipped my head up to the sky, gathering my thoughts. "I have a lot riding on this. I'm not doing this simply to get my mother off my back."

"Like I am," Fynn mumbled, still loud enough for me to hear. "Got it."

"Are you—are you mad at *me* now?"

Fynn sighed, shaking his head. "No, of course not."

He smiled, but the smile didn't reach his eyes. When he made to turn around, I grabbed his arm. If I had to talk about my feelings, so did he.

He looked down at the spot where my fingers curled around his arm, holding him in place. "Let go of me, Dani."

"Tell me what's wrong first."

"I have a lot on my mind today. Terin said something earlier to me that must still have me shaken."

My grip around his arm loosened. "What did he say?"

Fynn stepped back, forcing my hand to fall. He picked up his sword. "Nothing for you to worry about."

My brows scrunched together. Everyone's thoughts might have been wide open for Fynn to take, but it was often hard for Fynn to voice his own. However, there was only one thing in this world that

Fynn refused to discuss, one thing that put him on edge and made his anger quick to rise.

"We'll get her back, Fynn," I whispered.

Fynn sheathed his sword, his gaze fixed on the ground. "It's been fifteen years. Who knows if she's even the same person she was before she was taken?"

My hand wrapped around his. The gesture was not forced or hidden behind some pretense like the other night but rather from years of friendship. "The Nadareans are fighters, remember? She's stronger than you think."

"Historically speaking," he mumbled, "we're rulers, not fighters."

"Fynn, there are different kinds of warriors. One does not need to wear a uniform or carry a sword to be deemed a fighter."

Fynn's gaze met mine at last, and a small smile rose to his lips.

Moments like these, when I saw the real Fynn—the man who cared deeply, never gave up on his friends and family, and wanted to fix the world—it was hard not to let old feelings rise. This version of him was so rare that I often forgot it existed in the first place. But as the shadows spread across his face, I couldn't help but think that this quiet, reserved version of the prince was my favorite. Because when he showed this side of himself, there were no pretenses or masks.

But then Fynn took a step back, and the normal Fynn reappeared. Whatever old feelings that had been stirred up in the previous moment vanished.

"It's been a long day," he said.

I squinted at the sun as it beamed down on us. "It's barely even past noon."

Fynn rolled his eyes. "Fine, it's been a long morning, all right?"

I snorted.

And this was the future king of our kingdom, I thought to myself after having made sure my mental shields were up.

"The *point* is I have things to do, so if you don't mind. . ."

"Fine," I mumbled, only half listening now, my thoughts elsewhere. Maybe Fynn needed this fake courtship as much as I needed it.

"Dani?" Fynn asked.

"Huh?" I asked, blinking away the previous concerns that occupied my mind.

"I asked if you knew what event we should attend next?"

"Oh, right," I said, nodding my head.

Recognizing the hesitancy filling my voice, Fynn sighed. "What is it?"

I pursed my lips, shaking my head and dragging my attention away from him. "Nothing. It's silly."

His shoulders sagged. He grabbed my arm and tugged, forcing me to face him. My muscles beneath his fingers flexed, and he dropped my hand.

"All right, but before you say no, hear me out."

His gaze narrowed. "One date, and you already want to change the plan, Ferrios?"

I kicked the dirt. "Sometimes strategies must be adjusted."

"Out with it then, Ferrios."

The words spilled out in a rush. "I think we need to show the leaders that we are more serious about this—this *relationship*. I think we need to court each other properly."

"What do you mean?" he asked, brows arching.

Shrugging, I picked up one of the swords hanging from the rack and tested its balance. I recognized Xander's work immediately—the beauty in the craftsmanship. "Casual walks through the village, dinners. You know, whatever one does when people are courting one another."

"Whatever one does?"

"Mhm," I mumbled, twisting the blade in my hand. I sensed Fynn's gaze, but I continued studying the sword.

"Dani, when was the last time you were courted?"

A prickle shot through the back of my neck when I met his gaze at last, his head cocked to the side.

"I—" My tongue grew heavy as I placed the sword back on the rack.

I might have slept with several people, but none of them were a result of a serious relationship. For me, intimacy was about attraction and chemistry. A courtship never mattered. Never having officially courted someone never bothered me before.

Until, that is, amusement peppered Fynn's countenance.

"Do you mean to suggest that you have never been courted?"

Heat flushed my cheeks, and I dug my nails into the flesh of my palms. "Get out of my head, Fynneares."

"Ha! See, that's how I know I'm right." He leaned forward, the crisp scent of the ocean breeze surrounding me. With a finger, he poked the side of my head. "I don't need to be in your head to know when you're lying, Ferrios."

With a scoff, I flicked away his hand. "I have. There was that—that one guy. . ."

"The one who threw up on your boots, or are you referring to the second man who did that?" Fynn quirked a brow. "I'm not sure your mother's suitors count based on what you have told me about those outings."

The muscles in my jaw ticked.

"It's fine if you haven't," Fynn continued, dragging the tip of his blade through the dirt. My fingers flexed along the top of the rack as he walked in a circle around me. "I'm surprised, that's—"

A throwing knife flew from my hand, spiraling in the air. Fynn jumped back, narrowly missing the blade. Inches from his feet, the hilt of the knife wobbled.

"Shit, Dani. What was that for?"

"You're simply lucky I can't hear your thoughts because seeing them spread across your face is more than enough."

He snatched my wrist and pulled me toward him. He tipped my chin up with a finger, and my breathing hitched in my throat. "Because of that, Ferrios, I'm going to ruin you for any future suitor."

His closeness, his words—it was all too much. The pit of my stomach stirred, and my brows drew together. My eyes bounced across his face, unsure where to look. His dark brown eyes swirling with gold, the strand of hair falling across his forehead and brushing against the top of his cheek.

Snap.

The sound of a twig cracking in half forced my attention away. Behind Fynn, Jorian walked toward us.

Fynn smirked down at me.

The fluttering in my stomach extinguished into a puff of smoke. The closeness, the gaze—it had all been a part of the charade. One we *both* had agreed to, I reminded myself as the jealousy rolled in my stomach.

I shook out of his hold. "I have things to do."

With each step, I ignored the lingering warmth of his touch on my face and let the breeze sweep it away.

Fynn was only pretending, but I no longer knew if I was.

CHAPTER 12
DANI

I TWISTED THE MUG BETWEEN MY HANDS, THE DARK ALE SLOSHING dangerously close to the rim. Laughter and music filled The Splintered Oar, but tonight, I couldn't bring myself to join in it.

Since we were privates, Sylvia, Moris, and I had been coming to the tavern near the soldiers' barracks. At the end of a hard week of training, we would head to The Splintered Oar to drink our sore muscles and fresh bruises away. Although the drinks never made the bruises disappear, and often, we would hurt more the next day than we did before we stepped foot in the tavern. Still, we kept coming.

Soon enough, the table in the corner quickly became our spot.

The tavern was one of the oldest establishments in the capital's village and had been in the current barkeeper's family for generations. The barkeeper's wife was constantly changing things and updating the place despite the history worn into each piece of pavement. Once, I asked Roth how he dealt with all the changes. To which he said, "I couldn't care less what this place looks like, but if it puts that wide smile on Bernie's face, who am I to interfere? There is no greater joy than seeing my wife happy."

I hadn't known how to respond to that. Why change something if it worked? If it held such history within the grain of the worn wood?

Some things, I supposed, weren't meant to be understood.

Like the amount of heads that now turned in my direction wherever I went.

No one had ever cared that I was best friends with Fynn. But now that he was courting me? It changed everything. Wherever I went, more eyes turned my way, more cursory glances tracked me, more whispers trailed every step I took.

I only agreed to come to The Splintered Oar tonight because Sylvia wouldn't stop begging me. And once the patrons drank a few more pints of ale, their gazes would surely fade.

I hoped.

I hadn't seen or spoken to Fynn since storming onto the castle's training grounds. Going days without seeing him shouldn't have made me anxious, yet my knee shook beneath the table. He said he would take this seriously, but I didn't know if I believed him.

And when I told him I hadn't courted anyone? The look on his face?

It made me question why I had agreed to this plan in the first place.

To make matters worse, my mother had dismissed the news about our courtship with a wave of a hand, saying she would believe it when she saw it herself. Sooner rather than later, we would need to make an appearance before her.

"Another?" the barkeep asked, approaching our table in the corner.

"When have we ever said no, Roth?" Sylvia asked, sliding their mug across the table.

Moris cheered in response, his mug crashing into Sylvia's. As Roth refilled the mugs from the pitcher of ale he carried, he looked at me expectantly.

I shook my head and brought the half-filled mug closer to my body. "Still on the first."

Deep wrinkles creased his rich black skin, and I dropped my gaze to the ale as I sunk back into the worn leather bench. Typically, I was the first in our trio to wave him over, but today, the ale wasn't sitting right.

"She's had a rough week," Moris said, a hand covering his mouth—as if that would prevent me from overhearing him when he hadn't even bothered to lower his voice.

"I have not," I mumbled.

"Oh, come on, you can't fool us. You know you expected—"

I kicked Moris' leg under the table, and Moris glared at me.

"I'm all right for now, Roth. Thank you," I said, ignoring Moris' pointed stare.

Roth raised his pitcher, disbelief still deepening the wrinkles on his forehead. "Holler if you change your mind, all right?"

I nodded, even though I knew I wouldn't.

Roth walked away, turning his attention to another table as the band began strumming a lively song. Moris and Sylvia fell back into casual conversation, but I was only half listening, my thoughts wandering elsewhere. It was still early in the night, and spirits were high at the end of the work week. Yet, I couldn't help but feel a nervous energy filling the ale-soaked air. However, as couples moved toward the band, it seemed only I had noticed. Everyone's limbs were already sashaying to music, their lips loose as the chatter around the room increased in volume and excitement. Song after song passed, and the longer I sat there, the more the nerves grew.

Sylvia poked me in the side, jostling me and pulling my attention back to the table.

"What?" I asked.

"You didn't mention your new beau was coming, Ferrios," Sylvia said, wiggling their eyebrows.

My brows furrowed. "What are you talking about? He's not—"

I choked on my words when Sylvia elbowed me in the side again and tipped their head toward the tavern's entrance.

Sure enough, none other than the Crown Prince was walking into the soldiers' tavern, the doors slamming closed behind him. Wearing tailored trousers and a linen suit jacket, Fynn stuck out among the crowd like a diamond in a pile of coal. His jacket was left open, revealing a freshly pressed button-down with silver embroidery that shimmered in the sunlight. When his gaze met mine, he smiled, teeth sparkling as he waved.

Moris reached across the table and grabbed a handful of peanuts. He shoved them into his mouth and asked, "Now that you two are courting, does this mean that drinks are on the house?"

"Moris!" Sylvia chided. "You can't just ask that!"

"Why not? It's a simple question."

"It's rude." Sylvia sat back, arms folding over their chest. They tipped their head in my direction and arched a brow. "But are they?"

I snorted. "In your dreams."

Meanwhile, Fynn weaved through the bustling crowd, tipping his head toward the patrons who greeted him. A few tried to stop him, but he shook his head and pointed in my direction.

I looked away.

"Are you blushing, Ferrios?" Moris asked through another handful of peanuts.

"What? No, why would I—"

"She most certainly is," Sylvia interrupted, nudging me again. If Sylvia kept it up, my side would be covered in bruises before the night's end.

Nerves be damned, I raised the mug of ale to my lips, chugging it as Fynn reached the table. I was *not* blushing because of the Crown Prince.

I refused to.

"Your Highnesses, what a pleasant surprise!" Sylvia said, tipping their head in respect.

Fynn's thick brows bunched together as he tilted his head, a silent question on his lips as he looked at Sylvia.

My gaze bounced between Sylvia and him, watching them as Fynn tried to wipe the confusion from his face.

Sylvia pursed their lips and pulled the mug to their mouth. Sylvia might have been a great arsonist and alchemist, but their gift certainly did not enhance their ability to be sly.

I snorted, realizing that Fynn, in fact, hadn't come here by chance. Leave it to Sylvia to butt into something that had nothing to do with them.

"Yes, *Your Highness*," I hissed, "a surprise indeed."

Fynn scratched the back of his head and smiled down at me. "They said I should come, so—"

"Here," Sylvia cut in, hurrying out of the booth. "You can take my seat."

I tried to grab Sylvia's hand before they got up, but Sylvia swatted it away.

"Oh no," Fynn said, shaking his head. "That's not necessary. I can sit—"

"I insist, Your Highness," Sylvia said, already up and pointing a hand at the seat.

"Very well then," Fynn mumbled, nodding in thanks before taking the offered seat.

"Moris, do you want to come with me to the latrine?" Sylvia asked.

Moris' face contorted as he looked up from the empty bowl of peanuts. "Why would I—"

With an exasperated eye roll, Sylvia dragged him out of his seat. As they walked away, Sylvia mumbled something about wanting to give the two lovebirds a moment of privacy.

I wanted to gag. Instead, I shifted in my seat, turning to Fynn as I slammed my mug down. "What are you doing here?"

Fynn jerked back slightly. "You said I needed to take our relationship more seriously."

"And showing up to a dingy tavern is taking things more seriously?" I asked, giving Fynn a skeptical look.

"First of all, Sylvia sent me a note and said this was your favorite tavern in the entire kingdom." He scratched the back of his head, tussling his hair. Then he added, "They also might have added a sentence or two that was borderline a threat that I simply could not ignore."

"I'm going to kill Sylv," I groaned, staring at the beams running across the ceiling.

"Lance threatened the same thing when he first read the note. I told him it was unnecessary." Fynn shrugged. "Anyway, if you want the leaders to know we're serious, your comrades should see us together. It's only natural, and clearly, they care about you."

"Whatever. Just"—I took a swig of ale—"remember the rules."

"I always remember the rules, Ferrios," Fynn said and winked, sending a spiral of anxiety running to meet the ale. He leaned closer. "Doesn't mean I always listen to them though."

"Fynn, I'm serious, you can't—"

But then his hand squeezed mine beneath the table, causing the words to disintegrate on my tongue.

I blinked.

After a second that lasted too long for a pretend courtship, he tipped his head.

My gaze flicked to the crowd.

Sylvia and Moris were heading back. Sylvia was grinning and wiggling their brows like a child who couldn't keep a secret even if their life depended on it.

"Fine," I sputtered to Fynn.

The right corner of his lip twitched up, and he leaned back in his chair, stretching an arm across my shoulders. He cocked his head toward me expectantly. "Trust me, Ferrios."

I took a deep breath.

I could do this, I told myself before sinking against the cushion.

This was *almost* normal. There was no kissing, no weird touches. It was simply a casual outing with Fynn. Years ago, I had frequented plenty of taverns with him—before he favored the gambling hall or lavish nights spent with various women.

Then, Fynn scooted closer. His thigh pressing up against mine, his heat wrapping around me.

This was definitely not normal.

I swallowed as Sylvia and Moris sat down.

Fynn flicked his free hand in the air. Roth tossed a rag over his shoulder. The old barkeeper was among the few people I had ever seen meander over to a prince. But after knowing Roth for years, I knew he was the type of man who held his head high no matter who entered his tavern. Because at the end of the day, this was Roth's tavern, his place of business. He wore the crown here—at least, that's what he said whenever someone tried to argue with him about prices.

"What can I get ya?" Roth asked.

Fynn tilted his head to the side, assessing the bar behind Roth. An assortment of bottles in various shades of liquids and stained glasses lined the shelves. "Have any house cocktails?"

"Cocktails?" Roth snorted and scratched the side of his beard. A devious glint sparkled in his eyes, the crow's feet deepening at the corners. He spread out his arms. "If a cocktail is what ya want, I have—"

"An ale, Roth," I blurted out, interrupting.

Fynn turned to me, eyes wide. "But I—"

I stomped on his foot, cutting him off. I saw right through those wide, doe eyes.

Fynn cleared his throat. "An ale sounds great," he said with a grimace.

Laughter threatened to burst from Sylvia and Moris' lips, but somehow, they managed to restrain themselves. Ale had never been Fynn's preferred choice, but none of us needed to hear about Roth's *creative* alternatives.

"Are you sure?" Roth asked, disappointment shading his face now that he wouldn't get to tell his piss-poor joke.

"He's sure," I said. "I'll take another ale as well, Roth."

"You got it, Ferrios."

As Roth made to turn, I said, "Oh, and Roth?"

"Yes, ma'am?"

"Keep 'em coming."

Roth winked. "Anything for my favorite gal."

Once Roth was out of earshot, Fynn placed an elbow on the table and sat his chin atop his curled fist. "Favorite gal, huh?"

"Mhm," I mumbled, throwing back the last remnants of ale.

"You might want to watch out, Your Highness," Sylvia said from across the table, chuckling. "I've heard that Roth is Ferrios' favorite barkeeper."

"Is he now?" Fynn asked, his eyes locked on mine.

I leaned against the table, propping myself onto my elbow and cocking my head in Fynn's direction, mimicking his position. "What can I say? I'm a sucker for a man who makes a good cocktail."

Sylvia spat out a stream of ale onto the table.

"So, he *does* make cocktails," Fynn said, leaning closer.

Moris snorted. "Not the kind of cocktail you're looking for, Your Highness."

"Then what kind?" Fynn asked, turning to Moris, his brown eyes wide and innocent.

I knew that look all too well. He knew precisely what Roth had meant, for he had seen it within the barkeeper's mind. Fynn was playing the role of the foolish, naive prince to get a rise from everyone around him.

Two could play at that game, though.

I grinned, my fingers tapping on my jaw. "Why don't we ask Roth himself, hmm?"

"Ask me what, darling?" Roth asked, setting down the pints.

"Oh, the prince here was wondering—"

"If I can buy a round for everyone," Fynn finished, standing up, his knee banging against the table. Liquid splashed onto the wood.

Sylvia and Moris snickered.

Meanwhile, Roth's jaw dropped. Wiping his hands on his apron, he asked, "Everyone?"

"A gift from the crown," Fynn said.

As if the mere promise of coin was pulling the corners of his lips up, Roth grinned and shouted to the rest of the tavern, "Next round's on the Crown Prince!"

It seemed Sylvia and Moris would get their free drinks after all.

Cheers erupted across the tavern, and Fynn lifted his mug to the cheering patrons.

A nearby drunken patron slapped him in the shoulder and leaned heavily against him. Fynn quirked a brow. When the man met Fynn's gaze, he stumbled back once he realized whom he was touching. But Fynn, being the man he was, only laughed and nodded at the patron before another man guided the drunk away.

Fynn sat back down in his seat and leaned over to me. "Do you think he'll put it on my tab?"

"Your tab?"

Fynn's brows rose in shock. "You think I carry that much coin? Or *any* coin for that matter."

"You mean you don't—"

Fynn blinked. "I'm the Crown Prince. Things I buy usually get charged to the crown."

"Oh, Fynn," I said, patting his cheek, the light beard covering his jawline tickling my palm. "My naive little prince. This isn't that kind of establishment."

ONCE FYNN HAD SHOWN UP, our mugs were never empty.

Roth may have preached about how little titles meant inside his tavern, but his attentiveness to our table would have suggested otherwise.

Two and a half ales later, Fynn glanced around the table, the buzz reddening his cheeks. "Anyone up for a game of cards?"

"I'm always up for a good game," Moris said, raising his glass.

"Count me in, too," Sylvia said.

"Dani?" My name was light on Fynn's tongue; his gaze soft, almost hesitant. "You in?"

Across from us, Sylvia tipped their head to the side, grinning. The haze of the three pints of ale, a shining coat over their amber eyes.

I didn't know how much time had passed, but my ability to keep up this act was draining, and the ale didn't help. The more I drank, the greater the chance I had of slipping up. I had almost outed myself one too many times tonight.

Lying to the public was one thing, but to my friends, it was proving to be a challenge.

Fynn, however, didn't seem affected at all. Honestly, it was annoying how *good* Fynn was at pretending to court me.

"Come on," Sylvia begged.

"Yeah, Ferrios," Fynn piped in, gently nudging me with his elbow. How can one game hurt?"

I pursed my lips and leaned back. "Deal 'em, Nadarean."

"That's my girl," Fynn said with a wink as he began shuffling the deck of cards. "Everyone familiar with fifteen hundred?"

Sylvia and Moris nodded, but I narrowed my gaze. I knew the game, but I also knew Fynn.

"Good," Fynn said, ignoring my cold stare. He split the deck into two neat piles and bent the stacks, the cards arching slightly between his hands before he released them. With a quick movement, the cards shuffled back together, Fynn's long, delicate fingers keeping them from spilling onto the table. "Moris, you're on my team. Sylvia and Dani, you're together."

"But—" I interjected but swallowed my words when everyone's gazes snapped to mine.

"Is there a problem, Ferrios?" Fynn asked, head cocked to the side, the smugness dripping from his gaze.

The Crown Prince knew exactly what the problem was.

I had played this game countless times growing up. Back then, however, it served a greater purpose. When Fynn had revealed his gift to Graeson and me, we played to help strengthen my mental shield. One too many drunken nights spent in the Nadarean's family cottage, I had fallen into the trap of playing against Fynn and Terin. But I wasn't drunk enough to make that mistake tonight.

Not yet, anyway.

When it came to Fynn, I knew better than to step foot near a game like fifteen hundred if the rest of the party was ignorant of his ability. After all, what fun was it when your opponent could read your mind and not only see your moves but also know the cards their teammate would play? It made for a rather quick and unfair game.

"Are we sure we have to play fifteen hundred?" I asked. "Isn't there some other game we could play? Something. . .I don't know, more fun?"

"What did you have in mind, Ferrios?" Fynn quipped.

"Uhm," I chewed on my bottom lip. I knew few card games, but I also wasn't willing to lose a game against Fynn simply because of his ability.

"Oh, I know a game we could play!" Sylvia said, countenance lit with mischief.

A grin tugged at the corner of Fynn's lips. "Let's hear it then, Larpos."

"Odds and evens."

"How do you play?" I asked.

However, between Fynn's devilish smirk and Sylvia's bright amber eyes, I wasn't sure I wanted the answer. Still, I couldn't back out now.

"Put the stack of cards in the center of the table. When it's your turn, you pull a card. If it's an even card, you get to ask someone a question, which they either must answer truthfully or drink," Sylvia said.

"And if it's an odd?" I asked, swallowing.

"You get to dare someone to do something. If the person refuses, they drink."

"In!" Moris shouted, slamming his mug onto the table.

Sylvia turned to Fynn and me, the silent question between us.

"Isn't this a little childish?" I asked.

Fynn slid the stack of shuffled cards to the center of the table. He leaned closer to me. Pieces of his hair fell in front of his face, over his brown eyes shadowed in darkness. He cocked a brow, his voice lowering. "Come on, Ferrios. What do you have to lose?"

He brushed his hand across the deck and swiped the card through the air. He held it in between two fingers.

The five of hearts stared back at us. "Play or drink, love?"

A challenge sparkled gold in his eyes. While many things might have changed over the years, my inability to back down from a challenge did not.

I clicked my tongue, shaking my head. "Such a pity."

"What?" Fynn asked.

I snatched the card from him, his empty fingers hanging in the air between us. "What a waste of a card on such a silly question."

Moris whistled and rubbed his hands together as he scooted closer to the table. "Let's see who our Crown Prince really is."

I cocked a brow in Fynn's direction.

"Ask me anything," he said, his eyes still locked on mine. He turned to Moris and draped his arm across the back of the bench, the tips of his fingers brushing across my shoulder. "I'm an open book. As for you all, I don't know if I can say the same."

As my heart thumped, now, more than ever, I was thankful for my strong shields.

I turned to Sylvia. "Your turn, Sylv."

Sylvia picked up a card and flipped it over to reveal the eight of clubs. "Fynn," Sylvia called, formalities long gone after a few drinks.

"Hit me, Larpos."

"What do you like the most about Dani?"

Humming, Fynn spun his mug on the table as he surveyed me.

Unable to hold his gaze, I picked up my drink, breaking the connection. I took a sip. A *long* sip.

Only when I swallowed did Fynn finally answer.

"Her tenacity."

"Her *tenacity*?" Sylvia repeated.

"Mhm. When she puts her mind to something, she is determined to keep her word and hold herself to it. It's one of the qualities I have always admired about her."

Moris picked up his glass. "By the gods! Why couldn't you have been. . .I don't know? *Less* thoughtful?"

Fynn shrugged. "You asked for the truth; I gave you the truth."

"Your truth isn't very entertaining, now is it?" Sylvia mumbled, lifting the mug to their lips.

"My turn," Moris said, his hand smacking the deck. He flipped the card over. "Ugh, even again! Are you sure you shuffled these?"

"He shuffled them, Moris," Sylvia said with an eye roll.

"Whatever," Moris mumbled. He slapped the card against the table, looking around the table.

When his gaze finally landed on me, I straightened in my seat.

"How do you truly feel about Quint being promoted instead of you?"

I reached for my mug, but Sylvia slapped my hand away.

"Come on! What's the fun if you drink to every question?" Sylvia asked.

I quirked a brow and sneered. "First of all, I haven't drunk to a question."

"Yet," Sylvia retorted. "It's still early, and if this is any indication—"

Ignoring them, I continued, "Second, how else will I get drunk if I don't drink anything?"

"But this is an easy question!" Sylvia whined.

"Fine." My shoulders sagged as I gripped the mug between my hands. "I'm fine with Quint being promoted. What type of leader would I be if I questioned my own leaders' choices?"

Moris slammed his pint on the table, the golden liquid spilling over the rim and splashing onto the oak. "That's a bunch of horseshit, and everyone at this table knows it. Gods' breath! Everyone in this tavern knows that!"

I flipped my hair over my shoulder, lifting my chin. "I have no idea what you're talking about."

"You mean to tell me," Moris said, leaning forward, "you're not somewhat annoyed? A *little* jealous?"

"What do I have to be jealous about?" I said with a nonchalant shrug. "I obviously have more training to do. I just need to work harder to show them that I'm fit for the position. It's not my time, and that's all right."

Beside me, a huff escaped Fynn's lips, and I snapped my gaze toward him, eyes narrowed. He looked away as he raised the mug to his lips, nose twitching and lip curling as he swallowed the ale. The bitter taste of wheat was only marginally easier for him to swallow on his third pint. He shook his head, disappointment tousling his hair. "You're not fooling anyone, Dani. But if you want to lie, drink up, love."

"I'm telling the truth!" But when everyone groaned in disbelief, I sighed. "Fine. I'll drink."

Perhaps fifteen hundred would have been a better choice.

AT FIRST, the questions were light and easy. Everyone was merely dipping their toes in the water to see how far we could push one another and what lines people would and wouldn't cross.

Everything Fynn had asked Moris and Sylvia and everything they had asked him were things I already knew.

"When was the first time you were drunk, Fynn?" Moris asked.

"The winter solstice eight years ago," Fynn said.

I recalled the night easily. The four of us—Fynn, Terin, Graeson, and I—had snuck into the castle's alcohol cabinet. The three boys had drank nearly the entire bottle but had only let me have a sip. I was too young, they had said. At first, I was mad. But when I saw how terrible they looked the next day, I was grateful.

"Who was the first person you courted, Fynn?" Sylvia asked one round.

"Rosalina."

"Who was your first kiss?" Moris this time.

"Rosalina."

Again.

Easy questions. Questions that only made me sink further back against the bench as they dredged up memories of Fynn that I had tried to forget years ago.

When he was fresh-faced and wide-eyed.

When my heart fluttered every time he turned my way.

Those years had once felt miles away, but now, they seemed as close as ever. It made me realize how foolish I had been back then.

If thirteen-year-old me had known then that we would only be courting Fynn because of a deal, she would have been embarrassed and outraged. But most of all, she would have been heartbroken.

Childhood crushes, however, weren't meant to last.

Clearly.

"All right, my turn!" Moris shouted several rounds later. Swaying slightly in his seat, he reached forward and flipped over the next card. "Ha! An odd!" He pointed at Fynn, his finger waving in the air. Moris seemed to have forgotten that you only drank when you *didn't* answer the question, not every time a question was asked or a dare was posed. "Prince Fynneares," he slurred.

"Lieutenant Monistare," Fynn said, leaning forward.

Moris chuckled, his head falling onto the table as he pounded his fist against the wood.

Fynn raised a brow in question, glancing at Sylvia and me.

"Moris," I said, nudging him with my foot beneath the table. "You know you're supposed to ask him to do something, right?"

"I know, I know." He snorted, wiping his mouth with the back of his hand as he lifted his head from the table. "Go ask Bernadette about Roth's cocktails. "

"Isn't that—" Fynn began.

"Hilarious?" Moris supplied, interrupting Fynn.

Brows raised, Fynn said, "Not exactly what I was going to say, but—"

"You can always drink instead," Sylvia suggested.

Fynn dropped his gaze to the dismal ale before him.

Amusement rose in my throat as I watched him debate whether to go through with the dare or drink.

The moment he decided, his shoulders sagged. He brushed a hand through his hair and scanned the crowd. "Which one is Bernadette?"

"There we go!" Moris shouted, slapping a hand against the table.

I leaned closer to Fynn, reaching over him and pointing across the room toward the musicians. "Over there. She's the one in the yellow dress."

His eyes landed on the older woman dancing with her hands in the air as the musicians played a light jig on the small platform.

Shaking his head, he stood and weaved his way through the crowd. Once behind the woman, Fynn tapped her shoulder to get her attention. Bernadette spun around, almost slapping him in the face with her wild movements. Bernadette's dancing had always been borderline chaotic. One never knew when to expect an elbow in the air.

When recognition of whom she almost hit settled in, she slapped her hands over her mouth, muttering an apology. She immediately tried to curtsy, and I chuckled as her outburst began to catch the attention of the nearby patrons.

Fynn shifted on his feet and tugged at the ends of his hair at the base of his neck.

Soon, Bernadette folded over in laughter, and Fynn stared down at her. Unsure what to do, he looked back at us.

Moris pounded his fist against the oak table like a child cheering about dessert.

Once recovered, Bernadette stood and wiped a finger beneath her eye. She said something to Fynn and then patted him on the shoulder before giving her back to him and returning to her wild movements.

"What did she say?" Moris asked once Fynn returned.

"She said that uhm. . ." Fynn scratched the back of his head as he sat, "Crown Prince or not, I wasn't her husband's type."

Moris' head fell onto the table, muffled laughter spilling from his lips.

It was stupid.

So utterly stupid, but also such a Moris thing to ask someone to do. Borderline awkward and weird, yet harmless at the end of the day. Sylvia and I exchanged glances and then burst into laughter, joining Moris.

Soon, Fynn had joined in too.

CHAPTER 13
FYNN

AFTER THREE PINTS OF ALE, I HAD LOST COUNT OF HOW MANY I DRANK.
Enough that my tongue was now as loose as ever. And maybe that
was how I ended up spinning Sylvia around the tavern while avoiding
the tables and patrons as best as possible in the crowded tavern.

The ale twirled in my stomach, filling my veins with a warm buzz.
While ale was still not my drink of choice, my feet were lighter, and
the rush of thoughts was almost nonexistent. It was a nice change of
pace from the usual establishments I frequented.

"She's a good one, you know."

"Hmm?" I mumbled, leaning closer to Sylvia to hear over the band.

"Ferrios—she's one of the good ones."

"Do you mean to imply that I am not, Larpos?"

Sylvia narrowed their eyes at me. "That remains to be
determined."

I spun Sylvia around, the narrowed gaze disappearing just as a
grin appeared.

When they faced me again, they said, "If you ask me, she can be
cold and closed off at times, but she's got a big heart."

"Does she?"

Sylvia nodded. "And she's clearly smitten with you."

"Oh?" Laughter threatened to spill from my lips.

Dani was definitely not *smitten* with me. If anything, she was annoyed that she had to pretend to be in a fake relationship with me tonight when she hadn't expected to.

At least Dani was doing a good job selling it if Sylvia thought she was smitten.

"Oh, come on, now," Sylvia said, slapping me lightly in the chest. "That royal education had to teach you a thing or two."

"It sure did. Ask me anything about Pontia's history or give me an equation to solve, and I'll answer it. No problem," I said with a wide smile.

Sylvia snorted. "Perhaps you are dafter than you let on. I see the way you look at each other as if you have a secret you're hiding."

The back of my neck prickled, and I almost missed a step, nearly tripping over my feet. I reached for the thread to Sylvia's mind, but it was as wobbly as my feet and slipped through my grasp.

I should have considered the possible repercussions when I asked for another pint. But at this point, if anyone was questioning mine and Dani's ruse, they wouldn't even remember it come morning.

"You two think you're so slick, but I see through your little smirks and side-eye glances. This courtship of yours started a long time ago, didn't it?"

I laughed nervously. "No, Larpos, it's still very new."

"Oh, fine. Don't tell me. But if that's the truth, I'm surprised. You two have been friends for so long. It was only a matter of time before you got together."

I hummed as we let the music lead us after that.

Once the song slowed, I released Sylvia's hand and folded a hand behind my back, bowing. "It was a pleasure dancing with you, Sylvia."

"Oh, please. Call me Sylv," Sylvia said with a wink.

THE GROUP of patrons had dwindled, and the drinks had since slowed. Outside, the streets had cleared, and only a few wanderers strolled beneath the stars. The rest of the village was already in their houses, tucked under blankets as the midnight sky draped its shadow across the kingdom.

The water I had been nursing had diminished the drunken fervor, but I could still feel the buzz heating my veins. Despite the instruments still thrumming and the boisterous laughter from the drunken group at the bar, my mind was quiet.

Or at least almost quiet.

I cleared my throat and tapped the table. "I think I'm going to head out."

"Are you sure?" Sylvia asked, their words slurring slightly.

"Unfortunately, yes. I have an early meeting with the advisors tomorrow. If I'm late, my mother might have my head at long last."

"Esmeray would never do that," Dani said with a huff.

"Perhaps. I mean, I am her favorite," I joked.

Dani laughed, and the sound was so pure and light-hearted I couldn't help but smile. "Ha! Terin's her favorite, and we all know it."

I gasped, rubbing my chest with my palm as if her words struck me in the heart. "Ouch, Dani. That hurt."

"It's true," she said with an amused grin as she drained the last few droplets of water in her glass.

I wrapped my arm around Dani's shoulder and tugged her toward me. "I'm *your* favorite, though, right?" I teased, nuzzling her hair with my chin, knowing it would get a kick out of the others and simultaneously annoy Dani to no end.

Dani scoffed and shoved me away. "Yeah, right. Terin's always been my favorite, too."

I arched a brow, tilting my head.

Dani rolled her eyes. "But you're a close second." Dani tapped her chin. "After Graeson, that is."

"So, third?"

"Mhm." Dani raised her mug to her lips, even though she had already emptied it of its contents.

"Will you two go somewhere else with those love-bird eyes already?"

I surveyed Dani. The nerves that had run through her leg, causing it to bounce earlier in the night, had since disappeared. She was relaxed, happy even. It was nice to see.

"Walk me out?" I asked after a moment passed. When Dani's brows knitted together at my question, I added, "Please?"

Dani chuckled. "If the little prince needs someone to hold his elbow, very well. It would be my honor."

She might have switched to water recently, but her cheeks were still rosy, the bottom of her ears red.

I stood and held out a hand. Dani, of course, ignored it and stumbled to her feet. She wobbled on her feet, the careful facade of the obedient soldier slipping as she leaned against me.

I wrapped an arm around Dani's waist, tugging her closer and stabilizing her. Dani's fingers dug into my arm, but I smiled harder and placed my chin on her head. The faint notes of cinnamon surrounded me, quickly becoming intoxicating.

"It was a pleasure getting to know you both," I said, tipping my head to Sylvia and Moris.

"I mean, how could it not be?" Moris asked, still slurring his words despite drinking water instead of ale for the past half hour. "We're an absolute joy to be around."

Sylvia snorted. "What he said."

"I'll be right back," Dani said as I led her away from the table.

"Or not!" Sylvia said to our backs.

I chuckled, and Dani's nails bit into my arm even harder.

With Dani tucked against me, we weaved through the last of the drunken crowd. When we reached the door, I guided her in front of me and reached over her, pushing the door open. The crisp night air swept through Dani's hair, sending a spiral of cinnamon my way as the air kissed my cheek. Dani walked outside.

However, once the doors closed behind us, she spun toward me, glaring, the moon's rays slicing across her hazel eyes. She stumbled and pointed a finger at me. "Cut the crap, Fynn."

"Huh?"

Dani lifted her other hand—the hand I was still holding tightly within mine. "It's just you and me now."

She tried to snatch it back, but I leaned toward her instead.

Her back hit the wall, her boots slipping slightly on the pavement as she caught herself. I pressed a hand on the spot above her head, the red brick coarse against my palm.

Her brown curls flatted against the brick. "Fynn, what are you doing?"

"They're still watching," I mumbled, shifting to shield her from their view.

With the alcohol having worn off slightly, I could hear Sylvia and Moris' thoughts buzzing at the back of my mind. Dani might have done a decent job pretending inside the tavern, but the second we were outside, she had let go of the act. If our courtship were to work, we not only needed to convince our parents and friends that we were together, but we had to convince the entire kingdom as well. If one person thought we were faking—if one person didn't believe this was real—the charade was over.

And I was beginning to enjoy it.

So, even though I knew invading her space would annoy her, I stepped closer. The temptation to push her buttons was too enticing to ignore.

Dani's brows knitted together in the center of her forehead, deep creases marking her otherwise smooth, russet brown skin. Her hazel eyes bounced across my face, confusion sparkling within the gold flecks that swam among the forest of green. "But they can't—"

"The window," I interrupted with a small tip of my head.

She peered beyond my shoulder, and her shoulders sagged, the only sign that she saw what I already knew.

I leaned down, my lips almost brushing her ear. To everyone else, it would seem like I was whispering sweet nothings into her ear. But this was not some woman I was courting. This was Dani, and I needed to make up for her inability to read the room.

"So, Ferrios, whatever you're about to yell at me about," I whispered, "you're going to need to put on your best smitten smile while you do it."

I pulled away as Dani cocked her head to the side, hip popped out. She tried to grimace, to push forth the annoyance brewing beneath her skin, but she failed to restrain the small, amused grin.

"My best *smitten* smile, huh?"

Chuckling, I shook my head. "Something Sylvia said."

"Ah, that explains it. Sylvia is always talking nonsense." The smile faded from Dani's lips too quickly, though. "Fynn, why'd you need me to walk you out?"

"I wanted to talk to you."

"About?"

She blinked at me, her brows still drawn together. I suddenly had the urge to smooth the wrinkles from her face, but I didn't.

I shrugged. "Nothing."

Dani blinked. "You wanted to talk to me about. . .*nothing*?"

I brushed my hair back, my other hand still resting on the wall. "All right, not *nothing* exactly. I wanted to let you know that it seems to be working so far. Moris and Sylvia seem to be buying the act. Most of the villagers, too. But. . ." I hesitated.

Eyes squeezing shut, she rubbed her right temple with two fingers. "Just say it."

"Say what?"

"We're going to have to kiss at some point, aren't we?"

I cocked my head to the side and stared down at Dani. Nervous amusement rose in my throat, and without thinking, I chuckled.

Dani shoved me in the chest. "Don't laugh!"

"What?" I asked. "I know it's only logical, but we don't have to if you don't want to. Rule number three: only necessary touches."

Dani shook her head. "No. Like you said, we need to take this seriously. If there is even a sliver of doubt in my mother's mind when we inevitably see her, she will dismantle this entire scheme in the blink of an eye."

"I've always said that the Ferrios women are too smart for their own good."

Dani rolled her eyes, and I grinned. But then my smile faltered when worry creased her forehead once again.

"It's just kissing, Dani."

"Right." She nodded. "We're friends. It doesn't mean anything."

"Exactly."

"You're like a brother, after all."

I nodded. "And you're like a sister to me."

Dani continued, rambling on. "There's nothing to it, really. It's the logical thing to do. It doesn't—"

Enough.

I grabbed Dani's chin and tilted it up. Without thinking about it or debating the logic of it, I kissed her.

It wasn't long.

It wasn't explorative.

It was quick and straight to the point.

When I leaned away, Dani's eyes were wide. "Wh-what was that?"

"Might as well get it over with," I said with a shrug.

Dani nodded. "Right. Good idea." She raised her hand to her lips, but I snatched her wrist, stopping her. "What are you—"

I peered down at her, arching a brow. "They're still watching, remember? Would you wipe your mouth if you had just kissed the man you were truly courting?"

"I mean, no, but—"

"But nothing," I said, weaving my fingers between hers and guiding her hand back down.

Silence thickened the air, awkward and unyielding, as her hand remained in my grip.

Perhaps kissing her had been a mistake.

After a long, quiet moment, Dani leaned forward, her voice barely above a whisper as she asked, "Did they believe it?"

I reached out, finding the strands connecting to Moris and Sylvia's minds. I chuckled as Sylvia's thoughts filtered into my mind.

How cute.

Meanwhile, Moris' thoughts were less sweet and more set on some woman in the bar.

I quickly released that thread.

I nodded. "However, let me tell you. Moris' mind? It's not a place I want to spend much time in."

Dani chuckled, the previous tension breaking. "Not surprising. Moris is a buffoon. A good soldier, but clueless at times," Dani said, shifting on her feet. She glanced over my shoulder. "Well, now that that's over. . ."

I pushed myself off the wall and stepped back, brushing my fingers through my hair. "Right. Well. . .same time next week?" I asked.

"Huh?"

"You come here every week after training, don't you? At least that's what Sylvia said."

"Oh, right," she said, nodding. "Yeah, sure. Same time next week."

"Great."

"Great."

For a moment, we stood there like that. Gazes locking and unlocking. Until Dani offered a quick nod before pushing herself off the wall and heading toward the door. A utility belt hung off her hip, and as I watched it dip as her hips swayed, I wondered how close I had been to being stabbed with one of the throwing knives strapped to it.

The door swung behind her, the bell atop the door ringing. I tracked her through the windows as she returned to the table. Sylvia smiled at Dani, slapping her playfully on the arm. When I tried to slip into Dani's thoughts, her shields were still up and reinforced with steel.

Shaking my head, I stuffed my hands in my pockets and turned away, heading down the street toward the castle. Before I had entered the tavern that night, I had told the guards not to wait up. Now, I was thankful for the foresight because the light breeze was a blessing on my heated skin.

When I licked my lips, the taste of ale and something sweet lingered there.

The kiss had lasted barely more than a second, and yet my chest tightened as I recalled the warmth of my best friend's lips on mine.

CHAPTER 14
DANI

"I know you said you and Fynn were courting, but until the other night, I didn't believe you."

"Why not?" I asked Sylvia as we ran down the worn path.

Three days had passed since Fynn had shown up at the tavern. For the past two days, I had been with my father at one of the military schools in the north, overseeing the cadets' training. Every year, the commander took time out of his schedule to lead at least one weekend of the training. He believed getting a first look at the cadets and seeing the potential tracks for each recruit was important. I had been tagging along for years, at first simply as a daughter, but now I went as a leader. I also wanted to know who would soon be under my wing.

During our short trip, I had expected my father to ask about my relationship with Fynn at least once, but he hadn't. While I was not completely surprised, for my father had always avoided the topic of me courting anyone, I had thought my mother would have forced him to inquire about it. Still, I was grateful for the reprieve. Two days without my faux-courtship as the focal point of the conversation was a blessing granted by the gods themselves.

The break, apparently, was short-lived.

Sylvia huffed, pushing back the auburn strands of hair that had fallen from their low bun. "You're not the courting type, Ferrios."

"What's that supposed to mean?"

Sylvia waved me off. "You're so focused on your training. You've never given yourself time to court anyone. How often have I tried to set you up with one of my friends from my village?"

"Too many to count," I mumbled.

"Exactly. And every time you said you were too busy for a relationship."

"I am!"

Sylvia quirked a brow.

"I mean, I *was*." I shook my head, tripping over my words as I tried to keep my pace steady. "I *still* am, but that's why my relationship with Fynn is perfect. We both have our own responsibilities. He has a duty to his kingdom, and so do I."

"Hmph." Sylvia shrugged. "In any case, I have to admit you two are adorable together. It's nice."

I stumbled. "Nice?"

"Yeah." Sylvia nodded beside me. "It's nice to see you happy. I mean, you haven't stopped smiling since he kissed you."

"Now that's definitely not true!" Despite having meant the words, heat flushed my cheeks.

Sylvia laughed. "See? I've never seen you like this. So. . ." Sylvia ran ahead and turned around, jogging backward as we slowed. "I don't know! Carefree? Normal? *Human?*"

"Normal? What are you—"

"Come on, Dani." Sylvia opened their arms up, lifting them wide in the air. "Don't get me wrong. You're great to have around. Get a few drinks in you, and you're the life of the party sometimes. But other times, you're. . ."

My eyes narrowed. "I'm what?"

Sylvia sighed, spinning back around and returning to my side. "Strict? A rule follower? Single-minded? It's like once you entered the military and put on the uniform, you never took it off. It's great to see you stumble for a change."

"You're ridiculous."

However, the words did not sit right on my tongue. If Sylvia believed that, then perhaps the leaders did have a point.

"Maybe," Sylvia said with a half shrug. "But then again, maybe there's something to be said about not dedicating your life to one thing."

My pace slowed, and I let Sylvia race ahead as we turned the corner and started running up the hill.

Fynn and I had only been courting each other for two weeks. If Sylvia already was seeing some change, could that mean the leaders were, too?

My smile grew wider.

Maybe this deal wasn't as foolish as I thought.

WEEKS PASSED, and Fynn and I fell into a natural rhythm.

It was almost easy to pretend to court him. I didn't have to explain why I was tired after training or provide some excuse not to see him every single day. It was simple.

If only a real courtship were that easy.

It was both a blessing and a curse that our schedules often conflicted. On the one hand, I didn't have to pretend to be courting Fynn every single day, but on the other hand, we needed our family to see us together. Every time we tried to schedule a dinner with my parents or his mother, something got in the way—an advisor meeting, a strategy meeting, a training session, a court session.

The one time we could see each other during the week also ended up being the night when our parents were both busy.

At the end of each week, Sylvia, Moris, and I headed to the tavern, and more often than not, Fynn was already waiting for us at our table. Some nights, Terin tagged along, dragging Riley with him; other days, he didn't. When Terin was there, Fynn was touchier than usual.

I couldn't blame him. If anyone were to realize that this courtship was a farce, it would be Terin. He knew us better than anyone.

On those days, either Fynn's hand was squeezing mine to the point where our palms were sweating, or his arm was wrapped around my shoulders, crushing me to his body.

Thankfully, though, there was no more kissing.

Not that kissing my best friend was a big deal.

Not that it brought up old feelings that I kept trying to extinguish and pretend never existed.

Sometimes, however, old feelings had a way of creeping back up no matter how much we tried to ignore them.

Such as when Fynn and Terin teamed up against Sylvia and Moris during a game of fifteen hundred after I had declined the offer to play. Fynn had let them win the first round, which only gave Sylvia and Moris a false sense of hope. After that first round, though, Terin and Fynn worked in tandem, taking them down. I watched from the sidelines as Fynn undoubtedly crept into my friends' thoughts to anticipate their next moves. Occasionally, though, Fynn would 'mess up' by putting down the wrong card or by doing something that would grant Moris a chance to gain a small lead to keep him and Sylvia off their trail.

However, in the end, Fynn and Terin would typically win. They would high-five and raise their pints of ale, which Fynn drank with less distaste every week.

As far as I knew, Fynn only read his opponents' minds when there were no bets or stakes in the game to keep it fair. But I often wondered if he ever felt guilty for the invasion. While he sometimes poked and prodded at my mind, he usually respected my privacy. But fifteen hundred was just a simple card game. Perhaps he didn't feel guilty about it since no harm was done.

Or perhaps Fynn never felt guilty about anything he did.

When Moris whined, Fynn wrapped his arm around me, pulling me closer and saying, "What can I say? I'm a lucky man."

He would wink down at me, and then, despite my best intentions not to be affected by the man, a fluttering would erupt in the pit of my stomach.

I didn't *want* to like Fynn.

After all, I had thought I was over that foolish childhood crush years ago. But the more time I spent with Fynn, the more I realized the feelings had only been slumbering at the bottom of my stomach. Asleep and almost forgotten, but not nonexistent.

They meant nothing, though, I told myself.

There was no point in dwelling on them because what was happening between Fynn and me was purely platonic.

It had to be.

CHAPTER 15
FYNN

"You and Dani seem serious," Lukas said, the pieces of thick parchment sliding through his fingers as he shuffled the cards.

"That is because we are," I said, swishing the whiskey in the glass, the ice clinking against the sides.

It was the third day of the week, which meant Terin and I were at the Wilton manor, playing cards. We had been meeting the Wilton brothers for a game of cards for years, but suddenly, I craved ale and sticky floors.

Lukas hummed.

Over the rim of the crystal glass, I peered at my friend. "Lukas, you have never been one to hold your tongue. Do not bother now."

Lukas snorted. "Perhaps you should tell Rosalina that."

Groaning, I rubbed a hand across my face. "I have told Rosalina many times that she and I will never amount to anything."

"Is that so? From what I've heard, she's waiting for you and Dani to end whatever you have going on so she can stake her claim."

"The only thing Rosalina has a *claim* to is her haughty attitude and upturned nose."

Across from me, Terin snorted and took a sip of his whiskey.

"

"Is Dani the one then?" Riley asked, his light blue eyes stark against his brown skin.

"The one?" I asked.

Riley nodded. "You know, your soul bond? Haven't you been searching for—" Riley jerked back. "*Ouch.*"

My gaze snapped to Terin, who avoided meeting my gaze. *I told him that in confidence,* Terin thought.

I rolled my eyes. Leave it to my brother to gossip to his boyfriend about things that had nothing to do with him.

"Dani might not be my soul bond, but she's—she's different," I said at last.

"That's what he keeps saying," Terin whispered to Riley, who huffed a laugh.

Lukas ignored both of them and turned his attention to me. While his brother's eyes were bright blue, Lukas' were a sea of colors, browns and green and hints of blue depending on the lighting.

Lukas leaned forward. "Are you telling me you're ready to settle down? Only—what?—three or four months ago, you were talking about being with this girl and that girl. Now, you're telling me you've changed?"

The previous buzz from the whiskey disappeared, the accusation sobering me up quicker than an ice bath. My fingers wrapped tightly around the glass. "What's *that* supposed to mean, Lukas?"

Lukas shrugged, apparently unaware of the shift in my tone; Terin and Riley, however, were not. They both sunk back into their chairs, drinks pressed to their lips. Terin tried to throw his thoughts down the line, but I swatted them away.

Lukas shrugged and split the deck. "Don't get me wrong—I admire you a lot—but you're not the long-term relationship type. You never have been. There's always been an end date, always something that prevents you from taking the courtship to the next stage." Lukas began passing out the cards. "Do you really see Dani beside you for the rest of your life?"

Parchment slid across the table as he divvied the cards.

Mine and Dani's courtship might have been fake, but either way, I didn't appreciate whatever Lukas was implying.

"She's been one of my best friends for my entire life. Why would it be any different going forward?"

"But the *role* she plays will be different. Eventually, Queen Esmeray will step down, and you will take her place. Does Dani wish to be your queen? Have the two of you even had that discussion yet?"

I grabbed my glass and tossed the whiskey back, the liquid burning my throat as it went down. "Shut up and deal the cards."

With the Summer Solstice Ball less than a month away, the ball consumed the council meetings. For the past few weeks, Lord Cunningway had reassured the rest of the council that everything was in order. However, despite his reassurances, the rest of the advisors made him walk through the details of the event—the menu, the itinerary, the entertainment—at today's meeting. All the frivolous details I couldn't have cared less about.

But as they talked, I became painfully aware of two things.

First, my mother hadn't once asked me whom I was attending the ball with. I supposed it was a good sign, for it meant she believed my courtship with Dani was real. But then again, I never felt reassured when my mother *didn't* bring up something.

Second, I had yet to confirm with Dani that she could accompany me. There was no possible way that she didn't assume that she would be attending it with me. However, I had been so busy that it had slipped my mind to ask her. We mainly saw each other at the tavern at the end of the week—which was quickly becoming my favorite pastime. While I assumed she would accompany me, perhaps it was selfish to think she was available. Her schedule was just as busy as mine, after all.

When I was deciding how to broach the topic, the meeting took a turn for the worse.

After the discussion of the ball concluded, my mother opened the floor to Yelsania, the Royal Seer.

"The future is wrought with danger."

Teacups clattered atop porcelain saucers at the sound of the seer's voice. The cheerful laughter that had previously filled the room abruptly stopped.

Only a few years older than Terin and me at five and twenty, Yelsania pushed the thinly rimmed thick glasses up the bridge of her nose, her hands trembling slightly.

The seer spent most of her time nose-deep in either books or journals belonging to the former seers. As a result, her alabaster skin rarely saw the light of day. Her skin and paper-white hair were nearly transparent in the sunlight seeping through the large windows.

Although Yelsania had been sitting in the Royal Seer's seat since she had completed her training with the priestesses in the north four years ago, she acted as if every day was her first day among the council. Whenever she spoke, her voice was filled with trepidation and fragility, neither of which bode well for someone on the council. Yet, despite this, her quiet words always sent a creeping prickle crawling up my arms that I could never shake, even hours after the meeting ended.

Seers, especially powerful ones, were rare, and unfortunately, Yelsania wasn't a particularly strong gift user. Her mental shields were also weak as if she was always too focused on deciphering the visions spinning in her mind. Unlike most people, whose minds were a flurry of words and half-strung sentences, Yelsania's mind was filled with fog-encased images, unfinished scenes, and half-painted portraits.

With no more than a push, I slipped into the young woman's mind.

Burnt oranges and brilliant yellows flashed across her mind. At first, I thought it was the sun setting, but on closer inspection, I knew I was wrong.

Fire. So much fire filled her mind.

I pulled back out, my hand trembling as I put it underneath the table. I sensed Graeson's pointed stare, but I ignored him, turning my attention to the advisors.

"Do you know a specific date for when this future will take place, Yelsania?" Menides asked.

The seer shook her head. "My visions still remain. . .uncertain," she said, sinking in her seat.

Graeson groaned. "What is the point of sharing them then?"

Pain laced the creases in Yelsania's pale skin as if she had been slapped.

Graeson, however, did not care if his words hurt the young woman, for he pressed on, "Your visions have provided us with nothing of use. We know as much as we did when my mother sat in that same seat over two decades—"

"Graeson," my mother hissed.

The council shifted in their seats, unsure what to do as Graeson's burning gaze turned as bright as steel.

Graeson was not a cruel man, but he was not a kind man either. He knew what he wanted and did not care if someone got hurt in the process. He didn't enjoy the games of politics nor appreciated the need to ask for more information. Many advisors questioned his presence in these meetings—at least, they did so within the safety of their minds.

When Graeson was younger, he lacked control over his gift. Even to this day, he struggled to keep ahold of it. But he was like a son to my mother and a brother to Terin and me. His place was here, no matter who questioned it.

But being here seemed to be the last thing Graeson wanted to do.

The muscles in his jaw flexed, and a sea of emotion swam in his gray eyes, a storm of anger, incredulity, and hunger.

I sympathized with his anger. His mother was the best seer to have graced Pontian lands, and she, like my father, had been taken from the world too soon. From what my mother told us, Lysanthia's visions were clear, precise, and nearly always accurate.

What I did not sympathize with, however, was him taking his anger out on the young seer. Any chance Graeson could get, he questioned Yelsania.

No matter his reasons, she did not deserve his wrath.

I peered at Graeson with his hands rolled into little balls and his tan knuckles blanching. I knocked on the doors of his mind, and his gaze met mine instantly.

After a tense moment, his fists uncurled.

"Our island, once impenetrable, is changing." My mother folded her hands in her lap as she rolled her shoulders back. "Captain Squires and his crews have relayed that they have seen the kraken less and less on the Red Sea each passing year. It is only a matter of time before our enemy decides to try their luck and venture north."

Graeson pounded a fist on the table, shaking the goblets filled with water. "Then we must—"

My mother lifted a hand. "In time, son."

Graeson sat back with a sneer, his anger seeping into the air. His gaze met mine, and I merely arched a brow.

Since he came of age, Graeson had been begging to take revenge on the kingdom that attacked us. How could I blame him, though? We had all lost something that night.

One day, they would pay.

Unfortunately, today was not that day.

Nor was it a month ago.

Or two years ago.

Or fifteen years ago when the enemy kingdom first attacked.

At first, I was angry like Graeson. I *still* was. Over the years, however, I had learned to sit and listen. To study the way my mother led. How she remained calm even when the seer brought news of yet another vague vision of fires burning the sea, of the Red Sea earning its name as its waters became tainted with Pontian and enemy blood alike.

I had learned that my mother's calmness was not a sign of indifference. It was a sign of strength, a sign that she was calculating the perfect time to strike. But the question we were all wondering was *when?*

My father might have been gone, but my sister was still out there.

Last time, we had been unprepared. This time would be different.

So, maybe it was the new title or the desire to prove myself worthy of it, but I had enough of sitting and listening.

"We have spies in the southern kingdoms," I said, cutting through the silence.

My mother nodded.

"The spies have information. That is their purpose, is it not?" I asked.

"Among other things," Menides said.

I swept my gaze across the table of advisors. "Then let us use them. Send a group out. See if we can gather insight into the current climate. We sit here on our island, waiting for information to come to us. Waiting for Yelsania to have a vision. For once, perhaps we should go searching for the truth instead."

"But that's not—" Lord Cunningway began but stopped when my mother held up a hand.

"My son is right. We have hid inside the safety of our kingdom's walls for too long. This is not Yelsania's first vision of war. As Graeson noted, Lysanthia also had visions of darkness sweeping our kingdom. It is time for the tides to change," my mother said. "Menides, arrange for a squad to go south. Have them follow the standard protocol, for the treaty is still in effect. We cannot afford to make any mistakes. We will send a message to one of our contacts to arrange a meeting."

CHAIRS SCRATCHED against the pine floor as the advisors stood.

The letter to one of the spies had been written and sealed, sent off by way of messenger. It would take time to get things moving, but at least it was a start.

Graeson and Terin stood, the goblets on the table rattling in their wake. As I pushed myself up to follow them, my mother's cool hand landed atop mine.

"Stay a minute."

I hesitated, staring after Graeson as he headed for the doors without a second glance back. His eyes may have always been forward, but his mind was always stuck in the past.

I swallowed. "I really should—"

"I got him," my brother interrupted.

"I am *fine*," Graeson growled as he exited the room.

"Have fun with the beast," I whispered, sitting back down.

"Always do." Terin nodded. Then, after squeezing our mother's hand, my brother left, too.

"Airos, would you mind waiting outside?" my mother asked, turning to the man beside the door.

"Of course, Your Highness," Airos said, bowing to my mother. Although Airos had been the captain of my mother's guards for over two decades, he never dropped the formalities. But sometimes, when he didn't know others were watching, he looked at my mother with something other than formality lingering in his blue-grey eyes.

Airos had lost his wife twenty or so years ago. When we lost my father, he helped my mother navigate the pain of losing a soul bond. I was glad they found solace and comfort in each other's company.

Once the door shut behind Airos, my mother said, "One day, Graeson will work through his past." She sighed, the first sign of exhaustion flashing across her face. She shook her head. "Just as soon as he is honest with not only everyone around him but himself as well."

She stared at the closed door, her brows knitting together and concern covering her soft features. She cleared her throat and straightened. The previous emotion cleared from her countenance as if it had never been there in the first place. "You and Danisinia have been spending a lot of time together lately," she said.

I blinked. "I wouldn't say once a week is a lot, Mother."

Her eyes narrowed, the sun streaming in from the window, making her blue eyes even more piercing. "It seems she finally spoke up."

"What do you mean?"

"For years, she followed after you boys—you in particular, as if you held the world in your palms."

My brows drew together. "I—I'm not following."

My mother sat back in her chair, her fingers tapping the armrests. "You don't mean to tell me that you never noticed?"

"Noticed what?" I asked.

"That Danisinia has had a crush on you since you were children."

I snorted, leaning back in my chair. "Impossible."

My mother cocked her head to the side, and the laughter died in my throat.

Tap. Tap. Tap. Her nails clicked against the twisted oak.

"Is it? Or did you not wish to see it?"

"Why would I—"

"The mind is a strange place, Fynneares," my mother interrupted, her bright blue gaze boring into me and causing me to twist in my seat. "You more than anyone should know that."

Her stare was too heavy to bear, so I fixed my gaze upon the grain of the wood, the twisting lines and knots that ran throughout the table's surface.

My mother was wrong. Dani hadn't liked me. As a friend? Sure. But nothing more.

What did Dani say when I kissed her nearly a month ago?

You're like a brother to me, after all.

My mother's dainty hand entered my vision, her fingers flexing in the air. "I can show you if you need me to, son."

I stared at my mother's outstretched hand. For a second, I debated on saying yes. But there was no way she was right. If she was right. . .

I shook my head.

"Very well." She stood, smoothing out the wrinkles that had formed on the lavender fabric of her skirt. "Danisinia has always been strong. There's no question about it. But despite all that armor she wears, she still wears her heart on her sleeve. Do well to take care of it, son."

Before I could give my mother a response, she was already walking out of the room.

Guilt swam in the pit of my stomach. This deal was supposed to be simple. I had suggested it because Dani and I were friends. Since we had no feelings, we didn't need to worry about anyone's heart breaking once the arrangement ended. But if my mother was right. . .

She wasn't, I told myself.

She couldn't be.

Dani and I poked and prodded each other, but that was because we were best friends—nothing more.

Surely, if Dani had harbored feelings for me, there would have been more to the kiss we shared. It would have been more than a simple peck.

Still, a small voice at the back of my mind wondered if my mother was wrong, why did Dani always lock me out of her mind then?

I scoffed and grabbed my tea, sipping the lukewarm liquid. Herbs melted on my tongue, but for some reason, the ginger tea left me craving something else.

Something with cinnamon.

CHAPTER 16
DANI

"Delivery for Captain Ferrios!"

My sword fell to my side. "Delivery? I'm not—"

I choked on my words as my back hit the ground with a thud. A cloud of dust wafted into the air around my face. Tiny dust particles swam in the air as I squinted at the sun.

"Nice one, Moris!" Quint called out from the group of soldiers gathered around the mat.

I should have been thankful that the group of soldiers who witnessed me falling was smaller than usual, but it only made it worse.

For the past few days, the lieutenants and captains of the First Battalion had been asked to stay behind after our regular training for additional advanced sessions. General Walen said little else when he made the announcement. But when my father showed up, I knew something was up—something I *needed* to be a part of.

For the past three days straight, I worked myself tirelessly.

My body was covered in bruises from the additional combat training, and my limbs were so sore that even an ice bath did little to soothe the ache.

If only that was why Moris was able to knock me on my ass.

"That's what? Two losses in a month, Captain?" Moris squatted down beside me, his hands resting on his knees. "Dare I say you're losing your touch?"

I shoved him before rolling over and pushing myself up. "I am not. I was just distracted."

"Distractions will get you killed." A wide smile split across his face. "Isn't that what you always tell us?"

"Oh, shut it," I spat over my shoulder as I dusted off my backside and headed toward the man holding a package.

"What is it?" I asked the messenger as he held out the large rectangular box.

The man shrugged. "How would I know? I was told to deliver it, so I'm delivering it."

The box was simple and nondescript, with no letter on the outside. I couldn't remember the last time someone sent me something, especially in the midst of training.

"Can you at least tell me who it's from?"

"Prince Fynneares, ma'am."

My tongue was lead in my mouth as I gripped the box. The cardboard dented where my fingers pressed into it as whistles and hollers spread across the soldiers behind me.

I snapped my head in their direction, eyes narrowed. A few quickly dropped their gazes, but others were not as smart and snickered behind their hands.

"Thank you," I mumbled to the messenger. I turned the box and hugged it between my hip and arm.

Fynn had another thing coming if he thought I would open it in front of—

"What's in the box, Cap?" Sylvia asked.

"Nothing," I said, tightening my grip.

"Nothing? That's a big box for a whole lot of nothin'." Sylvia grinned and reached for the box.

As I shuffled it behind my back, it slipped from my hands.

Gasping, I spun, only to find Moris hopping away. I made to grab it, but as I reached forward, my body froze.

Internally, I screamed, but none of them heard me as Moris' gift swept over me, paralyzing me from my toes to my fists to my damn eyelids. I couldn't move; I couldn't speak.

But most unfortunately, I could still hear them.

Giggling, Sylvia ran over to Moris. "Quick, open it!"

Moris peeled the lid of the box open. Sylvia reached inside and snatched something from inside the box. She flipped over what looked to be a card with my name written in neat, fancy penmanship.

By the gods, I wished I could scream.

They were all dead. *All* of them. Sylvia, Moris, Fynn. I didn't care if leadership would need to find replacements for them or if Terin would need to take Fynn's place.

I didn't know who I wanted to kill more: Moris for paralyzing me or Fynn for putting me in this godsforsaken position in the first place.

Moris had no right to use his ability on me. It was strictly prohibited during combat training. And for good fucking reason. I could feel my cheeks turn bright red as Sylvia cleared their throat and began reading Fynn's letter.

Paper crinkled, and Moris cooed as he lifted beautiful silk fabric from the box.

Is that—

Internally, I shook my head. I thought Fynn didn't like that dress when we were at the boutique, yet here it was.

"Dearest Danisinia," Sylvia began, lowering their voice in some horrid impression of Fynn as they read, "it would be my honor if you would be my guest at the upcoming solstice ball. In anticipation, I have taken the liberty of choosing the dress for you so you do not have to put up with Lorallye's shenanigans for a second time. I hope it meets your high standards. With love, Fynneares Andros Nadarean, Crown Prince."

The soldiers burst into laughter. As Moris keeled over with the box squeezed against his chest, the effect of his gift melted away. I stumbled forward, my rage propelling me.

On wobbly feet, I snatched the letter from Sylvia's hands and pointed it at them, fire brewing in my eyes. "You're all dead."

Moris tried to say something, but he couldn't through his fits of laughter now overtaking his body.

"With love—" one of the soldiers behind me began as a few others finished with, "Fynneares Andros Nadarean, Crown Prince."

"Are you sure he didn't mean to send this to me?" Moris asked in between laughs, handing me the box. "Purple is more my color than yours."

More snickering sounded from the crowd, and I bit down on my tongue.

"Fuck off all of you," I said before spitting on the ground. I slammed the lid back onto the box and squished it between my arm and side, the material of the box crinkling.

"I'm leaving," I said as I stomped off the training field.

"Why? Do you need to prepare for some fancy ball?" a soldier asked—Gabriel, perhaps?

"Don't step on the prince's toes, Captain!" Moris shouted after me.

"We'll see about that," I mumbled as I stormed away, the soldiers' laughter a faint echo at my back.

Perhaps what Fynn needed was just that. His toes to be stepped on.

I SLAMMED the box onto the table, and Fynn arched a brow.

The guards at the castle's gates did little else but blink as they watched me storm past, box tucked beneath my arm, half-smashed, and pure fury bleeding through my eyes.

Fynn didn't even flinch. He looked up from the book in his hand and tilted his head. "Do you not like the dress? I recall you liked that one well enough at the shop. But if your opinion has changed, I can—"

I screamed in frustration, and outside the room, a few passing servants peeked in through the door. Lance and Telis, who were standing outside the sitting room, peered inside with concern furrowing their brows.

Fynn stood, waving them off. "It seems I've chosen the wrong dress color," he said.

Telis nodded as if that explained everything—as if that was a reasonable thing to get upset about.

Morons. The lot of them.

"Best we settle this in private. Wouldn't you agree, lads?" Fynn said as he shut the door.

My jaw fell open, and my nails bit into my palms, carving sharp crescent moons into my flesh.

"Can you not be so loud, Dani?" Fynn hissed, turning around. "We are supposed to be happy and in love, remember?"

I snapped my jaw shut, anger overriding the shock.

He brushed a hand through his hair. "Come on. Tell me what's wrong with the dress, and I can—"

"Fuck the dress, Fynn!" I slammed a fist against the table, the bright pain slicing through my arm. "This isn't about the damn dress!"

He leaned against the door, his ankles crossing and his arms folding over his chest. "Then what is it?"

"You sent a delivery man to training."

"And?"

I held up a finger. "Rule number one, Fynn."

"Mhm." Fynn nodded. "Right, the rules. Did I mention that rules are often made to be broken?"

My fists tightened at my side, my frustration about to boil over. "Second, do you know how embarrassing that was?"

He smirked.

He fucking *smirked*.

Holding up a finger, he said, "To your first question: I told Patrick to deliver the package *after* your training. But if you wish to blame me for Patrick's inability to follow a simple set of instructions, so be it." He held up a second finger. "Second, now I'm an embarrassment?"

I groaned and pulled the ribbon holding up my hair, hoping to release the headache that was forming.

It didn't.

"It was careless, Fynn."

"How? People who court each other often send one another gifts."

Point taken, I thought, but I refused to admit that to him.

"General Walen retires in less than three months, Fynn! What if that letter revealed the truth? And Sylvia had read *that* letter to the leaders of First Battalion? What then? Everyone would have known this is—"

"Dani, stop." Fynn pushed himself off the door and took a step toward me. "Do you think I am that foolish?"

"Yes, I do!"

"Wow, all right." He clicked his tongue. Something akin to hurt flashed across his countenance, but it was too quick to decipher.

I exhaled, long and hard. Pressing my palms flat against the table, I dropped my head, my anger simmering as I squeezed my eyes shut. "Fynn, I didn't—"

"No, it's fine. I get it. I'm the daft prince who had the misfortune of being named heir. Terin is too timid, too quiet. That's the real reason I'm the Crown Prince, right? If Terin had fought for it, the title would have been his." Fynn grabbed the crystal decanter and poured a glass. Once filled, he picked up the glass and spun the clear liquid before shooting it down his throat. He peeled his gaze away from the drink. His chocolate brown eyes met mine, a flurry of emotions swimming within his irises. "I know what people think about me. I just didn't realize you thought that, too."

My shoulders dropped, and the anger vanished. "Fynn."

He offered me a small smile, but it was far from convincing.

With soft, quiet steps, I stepped closer and placed a hand on his shoulder. The muscles in his shoulders softened, the tension lessening.

When he spoke next, none of the fire or anger that had been there previously was present. "I'm sorry. Today's meeting was rough. I know it's not an excuse, but—"

The change in Fynn's demeanor wasn't some ploy to trick me into calming down. Something was clearly bothering him.

So, instead of holding onto my anger, I nodded, squeezing his shoulder. "Do you want to talk about it?"

He shook his head

"When you do, I'm here."

He nodded.

My hand fell to my side. "Fynn, I swear I didn't mean it like that. I've told you before that I think you will be a great king."

He scratched the back of his head, making a mess of his hair. His cotton shirt stretched across his arm. "I know. I'm not upset about what you said."

"Then what is it? I know you said you don't want to talk about it, but—"

Fynn lifted his head, dark strands of hair falling in front of his face.

The sun was beginning to set. Golden light streamed into the windows and splashed across the exterior wall of the advisors' room.

Without thinking, I brushed the hair from his face, and the hair ran through my fingers like silk. When Fynn looked up at me, a hint of gold shimmered in the otherwise pool of dark brown that even the sun could not penetrate.

He blinked, his long eyelashes brushing his cheek. I dropped my hand.

One day, he would talk about the trauma of his past. If not with me, then with someone.

"The dress is perfect," I whispered. "Thank you."

He offered me a small smile as he lifted a hand and brushed a curl behind my ear. The pads of his fingertips were coarse against my skin from years of training with a sword and countless hours of studying, flipping through old books.

Fynn might have been daft at times, but he had not earned his title simply because his brother was too reserved. Fynn worked for his position just as hard as any soldier I had seen rise in the ranks.

But Fynn didn't see it that way. He never did.

If only he saw what I saw when I looked at him.

My lips parted, but before I could say anything, Fynn dropped his hand and said, "All the details are in the letter. The ball is in two weeks."

I nodded. Then, taking it as a dismissal, I turned around, heading for the door.

As my hand gripped the cold metal door knob, Fynn said to my back, his words quiet but sharp enough to cut through my heart like a blade, "If we're reminding each other of the rules, let us not forget the other three."

I bit down on my lip and nodded again before pulling open the door without a second glance back at the prince, whose touch still warmed my cheek.

His touch, I reminded myself as I walked through the cold halls, didn't belong to me.

CHAPTER 17
FYNN

"Where's Dani?" Terin asked as we settled into the carriage.

Sinking back against the gray crushed velvet cushion, I plucked off a piece of lint from my lapel. "She had a training early this morning that she couldn't miss, so we decided it would be best if we rode separately."

"Menides sure is working the troops hard lately, isn't he?"

"Seems so."

The carriage started forward. The muffled sounds of the horses' hooves pounding against the ground seeped inside.

Terin rubbed the top of his head, exhaustion coloring the bags beneath his eyes purple. "Any word about the scouting mission?"

I leaned my head against the carriage wall. "You've attended the same council meetings I have. There's been little talk about anything other than this ball."

"Yes, but I would have thought Dani would have mentioned something if she had heard anything."

I shook my head. "Our schedules haven't exactly aligned lately."

"Trouble in paradise?"

My eyes sprung open. "No. Why would you think that?"

Terin put a hand on my knee, stopping its rocking. "You haven't stopped fidgeting since we've sat down, brother."

I shook off his hand. "Dani and I are fine, Ter."

"Then why do you keep looking out the window toward the training grounds?"

The curtain slipped through my hands, the fabric swaying as the carriage rocked.

I folded my hands in my lap and turned to Terin. "Dani's training is important to her. I wouldn't want to get in the way of that. If Mother wasn't forcing me to arrive early, I would have stayed back and traveled with Dani instead. But according to Mother, I need to mingle and talk politics." I rolled my eyes, running my fingers through my hair. "I thought that was what council meetings were for?"

Across from me, Terin put his back to the side of the carriage and hoisted his feet onto the bench with a heavy sigh. "I do not pity you, brother. That is for sure." He folded his hands behind his head. "I suppose I should be happy, though. I've barely seen you in the past three months. Between your studies and little rendezvous with Dani, you're busier than ever."

I stared at my brother, confusion twisting my features. "What do you mean? I see you all the time."

Terin cocked a brow as he peered at me. "Advisor meetings don't count, Fynn."

"You've joined me at the tavern," I countered.

"You're too focused on staring at Dani for that to count, either."

"But—"

Terin shrugged as he crossed his legs. "It's fine. Truly. At least we can use this time to catch up."

The carriage hit a hole and jolted us. My stomach twisted, but I could no longer tell if it was from the ride or the guilt biting at my insides.

Nevertheless, I said, "You're right."

"Before we do, I'm going to try to sneak a nap in."

"All that fuss, yet you decide to nap?"

"What can I say?" Terin yawned and moved into a more comfortable position on the bench, cramming himself on it. "I'm exhausted."

Terin closed his eyes, and silence filled the carriage once more. As we rode across the winding path north of the castle, I peeled back the curtain again and pushed open the window, letting the cool morning air filter inside the stuffy space. Outside, sweeps of burnt oranges melted across the early morning sky.

My brother's presence and the quiet carriage should have been a reprieve, yet guilt twisted in my stomach. However, lying to my brother wasn't the only reason for the sourness.

Over the past few days, I had been training with Graeson extensively. I had foolishly thought that if I exhausted my body, my mind would quiet as well. Granted, it had worked when the sword was in my hand. But the moment I set that sword down, the thoughts came spiraling back.

I never would have guessed, though, that the thoughts I was most terrified of were my own.

Yet here I was, spiraling over my best friend.

It had been almost three weeks since I had last spoken to Dani. After what my mother had told me, I needed some distance to figure things out.

I was unsure if I believed my mother about Dani liking me when we were younger. But I wasn't sure if the answer mattered. Childhood feelings were as fleeting and fragile as youth itself. If Dani liked me then, she surely didn't like me now.

Nothing about the fury fuming in her gaze when she stormed into the castle after I had sent the dress to her suggested that she still had feelings for me. At some point, she must have seen what I already knew.

Dani wished to save the world. And I? Well, I could barely even save myself most days.

"You'll see her soon."

"Huh?" I peered at Terin, but his eyes were shut.

"Dani," Terin mumbled, sinking deeper into the cushion. Soon, his breathing shifted, and he began to snore as sleep finally embraced him.

THE SUMMER SOLSTICE was the largest event in Pontia, bringing people from across the island together to celebrate the longest day of the year. The food was plentiful, the music was grand, and the wine barrels were never empty. Laughter filled the space as people mingled with one another.

For the past several years, the Summer Solstice Ball had been an excuse for me to drink and fall into some woman's lap, head first.

This year, however, only one of those things would be happening.

I pressed the cold crystal to my lips. Notes of honeysuckle and orange wafted from the white wine, brushing my nose. The fresh citrus was a much-needed reprieve from Lord Alabas' overly sweet plum and oak aroma.

The Alabas family was one of the prominent families in northern Pontia. I didn't particularly care for the family, but their purse was immense and their gifts were useful. But no matter how valuable the Alabas family was, it didn't prevent my gaze from wandering to the large oak doors behind the lord as he prattled on about his latest hunting retreat.

Flurries of people still flooded through the doors, but none of them were the person I was looking for. The thoughts coming from the surrounding guests did little to soothe my wayward thoughts.

I thought he was courting that one soldier.

Did she stand him up?

This is why nobility should not court soldiers. Soldiers are meant to rule the field; they know nothing about court etiquette.

My sister owes me ten shillings.

Squeezing my eyes shut, I rubbed my temples as I took a swig of the wine. The alcohol was a relief for only a moment before the nausea returned, though.

When I opened my eyes, my gaze locked onto Terin. He stood beside Riley, his arm casually draped across his shoulder. Terin had been fawning after Riley for months. I couldn't say I blamed him. I might have preferred women, but I could appreciate an attractive man when I saw one. And Riley was good-looking. I had heard one too many times how mesmerizing his eyes were. Especially once Terin had drunk a glass or two of whiskey. Every cliché that existed passed through Terin's thoughts before I could block him out.

My brother met my gaze, and his smile faltered. I instinctively reached out to him.

She'll come, he said down the line.

I gnawed on my lip and nodded back.

Terin returned his attention to Riley and Lukas. Normally, I would have been with them, laughing, drinking wine, and finding the next woman I wanted to spin around the room. But as the crown dug into the top of my head, I didn't feel like doing any of those things.

A gentle hand landed on my shoulder, and my heart jumped. When I spun around to see who it was, I was only greeted with disappointment.

My mother smiled at the northern lord. "Lord Alabas, a pleasure. May I have a private word with my son?"

"Of course, Your Majesty," the lord said, bowing low. He spun on his heel, a waft of plum smacking me in the nose. His head swiveled as he searched for his next victim.

I should have been thankful for my mother's interference. Lord Alabas would talk nonstop to anyone who stood still for more than a second. Once he started talking, it was hard to get him to stop. Yet when my mother quirked a brow at me, I knew I had traded one dreaded conversation for another.

With her blonde hair knotted at the base of her neck and each strand perfectly in its place, she was the picture of calm and control. In the light, her pale purple dress appeared white. Amethysts and brilliant clear crystals covered the top of the chiffon fabric that then spilled onto the floor.

In the window behind her, I saw my own reflection: the ends of my hair were sticking up in different directions. Tugging my hair was a nervous habit I had developed as a child, one I would need to break when I became king.

Kings were never nervous—my mother taught me that.

But I wasn't a king. Not yet.

"No sign of Danisinia yet?" My mother kept her tone light, but I could hear the sounds of disappointment and expectation coating her tongue.

"She's coming." I stopped myself from brushing my hands through my hair and instead scratched the scruff on my chin. It was progress, I supposed. "She's only running late."

"Oh, so you're a seer now?"

I bit down on my tongue, then released it, forcing a small smile. "If Dani said she'll be here, then she'll be here."

"Very well."

As guests bowed and curtsied to my mother and me, we smiled back at the patrons, wishing them a happy solstice.

After a moment, my mother leaned closer to me, her voice barely above a whisper. "I must be honest with you, Fynneares. I was, at first, surprised that you and Danisinia were courting each other, but of all of your former partners, she is by far my favorite."

"Mother!" My eyes widened as I scanned the passing guests. "You can't say that," I hissed.

"Why not? It's true." She pushed her shoulders back, an amused smile twitching at the corner of her lips. "And I am queen, Fynneares. I may say whatever I please."

I snorted, shaking my head. If I hadn't known better, I would have said my mother was in a good mood.

"Although, I might be a little biased. The Ferrioses have been some of our closest friends for a long time." She tipped her head. "Rosalina, however, has always been after your crown."

I turned to my mother then, my jaw dropping.

Although I had known this for a while, my mother's words shocked me. She had only ever said kind things about Rosalina.

"Sweetie, mouth closed, please. It is unbecoming of a prince."

I blinked, stumbling for the words I wished to say.

She scoffed, the amusement slipping through her regal demeanor, a crack in the porcelain. "Do not act so surprised. She neither has been nor is *that* discrete about her desires for her future."

"Why were you pushing me to court her then?"

My mother tapped a finger along the glass she held in her hand. "The idea of her, I think, made you happy. All I have ever wanted for you was for you to be happy, son."

I stared at my mother, unsure what to say, as she looked up at me.

She tilted her head ever-so-slightly. "Danisinia makes you happy, does she not?"

I chewed on my cheek, glancing back at the oak doors. The guests flowing through the entrance had begun to dwindle, and the start of the ball was quickly approaching. Yet I still had not seen Dani walk through those doors. She said she was coming with her parents, but even her parents had yet to show.

"Dani is my best friend, Mother. She has always made me happy."

"Have you told her that?"

My brows twisted together. "What do you mean?"

"Have you told Dani how you feel about her?"

"Mother, we are courting."

She sighed. "Sometimes, it is not enough simply to put a label on something. After all, just because the castle is a house does not make it a home."

Now, she was indeed not making any sense.

I rubbed my temples and peered down at my glass.

My mother reached out, wrapping her delicate fingers around my hand and squeezing it once. Her sea-blue eyes peered through me, waves of emotion swimming inside them. "You are young, but you will not be young forever. Do not let the fear of the unknown hold you back from living, son. We are only granted so much time; use it."

When I still had yet to make sense of her words, she released a long sigh. "You have looked at the door more times than I can count."

"How did you—"

"I listen, and I observe. You may think your and Terin's gifts are different, but they are more alike than you realize. You float through everyone's minds, but how much time do you spend in your own?"

I pressed my lips together, unable to answer her truthfully.

"You worry too much, Fynneares."

"Mother, I—"

"Listen and observe," she said, interrupting and tapping my arm. "You do not need to be anyone else but you to be a good king. While your eyes may drift during conversations about the kingdom's coin or the status of ongoing trades, you care about the kingdom's heart. That alone will make you a good king. What I do worry about, however, is your ability to be happy." My mother's voice grew somber, a small line deepening between her eyebrows. "For your entire life, I have watched you push people away out of fear of loving them too much and having them ripped away from you. I have watched you stretch a smile across your face simply because you thought it was what you had to do. You are allowed to be sad, Fynneares. But please, listen to me when I say that, more than anything, you are allowed to be happy. Ruling is already a lonely act. Do not let her go simply because you are afraid."

I swallowed the lump in my throat and whispered, "Thank you, Mother."

She squeezed my arm and walked off, weaving her way through the crowd with her head held high.

Despite myself, I turned to the doors once more.

"She'll come," I said to myself. "She has to."

But the more I repeated it, the more I began to question it.

CHAPTER 18
FYNN

Her parents, brothers, and sister-in-laws stood in the crowd, but Dani was nowhere to be seen.

Dani's absence, however, did not prevent Lord Cunningway from stretching out a hand and saying, "Prince Fynneares, if you will lead us into the night."

I glanced at the doors, now closed. It didn't matter how many times I looked at them. It wasn't going to force her to walk through them. My gaze flicked to my mother standing beside Lord Cunningway, sadness filling her countenance.

I rolled my shoulders back before tipping my head at Lord Cunningway. "It would be my pleasure."

I strolled toward the center of the dance floor, and everyone's heads turned, watching my every step with bated breath. I didn't let my eyes wander the room, nor did I show an ounce of hesitancy or worry. I shoved it all down—the disappointment and the regret—and forced a steady smile to my lips.

As my gaze rounded the inner circle of the guests standing on the edge of the ballroom floor, Rosalina gave me a knowing look. When I slipped into her mind with little effort, her thoughts were a torrent of egotistical and power-hungry sentiments.

Did he truly think he could do better than me? The queen's crown was always meant to sit on my head.

I gritted my teeth, my jaw popping.

I might not have loved these events. I might have often spent my time drinking too much wine or dancing with too many women. More often than not, these balls were a frivolous display of wealth and prosperity. However, they were also a visual representation of our kingdom's unity, culture, and strength.

And today, I had a responsibility to my kingdom.

But what about the responsibility I have to myself?

I tried to push the thought aside, but it was persistent.

My gaze flicked to Terin, and a sad smile appeared on my brother's lips.

This was not what I wanted.

My fingers shook as I held them tightly behind my back. My tie suddenly became too tight.

I peered at my mother again, but her attention was no longer on me.

The doors creaked open, ripping through the silence.

MY HEART PLUMMETED as the doors opened, sending a shiver spiraling down my spine. I turned, and there she was.

Dani stepped inside the ballroom, drawing the attention of the entire ballroom. Golden sunlight streamed inside through the tall windows covering the walls, and Dani froze beneath it. Her eyes widened as she took in the room and the thousand faces staring up at her. Then, our gazes met, and a wide smile split across my face.

Perhaps I should have been furious that she was late. Or, at the least, disappointed and frustrated.

But I wasn't.

Because she was *here*.

Hundreds of people stood in the room, but their faces blurred into the background when I locked eyes with Dani. The guests' thoughts were only a dull buzz in the back of my mind, yet I was nearly sober. Because when I was with Dani, no one else mattered. Her thoughts were the only ones I cared about, even if she kept them locked away.

And atop the stairs, Danisinia Ferrios was radiant.

The seamstress' assistant, Lorallye, had been right. The purple dress had been made for Dani. When she first tried it on, I was rendered speechless. The woman before me had no longer been the girl I grew up with. She was so much more.

When I requested the dress from the boutique, I had the seamstress alter the dress slightly. At the bottom of the dress, tiny crystals were now embroidered into the material. With each step Dani took down the steps, the dress sparkled, a trail of shimmering diamonds trailing behind her.

Her curls hung loose down her back. Her collarbone, shown off by the low-cut dress that dipped between her breasts, sparkled in the gleam of the golden light. Above the crook of her elbow, thin gold bands wrapped around her arms. Dani was the sun itself, brilliant, beautiful, and absolutely blinding.

The crowd split as she made her way forward.

From several yards away, I couldn't make out the freckles on her nose, but I could see the fire burning in her eyes. Neither a nervous smile nor a late entrance could extinguish that.

At that moment, more than ever before, I wanted to know exactly what was happening inside Dani's mind. However, with her walls locked shut, there was only one way I would find out.

I shook myself from my stupor and signaled the small orchestra set up to the right.

The conductor tipped his head and picked up his baton, calling attention to the group of musicians. The strings of the violin vibrated, ringing through the ballroom.

Then, like a magnetic force, I was pulled toward her. I didn't know when things had changed between us—when I had stopped viewing her as a childhood friend. Perhaps I had been so blinded by the desire to find a soul bond that I had ignored the person who had always been there.

Because even if we only had each other for a blip of time, it would be worth it. No matter how long it was. All I wanted was to have Dani spinning in my arms.

I didn't know what that desire meant. All I knew was that whatever I felt was anything but platonic.

Dani dipped her head and began falling into a curtsy as she said, "Your—"

I stepped forward, my fingertips brushing the soft skin of her chin. She froze, mid-curtsy. She lifted her gaze to meet mine, and I encouraged her to stand.

Slowly, she rose.

I slipped a hand behind my back and bowed, low. Small gasps skittered across the room beneath the sounds of the orchestra. I smirked.

When I straightened, I held out a hand. A question furrowed across her forehead as she placed her palm on mine. Ignoring her question, I placed my other hand on her waist and pulled her closer. Then we were dancing.

"You came," I said.

Dani's throat bobbed. "I almost didn't," she whispered.

"Oh?"

The right corner of her mouth twitched, but she only nodded.

My eyes bounced across her face. Something was wrong, but as much as a part of me wished to break through her mental shields, it felt. . .wrong.

Dani swept her hazel gaze across the crowd behind me, worry wrinkling her brows.

"Hey." I squeezed her waist, and her attention returned to me. "It's just you and me, Dani."

She didn't say anything, but she didn't look away from me either as I guided her across the floor. The music swept through the air, the entire orchestra having joined in now. The light fabric of Dani's dress floated in the air as I led her through the steps.

Soon, the world around us melted away.

I leaned forward and whispered, "You're no longer fighting to lead, I see." When we were children and forced to take dancing lessons, Dani often fought the three of us boys to lead when she had to dance with us. "Madam Karina would be proud."

A grin cracked through Dani's focused countenance. "Oh, what I would do to snap Madam Karina's ruler in two. Do you know how often she tapped me with that stick while forcing us to dance?"

"If you would have just listened—"

Dani scoffed. "Like you were so innocent? If I recall correctly, you almost made her quit teaching lessons numerous times."

I chuckled.

"For the record, I would be more than happy to lead right now," Dani added.

"I would rather you lead than have danced with Rosalina." My face twisted, and Dani cocked a brow. "Right before you had shown up, Rosalina was one a step away from following me onto the dance floor, etiquette be damned."

"Oh, I'm sure Rosalina would have loved that."

I scoffed. "She's not too happy since she no longer gets to. She's pretty upset about it, actually. She's been shaking with anger ever since you arrived."

"Has she now?" Dani asked, eyes lit with amusement.

"Mhm."

"She must be upset that she can't show off her dress, huh?"

I laughed, my head throwing back as my hands gripped Dani's waist tighter, keeping me steady. "Have you adopted a second ability all of a sudden?"

Dani snorted. "Fynn, no one needs an ability to read Rosalina's mind. She may be pretty, but she's not very subtle."

"My mother said the same thing," I murmured, the laugh lines flattening.

Dani continued, "I still can't believe your mother would want you to be with her. I mean, after what she and your father had?"

I spun Dani, twirling her away as I straightened my countenance. "She only wants me to be happy."

Dani offered me a sad, knowing smile.

While the memories with my father were few and far between, the relationship he and my mother had was one that was hard to forget. Seeing them in the mornings at the breakfast table, my father pouring my mother her tea, giving her light kisses on her cheek. The way my mother would squeeze his shoulder as he worked in his office, hunched over towering stacks of formal requests from across the kingdom. How they would hold each other's hands as they walked through the park with us children in tow. Most parents hid any soft touch from their children, but my parents never did. Their love for each other was on full display for the entire kingdom to witness.

Perhaps that was what made my father's loss even harder to bear than it already was. As soul bonds, they were two halves of a whole, but one not less than the other. Two complete people who, once together, enhanced the other's gifts, the other's soul, the other's life.

That's what I wanted.

A partner for life.

The inexplicable joy that came with finding the person one's heart sang for. The person that, no matter how dark the clouds were or how long the storm was, could make the sun appear with just one glance.

I might not have had a soul bond, but looking down at Dani, I was still one of the lucky ones.

A forest burned bright within Dani's gaze. The yellow flecks in her irises were flames against the surrounding green. Her fingers danced atop my shoulders, and she cleared her throat, the fire in her eyes simmering. "Well, are you going to lead, or do I have to do all the work here?"

I smiled—the first true, genuine smile of the night. Even though thoughts of my father were now swirling in my mind, Dani had a way of easing the pain.

"And miss out on my one chance to lead one of the famous Ferrioses? The future of our military? I don't think so."

Dani's dress swept across the floor as my feet followed the steps, without more than a passing thought. These steps were engraved into my very soul ages ago.

It should have been awkward to dance with Dani, but I knew her like I knew my own mind. She was unpredictable at times. But if you watched her closely, you could see the change in emotion flick across her eyes. You could see her mind at work as she took in the scene before her.

Even now, as hundreds of people watched us, she had a way of carrying herself that was addictive. It made you want to be inside of her mind, to know what she was thinking.

And there was one thing I couldn't go another minute without knowing the answer to.

"Did you arrive with your mother and father?"

I could almost taste the lie on the tip of her tongue as she dropped her gaze.

I hummed. "So, you weren't late."

Dani worked her lip, her teeth scraping across it. "I—"

My fingers flexed on her back. "Dani, if you're going to keep your shields up, at least do me the decency of not lying to my face."

Her shoulders sagged, the muscles in her back loosening with the movement. "I didn't know if I wanted to come," she finally admitted.

"Because of the dress? I told you if you didn't like it, we could have—"

Dani shook her head and interrupted, "That's not it, Fynn. This"— her eyes danced across the room, surveying the spectators—"this isn't my scene. You know that. . ."

My brows drew together. "You've been to plenty of balls before."

"But this one is different."

"How?"

Hazel eyes met brown. "I'm normally not the one dancing in the center of the room, for starters," she mumbled.

"Dani, you're doing fine."

When I pulled her close, she pulled back, and a prickle spiked across my neck. Dani's gaze flicked somewhere behind me.

Her caramel hair brushed across my jaw.

"Forget about them."

"Easier said than done," she mumbled.

Her fingers lightly gripping my hand, she spun, her dress swishing across the floor, spinning around her ankles and into the air. As the purple fabric danced in the air, I could feel Dani pulling away. But I wouldn't let her. Not now.

Dani ran toward every fight, yet for some reason, she wanted to run away from this one, and I couldn't stand by and watch any longer.

I pulled her back in, twirling her toward me. The fabric fell and cascaded onto the floor, diamonds glittering beneath the crystal chandelier. My hand skated down her bare back, her skin warm beneath my palm.

"Dani, whatever reason you are telling yourself—whatever thought is flying through your mind telling you that you shouldn't be here—silence it."

Dani blinked up at me, a deep crease forming across her forehead. The freckles across her nose shifted. "Why? This is not real. What does any of this matter if they do not believe it?"

I swallowed the truth I wished to say and opted for another. "You have never once questioned who you were or if you deserved your spot among the leaders before they promoted Quint. You haven't lost, Dani. We can still show them who you are. We can still prove they made a mistake when they didn't choose you."

"How?" She stared at me, blinking, worry drawing her brows closer together.

"Kiss me."

"What?"

Her surprise mimicked my own, for the two words had escaped before I could call them back.

Friends didn't kiss friends.

But I wouldn't take them back now that they were in the world.

I twirled her away, not stopping the momentum of the dance. The song was ending soon, and we were running out of time.

I pulled her body tight to mine, my nose brushing against the side of her face. The sweet and acidic notes of cinnamon and orange consumed me.

"You heard me. *Kiss* me, Dani."

"Why would I do that?"

"It's just one kiss," I whispered.

We had already kissed once. While it hadn't changed anything per se, there were some nights when Dani consumed my dreams. When my subconscious dreamed up scenarios that friends should never consider between one another.

That kiss at the tavern was only supposed to convince her friends, but instead, it left me confused and wanting.

In truth, one kiss might have ruined everything for me.

I needed to know if it was a fluke—if it was the ale or the lie.

Or if it was something else entirely.

Dani peered beyond my shoulder, toward the crowd behind me. I sensed her debating—analyzing the situation and figuring out the best solution.

"Dani, I need an answer. The song is about to end, and I won't do it unless—"

"Fine," she spat, cutting me off. "But just—"

I spun her away, the light fabric flowing up and into the air around her feet, and then I tugged, pulling her back toward me before dipping her low. Her loose curls flew into the air, surrounding me. Her cheeks tinted pink, and large hazel eyes stared up at me.

I gripped her thigh, pulling it up my leg with a devilish smirk.

Then, I kissed her.

With no hesitation.

I kissed her as if this wasn't a fake courtship. As if this wasn't a part of the deal we had made together to get our mothers off our backs.

I kissed her like I meant it.

I kissed her as if she was the only one in the room.

Because, unlike the first time outside the tavern, I hadn't heard anyone in the ballroom question whether Dani and I were together as we were dancing. Because who could have questioned us?

Dani might have thought I was a good actor, but I couldn't even fake how the blood in my veins sparked every time we touched. I couldn't fake how much my cheeks heated every time she smirked up at me with that glance that suggested that she and I knew something the rest of the world didn't.

I kissed her long and hard because, unlike the first time, I wasn't pretending anymore. And I couldn't stop myself from taking as much of her as I could—before she would inevitably pull away, before the song would end and the next would begin.

I kissed her with the wish that I wanted this to be real, even if she didn't. Even if she was pretending when she kissed me back.

The violin strings dissipated into the air, and clapping echoed in the hall. Yet, my mind was completely silent for once as I peeled myself away from Dani and stared into the forest aflame in her eyes. There were no wayward thoughts, no foreign voices within my mind that weren't my own.

Because when I looked at Dani, with her cheeks flushed and wide eyes, all I saw was her. All I heard was the beating of my own heart—a song filling my veins that I never wanted to stop.

Dani cleared her throat, and I forced myself to right her. Her thigh slid down my leg, my hand sweeping over the silk fabric of her dress, over the curves of her leg.

Then Dani curtsied.

And that small movement alone—a gesture meant to show respect —felt like a slap in the face when she whispered, "Do you think they believed it?"

I cleared my throat, bowing in return. "I think so."

Because how could they not? I had believed it, too.

CHAPTER 19
DANI

FYNN'S LAUGHTER CUT THROUGH THE SURROUNDING NOISE AS THE actors crashed into one another, their performance bringing tears to the spectators.

"What did I miss?" Terin asked as he came up behind us and wrapped an arm around Fynn's shoulders, knocking Fynn into me.

I took a small side step.

Riley trailed behind Terin, cheeks flushed, but I was too distracted by Terin's question to give it any thought. My eyebrows twisted together as I tried to recall what happened in the performance I hadn't been paying any attention to.

In fact, I hadn't been paying much attention to anything since Fynn kissed me in the middle of the ballroom.

Since his hand gripped my thigh.

Since his fingers brushed the bare skin of my back.

The ghost of his gentle touch still lingered there as if he had somehow marked my very soul.

Hours must have passed, yet I couldn't get the taste of his lips off my mind.

Movement flickered in my peripheral vision—a staff member

strolling by balancing a precarious number of thinly stemmed glasses on a silver platter. I grabbed a glass as he passed and drank, letting the cool wine simmer the rising heat in my stomach.

"Oh, you missed it, Ter and Riley," Fynn said. "The two comedians were making a joke about the bull king and his—"

"I'm going to get some fresh air," I said as Fynn prattled.

Not bothering to wait for a response, I weaved through the crowd. As I downed the rest of the wine, I tried to drown out everything around me: Fynn's voice, his laughter, the phantom warmth on my back, on my lips, on my—

"By the gods," I groaned.

I kept walking until the fresh air swept across my face. But Pontanius himself must have cursed the sea's breeze, for it did little to soothe the burning consuming me.

I had set aside these feelings a long time ago. There was no reason I should have been getting heated about Fynn.

It was all pretend, I reminded myself.

He kissed me to ensure the kingdom believed we were serious. Yet the only thing it did was seriously confuse *me*.

I rubbed a hand across my face, groaning.

What am I doing? I asked myself.

"Danisinia."

I straightened at the queen's gentle voice and turned, curtsying. When I stood, Esmeray smiled. I could barely make my lips twitch, though, as her searing blue eyes bore into me. I had only known Esmeray to be a kind woman, but I had heard rumors about her gift— how she could rip memories from one's mind and claim them for her own. I had never feared her before, but now. . .

"Where's Fynneares?" Esmeray asked.

"Oh, uhm." My gaze flitted across the garden. "He and Terin are watching the rest of the performance. I came outside to get some fresh air."

She nodded, her gaze slipping to the manor behind me before her attention returned to me. "These events can be a lot sometimes."

"Indeed," I mumbled, twisting a curl around my finger behind my back.

"Walk with me for a moment?"

I tipped my head, unwilling to deny the queen. "Of course, Your Highness."

Esmeray strolled forward, and I walked beside her.

"Now, Danisinia, how many times have I told you? There is no need for such formalities. I have known you for your entire life. By the gods, I was there when you first started walking. We are practically family, so please, call me Esmeray."

I chewed on the inside of my cheek, the discomfort of the lie growing thick in my throat from the Queen's words. I had always been comfortable around Esmeray, but now she wasn't simply looking at me as her boys' childhood friend. In her eyes, I was now something. . .more.

But it was all a lie.

"Of course," I said with a tight smile, keeping my hands close to my body as she led us through the garden.

The captain of her guard walked several paces behind us. While his hands were folded behind his back, he remained alert as people celebrated the solstice all around us.

Despite only three or four hours left before midnight, there was still plenty of daylight ahead before night fell upon us. Music from the ballroom swirled around the manor's land, wrapping around the jovial faces of the guests who ran and danced and rejoiced in the gardens.

A group of children ran toward us, laughter filling their mouths and their attention lacking as they nearly ran into the queen. Esmeray, without blinking, moved to the side, smiling. As the children rounded the corner of the manor, their voices faded. The queen turned to one of the flower beds lining the paths. Different types of flowers in various vibrant shades of purple, pink, yellow, and orange filled the beds. Esmeray bent down, her lavender dress pooling at her feet and into the dirt.

Behind us, Airos made to step forward, but the queen stopped him with a lift of her hand. She brushed her fingers delicately across the sea of colors until she separated one from the rest.

"Dahlias were Marc's favorite flower," she said after a moment.

Fynn had told me that a month or so ago when we were strolling through the castle's gardens. Dahlias bloomed all over the castle's property with entire sections of the magnificent gardens dedicated solely to the flower. Here, the dahlias were sparse among the other brilliant blooms.

"They are beautiful," I said quietly.

"Indeed, but their beauty is not why my husband favored them of all the rest." Esmeray plucked the bloom with a quick snap of its stem and stood, a palm pressing against her thighs. Specks of dirt spotted her dress where her hand touched, but she didn't notice. She twisted the stem between her fingers, the pointed petals of the Dahlia spinning and melting into a sunset. "Do you know what dahlias signify, Danisinia?"

I pursed my lips, but none of my studies had ever revolved around flowers besides their medicinal and poisonous qualities. Neither of which were helpful in this situation.

"I cannot say that I do."

Esmeray smiled, still spinning the flower. "Dahlias represent a sort of inner strength, one that is not so easily shaken by external conditions." She sighed, stilling the vibrant flower. "Before we were engaged and found out we were soul bonds, Marc never pictured himself having a prestigious title. While he was set to inherit his father's title of lord, he had always planned on surrendering it to his sister, Marsella. Marc did not enjoy all the pomp and circumstance that came with bearing a title. When he discovered that our fathers had arranged for us to be married, he was outraged."

"He was?"

Esmeray nodded, amusement flashing across her eyes as she recalled the memory. "So much so that he even ran."

"Were you upset?"

The queen laughed, loud and unrestrained. "Upset? Oh no. Not at all. How could I be upset when I had done the same thing?"

"You ran away? The boys never mentioned—"

Esmeray waved a hand and interrupted, "Those boys only listen to half the things I tell them." She brought the flower to her nose and sniffed. "Then again, I never told them *that* particular part of the story."

"Why not?"

"Could you imagine how often Fynn or Graeson would have used that against me growing up? As unfair as it may be, we live in a different world now than we did then." Sighing, she continued, "Anyway, that is not the point of this story. When Marc and I finally came to terms with our arrangement, he still fought the title of King Consort."

"I had always heard he wore the crown well."

"He did indeed, but that does not mean he always enjoyed sacrificing his personal time for the sake of the crown."

Guilt rose in my throat, and sweat licked my palms. "Your Highness, I apologize for—"

Esmeray raised a hand, silencing me. "You do not need to explain yourself to me, Danisinia. While you may have been late, you showed up when you were needed. *That* is what matters."

I bit down on my tongue.

She swiped a hand down her dress, finally brushing off the dirt. "I do not tell you this because I believe you must follow in my late husband's footsteps. You've always been career-driven, and I deeply admire that about you. Truth be told, it's one of the many reasons I was thankful when you first started studying and training with my sons. It was my selfish hope that some of that would rub off onto them, Fynneares especially. He can be so. . ."

Amusement wrinkled the corner of my eyes when the queen's words fell off. "Heedless?" I suggested.

"And then some." The queen chuckled softly as if recalling another memory. "Now, Danisinia, do not take offense by what I say next."

I nodded, although a sourness filled my stomach as nerves tingled my fingertips.

"At first, I was unsure if this courtship between you was any different from Fynneares' last ones. But after seeing the two of you together tonight, I cannot help but think it is different."

My lips parted, the guilt rising too high to keep restrained, but Esmeray continued before I could speak.

"Fynneares is like his father in more ways than he realizes. And for that, I am thankful that he has you standing beside him."

I took a deep breath and met the queen with an even gaze. "If I may be frank, Esmeray?"

"Always, my dear."

I rolled my shoulders back, steadying myself. "Fynn doesn't need me or anyone at his side. He may be more reckless than not, but he cares deeply about this kingdom and will be a great king no matter."

Esmeray gave me a sad smile. "You and I may believe that, Danisinia, but does he? Often, we are the last ones to see the truth within ourselves."

ONCE A COUPLE of council members whisked Esmeray away, I walked further away from the castle, finding a solitary spot on the hill where the music was no more than a dull buzz in the background. While Esmeray meant well, I couldn't help but drown in my own guilt.

I thrived on facts and logic, but nothing about the courtship with Fynn was logical or factual.

Not anymore.

As my mind got lost among the stars finally appearing in the sky, a twig snapped somewhere in the distance behind me. The back of my neck prickled. Without turning around, I took a long breath before saying, "Fynn."

"There's no sneaking up on you, is there?" Fynn asked.

I huffed a laugh, but it came out coarser than intended.

Fynn sat beside me with an *oomph* and stretched out his legs. "You disappeared during the performance. I tried searching for you, but. . ."

It had been over half an hour since I had left the small theater. If Fynn had been trying to find me, he hadn't searched hard enough.

"I needed some fresh air," I said with a shrug.

"Ah."

"What are you doing out here, anyway?" I asked, peering at him from the corner of my eye.

He raked his fingers through his hair. "I needed some fresh air, too, I guess. In truth, I probably would have found you sooner, but your father stopped me before I could get too far."

Despite the summer heat, my skin grew cold. "Did he—"

Fynn shook his head. "He doesn't suspect anything. He didn't even bring it up."

"I suppose that is unsurprising. Whenever my mother brings it up in front of him, he stays quiet or finds some paperwork that suddenly requires his attention. I can't tell if it's good or bad that he hasn't asked any questions."

"I would say it's good," Fynn said, his tone calm as he leaned back on his palms. "His shields are strong—always have been—but he didn't seem suspicious. We were actually talking about one of my recent proposals."

"Oh?"

Fynn's jaw flexed. He fixed his gaze upon the sea where the sun hung low in the sky, hovering above the horizon. "It's been fifteen years."

There were no words to give that would lessen the pain, so instead, I kept quiet and let him talk.

"The council had a meeting a month ago, and I recommended sending a squadron to get more accurate intel."

My eyes widened, but I quickly flattened my expression before Fynn could notice. This must have been the reason for the extra practices. They were trying to identify who they would send.

Before I could say anything, Fynn sighed and continued, "My mother keeps telling me to be patient, but—" He swallowed, pulling one knee closer to his chest and resting his chin atop it.

"It's okay to be sad, Fynn." I bumped my shoulder into his. "It's even okay to be angry."

"I'm not—"

"Fynn," I said, cocking my head to the side.

"Fine. Usually, I'm better at holding it in—at compartmentalizing these things. But my mother has been bringing my father up more and more these days."

"He was her soul bond. I don't even know what I would do if I lost my other half. The pain she feels is unimaginable. For her to be able to talk about him, though, that's a good thing, Fynn."

"I know it is, and I don't want her to continue hiding from those memories. But when she compares me to him, it feels like I'm disappointing her." His hand grazed the grass. He plucked a single blade. After inspecting it briefly, he discarded it. He repeated the process, ripping blades of grass from the soil, his brows twisting. "I'm not him. I'm not even close," he mumbled.

"King Marc was a wonderful man, Fynn. He was a great leader, a great friend, a great father and husband." My hand landed on his hand, stilling it. "But you will be, too."

Fynn was quiet for a moment as he stared at the ground. After a moment, he dragged his attention up to meet my gaze. Disbelief was written in his brown eyes. "How do you know?"

I squeezed his hand. "Because you care."

His fingers twitched beneath my palm, but he didn't move away. "So?"

"People who don't care don't put in the effort you do."

His shoulders dropped, and he faced the sea.

"Can I give you some friendly advice?" I asked.

Fynn tilted his head toward me slightly. "Only if it's friendly, Ferrios." He winked, his classic smirk returning. Yet neither his gaze nor the quirk of his lip held any of its usual cockiness. Instead, when I looked at Fynn, I only saw a sad prince trying to make everyone but himself happy.

"Stop trying to be your father. You're not him."

He turned his gaze back toward the sea. "This doesn't sound too friendly."

He went to pull his hand away, but I tightened my grip around it.

"I'm not finished," I said. "You're Fynneares Andros Nadarean—being *you* is more than enough. You might have been born twenty minutes before Terin—"

"Ten minutes, actually," Fynn said, interrupting.

I rolled my eyes with a tsk. "*But* that's not why you were named heir."

When his lips parted as if he was going to interrupt again, I added, "Nor is it because of your gift. Your mother and the advisors chose you because of *who* you are. You care about this kingdom more than anyone else I know. You go into town, you talk to the shopkeepers, you befriend anyone you see simply because you can. You connect with them; you laugh with them. You stand up for what you believe in. You know the rules, but you also know when you can break them. You may not be your father, but you will be a great king one day, Fynn. I can promise you that."

His eyes stayed fixed upon the sea. If I hadn't known better, I would have thought he wasn't listening, but then I felt the brush of his hand as he flipped it over, followed by the weaving of his fingers between mine.

"Thank you, Dani."

I turned to watch the sun fall. "That's what friends are for, right?"

CHAPTER 20
DANI

We sat atop the hill until the sun had vanished, leaving only the stars and the moon to light the sky.

Outside, Fynn and I had fallen into a comfortable silence. Together, there was never a need to fill the space with small talk or other nonsense. Atop the hill, all the worries plaguing my mind were pushed to the wayside. For a moment, it was as if we weren't pretending to court each other, as if he hadn't kissed me, as if old feelings hadn't been rekindled despite years of shoving them down. As if nothing had changed between us at all in the past few months.

Until we walked into my room.

Or what I thought was *my* room.

"Wait, this can't be right," I said, twirling around as the door clicked shut.

My lungs were in my stomach as I stared at the luggage by the wall—more specifically, at the *extra* luggage sitting beside mine. This was most certainly *wrong*.

"I told them to bring my bags to my room."

"Are you missing something?" Fynn asked, placing a gentle hand on my back as he scanned the bags. "I can go ask—"

I quickly stepped away and cut him off, "No, Fynn. I am not *missing* something. Don't you see what the issue is?"

Confusion twisted his facial features as he surveyed the room. Was he purposely being ignorant? Did he truly not see the problem?

Groaning, I waved to his belongings sitting beside mine. "Why is *your* stuff in here?"

"Because—" Then his eyes fell onto the bed. The *single* bed that occupied the space. "Oh."

"*Oh*," I repeated, rolling my eyes far back into my head. "Why would they put us in the same room?"

Fynn scratched the back of his head. "Well, we are courting."

"Courting but not married!" I pressed the heels of my palms to the side of my head.

Even though Fynn was right, that wasn't the problem. *We* were the problem. I couldn't possibly stay in a room with him.

Fynn chuckled. "Dani, it's not a hundred years ago. Times have changed. No one cares if two people bed each other before—"

My eyes sprung open. "Bed each other? We're not—"

"Wait," Fynn said, stumbling back and waving his hands. "That's not what I meant."

"Of course you didn't! But now I can't stop thinking that everyone *else* is thinking we're bedding each other in here. I couldn't possibly bed you. I mean, look at you," I sputtered, pointing at him.

"What about me?" Fynn arched a brow as he leaned against the wall. His arms were crossed over his chest, sleeves rolled up, and the veins running across his forearms were on full display.

By the gods.

Veins simply pumped one's blood. There was nothing attractive about them, and yet. . .

My cheeks flushed as I snapped my gaze up to meet his, and Fynn stared back at me, that smug mouth cocking up.

He was absolutely, positively infuriating.

"You're. . .you!" I finally spat.

"I'm *me*? Would you rather me be someone else?"

Yes, I wanted to shout. But every part of me inside screamed, *no*.

I shook my hand in frustration, more annoyed with myself than the situation. "We can't possibly sleep in the same bed together. That's crossing a line, isn't it?"

"We have shared beds before," he said with a shrug.

"When we were children!"

"And what's the big deal?"

I snapped my mouth shut and bit my tongue. How could he not be reacting the same way as me? How could he ask that with a straight face? Was I the one making it a bigger deal than it needed to be?

I twisted my hands together and said, "Nothing. I just. . .I don't like the idea of people thinking we're sleeping together. We're friends, Fynn."

He quirked a brow.

Internally, I screamed.

Why did even that tiny movement send heat rising all the way from my toes to my cheeks?

"Friends who are pretending to court each other," he said.

Sweat dampened my neck, the bottom layer of my curls sticking to my skin.

When I still hadn't moved, Fynn shook his head with an exasperated sigh. "I can see that this bothers you. I'll ask one of the staff members if another room is available."

I nodded but then froze once I recalled what the doorman had said when I arrived.

"There's no point," I said with a groan. "There are no rooms left."

Fynn's hand fell from the door. "I'll sleep on the floor then."

Placing a hand on my hip, I asked, gaze narrowed at his back, "Have you ever slept on the floor, Fynn?"

He turned. "No, but—"

"But," I said, interrupting, "it's not comfortable. I am not going to make you sleep on the floor. I will."

Fynn snorted, folding his arms over his chest and stepping forward. "Over my dead body, Ferrios."

"Fine," I said, nibbling on my nails as I stared at the bed. It was just one night. "We'll share the bed."

"Are you sure?"

"Yes." I shifted on my feet, unsure if I was sure or not about it. But either way, it was too late. A decision had been made.

Fynn took several steps forward, his shoes light on the floor yet heavy in my mind. "But I'm so *me,*" he whispered, his words sweeping across my skin like a breeze.

A small smile cracked through the panic.

I quickly shook it away.

"We're both tired. Let's just get some rest," I said.

More steps.

"If you insist."

The click of the lock ripped through the room, and suddenly, the room felt too small to breathe despite its grandeur size.

"Do you want to change first?" Fynn asked.

"No." I waved him off. "You can. I'm going to open some windows. It's rather stuffy in here."

Fynn nodded. He removed his shoes, scuffing the toes as he did so. He tossed them out of the way of the door, and they landed with a *thunk*. Grabbing his bag, he headed into the adjoined bathing chambers. The door clicked shut behind him.

Through the door, I could hear the soft patter of his feet against the tile floor. Then, the thud of clothes hitting the ground.

Sweat licked my skin.

It might have been the shortest night of the year, but tonight was going to feel like the longest.

I pushed open a window, letting the night breeze rush in.

The Cunningway's manor was on the west side of the kingdom. In the distance, waves crashed against the cliffs surrounding Pontia.

I dug my fingers through my hair and lifted the curls off my neck. Yet, despite the mist in the air, the breeze did little to cool my skin.

"What are we doing?" I whispered as I stared out the window. The sea sparkled with the stars, and the full moon's reflection spilled across the water's surface. "This is insane. This is a—"

"Did you say something?" Fynn asked, the door creaking open.

I spun around, releasing my hair. My back hit the windowsill, and the curtain rod rattled above me. "I was admiring the view."

But the better view was standing in front of me. The button-downs and suit jackets Fynn wore hid his muscular build well—*too* well. As Fynn stood shirtless, leaning against the doorframe, his pectorals flexed beneath his crossed arms.

Had he always leaned on things so much?

"The view, huh?" Fynn asked, forcing my gaze up.

And there was that stupid, cocky smirk on his face again, as if he knew he was attractive and knew I was ogling him. He must have overheard the thoughts of countless women commenting on how good-looking he was over the years.

I refused to be another one on that list, though.

"Are you done in there, princess?" I asked.

Fynn held out a hand, ushering me forward. "All yours, Ferrios."

I hurried into the bathroom, shutting the door behind me.

I quickly dipped my hands into the water basin and splashed the water onto my face, spreading it across the back of my neck. Gripping the sides of the bowl, I leaned over the basin and glared at myself in the mirror.

What am I doing?

Nothing good would come from gawking at Fynn. Yet I couldn't deny that I was, on some level, attracted to him.

Objectively speaking, Fynn was attractive. He was tall, muscular, smart.

And the way he kissed me? My legs still trembled.

But that kiss was only for show, I reminded myself again.

It might have *felt* real, but Fynn had plenty of practice over the years to be able to fake a kiss decently.

I grabbed a clean towel on the counter and dabbed the water off my face. The summer heat had turned my curls into a frizzy mess. After detangling them with wet fingers, I twisted my hair into a simple plait and let it hang loose down my back. Quickly stripping out of my dress, I changed. For once, I was thankful for my expensive taste in sleepwear. After wearing a uniform most days, loungewear was one of the few luxuries I allowed myself to indulge in. Slipping the simple black slip on, I inspected my reflection.

I groaned.

Good taste or not, if I had known I would share a room with Fynn, I would have picked something that offered more coverage. The slip's neckline barely covered the tops of my breasts, and the hem barely reached the middle of my thighs.

My nails bit into my palms.

Then, something in the corner of the mirror caught my eye. Fynn's clothes were piled in the corner, discarded. I rushed over and picked up his shirt, holding it up. I rubbed the fabric between my fingertips.

With a groan, I dropped.

The fabric was too thick. At least the slip was light enough for the stifling summer heat. His shirt would be suffocating.

And his shirt smelled too much like him.

"Get it together, Dani. It's just one night," I whispered. "I can do one night."

With one final nod at myself, I picked up my belongings and left the bathing chambers.

A lit lantern sat on the bedside table, casting a golden hue across Fynn's features as he lay on the bed. His head was propped up on one of his hands as he held a book in his other hand.

"You brought a book?" I asked.

"You didn't?" Fynn asked, his attention glued to the book. His brows were scrunched together, and his eyes were slightly narrowed.

"I didn't expect to do any light reading," I said, fidgeting with the hem of my dress that kissed my thighs. If Fynn's current behavior was any indication, I shouldn't have been nervous. When it came to him, it didn't matter what I wore. And yet. . .

"What did you expect to do then?" Fynn asked, quirking a brow. He flipped to the next page, the page rubbing against his fingers.

Despite myself, my cheeks heated, and I rolled my eyes, hoping to cover it up. "I don't know. Sleep?"

"If only it were that easy for some of us," he mumbled. However, his comment seemed directed more at himself than in response to my statement.

"So, you read to sleep?" I asked, walking forward.

He tilted his head. "Sometimes it helps. Sometimes it doesn't. If I'm interested in the book, the story keeps me up late into the night instead. Either way, the books do what they need to do."

I was at the edge of the bed when I asked, "Which is?"

"Distract me from the thoughts spinning in my head." He finally looked up, and an emotion I couldn't quite place flashed across his brown eyes. But before I could identify it, it vanished. He shifted, folding up a leg and returning his gaze to his book. Clearing his throat, he asked, "Are you going to stand there all night, or are you going to get into bed?"

I blinked.

Did his—

No, I was *definitely* imagining it. Fynn's voice didn't wobble.

Yet, I still could not move forward, as if a line had been drawn in the sand, one I was unsure I wanted to cross.

Fynn sighed as he flipped the page. "We're friends, Dani. Sharing a bed means nothing."

Rolling my shoulders back, I tried to relax my jaw. I cleared my throat and walked to my side of the bed, my feet a soft patter against the wood.

Growing up, I had seen the twins shirtless countless times when we used to train together in the castle's private training grounds on hot summer days. As a soldier, I never gave a second thought to the men in the battalion when they stripped off their shirts.

This should have been no different.

But then why did my fingers tremble as I grabbed the duvet and flipped it over? As the cotton rubbed against my overly sensitive skin when I slipped between the sheets?

Why was I cognizant of how loud my breathing was?

Or how loud each turn of the page of that damned book was?

I took a quiet breath and exhaled softly.

Friends. Just friends.

CHAPTER 21
FYNN

I HAD FLIPPED THROUGH EIGHT PAGES OF MY BOOK YET HADN'T comprehended a single word.

I think someone died on the page, but I couldn't even explain why or how.

How could I when Dani was lying next to me?

The only thoughts that came to my mind as Dani slipped beneath the comforter were the exact things a friend shouldn't have been thinking about. How would her short black silk slip feel beneath my palms? Would it be like water running down her smooth skin as I grabbed her waist and explored her body? How would it feel as I cupped—

Fuck.

I flipped the page, the parchment coarse against my fingertips and nearly ripping from the book's seam. I scanned the words, but they were no more than splotches of ink. As if the book were written in the ancient language of the gods, I couldn't comprehend a single sentence while my attention kept returning to Dani.

Her chest rising.

Her legs sliding beneath the sheets.

The cotton duvet shifting when she turned to her side.

I exhaled. "Is something wrong?" I asked, my muscles growing taut.

"Why would something be wrong?"

My brow arched as I peered at her from the corner of my eye. The braid she had twisted her hair into was draped over her shoulder, curving over her breast.

"You seem. . ."

She shifted again, and one of the thin straps of the slip slipped down the soft curve of her shoulder.

I swallowed, blinking and forcing my gaze back to her eyes. "Restless."

She fixed the strap and swept a hand across her collarbone. A sweet golden hue hummed across her skin in the lantern's flickering light. "It's just warm in here, that's all."

Peeling my gaze away from her—a task more difficult than it should have been—I surveyed the windows lining the exterior wall. "Do you want me to open up another window?"

"No, I got it."

She moved, and because I was a glutton for punishment, I watched her from the corner of my eye. My book slipped an inch in my hand as she threw off the covers. Her slip had ridden up slightly, revealing more of her toned thighs. She threw her legs over the side of the bed and strolled to the window. Her hips swayed, and with each step, the slip rose.

When she reached the window—a distance that I selfishly wished to be longer—she pushed it open. The breeze that rolled in swept over the loose strands of hair surrounding her face, picking them up and twisting them into the air.

Dani leaned against the window, and my gaze dropped to her backside. As she leaned against the window with her arms on the windowsill, her back arched, and the fabric rose higher.

And for a moment, I let myself admire the woman before me.

As she stood in nothing more than a slip that barely kissed her thighs, her physique was proof of the work she had put in over the years.

She was bewitching.

Months ago, those words would not have entered my mind so easily. I had never looked at Dani that way before, not really, anyway. Not so. . .absentmindedly.

When we were kids, the thought did cross my mind once or twice —especially when I was a hormonal teenager who was easily distracted by any woman who looked at me. I once made the painful mistake of mentioning that Dani was attractive—perhaps not in such respectable terms, but the point was all the same. Instead of taking my comment about her growing curves as a compliment, she had kneed me in the balls.

Rightfully so, of course.

Back then, however, I didn't even realize what I had said was wrong. As a child and teenager, I struggled to keep my mouth shut. When you have so many thoughts running through your mind, you were bound to blurt out a thing or two by accident and at inappropriate times.

After Dani made me keel over, I tried never to repeat that mistake.

But on the shortest night of the year and in the privacy of my mind, I admired her.

She was lethal with a weapon.

She was powerful in a dress.

She was as beautiful as a freshly forged sword.

She was feminine and strong. Two words that so many men kept separate, as if they were opposites on a spectrum. And yet, Dani was the embodiment of both. Her strength was not diminished because of her femininity, nor vice versa. Instead, like a recipe requiring salt and sugar, they only enhanced one another.

I set my book on the bedside table, not caring to save the page at this point. I was more interested in the story unfolding before me.

Because, as if she was the moon and I was the sea, some magnetic force I could not explain pulled me toward her.

I kept my footsteps soft across the pine floors as if she was a doe in a forest. When I approached, Dani didn't move. She didn't even look at me as I leaned against the windowsill beside her.

We stood there in silence. As if were we to speak, whatever magic twisted in the air would disappear. So, instead, we watched the waves tumble over one another out at sea. As a cool gust swept in, the smell of sea salt wrapped around us. Beneath it, though, I could make out the faint notes of cinnamon kissing my cheeks as the breeze brushed past Dani's hair. A loose curl fell from her braid, and it took everything I had not to brush it behind her ear.

Her brows were drawn tight together, and a deep crease formed in the center of her forehead. I had the urge to wipe the worry away, too, but I kept my hands to myself despite the buzzing spiraling through my veins.

Earlier tonight, I had thought that maybe, just *maybe*, Dani felt the same about that kiss that I did. I thought I had seen a flash of something slip through her tightly sealed walls, but I couldn't be sure.

She never used to be so closed off. When we were children, she was an open book. But at some point, things had changed. I didn't know when. I didn't know why. All I knew was that as we grew up, her walls grew taller.

I would do anything to tear down those walls now, though.

"What are you thinking about?" I asked.

At first, I wasn't sure she would answer as the silence deepened. But then she whispered, "What are we doing?" The question was almost too faint on her lips, and I was unsure I had heard it until her fingers flexed around the windowsill.

That was not the response I had been hoping for. Still, I chuckled, but the once easy sound felt too heavy, too forced. "Standing here?"

"No, Fynn. What are *we* doing?"

"I—" The words disappeared on my tongue. I didn't want to lie to her, but I also couldn't fabricate a story that wasn't entangled with the truth. I couldn't tell some joke or brush off her question with a smug smirk or a wave of my hand because, in truth, I didn't know what we were doing. I didn't know what *I* was doing.

All I knew was that I needed to be by her.

Dani shifted on her feet, her hazel eyes wide as she peered up at me. "You want to know what I'm thinking?"

There's nothing I want more, Ferrios, is what I wanted to say, but I only nodded.

Her nails tapped the windowsill. "I'm trying to figure out why you kissed me."

I blinked.

"Was it for show?" Dani asked as she turned to face the sea.

I mimicked her as if we would find the answer somewhere in the depths of the water.

I could have blamed the kiss on the alcohol.

I could have blamed it on the need to make everyone else believe we were a real couple.

But I would have been lying if I had said any of those things.

Because, while the buzz of the wine had dissipated long ago, I still wanted to recreate that kiss even if there was no one here to put on a show for.

There was only Dani.

Only my best friend.

And maybe, if I could be honest with myself, I could be frank with Dani, too.

I took in a deep breath. When I exhaled, I let out the truth that I had been harboring inside since that first kiss outside the tavern.

"No, Dani," I said, shaking my head. "I kissed you because I wanted to."

With her gaze fixed on the sea, her hands tightened around the edge of the window, gripping the wood. "Why?"

This version of Dani was new—the one who doubted herself, the one who didn't see that I now craved the taste of cinnamon in my tea. And as cute as she was, this wasn't the Dani I knew.

This wasn't *my* Dani.

"Look at me."

When she refused, I shook my head in amusement. Reaching out, I finally brushed that incessant loose curl behind her ear. My finger trailed down her jaw, light and soft. Curling it beneath her chin, I turned her head toward me. "You are absolutely vexing."

Her lips parted, but no words escaped.

"There is no other explanation or reason. I could tell you I kissed you because we were in front of hundreds of people who expected us to. I could tell you I kissed you because we needed to make them believe. I could tell you that I kissed you because it is what two people courting each other do. But if I told you any of these things, they would all be lies. I kissed you because I wanted to. Plain and simple."

She shook her head as if she still didn't believe me. "But you said that some people didn't believe we were telling the truth."

A breeze entered through the window, wrapping around us and sending goosebumps crawling across Dani's bare arm.

"That was a lie."

"I don't understand." Dani took a small step back.

She was preparing to run—I could see it in her eyes. But I wasn't done talking about this.

I took a step forward, matching her. "Would you believe me if I said I wanted to kiss you right now?"

"Why would you—" Her head tilted to the side as she sucked on her bottom lip. Dani shook her head, releasing her lip, which was now plump and red. When she spoke again, her voice was quiet. "There's no one here."

"Does there have to be?" I asked.

"I—" Her gaze dropped to my lips. There may have been fear in her eyes, but there was also desire.

And desire looked good on Dani.

"Do you mean to tell me you're not replaying that kiss in your head right now?" I leaned closer, my lips brushing lightly across her ear. Her chest rose as she inhaled sharply, and a smile tugged at the corners of my mouth. "Do you mean to tell me you're not thinking about my hands on your back? My hand gripping your thigh? That you're not at all curious about what would have happened if I didn't stop kissing you?" I leaned back and tipped her chin up, my fingers coarse against her soft skin. "Because I am."

Her cheeks reddened, and her fingers curled around the hem of her slip, bunching the silk fabric in her palms. "What about rule number three?" she mumbled.

"I've never been a big fan of rules," I said, my thumb brushing across her chin, "especially rule number three."

She swallowed, her throat dipping. Her eyes flicked to my lips again as I licked them.

"Dani, tell me the truth," I said, noting every freckle on her face and every twitch of muscle. "We don't have to do anything you don't want to. If you tell me no right now, I will walk away. I will sleep in Terin's room and throw Riley out of his room. I will take his wrath if that's what—"

Dani cut my words off, pressing her lips against mine.

Her hand gripped the back of my neck as she pulled my head down with a fervor I wanted to drink up and never run out of. I wrapped my hand around her waist, pulling her tighter to me.

I smiled against her soft lips. I was right. The silk was just as smooth as the sea, leaving little to the imagination.

She peeled herself away from me, her chest rising hard and fast, but her fingers were still woven into my hair, locking me into place.

"This is a mistake," she said, her lip swollen.

We had crossed the line.

I knew it.

She knew it.

But with Dani, I was beginning to realize that I wanted to cross all the lines.

I wanted to throw the godsforsaken rule book out the window.

For at least one night.

We could blame it on the summer solstice, the stars, the sun, the pull of the moon. I didn't care. All I wanted was her lips on mine, her body atop mine.

"Then let's make the greatest mistake we can, Ferrios."

A SMILE SPLIT HER FACE, and without hesitating any longer, I picked her up. Her thighs wrapped around me tightly as I gripped her thighs and pressed her back against the wall.

Then, I devoured her.

I pressed my lips to her neck, nibbled the spot beneath her ear, and explored her body. When Dani wiggled against me, her gasp coming out more of a moan, I knew I had found the spot that would not only be her undoing but mine as well.

"The bed, Fynn," she said through heavy breaths.

"Is that an order, Ferrios?"

"Yes, now move," she growled as she gripped my head between her palms and kissed me.

A logical part of me told me not to listen, but who was I to deny Dani's command? So, when my legs hit the bed, I plopped her down. She unwrapped her legs, and I threw caution out the window.

Because when she looked up at me with fire sparkling in her irises and a devilish smirk slipping over her face, I couldn't move away.

And the worst part?

I didn't want to move. I was lost in her, completely and utterly.

She leaned to the side, and my length strained against the fabric of my trousers as she shifted. With a quick breath, she blew out the lantern. All that was left to light the room was the soft glow of the moon sweeping into the room. Shadows swept over her body, and I marveled at the glow of the moon hugging her skin. I had seen her in dresses that clung to her body, that dripped down her skin, but I had never allowed myself to observe Dani for long.

Looking was dangerous. Admiring a woman's body often led to other things, and there had always been a clear line between Dani and me.

But right now, all I could do was look.

And I reveled in the sight before me.

Her curves begged to be touched. The arch of her back had my body reacting in ways I knew it shouldn't. How she propped herself on her arms, her braid falling over her shoulder. How that pesky little strap hung off her shoulders yet again.

I had known Dani was a master at wielding many weapons: the bow, the sword, the dagger. But I had never imagined that she was a master of her own body as well—not in this way, not with such expertise that I would crawl on my knees for her.

"Are you going to do something or just stare?"

I dragged my gaze down her body. "Simply taking my time, Ferrios. Tonight won't last forever."

She stared back with a challenge sparkling in her moonlit eyes. "Tonight's only just begun, Nadarean."

She grabbed me by the neck, but as she pulled me down toward her, she froze. "Whatever happens tonight will not change anything come morning. Deal?"

I swallowed. I wasn't so sure about that because this moment felt like it might change everything.

Yet I nodded. "Deal." I hovered over her, only inches away from her face. My lips brushed the side of her cheek. "But Dani?"

"Yes?"

I dragged a finger down the side of her neck, over her collarbone, leaving a trail of goosebumps in its wake. When I reached the top hem of the slip, I ran my finger atop the thin frill of lace and over the swell of her breasts. "Most don't forget having slept with me."

"Most, huh?"

I nodded, her face brushing against the scruff along my jawline, sending a shiver down my spine.

"There's always a first," she whispered, her voice husky.

"We'll see about that, Ferrios." I chuckled, turning to kiss the spot below her ear.

Friends, I reminded myself.

But would a friend be snaking his hand up his best friend's collarbone? Wrapping it around her throat before finding his way to the back of her neck and tugging her closer to pull a gasp from those sinful lips?

Would a friend be thinking of how those lips would feel wrapped around his throbbing cock?

No, a friend would not.

But I was, and I wasn't sure what that made us.

However, I didn't think I cared what label we placed on this.

Friends.

Acquaintances.

Lovers.

I did not care as she slipped a hand beneath the band of my trousers and fisted my length. She pumped me, her hand firm but soft, twisting around me. My teeth ground together as my arousal grew even harder.

I was already wound up watching her walk across the room in her slip, hearing her laugh, and seeing her swollen lips.

Usually, I was in control.

Normally, I was reading the woman's thoughts.

But right now, even when I tried to reach out to Dani's mind, her walls were up and tightly shut.

If she didn't stop soon, the night would end sooner than I wanted, and I was not done with her. It might have been the shortest night of the year, but this was only the beginning.

I would show Dani why she would never be able to forget tonight.

I grabbed her wrist, halting her, and growled, "My turn."

CHAPTER 22
DANI

FUCK.

That was the only word that came to mind when Fynn's eyes darkened. His fingers curled around my wrist, and he locked my arms above my head.

And for once, I didn't care if I lost this fight. Not when Fynn was pressing hungry kisses across my jawline, down my neck, over my collarbone. With each kiss, a trail of fire raced over my skin, my worries burning to ash along with it.

This—whatever *this* was—was a fight I *wanted* to lose.

Fynn sat up, and my heart sank.

Because this had to have been it—the moment he realized the egregious mistake we were making.

But when his gaze met mine, I knew I was wrong. He hadn't realized that. Because my friend was gone. Only a primal animal remained.

His hand hovered over the cotton waistband of his trousers, and a question flashed across his countenance.

"Are you. . .?"

"Am I?" I asked, the two words raw in my throat.

He swallowed, then cleared his throat. "Are you taking anything to prevent—?"

I stared up at him. His sudden shyness was enough to force a laugh from my lips. "Yes, Fynn. I take a medicinal herb with my tea." With my hands still restrained by his, I twisted my hips. "Now, take them off."

He blinked, and the shyness vanished. He took off his trousers, kicking them off his ankles and grabbing his cock in his hand, pumping it once.

My lips parted, a small gasp escaping.

I had felt him press against me, but seeing his length was something entirely different.

I snapped my gaze up to meet his. "Are you simply going to play with yourself all night, Fynn?"

The corner of his lip quirked up. His teeth scraped across his bottom lip. "As tempting as it would be for you to watch me beat off, I have other plans."

Releasing his cock, he sunk lower. His fingers danced across the fabric of the slip, running up and down my ribcage, sending spikes of ice-cold shivers coursing through my body.

"Have I mentioned yet how much I love this slip?" His voice was low, hungry, and unlike any of his voices I was used to.

But I was rendered speechless as he pushed the slip up and over my hips, the fabric rubbing against my overly sensitive skin. Heat bloomed between my thighs. I should have felt self-conscious; I should have felt uncomfortable. But when he licked his lips, the hunger in his gaze palpable, the need between my thighs only increased.

"Gods, Dani, you are beautiful."

My fingers dug deeper into his shoulders. It felt too intimate, too close. We were already crossing the line as it was. I had sex plenty of times before, but it was just sex and nothing more. During extended training camps, we had little time for anything else. It was quick and straightforward, not explorative. Not like this.

And it most definitely never felt as if we had been starved of each other for decades.

But right now, I was *starving*.

"Fynn," I begged, raising my hips.

His head dropped, the fallen locks of hair hiding his features. He released my hands. Then, he was crawling up my body, his hand slipping between my legs. As he trailed his fingers up my inner thigh, my legs parted for him. He rubbed a finger over my clit. "Shit, Dani," he said.

"What happened to that royal vocabulary?"

Fynn huffed a laugh. "No time for it when you feel like this."

His lips met mine, and there was nothing sweet or light about this kiss. Not as he worked me, circling my sex. I released a strangled moan, unable to hold it back. He might not have been able to read my mind, but he found the rhythm and pattern I preferred quickly.

I arched, craving more of his touch.

This meant nothing, I told myself.

It was just two people blowing off steam—

I groaned, my head pressing into the pillow. My nails dug into his shoulders as his fingers continued to work. He was already bringing me to the edge. "I need—"

He dipped a finger inside me and then pulled it out too soon. He spread the slickness around, teasing me, asking, "You need what, Ferrios?"

Moaning, I squeezed my eyes shut. "You."

Chuckling, he rubbed his cock against my folds, circling me and driving me insane. When I thought I was going to have to beg again, he pushed the tip inside. He was gentle and slow and sweet. When he slipped his length out, I shivered and bucked my hips.

He forced me back down with a hand against my stomach. He leaned closer, his scruff brushing the side of my neck as he nibbled a spot beneath my ear. Another shiver raced down my spine as my back arched higher.

Chestnut hair fell in a halo around Fynn's face, casting shadows across his features. "Since you won't bring your shields down for me, tell me, Ferrios, do you want it slow or hard?"

He slipped inside me, and at first, it was slow, but then he slammed the rest of his length into me. My back arched further, his breath hot against my throat.

"Hard." The word was no more than a whisper on my tongue, but he heard it nevertheless.

And for once, the Crown Prince listened.

With the tip at my entrance, he thrust. He wasn't sweet or gentle about it; he was rough and hard.

Because this was just sex. It wasn't supposed to be gentle or loving.

We weren't supposed to be taking our time or whispering sweet nothings into one another's ears.

At that moment, we were not friends; we were not lovers. We were something else. And whatever we were, it wasn't sweet, it wasn't soft.

It was hard, fast, and quick.

Simple.

I lifted my legs and wrapped them around his waist, shifting the angle. He bit the tender spot behind my ear and picked up his pace. My hands dug into his hair, gripping his head as my other hand wrapped around his shoulder.

He pulled out, leaving just the tip in before thrusting. Hard. Again and again, hitting the back of me and driving my head further into the pillow. He grabbed my calf and lifted it over his shoulder.

My head tipped back, and a moan escaped as he stretched me.

"Tell me, Ferrios," Fynn said, driving into me once before slipping out. He ran a hand across my leg, still lying on the bed. "Has your training made you as stiff as you are outside this bed?"

"You tell me," I said, but the words didn't come out as snarky as I intended; instead, they were more like a plea.

Smirking, he tossed my other leg over his shoulder and bent me forward, folding me. "That's a good girl," he said.

He slipped a hand between us. He found my clit with his thumb as he pushed inside of me.

A smack sounded, my hand hitting the wall.

"Gods above," I hissed.

Fynn paused, his fingers digging into the side of my hip. His beard brushed against my chin. "There are no gods here, Ferrios," he said, his voice husky and sending a chill down my neck.

Something in me stirred when his voice went that low and turned that primal. The pit of my stomach filled with an untamable fire, roaring fiercely.

"Fynn, please."

"What was that?" he asked, pausing.

My eyes sprung open. My hand flung out, wrapping my fingers around the back of his neck and pulling him closer. "Fuck me, Fynn, or so help me—"

I gasped, and my hands slapped against the wall as he slammed into me, again and again. We breathed in tandem as if our bodies were connecting on a higher level. Sweat coated my skin and his, but I no longer cared about the heat licking my skin. All I cared about was climbing over that edge with him. With his fingers wrapped around my ankle, his grip tightening, and his teeth scraping, then biting my ankle, I fell over the edge.

And Fynn fell with me.

It was at that exact moment when I didn't know if we could be just friends after what we had just experienced. How could we revert to normal after our bodies connected and after I screamed his name as white stars filled the back of my eyes?

Fynn let my leg fall onto the bed. He leaned over, his teeth scraping the side of my neck and the stars spinning across the ceiling.

I had lied before. There was no way I was going to forget tonight.

CHAPTER 23

DANI

MY EYES SPRUNG OPEN AS A WEIGHT BORE DOWN ON MY CHEST. I turned my head to the side. Beside me, Fynn was sprawled across the bed, lying on his chest, with one arm propped beneath his pillow and the other atop me. He was facing the other way, but based on the dead weight of his arm, he was fast asleep.

I gingerly picked up his arm and slipped beneath it.

Tip-toeing into the bathing chambers, I quickly washed up with the rag and the leftover water in the pail. Based on the temperature of the water, none of the staff had been in the room, which I was more than thankful for despite the desire for a warm bath.

Last night, I told Fynn not to be gentle with me, and he wasn't. But now. . .

Now I felt like I needed to wash everything that transpired last night off me.

While I didn't necessarily regret sleeping with Fynn, I couldn't shake the creeping feeling in my gut that last night might have been the biggest mistake either of us had made. It twisted and pulled.

We had crossed a line—a line I wasn't sure either of us had been truly prepared to cross. It was a moment of lust, driven by the enchantment of the solstice.

I hated admitting it, even to myself, but I had never experienced anything like last night. The sex I've had with former partners had been fine—meaningless and quick. None had even been able to make me go over the edge before, so I was used to finishing on my own once the person had left.

But Fynn didn't need any help.

And I hated it.

I hated it more than anything because what had happened last night was never going to happen again. It was a fluke, a blip, a one-time event.

As it should be, I told myself.

After washing up, I dressed and hurried to the door, bags in hand. With a hand wrapped around the doorknob, I peered over my shoulder, my gaze falling atop the sleeping prince.

Peace blanketed Fynn's features.

I bit the inside of my cheek, my brows drawing together.

Then I cracked the door open and stepped out into the hall, putting the summer solstice behind me.

"Sleep well, Dani?"

I inhaled, my back hitting the door. The latch's click was loud and piercing in the otherwise silent hall.

I quickly smoothed out my features as I spun and faced Terin. "Yes, why do you ask?"

Terin shrugged. The skin beneath his eyes was a light shade of purple. There was no need to ask how he slept. "You all right? You seem—"

"I'm fine," I spat, peeling myself away from the door. "He's still sleeping."

Terin's gaze flicked to the closed door, then to me, a question in his expression.

I gripped my bags tighter and hoped I appeared more put together than I felt.

He yawned and rubbed a palm over his face. "I was about to head downstairs for some tea and a quick bite. Care to join?"

"Uhm. Actually," I said, adjusting the strap of my bag hanging on my shoulder. "I was on my way out. I have a training I need to get to later this afternoon."

"On the day after the solstice?"

I lifted a shoulder, then dropped it. "I don't make the schedule. I only follow it."

Terin stared at me, his features a carbon copy of Fynn's. Guilt bloomed in my stomach.

He nodded. "Very well then. Is Fynn heading out with you?"

"Nope, only me," I said, moving away from the door and slipping by him.

His gaze narrowed as I passed, his head tilting to the side. "Are you sure nothing is wrong?"

I twisted my hands behind my back and forced a smile onto my face. "I'm sure."

"All right. Have a safe trip back."

"You too!" I said, already racing down the steps.

I STEPPED INSIDE THE CARRIAGE, mumbling a quick thank you to one of the staff members. When the door clicked shut, I leaned my head against the back of the seat, trying to settle the rising nausea.

Last night was a fluke, I reminded myself for the one-hundredth time. I didn't care what Fynn said. We were so deep in this fake courtship that we could no longer tell what was real or fake. The line had been completely blurred, swiped through in the sand and washed over by an unsuspecting wave.

While we had both been drinking earlier that night, by the time we had stepped foot into our suite, we had been entirely sober. It was a piss-poor excuse to succumb to my needs.

I straightened.

That's all it was. I was human, and I had needs that needed to be fulfilled. And Fynn? Well, he had fulfilled them thoroughly.

What was done was done.

The next time we saw each other, nothing would be different. We had promised that and made it a rule.

I groaned, leaning back, my weight sinking into the stiff cushion. Even I no longer believed in the rules, though.

I couldn't help but wish that last night hadn't happened on the shortest night of the year, that it hadn't passed by so quickly.

My fingers tapped across my bouncing knee. We should have been on the way by now, yet we were still sitting in front of the manor. I leaned closer to the door. Shuffling sounded from outside, a murmuring of voices that I couldn't quite parse.

With a sigh, I pushed the door open. "Was there something I"—I swallowed, my lungs dropping—"forgot?"

"Yes, there was."

I quirked a brow, unable to say or do anything more as Fynn took another step closer to the carriage.

"Me," Fynn said. His fingers curled around the frame of the carriage. His hair was messier than usual, as if he hadn't bothered to brush it before he dressed and ran down the stairs. Dark brown strands fell in front of his face, masking it in shadows. The top button of his cotton shirt was undone and untucked. His sleeves were rolled up at different lengths as if he had pushed them up hastily.

Through the space between his arm and his head, I saw Jorian and Lance walking with Fynn's bags.

"Move over," Fynn said.

I didn't move. "Wh-what? Why?"

"I would like to sit."

My heart pounded against my ribcage. "In here?"

Fynn nodded.

I looked behind him. The sky was still a vibrant pink. "But it's early, you don't need to—"

"If you're leaving now, I'm leaving," he said, interrupting.

"But—"

Fynn shook his head and placed a hand atop the carriage to lean closer. "If you won't move, I don't have a problem moving you myself, Ferrios."

An image of Fynn flipping me onto my back surfaced.

I quickly dismissed the thought. With a groan, I moved back, if only to hide the unwelcome blush rising to my cheeks.

Once Fynn was inside and settled across from me, Lance shut the door, grinning at me.

Silence and heat filled the small carriage. Fynn's fingers tapped along the wooden arm of the bench. Then, the carriage shook, jostling us as it took off.

I forced my gaze away and peeled back the thin curtain. We would be home in a few hours. A few hours were nothing. I could—

"I woke up, and you were gone," he said, interrupting my thoughts. "Care to explain?"

"Training," I mumbled.

Fynn quirked a brow. When he realized I wasn't planning on elaborating, he added, "So Terin said."

The carriage jerked forward as the horses descended the hill toward the main road. The alder trees whizzed by the window, the manor growing smaller and smaller as we pulled away.

"He said you practically ran away from him."

I scoffed. "An exaggeration."

Fynn tapped his fingers on top of his knee. "Said you looked as if there was something wrong."

"Oh?" I could feel Fynn's gaze, but I refused to acknowledge it.

"Dani," Fynn said, my name a plea on his lips. In my periphery, he reached out as if to touch my face, but his hand fell as though he thought better of it. "Talk to me."

"About?" I asked, watching the morning sky melt into an array of colors. The summer solstice was over. Last night was over. We had nothing to talk about.

We made a promise.

"Everything? Anything? It doesn't matter, but don't shut me out now."

"I'm not." From the corner of my eye, I saw him lean forward.

"You are," he said. "If you could sink into that cushion right now, you would."

I snapped my head in his direction, my mouth opening to argue, but he cut me off, arching a brow.

"Don't try to lie to me right now." His attention dropped to my arms, pressed tightly over my chest.

My nails dug into my triceps as I pushed my back against the cushion. I loosened my grip, revealing crisp crescent moons marking my flesh. I tried to relax. I dropped my shoulders and uncrossed my legs, but no matter what I did, my heart still thumped in my chest.

"Why did you leave without saying goodbye?" The question was soft on his lips—lips I definitely was not admiring. He shifted to the front of the bench, his hands falling in front of his lap and dangling between his legs.

I shrugged. "I didn't want to wake—"

Fynn's lowered gaze forced me to swallow the lie.

"Dani."

I bit down on my tongue. He wasn't going to let this go. His eyes were as fixed on me as the roots of a thousand-year-old oak tree, ingrained into the very soil and unmoving.

"If you can't say whatever it is, perhaps. . ." The rest of his thought melted away.

But Fynn was right. I might not have been able to say the words aloud, but there were other ways of expressing myself when Fynn was around.

Focusing, I imagined a window in one of the tall concrete walls of the fortress I had spent years building within my mind. I cracked it open. Only prying it open enough for a single thought to release—a whisper on the breeze, barely there and easily missed if one wasn't looking.

"What were you scared about?" Fynn asked in response.

I sighed, squeezing my eyes shut.

Everything, I said through the mental window.

Fynn reached forward, but when I balled up my hands, his hand fell to my knee instead. His touch was warm and familiar, and somehow, it stabilized me. "Dani."

Last night was a—

"Dani," Fynn said, interrupting me, "before you even finish that thought, let me say one thing." He wrung his hands together.

If I hadn't known better, I would have thought Fynn was nervous. But what did he, of all people, have to be anxious about?

"We've been pretending to court each other for almost three months. We have two months left." He swiped a hand through his hair, his chest rising as he took a deep breath. "What if we. . .stopped pretending for the last two months?"

The window in my mind slammed shut.

"We're friends, Fynn, we can't just. . ."

"Can't what? Fuck?" He cocked a brow. "*Court* each other?"

I waved my hand as if I could grab onto everything he said. "All of it."

"Dani, I'm not sure if you're aware of this, but we already *have* done and *are* doing those exact things."

I shook my head, my neck quickly becoming sore from the repeated movement. "That wasn't the deal, though."

The wheels of the carriage continued to creak as we rode down the winding path back to the capital, back to normal.

What Fynn was proposing was the opposite of normal.

"Why does this scare you?"

"I—I don't want things to change between us. We've been in a good place. Relationships. . ." I twisted my hands together, my voice growing softer, less sure. "Relationships aren't for me."

"How do you know that?"

"Because I do, Fynn!"

I wished I was anywhere but locked inside a moving carriage, for there was nowhere to go. Nowhere to move.

"I'm too busy," I said, "I need to be focused on my career and getting promoted."

Fynn grabbed my hand, unfolding my tightly wound fingers before weaving his fingers between the empty spaces. When his palm pressed against mine, a honeyed warmth spread through my arm and to my gut.

"That doesn't have to change," he said, voice firm, solid. "We started this deal *because* of your goals. Why does that mean we have to end it?"

"Because!"

"Because *why*, Dani? You haven't given me a single good reason for *why* it can't work—why *we* can't work. Whatever happened last night —whatever is going on between us, I want to figure out what it is. We've been faking this courtship this entire time, but what if we stopped faking? What if we stopped worrying if people discovered this wasn't real? Simply because it was."

Fynn was saying all the right things, yet the words felt wrong, illogical, reckless.

I wasn't the relationship type.

That's what he had said years ago.

Fynn tightened his grip around my hand and scooted closer, his knees knocking into mine and enclosing my legs in between his. "Let me ask you this, Dani. Do you regret last night?"

My mouth fell open.

Yes. I should say yes.

But I couldn't. The word wouldn't come out.

Instead, I cracked open the window and asked within the safety of my mind, *Do you?*

He leaned forward, and his fingers brushed across the bottom of my chin. "Do I regret hearing you scream my name? No, Dani, I don't."

My cheeks flushed, and heat pooled between my thighs.

He sat back against the cushion, a smug smirk slipping across his face along with that godforsaken dimple. Because we both knew I couldn't deny that I had done just that.

However, I couldn't let what happened last night blind me. I promised myself it wouldn't change things.

"Whether we regret it or not doesn't matter. You cannot deny that what transpired last night isn't the reason for this...this *change* in the plan, can you?" I asked, folding my arms over my chest.

"Of course, it has changed things, Dani," Fynn said, matter-of-fact.

His words shouldn't have hurt, yet they did.

I scoffed. "Just because we had sex—"

His hand gripped my knee. "I'm not proposing we stop pretending because we had sex, Ferrios. As incredible as it was," he said, cocking a brow, "and it was incredible, I will never deny that. I wanted to make this real before that."

My fingers curled around the bench. "Then why didn't you say anything?" I asked skeptically.

Fynn sighed and brushed a hand through his hair. "Because, Dani, you mean too much to me to mess this—whatever *this* is—up. Perhaps sleeping with you was a mistake."

I tried to pull my hand away, but Fynn squeezed it.

His words came out in a flurry. "Shit. See? I'm already messing this up." He scooted closer, his knees bumping into mine. "It was only a mistake because now you doubt my intentions. I should have said no, but I didn't because when I'm around you, I can't help but say yes."

I was completely and utterly speechless as I stared at Fynn.

This wasn't a part of the plan. This was never supposed to happen.

Yet, last night wasn't either.

"So, tell me the truth, Ferrios. Am I the only one who can't stop thinking about last night? About what would happen if we stopped pretending?"

I stared at our conjoined hands, his knees pressed against mine.

Stars spun in the back of my eyes.

This was too much.

Too much.

Too much.

Sleeping together was one thing. Having my feelings rekindled was one thing. But admitting them to Fynn? Making this courtship *real*? That was an entirely different issue.

Fynn shifted and dug a hand in his pocket. He pulled out a playing card.

"Fynn, I don't think this isn't the time for—"

He slapped a hand down on the space beside me. When he peeled his hand away, a single card sat atop the cushion.

"The truth only, Dani."

But as I stared at the eight of spades, the truth wasn't that easy to confess. Because how could I tell him I had been in love with him since we were children?

Whatever Fynn was feeling wasn't love. Despite what he said, love didn't happen overnight. That was lust. But did I care?

Wasn't one moment—or two months—with Fynn better than none?

"No," I mumbled.

Fynn tipped my chin up, his thumb sweeping across it before pulling at my bottom lip. "What was that, Ferrios?"

I forced my gaze to meet his. The sunlight seeping through the thin space between the curtains streaked across his face. A fire of gold danced among the dark shadows within his irises.

Warning bells sounded in my head.

But the beat of my racing heart was louder than the ringing.

"I said, *no*, you're not the only one."

"So, no more pretending?"

"No more pretending," I said. I picked up the card and held it in the space between us. "If you answer one question for me."

"Go for it, Ferrios."

"How long have you been holding onto this card?"

A wide smile split across his face, but his answer never came.

In truth, though, I didn't care about the answer—not when his lips met mine.

The kiss was soft at first. Then, he parted my lips with his tongue, and the softness vanished. It was all-consuming, head-spinning. And without the lie sitting between us, Fynn was unrelenting.

CHAPTER 24
FYNN

WHAT HAS YOU SMILING LIKE YOU JUST CAUGHT THE BIGGEST BUCK OF THE season, brother?

I straightened in my seat and tried to wipe the grin off my face at the sound of Terin's voice in my mind. I failed miserably, though, the corners of my eyes wrinkling.

I hadn't stopped grinning like a smitten fool since Dani and I had parted ways two days ago. Despite my attempt in the carriage— because I had thrown caution out the window once I had gotten a taste of her—she had declined to go any further than kissing— something about not wanting Jorian and Lance to hear.

I could have cared less, of course. Lance had the unfortunate (or fortunate, depending on one's opinion) task of taking the night shift one too many times over the years. Overhearing what I did in private would have been nothing new to him. But then, when I kissed Dani below her ear, and that sinful moan escaped those soft, plump lips, I no longer wished to share that beautiful noise with anyone.

So, seeing her lips swollen, cheeks flushed, and breaths shortened had to suffice.

And that was precisely what I had been thinking about as the advisors discussed the success of the solstice ball.

I took a sip of my tea.

A success, indeed.

Never mind. I don't want to know, Terin thought.

I refrained from chuckling and propped my chin on my fist, pretending to listen to the advisors as they changed topics. They went back and forth about some dispute about a lord's land and a wolf infestation.

My mind, however, was still stuck on the solstice.

"DAISES OR ROSES?" I asked Terin as we headed down the hall in the opposite direction of the advisors.

Graeson walked ahead of us, his fists deep in his pockets. When we left the meeting, he shook his head after glancing my way and mumbled something unintelligible.

I didn't care about his sour attitude, though. Not today.

"Excuse me?" Terin asked as we exited the castle and headed toward the training grounds.

I shook off the stiff jacket and tossed it over my shoulder. "You're right—both are far too simplistic. Perhaps a bundle of those purple ranunculuses from Mother's garden."

"Are these for *Dani*?" Terin pulled me to a stop.

"Yes. One often gives flowers to one's partner. Perhaps you should try it, Ter."

Dani had said that she had never been courted—after all, those frivolous outings with her mother's suitors did not count. Not when they made a woman go running for the hills on horseback. While this might have started as a fake courtship, it would be impudent of me not to show her what it was like to truly be courted.

"While you two continue to prattle about *flowers*, I'm going to go do something worthwhile," Graeson grumbled ahead of us, not bothering to wait.

Terin rolled his eyes at him and slapped my arm. "Wait, is this why you've been smiling nonstop?"

I folded my arms over my chest, cocking my head to the side. "Is it a crime now to smile, brother?"

"No, but. . ." Terin's gaze swept over me, assessing me. He hummed and continued walking, trailing behind Graeson who walked as if his life depended on it.

"You truly are smitten with her then?"

"I—" I sighed, brushing my hair back. The crisp breeze of the ocean brushed across my face. "I really like her, Ter."

My brother's forehead creased with concern. "Don't break her heart, Fynn. She's our best friend."

My hands rolled into tight fists at my side, and although I didn't mean to reach out, I did.

Feelings of doubt and disbelief coated the invisible thread before Terin closed off our connection, throwing his shields up.

Terin closing himself off was a sword to the gut, but that wasn't why anger heated my skin.

It didn't bother me that Terin believed I was some man who played with women's hearts. He wasn't right, but he also wasn't necessarily wrong either. I knew what people said about me. I knew how many women I had courted over the years. But what was I supposed to do when every woman that I allowed to get close to me only wanted me for my crown? Was I expected to settle for someone who didn't care about me?

I always tried to give my past partners the benefit of the doubt. It was easy for someone to pass judgment before they got to know someone. But after a few weeks or months of courting, their opinions never changed. Even Rosalina, whom I had gone back to time and time again, never altered her reasoning for pursuing me.

But with Dani, it was different.

She *knew* me.

Her interest wasn't in the crown. Dani wanted to protect the crown, not wear it. By the gods, if I ever tried to make her my consort, she would probably throw the crown at me or try to stab me with it.

What hurt the most, however, was that Terin didn't believe I *could* change. That I would not treat her differently than the others.

She was my best friend, and that meant more to me than anything else.

"I won't break her heart," I said.

But as we headed toward the training grounds, a small voice in my mind whispered, *She might break mine, though.*

CHAPTER 25
DANI

"ANOTHER MILE?" I ASKED SYLVIA, BOUNCING ON MY TOES, ENERGY coursing through me.

"Are you serious?" Sylvia was bent over, hands on their knees as they tried to regain their breath. "We just ran ten miles."

I stretched my arms over my head, keeping the muscles loose as I continued shifting my weight from one foot to the other. I had to keep moving. If I stopped, my mind would spiral. *Again.*

"And? We do this all the time," I said.

"Sure, but not at that speed," Sylvia countered.

"That was a normal pace, Sylv."

Sylvia shook their head. "No, it wasn't. That was Gabriel-level of running." Sylvia shrugged when I quirked a brow, then added, "All right. Maybe not *Gabriel*-level, but still faster than normal."

I hummed. "That's a no, then?"

My gaze slid past Sylvia toward the path through the forests. The terrain was rocky, and the elevation constantly changed. As treacherous as it might have been, it would keep my mind occupied.

"Definitely a no," Sylvia snorted, folding their hands behind their head. "What's gotten into you, anyway? You're—" Their hands fell to their hips, their brows twisting. "Honestly, I can't tell. Are you happy or nervous?"

I laughed, trying to blow the comment off, but I didn't even believe the sound coming from my mouth.

Sylvia gasped. Grabbing my arm, they tugged, pulling me further away from the rest of the soldiers who had run with us. "You and Fynn had sex, didn't you?"

"What?" The blood rushed from my face, and I looked over my shoulder, checking to see if anyone had overheard. "Why would you—"

Sylvia clapped, bouncing up and down. Apparently, Sylvia still had *some* energy left despite what they had said before.

"You did! You have that whole I-just-screwed-the-Crown-Prince look on your face."

I scoffed, eyes rolling. "How would you know what that would look like?"

Sylvia shrugged, wiggling their brows. "Call it intuition."

I grabbed the water canister from my belt and drank, avoiding Sylvia's pointed gaze.

But Sylvia was having none of it. They grabbed my arm and pulled, causing water to spill onto my face and down my shirt. "When?"

I snatched my arm back. "I am not talking about this."

"Ah-ha! So you admit it then!" Bright excitement lit Sylvia's amber eyes, making me back up. Sylvia's grip, however, tightened, pleading. "Come on, Ferrios. My love life is practically nonexistent right now. Let me at least live vicariously through you, for once! How was it? Is he, you know, as good as they say?"

My mouth dropped, and a bud of jealousy bloomed bright green in the pit of my stomach.

I quickly squashed it.

"It was fine," I said after a passing moment.

"You mean to tell me knocking between the sheets with *the* Fynneares Nadarean was *fine?*"

I snorted. "You say that as if he's some god."

Sylvia curled a fallen red piece of hair behind their ear. "I mean, based on how some women talk about him? He might as well be. Wait? Are you *jealous?*" My eyes enlarged, but before I could deny it, Sylvia continued. "You are! By the gods! He *must* be some sort of god because I've never seen you act jealous about any man you've been with."

"I'm not jealous," I said, crossing my arms as if the very act would shield me from Sylvia's assessing gaze.

"If you say so, Captain." Sylvia smirked. "So, when did it—" They gasped, slapping me on the arm. "The summer solstice! Ever since you've come back, you've been giddy. I can't believe I didn't notice it until now! It's so obvious. I would even bet that the two of you haven't since, huh? That's why you have so much pent-up energy. The man had the nerve to send the stars spinning, but now you're just left hanging somewhere among them, waiting for—"

"By the gods, Sylvia!" I hissed, looking around us to make sure no one was listening.

Everyone mainly had cleared out, though. No one was ever keen on staying around for long out of fear of having to run more.

That wasn't the only reason I needed Sylvia to stop talking, though. They were saying everything I was refusing to even think about. But once I heard it said aloud, I no longer could deny it.

Fynn had royally screwed me—in more ways than one. And now I was left with this sickening feeling twisting inside my gut.

In the carriage, we had agreed to stop pretending, but I hadn't seen him since then. What if the time apart had changed his mind? What if—

"Oh, Captain. I can see your mind spinning even now. If you have that much nervous energy, go make him shake it out of you."

"That's not—" I groaned. "It's complicated, all right?"

Sylvia grabbed my shoulders and quirked a brow. "How is it complicated? He just puts his—"

"Not like that!" I slapped their hands off my shoulders, suddenly needing a bath. "Fynn and I have been busy. That's all."

Crossing their arms over their chest, Sylvia said, "You're always 'busy.'"

I waved a hand in the air. "Exactly."

"No, Dani. That's the excuse you always give when you're avoiding something."

I furrowed my brows. "I'm not avoiding anything."

"Are you sure about that?"

I looked toward the east, where the castle's spires pierced through the clouds.

Was I avoiding him? If I was, I wasn't doing it intentionally.

Perhaps that only made it worse, though.

My mouth flattened. I turned around, but Sylvia had already walked away.

Sylvia was wrong.

I wasn't avoiding him. I *was* busy.

Turning away from the castle, I ran another mile.

SWEAT STUCK to my skin beneath the layers of fabric and light armor. My muscles were aching, which meant the next two days would be excruciating once the real soreness settled in. The run had settled some of my nerves but not all of them.

It was half past noon, and all I wanted was a long nap before meeting everyone at the tavern. I tugged on the end of the ribbon and brushed my hair with my fingers, detangling the knots as I turned into my room. My hands dropped as I stared at the petite woman near my vanity.

"Mother, what are you doing in here?"

My mother clicked her tongue and continued to arrange a fresh bouquet of three dozen purple and white ranunculuses inside a crystal vase. "And your father says you're one of the brightest soldiers of your generation. What does it look like I'm doing, Danisinia? You're not going to arrange these."

I unbuckled my short sword from my waistband and sat it against the wall. "Did you. . .did you get me flowers?"

"Me?" My mother scoffed. "Of course not. I have much better things to do with my time."

My hand froze on the throwing knives tucked into my corset. "Then who did?"

"The prince."

"*Fynn?*"

My mother nodded, humming. "Are there multiple princes that you are courting, Danisinia?"

With a roll of my eyes, I started removing the knives that covered my torso.

"Give me one of those," my mother said, snapping her fingers.

"What for?" I asked as I held the last knife to my chest, twisting it between my fingers.

She had barely looked up from the flowers since I had walked into my room, and a small vein protruded from her forehead. The one that only ever appeared when she was stewing.

She snapped her fingers again.

With a sigh, I joined her at the vanity, preparing for whatever storm was about to come.

When I handed her the knife with the handle out, she scoffed as she snatched it from my fingers. She began snipping the ends of the stems with the blade held at a diagonal angle.

"Some things need extra attention if you want them to last as long as possible."

Snip. Snip.

The vein in the middle of her forehead throbbed, and I narrowed my eyes at her. I had a strange inclination that she wasn't talking about the flowers, but I wasn't foolish enough to ask her to confirm.

I removed the pieces of light armor strap-by-strap. The metal clanged as it hit the hardwood floors.

"Is that where that goes, Danisinia?"

Snip.

I looked down at the pauldron I had tossed and shrugged. "That's where it is."

Snip. Snip.

My mother quirked a brow. "What would the prince say about how you keep your room?"

I cocked my head at her. "I don't think the *prince* will care how I keep my room, Mother. If he is in here, I'm sure his primary concern will not be where I throw my armor."

She slammed the knife against the table. "Danisinia!"

I rolled my eyes as I unbuttoned the left vambrace. "I am only joking, Mother." I dropped the piece of armor, letting it crash onto the floor. "He would, of course, be the one who was throwing my armor onto the floor."

The blood drained from my mother's face, horror brandishing her eyes. She pursed her lips and quickly returned to the flowers. "Danisinia, I know times have changed since your father and I were young, but are you truly joking about your nighttime activities? No respectable woman would do such a thing."

I leaned against the vanity, my back to the mirror. "Mother, will you please tell me what is wrong?"

She plucked a wilted petal from one of the ranunculuses. "Prince Fynneares is heir to the throne, Danisinia."

"And you are upset because of this?"

She scoffed as she plucked another petal, dropping it beside the cutoff stems now littering the vanity's surface. "Of course not."

"Then what is it?"

Pressing her palms against the top of the desk, my mother dropped her head, her brows quivering. "I know you were upset with me when I brought the suitors here, but—" my mother sniffled.

I straightened. "Are you—are you crying, Mother?"

"No," she said with another sniffle. "Ferrios women do not cry."

It was a lie, but I did not say that. Instead, I grabbed a handkerchief from my desk and held it out for her. "Please tell me what's wrong."

Taking the napkin, she delicately patted her cheeks. "You and Fynneares make a beautiful couple, dear. You truly do, but I worry about you."

"Mother, there is no need—"

She turned toward me, her eyes streaked red. "I am your mother. Do not think that I have not noticed you fawning after Fynneares ever since he was a young boy."

I blinked. "I have never *fawned* after any man, let alone Fynn."

"Rubbish! Whatever you wish to call it, you have liked him for a long time. For the past few years, I had thought you put that childhood crush behind you. I had found the most suitable men I could find. All in the hopes that one of those men would be a good match, but none were good enough for you. Even when you started courting the prince a few months ago, I did not think anything of it. Fynneares is a nice boy, but I saw how he looked at you at the solstice ball."

"And?" I prompted, swallowing the vitriol threatening to come out as my mother teetered on the edge of insulting me.

"I do not want you to be another one of the women he leaves behind in his wake."

A sharp pain soared through my teeth and into my gums as I bit down. The piercing pain, however, did little to distract from the stab of my mother's words. My mother may not have needed to wield a weapon in her daily life, but she knew how to strike someone with her words, twisting them and driving them further into her victim's heart.

"What is *that* supposed to mean?"

"Come now, dear. The prince is not known for his serious relationships. You are supposed to be finding a *husband*. I mean no offense to the prince, but is he truly husband material?"

"He is my best friend. Isn't that what matters? You and Father—"

"Your father and I are soul bonds, Danisinia," my mother interrupted. "Is there a reason for me to believe that you and the prince are?"

My lips parted, but no words came out. I had no answer to give her.

My mother shook her head. "That is precisely why I am telling you this. I know how much he means to you, but Queen Esmeray has also told me how much the Crown Prince wishes to find his other half." Pain coated her eyes as she squeezed my hand. "Not everyone meets their soul bond, but what will happen if he does?"

I swallowed the lump in my throat. "If that happens, then so be it."

My mother sighed. "I do not wish for your heart to be broken, Danisinia. When you love, you love fiercely. But the prince. . .he only loves himself."

I squeezed my eyes shut, shaking my head and giving her my back.

My mother may have thought she had good intentions, but her words were only knives to my heart.

One after another.

My mother exhaled, and footsteps snapped against the hardwood floors. The door creaked open. Nails tapped along the wooden frame. "I'm only trying to look out for you," she said to my back.

I didn't move until I heard the door click and her footsteps fade down the hallway.

Even then, I stared at the heap of metal strewn across my floor. In the far corner of my room, swords and throwing knives hung on the wall, and a bare mannequin sat in the corner.

My gaze fell to the purple ranunculuses. I lifted a flower from the bouquet and twisted it between two fingers as I sniffed it.

My mother thought I didn't know who Fynn was. That I didn't know he liked to lead on the women he courted. That he never took his relationships seriously. But Fynn was my best friend. I knew who he was. I knew how his relationships had worked out in the past. I had heard all about his escapades since he started courting women years ago. I had witnessed the failed dates and the slaps he received after he had ended the courtships with various women.

Looking down at the flowers, I plucked the card from the bouquet and scanned the message written across it.

"Roses would have been predictable, and you are anything but predictable, Danisinia Ferrios."

Fynn might not have been King of Pontia yet, but he was the king of breaking hearts. And I couldn't help but wonder if he would break mine, too.

MUSIC AND CHATTER filled The Splintered-Oar as my knee shook beneath the worn table sticky with spilled ale.

Despite the run earlier, my body still buzzed with energy. Sylvia had thought it was from excitement, and I supposed some of it was. But most of it resulted from the man sitting next to me.

Fynn had arrived nearly an hour ago with a wide grin and hair wind-blown after riding on horseback from the castle. He was devastatingly handsome.

Yet when he tried to kiss me upon arriving, I moved, giving him a hug instead. The whole exchange was. . .awkward.

It was just so *different*, even compared to how we were when we were pretending to court one another.

So, I tried to focus on the things that were normal: Moris being the first to get sloshed, Sylvia's playful jabs, Moris losing against Fynn at cards. Still, everything that was different stuck out like a deer wandering a village.

How Fynn no longer squirmed when he drank ale.

How a part of him was always touching me.

How the bench simultaneously felt too small and too big.

How I still felt like I *should* have been sitting closer to the wall, hiding my feelings, rather than nestled in the crook of Fynn's side.

How my palms were sweaty beneath the table.

But despite my sweat-slicked palms, I wanted to scoot closer to Fynn and let his calmness envelop me like a sweet caress.

At least when we were pretending, my heart was still protected, hidden beneath a shield of armor. Fynn, however, had stripped me of that armor with graceful fingers, and now, his fingers were wrapped around my heart.

While I trusted Fynn, I didn't trust anyone with something so fragile.

I feared what he would do—what he *could* do with my heart in his palms. One squeeze too hard and it would burst.

"Fynn, are you attending the commander's dinner next week?" Sylvia asked.

The mug almost slipped from my hands.

Shit.

"The commander's dinner?" Fynn asked, his gaze flicking to me.

"It must have slipped my mind," I said. "It's only a casual dinner."

In these moments, I wished I was the one who could read minds.

While Fynn didn't appear mad that I hadn't told him, something twisted his features.

"Don't let her fool you, Fynn," Moris said through a mouthful of peanuts. "It's only a gathering of the most important leaders in the military and their partners. Every month, they invite a few select soldiers. So, like Ferrios said, *casual.*"

"For Fynn, that *is* casual," Sylvia said, rolling their eyes.

"Ah, right." Moris shoved more peanuts into his mouth. He wiped the salt from his lips with the back of his hand. "You know, sometimes I forget that you're a prince."

Fynn stiffened.

Beneath the table, I squeezed his knee (sweaty palms or not), and he relaxed.

To Moris, I said, "It's not that exciting, Moris. The leaders mainly discuss new strategies they wish to implement or some other boring topic."

"And how many have you been to, Ferrios?" Moris quipped.

"That's not a fair question. I'm the commander's daughter. Any time it's at our house, I don't have a choice but to attend."

"Well, at least you get to go," Moris mumbled, his elbow sliding on the table as he propped his head on his fist. Not a moment later, he perked up. "Anyway, this time I *will* be going."

"Have you received an invitation yet, Moris?" Sylvia asked, quirking a brow.

"No, but I can feel it."

"Oh, so you're a seer now."

"No, but—"

"A seer *told* you then?"

"No, but I know it!" Moris slammed his mug down, sloshing ale onto the table. "And with Fynn and I there, I'm sure it'll be less boring."

"*If* Fynn wants to go." I looked at Fynn. "You don't have to."

"Do you want me to come?" Fynn asked, his hand falling atop mine. He drew light circles on the back of my hand.

I bit my tongue. While the dinner would be a good opportunity for the leaders to see us together, it now felt somehow wrong to use our relationship to acquire the promotion.

I made to remove my hand from beneath his, but Fynn squeezed it, stilling it.

I peered down at our joined hands. While I may not have wanted Fynn there for my own career advancement, I couldn't deny that I wanted him there.

"If you don't want me to—"

I flipped my hand over, weaving my fingers in between his. "I do."

Fynn smiled softly before leaning back against the worn bench and pulling me closer. For once, I didn't find myself fighting him about it either.

The three of them fell into conversation again, but my mind was somewhere else, caught between the worlds of pretend and truth.

I didn't know how much time had passed or how many drinks Moris had finished when Fynn nudged me in my side. "Dani?"

My gaze snapped up to meet his. "Hmm?"

"Do you want to get some air?"

I blinked and wiped my palms on my trousers. "Sure."

Fynn scooted out of the bench, and I followed. He guided me through the budding crowd, his hand wrapped tightly around mine. Music was playing, but I couldn't identify the song. The noise was no more than an echo in my ears.

Fynn opened the door, the bell above the threshold faintly ringing as he ushered me forward. Outside, he led me around the corner of the tavern, down one of the small alleys.

He spun and grabbed both of my hands. "All right, talk to me."

I scanned the area, and my countenance twisted.

Dusk had long since settled, leaving behind heavy shadows to dance across the alley in the faint glow of the waning moon. On the main street, the occasional groups walked by, but we were too far away to make out what they were saying.

I quirked a brow at Fynn. "Why are we in an alley?"

"For some resemblance of privacy. There's something wrong, and I wish to know what it is."

I took a small step backward, freeing a hand. "I'm fine, Fynn."

Fynn cocked his head. "Do you make it a habit of lying to those around you?"

"I'm not lying," I said, rubbing my arm.

Fynn pushed his fingers into his hair. He looked up at the stars, the moon illuminating his features. "You've barely said a word to me."

"That's not true. I—"

He shook his head and interrupted, "Saying hello does not count."

His hands fell from his hair, the ends standing in different directions. I had the insane urge to run my fingers through his hair and fix the disarray.

Unaware of my thoughts, Fynn continued, "And *hello*? Dani, how is it possible that we appear to be in a fake relationship more now than when we were actually in one?"

I jerked back "What? That's not true."

Fynn sighed and took a step forward.

He shook his head, huffing an exasperated laugh filled with exhaustion. He pointed at my feet. "That's precisely what I'm talking about."

I looked down at the ground.

Fynn might have taken a step closer, but I had taken a step back, the gravel on the ground disturbed, showing my retreat. I didn't need my tracking skills to notice that.

"You're avoiding me, Dani."

"That proves nothing."

Fynn took another step forward, and my back hit the brick wall.

"Are you sure?" he asked, quirking a brow.

"Yes." I tipped my chin up, arms crossing over my chest.

Even in the shadows blanketing his face, the faint trace of sadness in his brown eyes was evident. The bump on this throat dipped. "Is it me? If I did something, tell me, and I'll fix it."

"It's not you. It's—it's—" I groaned, pressing my palms against the sides of my temples. I leaned my head against the brick, my loose curls snagging on the rough grooves. "Everything is different now. We promised nothing would change."

Fynn peeled my hands from my face, weaving his fingers between mine and tugging them down. "Nothing has changed, Dani."

"You like the taste of ale!" I exclaimed.

"I *what?*" Fynn's confounded face was enough to make me realize how utterly ridiculous I sounded, yet I continued.

"You hated ale before, but now you drink it as if you don't mind it."

He shook the confusion away and shrugged. "When you have something for a while, you grow to tolerate it."

"Is that what this is then, too? We've been fake courting for so long that now you tolerate it enough to make it real?"

Fynn flinched. "Is that what you think?"

"I—" I swallowed.

In truth, I didn't know what I thought. While I knew I was overreacting, part of me feared what would happen if this didn't work out. Part of me was still in disbelief that we were together because, in the past week, nothing had changed—at least not around me, not on the outside.

On the inside, I was eager. Eager to see Fynn again, yearning to be only inches from the scent of the sea.

Eager to kiss him again.

Fynn smirked. "Eager to kiss me, huh?"

Snatching my hand back, I shoved him in the chest. "Get out of my mind, Fynn!"

"But it's much more fun when you let me in, Ferrios. I mean. . ." His gaze flicked down before crawling up the curves of my body. When our eyes met, a hunger swirled within the flames of his irises. "You have to admit, a part of you likes me being inside you. I know I do."

I gasped.

"Inside your *mind,*" he said with a wink, his hand gripping my waist as he pressed his body against mine. "But I also enjoy being inside *you.*"

I opened my mouth to respond—once, twice. I failed to speak each time, though. The heat pooling beneath my thighs was not helping me either.

This was *not* the time to be thinking those thoughts. Yet, how could I not when the truth was that those thoughts had been consuming me for days?

Fynn pressed his hand flat against the brick wall above my head. "Did I not say it loud enough, Ferrios?" He leaned in closer, the tips of his hair tickling my cheek. His hand on my waist ventured lower, down my side, then high on my thigh.

My heart was in my lungs. "I heard you," I whispered, the words barely audible. Everywhere he touched, an inextinguishable heat bloomed, and an insatiable hunger stirred at my core.

He leaned down, the tips of his hair brushing my forehead, sending a shiver down my back. "No, I don't think you did. Because I've been thinking a lot about that night and how hasty it was, how I didn't get to take my time with you."

His fingers splayed across my thigh. His thumb moved in small circles along my inner thigh. He was barely even touching me, yet heat filled the pit of my stomach, and my body arched toward him.

A crash sounded. I jumped.

My gaze flicked to the streets, but it was only a storekeeper throwing their trash into a bin.

Fynn grabbed my chin and forced my attention back to him. "I told you I was done pretending, so why do you keep fighting this?"

My chest rose, my breaths coming faster. "We're in public," I mumbled.

"It's pitch dark outside."

"But—"

"But no excuses. Tell me right now, what do you want, Ferrios?"

I chewed on my bottom lip, and Fynn's attention dropped to the movement.

"Truth only," he said, his voice low and heavy and sinking straight to my core. "Do not make me beg to be inside your mind, Ferrios."

A hunger I hadn't anticipated darkened his eyes, but he wasn't the only one starving.

"You, Fynn. I want you."

"That's all you had to say," he said before grabbing my hand and guiding me down the path lit only by the partial moon.

CHAPTER 26
FYNN

I N THE TWENTY YEARS I HAD SPENT STUDYING THE MAPS OF PONTIA, I had never once thought that knowing the location of every storefront and hidden entrance would serve any purpose.

Until today.

I pried the door open of a nearby storage room and slammed it shut. Inside the small space, the moon's rays leaked in from a skylight, providing just enough light to make out Dani's features.

Dani leaned against the shelves, causing the glass bottles stored on it to clink together. "What are we doing in here, Fynn?" she asked.

I leaned back against the door. "That depends."

"On?" The single syllable on her lips was a whisper, yet it sent my insides turning.

I dug my hands into my pockets and held onto whatever restraint I had left.

"On you," I said.

"On me?"

I nodded.

I could have run to her then. By the gods, I wanted to press her against the shelves and claim those lips as mine. But I held my ground. This was not about my needs or what I wanted.

"If it is me you want," I said, "then why are you over there?"

At those words, something snapped within her. Her previous anxiety melted away as she drank me in with a burning gaze. When she stepped forward, the beam of moonlight flashed across her eyes, catching the golden flecks in her irises and a mischievous glint lit within them.

"Tell me one thing first, Fynn," she said, challenging my control more and more with each step as her hips swayed languidly back and forth.

"For you? Anything." I was awestruck, a puddle on the streets, as she trailed a finger over the edge of one of the shelves.

I had known Dani was a huntress since we were children, but I had never seen her gift appear in this way. I had seen countless times how she used her surroundings to her advantage, how she found the trail that led her straight to her prey.

But *I* had never been the prey.

And to experience firsthand how she stalked her prey, how she moved with careful yet predatory steps—by the gods, it was spellbinding.

Dani tilted her head. "What is it that *you* want?"

My gaze trailed down her body, from her collarbone to the bottom of her corset, where it outlined her wide hips. She was laying the trap, and I was falling for the bait like a fox in a rabbit hole.

"Because unlike you, Fynn," Dani continued, "I am no mind reader. If you want something, you have to say it." When she was a foot away, she tipped my chin up. "*Out loud.*"

"I want whatever you'll give me, Ferrios."

She dragged her finger beneath my chin, scraping it across the unshaven scruff. "Oh, come on now. You'll have to do better than that, Your Highness."

It was the way she said those two words, the sinfulness hiss, that finally broke my restraint.

I tugged her toward me, my arm wrapping around her waist, and spun her around, pushing her up against the door. My chin brushed across the side of her face. Despite the clothing that separated us, I felt the shiver that slipped down her spine. I heard the gasp that escaped her red lips.

But what truly unraveled me was the little crack in the mental shields she always held up around me and the single thought that escaped her mind.

A plea.

And hearing what she wanted, the words she couldn't speak aloud, whispered down the invisible thread, made a smirk appear.

"See, here's the thing about what I want," I said, pulling her tight against me. "A king, I have been told, never falls to his knees."

"Oh?"

"But I am not a king."

My knees hit the ground.

I COULD ALMOST HEAR Dani's jaw drop as I hit the floor.

When I peered up at her with that coy, boyish smirk that drove her insane in more ways than one, she snapped her mouth shut. I brushed a hand against her ankle, sending a shiver up her body.

Her nails dug into my shoulder. "Fynn, wait."

"What is it?"

"I—" Dani sighed, and my brows knitted together.

I didn't think I had misconstrued her desires—the wish she let slip beneath her shields—but something made her hesitate. I squeezed her thigh, reminding her she could be honest with me—with whatever it was.

She sucked in her bottom lip, her teeth scraping across it.

An insatiable hunger stirred, but I didn't act on it. I would deal with that mouth of hers later.

"No one ever has. . ."

"Tasted you?" I finished for her.

"No."

Embarrassment flooded her voice, but excitement filled mine.

"A shame, truly," I said, licking my lips. "But I cannot say that I am upset about being the first."

A faint blush rose to her cheeks. I ran my fingers across the waistband of her trousers and quirked a brow. "May I?"

She nodded, her chest rising quicker than before. I unbuttoned her trousers and tugged them down.

"Step," I commanded, holding her waist.

Dani pressed her palms against my shoulders, and I pushed the clothing away as she leaned on me.

The last time I was with Dani, it was too quick. And now, learning that no one had pleasured her this way before, I wished I hadn't let her persuade me from doing so.

This time, I would take my time.

I pressed kisses along the entire length of her leg. I had half a mind to kiss every inch of her, but this closet was not the best place to lay her out beneath me. Instead, I left a trail of goosebumps skittering up her leg as I made my way up her calf, over her knee, to her thigh. I nibbled, my teeth scraping against the apex of her thigh. Dani squirmed in my hands, forcing a smile upon my lips.

I had meant what I had said. It was indeed a shame that Dani had never been pleasured this way. But by the gods and beneath the moon, I would devour her.

I slipped my finger beneath the band of her undergarment as I continued to press light kisses on the inside of her leg.

Even though I had barely touched her, my cock was already throbbing. Tonight wasn't about me, though.

I tugged her undergarments down and glanced up. Dani's eyes were squeezed shut.

See, now that won't do, I thought, tsking.

I squeezed her thigh. "Look at me when I am on my knees tasting you, Ferrios."

When her gaze met mine, the fire returned—the hunger, the desire, the fight. "Is that an order?"

I arched a brow. "Think of it as my first order as Crown Prince."

She smirked. "The kingdom would be so proud."

At that moment, though, I couldn't care less about the kingdom.

I pressed a kiss on her hip bone and slipped a finger in between her folds. Dani deserved to know what it was like to be worshiped.

My movements were slow, my kisses sweet.

At first.

I pushed my finger inside her and curled it. My thumb brushed against her clit, and her breaths came quicker. Above me, she gasped as her hand slapped against the wall.

"Gods, Dani," I groaned and bit the sensitive spot on her inner thigh. "You are so wet." I pulled my finger out and spread the wetness around. Dani's breaths came faster as she braced herself. "If this already has you moaning, then I cannot wait to hear what other noises I pull from that mouth of yours."

As I felt her pussy tighten around my finger as she rolled forward, I slipped my finger out. A noise I never thought I would hear from Dani's lip sounded. A whine that was pleading, begging.

I looked up. "You will not be coming on my hand tonight, Dani."

Without blinking an eye as I stared up at her, my mouth fell onto her sex. My tongue swept over her clit, circling it, teasing it. Dani was as sweet as I had imagined. And now that I had tasted her, I never wanted to get up. I would live on my knees for the rest of my life if she let me.

Her legs shook as I licked and sucked. Her balance wavered, and my free hand ran up her thighs, squeezing and stabilizing her at the same time. Her fingers dug into my hair, and her head tipped back.

Something crashed, glass breaking, but I didn't pull away. Neither of us did.

Not until Dani came on my tongue as she screamed my name.

CHAPTER 27
DANI

I SAW FYNN ALMOST EVERY DAY THE FOLLOWING WEEK, AND I HAD TO give him credit. With the additional training, my schedule had grown increasingly packed, yet that didn't stop Fynn from finding the time to see me, even if it was only ten minutes.

The first day, training had gone longer than anticipated. When Sylvia, Moris, and I were leaving the barracks, I found Fynn lying on a bench, his hair spread across the seat as he held a book in the air. The sun was beginning to set, bathing him in a golden hue and forming a sun-kissed crown upon his head.

I didn't know how long Fynn had been waiting, but it was long enough for him to become lost in whatever story he read. If I hadn't known better, I would have thought he was so engrossed in it that he hadn't even noticed my approach. But Fynn always seemed to sense my presence.

I leaned over the bench, my palms pressing into the metal arm. The single braid holding my hair fell onto his page.

"Ferrios," Fynn murmured, his deep voice sinking to my core and sending a shiver down my spine.

"Am I interrupting you?" I asked.

Snapping the book closed, Fynn stared up at me, his pupils dilating as they adjusted to the shift in light. "Your timing is truly impeccable. I have been waiting for thirty minutes, yet you show up right when the battle is at its height. Typical."

I chuckled.

He twisted the end of my braid between two fingertips, then gently tugged it, pulling me closer.

Fynn had been right in the tavern. While some things might have changed over the past few months, most things had stayed the same.

At the end of the day, he was still my best friend, the person I could always count on to put a smile on my face and calm my nerves.

"Better late than never, right?" I asked.

He cupped my cheek with his palm, and I leaned into the touch.

"Always better late than never," he said, smirking.

As Fynn got up, I asked, "Don't you have some princely duty to attend to?"

He shrugged, tucking his book beneath his arm. "If you mean listening to the lords prattle on and on about trivial pursuits? Sure, plenty. But that's what my morning naps are for," he said with a wink.

I went to nudge him, but Fynn dodged it and curved an arm around my waist, pulling me close.

"What's with the extra trainings?" he asked.

"You mean to tell me you *don't* know everything that is going on in your kingdom?"

He bumped his hip against mine. "I know plenty, Ferrios, but there are some things I pay more attention to than others." He dragged his gaze over me as if he was drinking me in.

For a moment, I forgot all about my father's speech during today's training, the growing unrest in the southern kingdoms, and how the upcoming mission would help us gain an advantage over our enemies.

Perhaps I let Fynn's question go by the wayside because I did not want to get my hopes up.

While the leaders were getting closer to narrowing down the squad that would be assigned to the upcoming mission, it was still too soon to say anything. I didn't think I could deal with the ramifications if I told Fynn about it and wasn't chosen. I had been messing up so much the past few months that it seemed precarious to hope to be selected for this mission. And in truth, there wasn't much to tell. My father and the generals were keeping the details of the mission quiet until the squad was chosen.

To make matters worse, the scathing glances from some of the other captains in the battalion had recently returned. I had dealt with my peers' cynical gazes when I was a private, but I had thought I had proven myself to them already. But as several soldiers passed by, their sneers were only more caustic when they saw Fynn standing beside me.

Courting was supposed to make things simple, but perhaps that was a foolish thought to have had in the first place.

I did not want to give anyone reason to think Fynn had anything to do with me being chosen for a simple mission. So, unwilling to take that risk, I kept quiet as Fynn pulled me close, his warmth blanketing me, a shield from everything else going wrong in the world.

Not that Fynn seemed to notice as he tipped my chin up and leaned down, sweeping me into a dizzying kiss.

FOR THE REST of the week, Fynn continued to show up. Some days, he only had time to chat for a few minutes before he had to head out. On other days, we would walk through the nearby park, talking about nothing and everything all at once. On those days, I forgot why I previously had feared courtships.

But then again, courting Fynn wasn't like any of the days I had spent with my mother's potential suitors. There was no talking about the weather to pass the time or asking simplistic questions like what one another's parents did. Fynn and I already knew each other's past and present. And yet, somehow, the silent moments were few and far between. When there was silence, it wasn't awkward or uncomfortable. It was peaceful.

Whenever Fynn talked, I was hanging on to every word, and he mine.

It was easy.

It was simple.

It was like nothing I had thought it would be and everything I had once feared dreaming it could be.

The nerves were long gone because I finally realized I didn't need to be anyone but myself with Fynn.

Courting Fynn, I found, wasn't all that different from being friends with him—besides the fact that my hair was always a little messed up and my clothes were more wrinkled than they had been prior to seeing him.

However, I was finding that I did not mind that too much, either.

CHAPTER 28
DANI

The day before dinner with the leaders, I had almost forgone going to the tavern. Moris and Sylvia, however, had insisted.

There were only ten of us left whom the leaders were deciding between, and tomorrow, the leaders would finally make their choice. All three of us had made it to the final ten soldiers. Moris wanted to celebrate that; Sylvia had other intentions, though. Going to the tavern seemed like the last thing I should have been doing. And perhaps I should have listened to the creeping sensation crawling up my neck, but I didn't.

Before we could even wrap our hands around a pint of ale, Sylvia pulled us to the dance floor, where the truth came out. Last week, Sylvia had started talking to the band's singer, who was a gorgeous woman with flowing ebony hair and dark brown skin. While Sylvia gawked at the singer, Moris, Fynn, and I were all forced to dance.

After three or four dances, Fynn and I managed to sneak away to our table.

"How was training?" Fynn asked as I sat down beside him.

"Good," I said, reaching up and kissing his cheek.

Fynn pulled back. "Just good? Because you seem more chipper than usual."

I shrugged. "I'm in a good mood, that's all."

"Do you want to talk about it?"

I bit my lip. As much as I was delighted to be one of the last ten, I shook my head. "Not yet," I said.

Fynn's eyes enlarged. "Have you heard something about the promotion?" he whispered as Sylvia and Moris continued dancing.

Some of the excitement dwindled, but I kept the smile on my face. "Not yet, but I have a good feeling."

He arched a brow but didn't push the topic any further.

I wasn't purposely keeping anything a secret from him. However, I was too close to being selected for this mission. I did not doubt that leaders believed our courtship was real. Despite the reasoning my father had given me months ago, a successful courtship would not be enough to secure the promotion. Nor did I wish to let my relationship status dictate my career.

I *needed* to be chosen for this mission because of who *I* was, not because of who Fynn was. I didn't want him to try to sway my father and the generals if he found out about it.

After an hour, I had called it a night after a wave of exhaustion had swept over me.

Outside, Fynn leaned against the post of the stables across the street. "I'll see you tomorrow then, Ferrios?" Fynn asked.

I sighed. "I told you, you don't have to—"

Fynn grabbed my waist, pressing his lips against mine. His lips were soft and warm against mine.

No matter how many times Fynn kissed me, each time left me more breathless than the last.

He leaned back, his arms still wrapped around me. "If you tell me I do not have to come to the dinner tomorrow one more time—"

"You'll what? Hmm?" I narrowed my eyes, but the wide grin splitting across my face betrayed me.

If the past week had shown me anything, I had nothing to worry about when it came to my relationship with Fynn. Knowing Fynn would be by my side tomorrow night, not as my pretend suitor but as something more than a friend, tamed most of the uneasiness I had felt last week.

I had yet to tell my mother that Fynn would be attending dinner, which was a whole other reason to be nervous. Although my mother had known Fynn for his entire life, she acted as if she had never seen him running around the castle at age five, wearing a helmet that was too big for his head and wielding a wooden sword. When it came to the royal family though, none of that mattered to her. If I told my mother too soon, she would change the entire menu to make it more ostentatious.

Fynn brushed a finger across my lips, scraping his teeth on his bottom lip. "Honestly, Ferrios, I don't know, but I'm sure I could think of something." His gaze dipped down my body, sending heat up to my cheeks. "Give me a few minutes and a storage closet, and you'll regret those words in no time."

I chuckled. "Not tonight."

"If you say so," he said with a wink.

I poked him in the chest. "I'm serious. I have—"

"Training in the morning," he said, interrupting me in mockery. I probably had said that exact statement numerous times throughout the night.

He shoved his hands in his pockets and looked toward the horses. "Can I at least ride with you home?"

I shook my head. "I think some quiet would do me some good tonight."

"Very well."

I reached for the hood of my cloak, but my hand swiped at the air. I groaned. "I left my cloak inside. You go ahead."

He shifted, turning toward the tavern's entrance. "Are you sure? I can—"

I held out a hand. "Fynn, I'm a big girl. I can handle myself."

Fynn lifted his hands in the air. "I wasn't saying you couldn't, Ferrios. You've put me on my back plenty of times." He cocked his head to the side, a sinful smirk appearing. "Although I recall—"

"Night, Nadarean," I shouted over my shoulder as I walked away.

"Night, Ferrios," he called after me.

As I swung the tavern door open, I heard Fynn's horse take off down the gravel pathway. Thankfully, Sylvia and Moris were still dancing, so I was able to grab my cloak without being sucked back into the fold of the music.

Cloak in hand, I headed back through the growing crowd and slipped through the door unseen. Or so I thought.

Someone giggled, the sound girlish with a hint of vitriol coating it. A pang of nausea coursed through my veins.

"You are truly the last person I thought the prince would be courting."

My hand fell from the door. As it swung shut behind me, I asked, my voice even, "And why is that, Rosalina?"

I turned and found Fynn's former partner walking toward the tavern from down the street. Her caramel hair was tied back in a clean chignon. She wore a delicate light pink dress and short silk gloves over her hands that stopped just beyond her wrists with a white ruffle.

As I looked her up and down, she raised her chin. When Esmeray lifted her chin and rolled her shoulders back, she exuded power and stability; when Rosalina did it, she looked like a peacock fluffing up her feathers before a python.

Rosalina scoffed, flipping her hand in the air. "He's the heir to the throne, and you? Well, you're just a soldier."

Rolling my eyes, I glanced at the quarter moon shining down. "Is there some other obvious fact you wish to state? I do have places to be."

Her lips parted slightly as if she was appalled I would dismiss her.

She quickly flattened her expression and took a step forward, chuckling. "He was enamored with you at the solstice ball, I will say that. But if you put anyone in an elegant dress, they are bound to catch someone's eye. Everyone is watching you. They're watching and waiting for you to fall. For Fynn to see his mistake in courting you. Now that he has been crowned heir, whomever he marries will become Queen of Pontia. You do realize that, don't you?"

I cocked my head. "Are you planning a coup that I should know of, Rosalina? Because as far as I know, the queen is alive and well."

Rosalina's pale pink lip curled. She wrung her hands together. "I have heard the queen herself say that she will abdicate when she believes her son is old enough and mature enough to sit upon the throne. She is only waiting for him to grow up and to marry."

I placed a hand on my hip. "Let me guess, Rosalina, you believe you are the one he should marry?"

She smoothed a flyaway back down and clicked her tongue. "A queen is not a warrior, Danisinia."

Thinking of becoming Fynn's consort one day left a sour taste in my mouth. He had told me several times how he felt about his former partners being with him only for the sake of the crown. I wasn't Rosalina. I didn't want that title. I didn't know if I even wanted to be married, let alone be married to the future king. What had Esmeray told me the night of the solstice? That even Marc had to make sacrifices he did not wish to make.

Of course, it was too soon to even think that marrying Fynn was remotely a possibility; whatever we were, it was still too new.

Yet, I didn't wish to think about us going our separate ways after I received my promotion, either.

This entire relationship resulted from neither Fynn nor I wanting to be in a long-term relationship despite our mothers' wishes. Although we were no longer pretending, we hadn't outwardly discussed if there was a finite end to our courtship.

Still, there might not have been an official end date, but there was an end. That much was clear.

But I would not let Rosalina know that.

I took a step forward. "If you wish to be Fynn's consort simply to sit on a throne beside him and smile at the crowd, then you are gravely mistaken about what a queen is."

"Am I?" Rosalina asked, tipping her small, pointed nose higher into the air.

"A queen is whoever she wishes to be. Queen Esmeray may not be a soldier, but she is one of the fiercest and strongest people I know. And if you think even for a second that neither she nor her son have seen through your poor pursuits of the crown, then you are the one gravely mistaken."

Rosalina laughed, but the sound was strained, forced. Her hands fell to her side, rolling into a tight fist, the white cotton fabric stretching over her knuckles. "Whatever you and Fynneares have will pass. It always does with him."

"Here's the difference between you and me, Rosalina," I said, walking around her. My shoulder bumped against hers when I stopped beside her. I leaned over. "You've been running after Fynn for years, but I was the one he ran toward."

CHAPTER 29
FYNN

Dinner with the leaders was going exceptionally well, despite Moris stuffing his mouth with whatever he could get his hands on and Dani's bouncing nerves as we sat. Usually, I was good at reading Dani's body language, but tonight, things were muddled. One second, she looked excited; the next, that excitement bled into apprehension.

Before dinner, she tried to pull me aside, but her mother barged in and forced us to the dining room before Dani could get a word out. Soon enough, the dinner guests pulled us into different conversations.

Commander Ferrios, General Walen, and General Cornish filled the evening with stories of old missions.

After almost two hours of reminiscing, General Cornish's husband, Eryn, patted his spouse on the shoulder, saying, "Are you three so old that you have no new stories to tell besides the ones you've bored us with for the past decade?"

The three men scoffed and tried to recall a new story. However, all they could come up with was Menides' recent trip to inspect a military school in the west, where several cadets tripped over themselves upon seeing him. Not much of a story but more of a brag.

While the stories might have been tales the others had heard many times, I enjoyed them. It was nice seeing Menides away from the rest of the council. Even with the other military leaders sitting at the table, he was more relaxed than during the council meetings.

However, I did not miss how the commander avoided looking at me for too long at the dining table. Or how he had avoided me when I had spotted him once or twice after Dani's training during the days prior.

Although, in truth, I hadn't tried too hard to seek him out once I had seen Dani. When Dani was around, all sense was lost.

During council this week, I asked about the mission's status. Menides, however, simply said they were working on it. I should have trusted my mother's war strategist and the commander of our military, but this mission was too important. We needed to get ahead of the war before it started.

But I wasn't going to bring the mission up now. Not in front of everyone else.

I folded the napkin over my lap and pulled the crystal dish closer. Grabbing a spoonful of the chocolate mousse, I took a bite.

Dani nudged me gently in the side, pulling me from my thoughts. "You have something on your chin," she whispered, pointing to a spot on her face.

I grabbed the napkin and dabbed my face. When I pulled the napkin away, Dani rolled her eyes. She swatted my hand away and reached forward. With a gentle hand, she swiped a finger across my chin, near the corner of my lip.

When she sucked the mousse from the tip of her finger, my eyes widened for a second.

She might have been nervous about something, but at least she was no longer anxious because of our courtship.

Near the end of the table, metal *tinked* against glass. Everyone shifted their attention to General Cornish, who sat to the commander's right.

The general raised his glass, and everyone lifted theirs along with him. "Let me be among the first to wish the three of you and Quint well on your upcoming mission."

He tipped his glass up, and I looked around the table to see whom he was talking to.

My hand froze in the air, glass in hand, as Moris, Sylvia, and Dani nodded at the general.

I took a sip from my glass, the red wine bitter on my tongue as Dani refused to meet my gaze, shifting uncomfortably in her seat.

Dani always told me everything, yet she had kept an upcoming assignment a secret?

There were only a few reasons she would keep something like that a secret. It was either too dangerous that she knew I would be concerned or...

My attention flicked to Menides. "What mission would that be, Commander?"

Instinctively, I reached for the invisible thread leading to Dani's mind. Her walls were high, the cracks sealed shut. But I needed to know if I was right. For years, Dani had kept her mind locked away from me.

But this? I had a right to know. I searched the walls of her shields. I should have been proud of how strong they were and how tall Dani had been able to build them over the years. Instead, I was angry—no, I wasn't angry. I was hurt.

Which was so much worse.

Still, no castle was impenetrable.

But as I stared at the base of her shields, the hurt became palpable, a sourness soaking my tongue.

I pulled back, my fingers digging into my thigh. For once, I did not wish to find the answers by ripping them from someone's mind. I was sick and tired of people hiding behind their shields.

I wanted the truth said aloud. I glared at the commander, who had been avoiding me for the past week.

"And where is this mission taking place?" I asked, my fingers tapping the table.

Moris, however, was the one to speak. "We've been chosen to head to the mainland for a *classified* reconnaissance mission." His eyes lit with an unfiltered eagerness as he waved his spoon.

Lady Ferrios cleared her throat, glaring at Moris.

Moris straightened and added, "Your Highness."

"To the mainland, you say?" I asked.

"The mission," Menides said after sipping his wine, "actually was the Crown Prince's idea."

My jaw cracked as Dani turned to me and asked, "Was it?"

"Mhm," I hummed, my attention still fixed on the commander. "I didn't know you had already chosen the squad, Commander."

Menides peered over his glass, his features void of emotion. "The decision was made this morning, Your Highness."

"I see." My gaze slipped to Dani.

As her eyes met mine reluctantly, an unspoken question rose to my countenance.

A honeyed thought cut through the air in response, but her sweet voice did little to soothe the pain.

I was going to tell you.

But the words meant little when I knew the truth, for her eyes said everything.

She wasn't going to tell me.

Not until she had returned from Ardentol.

Not until the mission had already been completed.

CHAPTER 30
DANI

The moment I saw Fynn, I should have told him I had been chosen for the mission. But I couldn't. The words became lead in my mouth and concrete in my stomach.

This mission was too critical.

After my father had announced who was chosen for it, he finally told us what we had trained so hard for over the past few weeks.

The Royal Seer had another vision. Soon, bloodshed and death would mark Pontian soil. The previous attack was only a precursor, a prequel for the story to come. For years, our kingdom had not retaliated. With the peace treaty from the Great War still in place, retaliating would put our kingdom at risk. So, for fifteen years, we had waited.

And *waited*.

But now it was time to start acting.

Details of Fynn's sister were carefully guarded. Few spoke of her, and even fewer knew the details of her capture. According to the queen, her daughter was safe and alive. While this wasn't a rescue mission—not yet anyway—my father had said it would help retrieve the lost princess.

I was five when the princess was taken. Although my memories of her were sparse and quickly fading, I knew how much she meant to Fynn despite the years that had passed.

And perhaps that was why I didn't confide in him when I saw him. I knew how much this mission would mean to him if he knew the truth.

Hope, while one of the most powerful tools, was also the most dangerous.

I had no idea, however, that he was the one who had set this mission into motion.

I thought I was protecting him, but I was wrong. So incredibly wrong.

"Menides and Sorinia, dinner was delicious. Thank you. However, I must be going." Wood scraped against the floor as Fynn pushed his chair away.

Everyone around the table stood. I was the last one to do so, my legs numb and stiff.

"It was a pleasure having you, Your Highness," my mother said, offering him a small curtsy, her gaze bouncing to me for a moment.

Fynn nodded to the others and turned away, leaving the room without sparing me a glance.

My palms pressed into the wood as everyone else sat down. My heart thumped in my chest as my gaze bounced around the room, as the ghost of Fynn's handprint on my leg burned a hole through the dress my mother had picked out.

When I turned to my father, he tipped his head toward the doors. "Go," he mouthed.

I didn't hesitate. The stiff fabric of my dress wrapped around the chair, tugging it with me. The legs scraped the floor, and my mother gasped in horror.

"Sorry," I mumbled, quickly righting the chair before flying out the door. A sea of pink fabric chased me as my heels struck the floor.

When I turned out of the dining room, Fynn was already halfway to the door, his usual swagger long gone and his back rigid. I sped up, my footsteps quick across the freshly polished floors as I chased after him.

"Fynn, wait!" I grabbed his arm, but he shook my hand off and continued for the door. "Let me explain."

"There's nothing to explain, Dani," he said, his voice even, flat. *Cold.*

Pain pierced my gut, but I wouldn't let it stop me from reaching out again. "Fynn, please." I reached for his hand, my fingers brushing against it.

Yet he snatched his hand away. Stopping, he spun around so abruptly that I almost smacked into his back, barely catching myself before running into him.

"Fine," he said.

"I—" My tongue twisted, the words suddenly becoming too heavy to say aloud. I averted my gaze, unable to look Fynn in the eye. I glanced at the hall leading to the dining room, where everyone else still chatted and laughed the night away.

In a matter of minutes, I had ruined everything.

Fynn.

The promotion.

Everything.

He sighed, and the noise was full of all the words unspoken between us. He tugged me into the nearby sitting room and shut the door behind him. The last time I stepped into this room was when my mother had filled it with eager suitors. The room felt so small then, but now it was far too big and the air too stiff. The sun slipped in between the cracks of the curtain, yet despite the golden hue it cast, there was nothing golden about this moment.

Fynn crossed his arms over his chest. "Let's talk then. Dani. Were you going to tell me about the mission?"

As Fynn stared at me for a moment, time ticked by at a sluggish pace. I couldn't rewind time. I couldn't go back and tell him the truth the moment I saw him. And in seconds that ticked by, a heavy silence grew between us.

Until Fynn cut through it like a knife with three words: "The truth, Dani."

My brows quivered. Twisting my fingers together, I said, "I would have told you if I had known."

Fynn rubbed his palms over his face. "That is not the truth, and you know it."

"Yes, it is," I hissed, though I didn't believe the words I spoke aloud. "I was trying to protect you."

Fynn scoffed. "You thought you were *protecting* me?"

"Yes," I said, and for the first time since Fynn had found out about the mission, I looked at him—*really* looked at him. His countenance was painted with pain, his brows drawn together, and his hair ragged from his fingers running through it.

The truth was a burden, and I would not have wanted to burden Fynn with it—not this time, not unless I absolutely needed to. When it came to the Bull King, the less Fynn knew, the better.

At least, that's what I had thought. A part of me still did.

"The truth, Fynn." I took a step forward. "Are you mad at me because I didn't tell you, or are you mad that I was chosen to go?"

His lips parted, but no words came out.

I had my answer.

"What is the difference if it was me or someone else, Fynn?"

"Because, Dani!" Fynn dug his fingers into his hair. "That—that man has taken too much from me already. I cannot—" Fynn groaned, and the charming prince with smooth, sweet words disappeared before me.

Fynn was scared, and he was finally showing it.

While I could understand his fear, I would not let his fear deter me.

"I am not your sister, Fynn. I am not being taken against my will. We are not even going to Ardentol."

"It doesn't matter if you are going to the castle or not! Pontia was supposed to be the safest kingdom in Vaneria, yet we were still attacked! My sister was taken from us all because we weren't quick enough or strong enough. How am I supposed to protect you from him if he somehow discovers that a group of Pontians have been sent south?" He shook his head, stumbling over his words. "This isn't—you can't—"

And it was the sound of those two words that washed away any conflict in my mind. I no longer cared if I hurt his feelings. I was a warrior, and Fynn would do well to remember that.

"You may be the Crown Prince, but you do *not* tell me what I can or cannot do, Fynneares." I took a step forward. My heart beat faster and faster, but my voice was ice-cold and steady. "This is the job. My orders have already been given, and they come directly from the commander and the queen. At the end of the day, our lives—my *life* means nothing when it comes to protecting Pontia. When I joined, I made a vow to protect this kingdom at whatever cost."

"A vow?" Fynn's jaw popped as he clenched his teeth. His hands fell from his hair, the blood rushing from his face. "What is a vow compared to your *life*, Dani?"

When I spoke, my voice was steadfast, unwavering. "It is *everything*."

Once again, his mouth fell open, yet he didn't utter a word.

But I was done waiting for other people to make their judgments about my choices.

I pushed my shoulders back. "I am not a queen, Fynn."

His face twisted with confusion, deep wrinkles creasing his forehead. "How does that—that doesn't—"

I shook my head, lifting a hand and silencing him. "I am neither a queen nor a princess. I am a soldier. I love this kingdom. I love my family and friends. It is my home, and I will do anything and everything I can to protect it."

"You are more important than a mission, Dani." Fynn took a step forward. Only a foot or two separated us, yet it felt like a mile stretched between us.

He reached out a hand as if he wished to console me, but I did not wish to be consoled. I didn't *need* to be consoled.

My lip curled. "You don't get it. You're not a soldier."

His hand, having dropped to his side, rolled into a ball, his knuckles blanching. "But I am a servant to this kingdom. I know about sacrificing your life—your dreams, your wants—for the kingdom."

I scoffed. He still didn't get it, but I was beginning to think he never would.

"It's not the same thing, Fynn. You're the Crown Prince. When Queen Esmeray steps down, you will take her place. You'll sit on your throne giving orders. But who fulfills those orders? Who has to protect the kingdom while you sit in the safety of your castle walls?"

He jerked back. There was no sign of the smug prince, no smirk twitching at his lips, no dimple appearing at the corner of his mouth. The man before me was almost unrecognizable as he pointed a finger at me.

"You didn't have to join the military, Dani. That was your choice," he said.

I tipped my chin up. "And I will gladly make that choice over and over again because it is what I am meant to do. You might have been born to rule, Fynn, but I was born to fight."

He pointed in the direction of the castle, the tip of his ears turning red. "Do you think I want to sit in that castle all day in meetings?" He gripped his shirt, his fingers wrinkling the expensive fabric. "Do you think I would not rather be fighting for my kingdom—actually *doing* something worthwhile rather than planning frivolous balls?" As the words spilled from his mouth, something akin to anger flooded his face, tinting it pink.

No, it was not anger. It was hurt.

But I was hurting, too. "That's not how this works, Fynn."

"You may think this is only a reconnaissance mission, but that man is always one step ahead of us! There is a reason that my mother has not made a move against him yet. It is dangerous."

"The life of a soldier is dangerous, Fynn."

"But it doesn't have to be! You can—you could—" He swallowed the rest of his words and spun around, giving me his back.

I didn't know what I wanted him to say, but him saying nothing was almost worse. Because in the silence that filled the space between us, everything my mother and Rosalina had said within the past week spun in my mind.

If you put anyone in an elegant dress, they are bound to catch someone's eye.

You are a soldier. You were never meant to be a queen.

Whatever you and Fynneares have will pass. It always does with him.

I do not wish for your heart to be broken, Danisinia.

I might not have expected to be Fynn's queen, but knowing that he couldn't even say the words was more painful than it should have been.

I brushed my hair back and steadied myself. "You have known from the beginning that this is who I am."

He shook his head but didn't say anything. He didn't even turn around.

"This kingdom," I said, pointing in the general direction of the castle, "has been handed to you. While I know you love your kingdom, no matter what you do, you will become king. But that's not how it works for everyone else. We aren't all handed our parents' titles. Because my father is the commander, it doesn't make things easier for me. I've had to work ten times as hard to rise in the ranks and earn the respect of my counterparts. I have had to face constant ridicule *because* my father is the commander. And now? I practically have to ignore his mere existence when we are in uniform."

Fynn scoffed. "I never asked to be king. If Terin had been born first, if he had been given my ability. . ." Sighing, he cracked his knuckles before shoving them into his pockets. He rolled his shoulders back, shaking his head. "I can't change who I am. But you're right. It doesn't matter what I do. All that matters is that I marry a respectable woman who will bear the kingdom an heir. I'm a glorified figure-head. The advisors. . .they'll be the ones who get the final say in the policies. It doesn't matter what I think."

Fynn turned around and grabbed my shoulders, squeezing them gently. When he looked at me, his eyes pierced my soul. As he exhaled, his shoulders sank. He took a step closer and pressed his forehead against mine. His breath was warm against my face, a light whisper against my cheek. "But you? When you are promoted to general, it will be because you have earned it, Ferrios."

My mouth was sealed shut. There were a million things I could have said and a million things I should have said. With Fynn, though, I never had to say anything. He always knew. Before, it had always been a blessing, but now? Now, it was nothing more than a curse.

He released a small sigh. A tight, knowing smile pushed at the corners of his lips, but the smile didn't reach his eyes. Placing a gentle kiss on my forehead, he said, "I understand, Dani. It was never going to be me. You're my end, but I am only your beginning."

Before I could say anything, he turned, and all I could do was watch him walk away.

His fingers wrapped around the doorknob, and for a second, I thought he would turn around. I thought he would hesitate, but he didn't. He twisted the doorknob, saying, "Promise me you will come home safe."

Then, he yanked the door open without waiting for the promise he knew I couldn't give him.

Only fools promised their own safety.

It didn't matter if I wanted to grab his arm and force him to stay. My feet were frozen in place, as if bricks had been tied to the bottom of the sharp heels, preventing me from moving forward. I had been under Moris' paralysis many times, but this was so much worse.

This was why my mother had been worried. She knew this would happen—that I would be forced to choose between my duty to my kingdom and my best friend.

Maybe Fynn was right not to hesitate then.

Our paths were not supposed to be aligned, not in this world and maybe not even in the next.

Our courtship was doomed from the very beginning.

Yet, when the front door slammed shut, knowing its cursed fate didn't prevent the sound from shattering a piece of my soul. It ricocheted against the walls of my ribcage, within the confinements of my body that felt too constricting, the air too close.

And there was no way the guests in the dining room had not heard the bang down the hall.

It didn't matter if I went on this mission or not. I would not be getting the promotion. Not when the actual test had been whether I had ties holding me down.

I wasn't even someone who could hold on to their ties.

And yet, that wasn't why my body collapsed the moment I could no longer see Fynn's silhouette.

It wasn't the reason why my knees hit the ground.

It wasn't why it felt like a piece of me had ripped from my body.

I couldn't give a damn about the promotion at that moment. Not when I might have just lost my best friend.

And all because I had made a bargain with a prince.

CHAPTER 31
FYNN

OUTSIDE THE FERRIOS MANOR, WITH MY BACK PRESSED AGAINST THE brick wall and my head tilted, I watched the sky melt. Its brilliant shades faded into a muted orange, the honeyed glow dissipating into the air.

And I waited.

At first, I stayed because I couldn't get myself to walk down the steps to the carriage. When I came outside, Lance made to move forward, but with one single shake of my head, he retreated to the driver's bench. I needed to catch my breath before I could sit in a carriage with no way of escaping the weight of everything that had transpired.

But in truth, I waited because I had foolishly hoped that Dani would chase after me. That after months of our fake-courtship-turned-real, she would have learned to stop running from her problems somewhere along the way.

Yet her footsteps hadn't followed, and the door never creaked open.

I had never questioned Dani's strength or ability, but she still doubted herself. Because through the fire bleeding through her hazel eyes, I saw the doubt burning beneath it. Although she was making the choice she thought she needed to make, it didn't mean it hurt any less. That didn't mean that a piece of me wasn't crumbling inside.

I did not wish for Dani to betray her word. I did not want Dani to give up her career for me.

I would have never asked her that.

The mission might have been my idea, but it wasn't supposed to put more people I loved in danger. It wasn't supposed to put *her* in danger, as selfish as a thought as it might have been.

I would lay my life down if it meant she had a chance at happiness.

To me, Dani was everything—the light, the spark.

I did not wish for the enemy to take that from me. The Bull King had already taken too much.

If my words had insulted her, that had not been my intent. Nor had I meant to make a fool of myself. However, I hadn't known what to say when I had looked at her. I had seen so many women glare at me like she had, with anger and spite. But with Dani, that look was different.

Did she not realize that I would do anything to protect anyone in my kingdom? But more than that, that I would do anything to protect *her?*

But how could I protect her when Dani didn't even seem to trust me to protect her heart?

So, when the stars peeked out in the darkening sky, and the door still had not opened, I finally descended the steps, no longer wishing to be under the gods' watching eyes. I did not wish for Pontanius and Sabina to look down upon me and see that I had failed them and the kingdom they had built.

I was the prince with the cocky smile who broke hearts left and right. But who would have guessed that the heartbreaker prince would have been the one to walk away with his heart shattered into a million pieces?

I hadn't even known I had given my heart to someone until it was too late.

CHAPTER 32
FYNN

The door slammed shut behind me.

"Oh, Fynneares, is that you?"

My steps faltered as my mother's light voice called out from somewhere in the castle.

"Fynneares?" she called again when I had yet to respond.

At last, I grunted, unable to string together a single thought, let alone voice a sentence.

I never wanted to interfere with Dani's career or make her feel the need to make such a choice. I had never asked her to, yet she had made the choice anyway.

For me, it was never an either-or situation.

Dani might have thought I was overreacting, but I had been studying the Bull King and his movements for over a decade. Based on the little intel we received from our spies in the south, the man was unpredictable. He was conniving and cunning and always one step ahead.

That's how he was able to break my family the first time.

Every year, my family would go to our summer home for a month to escape the bustle of the capital. In their absence, my parents trusted the advisors to keep the kingdom running.

My father always told us, "Even queens and kings need to live once in a while."

But on that fatal day, we had lived *too* much. Our walls were down. Caution had been left behind in the castle. At night, the fire rolled over the house, burning anything it could.

As the smoke filled the hallways and slithered beneath the cracks of the doors, wrapping around our lungs, Terin had succumbed to sleep's embrace. Terin still had not gained solid control over his ability at the time. Unlike now, where sleep evaded him, sleep wrapped its heavy tendrils around his ankles, drowning him in its embrace. It took everything I had to drag my brother out of the house as the flames crawled over the building and ate away at its beams and walls.

When we at last made it outside, no one was there.

The smoke had not left my lungs yet, but I had to go back. I *tried* to go back. But as I ran for the house, the windows shattered as Graeson burst through the doors with my sister clawing at his face. She clawed and bit and scratched, hollering unintelligible words through a tear-stained face.

When she escaped Graeson's hold like the little mouse she was, my sister crawled to the house on her hands and knees. But she was only three and had been inside longer than I had. Her lungs were weak, her body feeble.

She was too slow, too small.

And then the Bull King came. His iron helmet, in the shape of a bull, glowed red and yellow as the flames slashed and roared around him. He was unfazed by the fire as he sped forward on his horse.

Before Graeson and I could process what was happening, the Bull King snatched my sister and threw her atop his black stallion.

I tried to go after her.

I tried to run.

I tried to fight the burning in my lungs.

But I couldn't.

I wasn't quick enough.

I wasn't strong enough.

My sister was taken that night because I had not been *enough.*

For centuries, our kingdom had been the safest place in Vaneria. Yet, in one night, that safety was obliterated.

Therefore, it didn't matter if Dani's upcoming mission was only for the purpose of gaining more information.

It didn't matter if Dani was one of the strongest people I knew.

One needed more than strength to outwit a man who had been able to slither past Pontia's defenses and discover where my family was without raising a single warning bell.

Yet Dani had brushed away my concerns, claiming it was her duty to go.

I knew about obligations. But more importantly, I knew all about failing them.

And perhaps that's where my problem lay.

As a child, I thought the title of prince granted me access to everything I wanted. I slacked off on my training because I didn't think it was worthwhile. The crown was all the protection I needed.

Or so I had thought.

When we were attacked, some of that changed. But in some ways, the ignorance and carelessness only grew worse.

As a teenager, I let my title open doors for me. I fell into bed with women because they wanted me for my name, my body, and little else. I had thought that was something to be proud of. I was wanted. I was *useful.*

For a while, that's all I cared about—to be wanted while drowning between the sheets of whichever woman occupied my bed for the night.

In recent years, though, the charade grew more exhausting than it was worth.

Then came the deal.

When Dani said she had never been courted, I had made it my mission to court her properly. I always thought that the formalities of courtships were futile and obnoxious, filled with clichés and superficial thoughts. I had never realized it could be *fun,* though. That it could be filled with so much laughter.

I had never realized that seeing the flash of someone's smile could twist my heart and paralyze me.

Until Dani, that is.

I couldn't pinpoint the exact moment when Dani had crossed the line from being a friend to being something more. I didn't even know what that *more* was. All I knew was the pain spiking in my chest.

I wasn't angry at Dani. I was simply. . .numb. My body, my mind, my *soul.*

I didn't want my mother's gentle words, nor did I deserve them. So even though she called after me, I continued forward.

But the gods did not seem to care about what I wanted because as my palm landed on the railing, light footsteps echoed in the hall, growing louder and louder.

"I thought that was you," my mother said.

I swallowed, trying to force the heartache back down my throat as my fingers curled around the railing.

"How was the dinner?" my mother asked.

A beat of silence passed, my vocal cords continuing to fail me.

She stepped closer. When she spoke next, her tone shifted in the only way a mother's voice could, "Fynneares?" Her hand fell atop mine, and my fingers tightened around the railing as my head spun.

I slipped my hand from beneath hers. "I'm tired, Mother."

My foot hit the first step, but that's as far as I got before her delicate fingers wrapped around my wrist, tugging me.

"Do not walk away from me," she said, not as a queen but as a mother worried for her son.

My shoulders sagged, but I relented and turned around.

"What happened?" she asked.

I leaned against the railing, the post digging into the middle of my back. "Does it matter?"

My mother's brows twisted together, light blue eyes dripping with concern. "Of course, it matters."

I bit down on the inside of my cheek, willing the pain to spike somewhere else—anywhere else but my shattering heart.

My mother quirked a brow.

"Dani and I. . ." I released a heavy sigh. "We got into a fight."

She nodded as if she had expected this, as if this was the only possible outcome of any of my courtships.

Was this why everyone close to me kept their shields up? Were they all hiding their true thoughts about my ability to care for someone other than myself? Did none of them believe in me?

I took a step backward and up the steps. "I don't want to hear it, Mother."

"Hear what?" My mother pressed a delicate hand against her chest, feigning ignorance, as if both of us didn't already know what she was thinking.

I cocked my head to the side. "The 'I told you so' or the 'you should have planned for this.' Come on, Mother. Let's hear it. Let's hear how your son, the Crown Prince, has once again disappointed you."

She stepped forward, the silk fabric of her silver dress sweeping across the floor. "Now, why would I say that?"

My fingers curled around the railing, my knuckles blanching, as I said, "Because it's what you always say when I do something disappointing. By now, you should be used to it. I may be the Crown Prince, but I am an even bigger disappointment."

My mother pressed both hands to my cheeks, tilting my face

down. Her fingers were soft against the scruff on my jawline. "Fynneares, you are not a disappointment. If your father could hear you now—"

I jerked away, and her hands fell. "Father isn't here though, is he?"

My mother's jaw ticked, and water glistened over her sea-blue eyes.

I squeezed my eyes shut, sighing as I rubbed my palms across my face. "I didn't—I'm sorry, Mother. I didn't mean to say that."

My mother tapped a hand against my cheek. When I opened my eyes, she offered me a small, sad smile. Pain still lingered in her gaze, but the anger I had expected was nowhere to be seen.

"Son, I have been through my fair share of heartaches to know not to take anyone's words to heart when they are hurting. Your grandmother has heard more than her fair share of painful words from me, no doubt. But—"

Here it comes, I thought to myself, *the moment I've been waiting for— when my mother passes on her wisdom while simultaneously proving to me yet again that I do not deserve the title I was given months ago.*

My mother inhaled. "Stop those thoughts, Fynneares. I may not have your gift, but I have known you for your entire life. I can see it when the self-doubt creeps in and you begin questioning your self-worth and ability to lead."

I stared at the ceiling, at the depiction of the summer sky splayed across the sprawling space. It was meant to give the illusion that the sky was within reach, that our limits were endless, even within the boundaries of the castle's walls.

Or at least that's what I had once thought as a child.

Now, I saw it for what it was: a farce—a mirage.

"I am no king, Mother," I whispered at last.

"As you have said time and time again, but one day, you will be. You and Danisinia have been friends since you were children, I am sure—"

"This is different," I said, interrupting.

Her mouth flattened as she looked up at me. "It might feel that way now, but it will pass."

My head fell, the weight of tonight becoming too heavy to carry on my shoulders any longer. The soft chestnut waves fell in front of my eyes, shielding me from the world around me, but its halo cocooning me could do little to protect me from the thoughts within.

My mother placed a hand on my shoulder. Tears stung my eyes, and for the first time all night, I let them fall.

The tears I shed rolled down my face, falling down the contours of my cheeks and chin, not in a torrent, but rather painstakingly slow. The adrenaline coursing through my veins when I stormed into Dani's childhood home was long gone. Without it, everything felt too heavy, too slow, too weighted. Each tear that slipped from the corner of my eye and left a slim trail of water on my face was more painful than the last.

"She's—she's my best friend," I whispered, my hand falling onto the railing beside me for support. "What am I supposed to do now?"

My mother didn't say anything, only wrapped her arms around me as my soul bled from my eyes.

CHAPTER 33
DANI

BETWEEN MY FIGHT WITH FYNN AND THE DAY THE BOAT SET SAIL, training and meetings filled my schedule. At first, I was thankful for the distractions. It meant I was too occupied during the day to think about the heartache that was trying to swallow me whole. Yet no matter how much my muscles ached or my eyes burned from exhaustion, when the night greeted me, so too did thoughts of Fynn.

Every night when I laid down to go to sleep, I replayed our fight in my head, despite knowing I shouldn't. It was my nature to review past events and study them for better alternatives. I tried to see if there was a way our argument could have ended differently, a way I couldn't have prevented the argument. But no matter how I looked at it, I knew nothing would have changed the outcome.

I understood Fynn's concerns. I understood why he was worried. Yet understanding his fears did not mean we could have avoided the inevitable.

And that fight? It was inevitable, no matter how we twisted it.

Fynn wanted to protect those he loved; I wanted to fight for them.

The morning before Moris, Sylvia, Quint, and I set sail, I stood on the dock with our closest friends and family—saying goodbye without uttering the actual word to those who came.

My parents stood with my brothers and their wives. After giving me a quick hug, Sawyer hurried after Ronan. My nephew ran up and down the dock, chasing after the fish swimming in the sea. When I was Ronan's age, I had attended several send-offs for my father. Back then, I didn't understand the dangers my father and the other soldiers often faced when they departed. It was strange being on the other side now, seeing the watery eyes of loved ones and the smiles of ignorant children as they played on the dock.

As I kissed my niece's forehead, I knew in my heart that the leaders were wrong. Everyone standing on the dock—my family and friends—was another reason I fought for my kingdom.

They were my why.

I should have never let the leaders' concerns with my love life get in the way of seeing that. I should have never let my father make me think otherwise. I had plenty of people to fight for.

My sister-in-law, Ambrosia, smiled at me as Lia reached for me. Chuckling, I gave her my finger, and her tiny fingers wrapped around mine.

"Come home safe, all right? You're the only sane one among your brothers," Ambrosia said.

My brothers' wives and I weren't close. Both were quiet women, focused on building their homes and families. But I liked them well enough. They made Sawyer and Xavier happy—and I especially liked how they kept my brothers out of my hair for once.

I laughed. "If only that were true."

Lia released my hand and reached for her mother's hair, tugging it. Ambrosia chuckled. After a swift embrace, my sister-in-law turned away and headed for Sawyer and Ronan.

Terin stepped forward, pulling me into a hug and squeezing me tight. All the words no one said were embedded into his embrace. But it was what he chose to say aloud that had me stumbling back a half step.

"I did ask him to come."

I struggled to swallow the rising lump in my throat. "I—I wasn't looking."

"If you say so, Dani." Terin's brown eyes met mine, and I dropped his gaze, offering him a terse smile, unwilling to admit the sourness in my stomach.

I shouldn't have been surprised. In truth, I hadn't expected even Terin or Graeson to show up. None of us liked goodbyes. But deep down, I had hoped Fynn would have shown up.

Captain Squires, one of the most experienced sailors, whistled. After one final look at my friends and family, I boarded the ship with the rest of my squad. Then, we were off.

And I forced myself not to look back.

IN THE FIRST couple of hours, everyone was lively, and the excitement of the voyage was fresh in the air. Leaving Pontia, the Red Sea was calm, as if the god Pontanius were blessing us on our journey south. But the trip from Pontia was always easy; it was the journey back that would prove to be treacherous, according to Captain Squires.

As we sailed, Quint tried to make small talk about the weather or his family, and I tried my best to listen. But when the nodding and smiling became too much, I gave up, my smile fading in the salt-filled air.

At some point, Sylvia and Moris tried to pull me into a game of cards, but I couldn't recall the rules of a game I had known since I was a child. Diamonds looked like hearts, and queens melted into kings.

As the sun beamed down on the dock, the loneliness crept in.

I tried to think about my niece's small, bright face, her tiny fingers wrapping around mine. I tried to think about Ronan chasing fish, his unfiltered laughter echoing across the sea. They were the future of our kingdom, my reasons for fighting.

Yet my thoughts kept wandering to the future king. To the man who would one day lead Pontia to a brighter tomorrow.

The leaders were foolish to have thought that giving my heart to someone to hold would encourage me to be a better leader. Fynn had held a piece of my heart since we were children, and it had done me no good all those years. But now that he held my heart in its entirety with more than a sea between us? It was soul-splitting.

When we landed near the mouth of the Lucien River and traveled along the stream on foot the next day, the voyage south remained quiet and unexciting. We should have been grateful for the silence, yet it only made my thoughts louder and my regrets more bitter.

I couldn't help but wonder how Fynn managed to exist with anyone else's thoughts inside his head. Mine alone were already too loud.

AFTER TEN DAYS OF TRAVELING, we finally arrived outside the rendezvous point.

Our mission was simple: meet with our contact and retrieve the intel that was too important to pass along by our spies' standard coded messages.

When we were chosen for this mission, I wondered why we needed four people to go. It would have been much easier and quicker to travel alone. But when I asked, my father had shaken his head.

"We're sending a full squad, nothing less," he had said.

Beneath his words, though, lay the real reason: a squad ensured that the mission, no matter what, would be completed. That if the gods were not on our side and one soldier was lost, someone would survive.

Our contact would not arrive until morning, so all that was left to do was wait.

The cave I had chosen for us was tucked away along the mountainside. Rocky cliffs nestled on one side of the entrance and a forest of trees to the right. The four of us hugged our cloaks tight to our bodies as we sat side-by-side around the dwindling fire. Although several weeks remained before the autumn chill crept onto Pontian shores, one would have never guessed that in the mountains separating the kingdoms of Borgania and Kadia. In the northeastern kingdoms, winters were long and hard. If the frigid night air were any indication, this coming season would be no different across Vaneria.

Moris handed me a flask. The time spent traveling had left Moris' usually clean-shaven face burly. His light brown skin beneath his eyes also showed more purple tones than usual.

With a nod, I grabbed the flask and twisted the cap off. However, when I brought it to my lips, the smell of oak and leather wafted to my nose. I put the cap back on and returned it to him, mumbling, "No, thanks."

"Come on, Ferrios," Moris said, nudging me. "We've been traveling nonstop for the last thirteen days. Enjoy the quiet while you can."

I shook my head, tugging my knees closer to my chest. "Someone needs to stay sharp."

With a shake of his head, Moris said, his mouth already to the flask, "More for us then."

He passed it to Sylvia, who drank from it quickly, sighing. They passed the flask to Quint and wrapped their cloak tightly around their body.

As they continued to pass the flask back and forth, I scanned the area outside the entrance. Moris might have been right about the long hike, but I knew better than to let the quiet of the woods fool me. The moment the air stilled and the noise of the wandering rabbits and squirrels dwindled, that was when one should be concerned.

Silence, after all, was not always a gift.

There were messages in the silence. Small, nearly imperceptible cracks of twigs, the rustling of leaves, the prickling of the back of the neck. The minute disturbances that the average person might have ignored were the things that I couldn't help but hear and latch onto. It was why my comrades called me the huntress, and it was one of the reasons I was here.

Apparently, another being that I was the only one wise enough to keep a sharp mind.

"Why is it so fucking cold?" Moris asked, his teeth clattering together. "Isn't liquor supposed to keep you warm?"

"Which idiotic question do you want me to answer first?" I retorted.

"Idiotic? They're not idiotic! They're practical," Moris argued, scooting closer to the fire as he shivered harder. "But the first one."

Quint snorted beside me, pulling the hood of his cloak lower.

I rolled my eyes. "Because we're on top of a mountain, dingus."

"And?"

I rubbed my temples, trying to soothe the headache that was quickly forming. "*And* do I look like a scientist?"

"No, but you usually know everything. You tracked down the rabbits on the way here. You knew which paths to avoid because you had *sensed* someone else's presence."

I scoffed. "I do not *sense* things, Moris. I listen to what my surroundings are telling me."

Rubbing his hands together near the flames, Moris shrugged. "Sounds like you sense it to me."

Out past the cave's entrance, leaves rustled as the wind swept through the woods. Goosebumps spread across my arms. I squinted at the shadows slithering between the trees as night fell. A breeze flew in, howling. The air ruffled our clothes and stirred the fire. The sun had begun its descent, and soon, we would need to blow the fire out. But until then, we needed to soak in its heat before the crisp breeze coated our uncovered skin as night fell.

Sylvia cleared their throat, bringing my attention back to the group. "It's cold up here because the atmospheric pressure is lower in the mountains, so—"

"All right, all right," Moris said, cutting Sylvia off. "I get it, Sylv."

"What? You asked."

"Yeah, but listening to you is just making it colder."

"That's not possible," Sylvia said with a sigh. "In fact, the more talking there is, the warmer—"

"Sylv," Moris whined.

Sylvia raised their hands. "Sorry for trying to educate you. I'll just shut up."

"Thank the gods," Moris sighed. "Pontanius himself could fall asleep to your *educating*."

Laughter filled our small circle. Even I couldn't help but crack a smile. But then Sylvia had to ruin it.

"Are you ever going to talk about it?" Sylvia asked, their attention turning to me.

"About what?" I asked, my smile fading.

Sylvia arched a brow.

I buried my chin into the crook between my knees and chest. "Do we need to discuss this right now?"

Sylvia looked around the cave. "What? Is there another way you would rather spend our time while we wait for dawn to rise?" Sylvia took a swig from the flask and passed it to Moris.

"Enough of this," I said, snatching the flask from Moris' hand. "We need to stay sharp. Don't we, Major Torian?" I asked Quint, hoping he would provide some resemblance of order—as a leader should.

Moris shrugged.

I shook the flask, but nothing echoed inside the container. Turning it upside down, a singly measly drop slipped out.

Empty.

I narrowed my eyes at Moris, whose eyes were already glass.

"Is that what this is about?" Quint asked after a moment.

"Is that what *what* is about?" I asked, tossing the flask onto the ground.

"This," Quint said, pointing at me before tugging his cloak tighter around him. "You've been acting cold this entire trip. Is it because of the promotion? If you care to know, I thought you would get it. I still think you deserved—"

I shook my head and cut him off before he could push the knife further into the wound. "I am not upset because of the promotion, Quint."

"But you are upset, aren't you?"

I clicked my tongue, hugging my legs. "I am not upset at all."

Sylvia snorted. "Don't let her fool you, Major. She is upset, but not at you."

"Then who?" Quint asked.

"Ferrios and Prince Charming had a fight at the commander's dinner."

"You should have been there, Major. It was—" Moris snapped his mouth shut when I chucked a throwing knife inches from his boot.

Sylvia snickered.

Quint continued, "Yes, well, I didn't want to miss my niece's birth. Family does come first," Quint said to Moris before turning to me. "You and the prince fought?"

I scoffed. "Of course not. Sylvia is exaggerating."

Sylvia, however, brushed me off, continuing as if I hadn't said a single word and wasn't currently reaching for another throwing knife. "The prince was upset that *someone* didn't inform him she was coming."

I tried to interject, my brows twisting, "It's not that. It's—"

"Was this your first fight?" Quint asked, turning a curious gaze toward me.

"Our first fight?" My eyes widened, and I wrapped my arms tighter around my legs. "I told you, we're not fighting."

We weren't anything *anymore based on how we left things*, I thought to myself.

"Come on, Dani. You were just complaining to me about—"

I elbowed Sylvia in the ribcage, and they hissed. "Hey! What was that for?"

"Shut up, Sylvia," I hissed.

When Fynn slammed the door shut on his way out after dinner, those in attendance figured something was wrong. According to Sylvia, no one had dared voice it, though. On the voyage over, Sylvia had asked me what had happened. And in confidence—or at least what I thought was in confidence—I had relayed some of the details about the argument.

"Fine. I won't say anything else. But"—there was always a *but* when it came to Sylvia—"if I were you, I would talk to him when we return and try to make up. Rumor has it there are women already lining up to be next."

My stomach twisted. "Next?"

Moris nodded and said, "You know, the next to court Fynn?"

My lungs dropped to the pit of my stomach. Our courtship—if one could even call it that—might have been short-lived, but I had thought Fynn would have at least waited to find his next conquest.

My conversation with him after the dinner resurfaced. I had told him I was not a queen. I had told him my career was important. But what did he say?

Nothing. Absolutely nothing.

Instead, Fynn only focused on the mission.

And what was that supposed to mean? Did he, too, think we were ignorant for believing we could have been something?

We had yet to talk concretely about what would happen after the deal was over. If we hadn't fought, would there have been an after?

Or was I just the latest woman in Fynn's line-up, as Moris had suggested?

"I'm going to get some sleep while I can," Moris said, stretching his arms up.

Sylvia looked at me.

"I'll take the first watch," I said.

"No, I got it," Quint said. "You get some sleep, Ferrios. You've already done most of the heavy lifting to get us here. It's the least I can do."

My gaze fell to the flask.

Quint shook his head. "I didn't drink any."

My lips parted. The question of why Moris only gave me a hard time was on the tip of my tongue, but I swallowed it.

I nodded to Quint and headed toward the edge of the cave, peering out.

The sky had turned to a muted purple now. A few stars dotted the sky, but most of the gods still hid among the clouds. I could only make out the constellation of Barinthian, the god of truth, peeking out.

I turned away from the god.

Right now, the truth was not something I wished to see.

I found my spot beside Sylvia and curled next to them on my side.

Soon, darkness filtered into the cave like a heavy shadow. When I closed my eyes to sleep, two deep brown eyes stared down at me, and a sharp pain twisted in my stomach.

CHAPTER 34
FYNN

GOODBYES WERE A FOREIGN LANGUAGE, ONE I HAD NEVER BEEN TAUGHT despite my years of studying the ancient language of the gods.

I had attempted to see Dani the day her ship set sail—I truly had. I even made it as far as having Telis and Lance take the carriage to the pier. But when I saw her standing on the dock, the ocean breeze kissing her cheek, I couldn't get myself to leave the safety of the carriage.

Nothing I said would have stopped her from leaving. And as I watched her wrap her arms around Terin and Graeson, I realized I didn't want to stop her. I didn't want to be the reason Dani held any part of who she was back.

She could handle herself. She always had.

She didn't need me protecting her.

Nor did she need me stumbling over my words as I prepared for her to set sail.

So, the ship set sail, and I remained inside the carriage. As Terin and Graeson waved from the edge of the dock, I ordered Telis to take us to the cottage north of the Whispering Springs.

Because if I was anything, I was a coward and an idiot.

Once alone at the cottage with only two of my guards to entertain me, I wallowed.

I drowned myself in my self-pity, in my ability to fuck everything up—in my ability to take something so sweet and destroy it because of my pig-headed brain.

It seemed Dani had been right all those months ago—the heir's crown had only made my head bigger.

And I was the one who paid the price for it.

On the eighth day, I stared at the wooden beams spanning the ceiling. On the tiled floor, the decanter lay empty on its side, and my book was just beyond my reach. I couldn't remember the last time I had moved. For days, I had been listlessly lying about, my hair unkempt, my clothes haggard.

At some point, the door creaked open, but I couldn't get myself to look.

With a groan, I tossed my hand in the air. "No, Lance. I do not wish to go outside today either."

Lance snorted. While I should have cared about his disrespect and apparent inability to listen to my wishes, I didn't.

Then, my head hit oak as the pillow was snatched from beneath me.

"Lance!" I shouted, my eyes squeezing shut as a sharp pain spiked through my skull.

"Fynn."

Shit.

I groaned. Even my mind seemed to be betraying me, for I hadn't even heard Terin's approach or noticed his thoughts swirling at the edge of my mind.

"Brother," I spat, "Now that was just rude."

"Get up," Terin commanded.

I rolled my eyes, turning away from him. "I am the heir, remember? You do not command me."

"Are you? Because, based on the man I am looking at right now, I would never have guessed."

"Piss off, Ter," I grumbled, stuffing another pillow from the couch behind my head.

He snatched that pillow, too. "You are *pathetic*."

"Add it to the list. Perhaps next to disappointment and coward."

Terin released a heavy sigh. Footsteps padded across the floor before the couch sunk slightly near my feet. "You've been here for over a week, Fynn."

"If this is about some princely duty, the council can handle it without me. None of them wish for me to be in that seat, anyway."

"Is that what this is about?" Terin asked, slapping my leg. "And here I thought it was because of you and Dani."

I kicked him. "I said piss off."

"Mother is worried. We are *all* worried."

"Go worry somewhere else then," I said, pressing the heels of my palms against my eye sockets, willing the burning to disappear. At least when Lance or Telis had bothered me, they buggered off when I commanded.

Terin hummed, but he did not move.

Groaning, I asked, "If you will not leave, then out with it already."

The silence that followed was a heavy weight upon my head. For a moment, I did not think Terin would give me a response, but then he finally did.

"I didn't think you would be this upset. You've never been this distraught over someone you have courted before. What makes this different from any of those courtships?"

I bit down on my tongue. However, the searing pain did little to distract from the ache in my chest.

"Dani," I said at last.

"What about her?"

"*She* is the difference."

"Why?" Terin asked. "I thought this was fake."

My eyes sprung open, and my limbs grew cold.

Terin wasn't supposed to know. No one was. If Terin knew—

"What did you just say?"

"Oh, calm down." Terin shoved my legs off the couch. "No one else knows."

"But how—why—" My tongue twisted in my mouth as I struggled to sit up.

Terin scoffed, scratching his head. "You and Dani are quite loud when you argue."

My brows twisted.

Terin continued, "The day she interrupted our training? Before I even got out of earshot, Dani had said something about the importance of making your courtship believable to the generals." He shrugged a shoulder and added, "Plus, you are not as good at keeping secrets when you are asleep as you are awake."

"You snuck into my dreams?" I asked, fear lacing my tongue.

"Is that really what you are concerned about right now?" Terin asked, quirking a brow.

"Yes! No—" I shook my head, digging my fingers into my knotted hair. "Are you telling me that you have known this entire time?"

Terin nodded.

My hands fell limp on my lap. "Why didn't you say anything?"

"Why didn't you?" Terin asked.

I chewed on the inside of my cheek as my brother stared at me, sadness spilling from his countenance.

My gaze fell to the floor, my arms leaning atop my knees. "I promised her I wouldn't say anything," I mumbled.

"It wasn't fake, was it?" Terin asked.

As I returned my attention to my brother, I caught my reflection in the window behind him. My eyes were bloodshot, my complexion ashen.

I swallowed the lump, tearing my gaze from my ragged reflection. "I'm not sure if it ever was truly fake, Ter."

CHAPTER 35
DANI

CRACK.

Sharp needles ran down my spine, and I jolted up as the air shifted around me.

But it was too late.

We were surrounded.

CHAPTER 36
FYNN

After two days of sulking with Terin, my brother finally had had enough and forced me to return home.

The day we returned was also the day I would typically head off to The Splintered Oar to meet Dani and her friends—which must have been precisely why Terin dragged me to the Wilton's manor before I could argue.

As I sat in the marble billiards room, all I could think about was that old, musty tavern. I missed the music, the drunken patrons, the old barkeeper and his wife. Coming to this manor, playing cards with Riley and Lukas, and drinking whiskey from crystal glasses were all things I had done *before* Dani and I.

I realized then that time was a strange thing. Our lives were split into a series of before's and after's.

For a long time, I thought you only experienced one of those moments in your lifetime. And for me, I believed that the night of the attack was the moment that defined the rest of my life. I had thought it was the single moment that would mark my life for the rest of my days.

But this moment between Dani and me? Something about it felt life-altering, even though our courtship only lasted a few months.

Maybe that was why the liquor went down quicker as the night wore on.

CRACK.

I jolted up as Terin's hand slapped against the table, his chair scratching against the oak floors as he reached for me. He held out his hand, waiting for me. I stumbled forward, nearly missing his hand as the floor beneath me wobbled.

Or was that me?

Either way, I shrugged it off and picked up my glass. I swirled the remaining droplets of amber liquid, then tossed the drink back before calling Jorian over for a refill.

Riley groaned, slumping back in his chair, his fingers digging into his short, tight black curls.

Lukas shot back the whiskey in his glass. With the back of his hand, he wiped the dribble of liquid dripping down the stubble of his brown chin.

Riley banged his glass against the table, his bright blue eyes locking onto Terin. "I call for a rematch!"

Terin chuckled and scratched the back of his neck as an amused grin stretched across his face from ear to ear.

A hint of bitterness pooled in my stomach, but I shoved it away.

A drunken, heartbroken fool or not—I would always be happy for Terin.

We really shouldn't. It's not fair, Terin thought.

An ounce of amusement flicked at the corner of my mouth.

Originally, Terin had wanted to go easy on his boyfriend and Lukas.

Since I was not in the mood for a game of cards, I had not argued with him. The game felt frivolous in the grand scheme of things. But once we started losing, Terin's competitive nature—a side he usually kept masked behind his quiet demeanor—slipped out. Then, all bets were off.

I feigned a smirk and took a sip of my whiskey. "Are you sure about that, Riley?"

Lukas' gaze snapped to mine. "Has that crown of yours made you cockier, Fynnie?"

I scoffed.

"That's not possible," Terin said. "His ego was already too large for that crown to begin with."

Riley spat whiskey onto the table as he fell into a fit of laughter. Terin's cheeks reddened, and he tried to cover it with a small drink.

I gasped, stabbing an imaginary dagger into my chest and twisting it. "Wounded—and by my own brother, no less."

"So, another?" Riley asked once his laughter died down. He began gathering the cards into a pile.

"Are you a glutton for punishment or something, Riley?" Terin asked.

Leaning back with his arm hanging on the back of the chair, Riley cocked his head as he held out the shuffled deck to Terin. "Or something."

I glanced at Terin, but his mind was sealed shut as he grabbed the deck from Riley.

Soon, the cards were dealt, and the game began again.

However, despite the smile on my face and the laughter slipping from my tongue, my heart was still aching. And for once, I was thankful that Terin's shields remained up, his love-sick thoughts kept to himself.

CHAPTER 37
DANI

A BLOOD-CURDLING SCREAM RIPPED THROUGH THE MAN'S MOUTH AS I ran my blade through his chest.

Everywhere I looked, men with unmarked clothes surrounded us. In the middle of the night, they had ambushed us, coming out of the woods and up the cliffside. And we were outnumbered three-to-one.

Somehow, we had been betrayed. Whether by our informant or by someone else. Either way, the traitor would die. I didn't care if it was by my hands or someone else's. Their death would come.

Once we made it through the night.

The lifeless body of my opponent dropped to the ground with a *thud.* Iron soaked the air as metal clashed and blood spilled onto the ground. The moon was just bright enough to distinguish friend from foe.

I pulled my blade from the enemy, preparing to identify my next victim—

"Dani!" Sylvia shouted, calling my attention.

I dove, tumbling forward as a man swung his long sword. My knees scraped across the ground as the gravel cut through the fabric of my trousers.

However, Pontanius must not have been watching over us this far away from his beloved kingdom. As I slid across the gravel, I realized too late that I had dove too far, straight toward the cliff.

I tried to stop.

I tried to dig my heels into the ground.

I tried to plunge my short sword into the earth, but the ground crumbled beneath me before I could stop the momentum.

I slid down the side of the cliff, clawing and scratching at anything and everything to stop gravity from tugging me down.

But gravity had already wrapped its tendrils around my ankles and pulled.

Up above, shouts and metal continued to soak the air, but I could do nothing to help them as I slid down, down, down.

I was going to die. I was going to—

Thump.

My feet landed on solid ground, my right ankle rolling. However, my foot slipped before I could steady myself. I flattened myself against the side of the cliff, my nails digging into the rough terrain. Pebbles peeled off the precarious ledge I now balanced on as the wind whipped at my hair, loud and rancorous. I never heard the sound of the pebbles landing beneath me, yet I didn't dare look down.

I swallowed. Sweat soaked the back of my neck. My heart pounded, and my lungs screamed.

The clanging of metal muffled the voices of my friends and shouts of the enemy as the fight above continued.

I had to help them.

I had to get *back.*

I inhaled, the cold air sharp in my lungs. I breathed past the pain and searched the face of the cliff, trying to find anything I could grab onto and use to hoist myself up.

I searched and searched.

I need something. *Anything.*

I gasped.

A branch!

A single branch barely within reach stuck out of the side of the mountain. For a split second, I inspected it, but there was no time to question whether it could hold my weight, not when my comrades needed me.

I took a deep breath and jumped, the small chunk of the cliff breaking off as I grabbed onto the branch.

The branch sunk with my weight, but I used my momentum to reach for the landing just above it before it could snap.

Arms burning and lungs screaming, I heaved myself up, my feet scraping along the face of the mountain.

Sweat dripped down the contours of my face and neck as I pulled myself up. My nails dug into the dirt, cracking, bleeding, splitting.

Then, when I looked up, my heart almost stopped entirely.

Moris' hands were outstretched, sweat gleaming on his brown face in the moonlight. His eyes were wide and bloodshot as eight men stood paralyzed around him.

But in the moonlight, I noticed the slight tremble in Moris' hands.

His strength was waning, and I didn't know how much longer he could hold the men.

Beside him, Sylvia was on the ground, and my heart dropped. The glow of the moon illuminated their freckled face as blood seeped the ground where she lay.

After a moment, though, her chest rose, her breathing haggard.

She was still alive.

For now.

If Moris could hold on.

If Quint—

Where's Quint? Panic rose in my throat as I scanned the area, the dead bodies, the paralyzed men, the—

There.

Blade to throat, Quint looked to the stars, to the god who seemed to have forgotten us in the mountains.

The arm of the man who held Quint twitched, and without thinking, I ran.

Quint would not die today.

Quint would not leave behind his children, his wife, his family.

I pumped my arms, harder, faster. I sprinted as hard as I could—as fast as Gabriel. Then I dove, shoving Quint out of the way without any hesitation.

Searing pain tore through my torso, blinding and piercing.

One faint thought spun in my mind as hot pain spiked through my body, where the metal ripped through my flesh. But as I tried to grab the blade, I fell into a sea of darkness before I could grasp the thought.

CHAPTER 38
FYNN

My cards slipped through my hands.

Someone said something—my name?

I couldn't focus on the question, though. Wrinkles creased my forehead as the thoughts of those around me became jumbled in my mind. The thoughts were a torrent, a sea of words mixing as if whomever they belonged to was panicking, barely even able to keep a grip on their own mind.

Failed mission.

Attack in the mountains.

Hurt.

Hurt.

Hurt.

"No," I whispered as my fingers curled around the edge of the table. "*No.*"

"Fynn, what's wrong?" someone asked. My brother? Lukas? I didn't know, nor could I tell.

I couldn't form any words as the thoughts of those racing down the hall came spiraling down the invisible threads.

A spout of nausea rose in my stomach, the alcohol turning, tumbling, twisting.

This couldn't have been happening.

Not again.

Not again.

Not again.

My chair crashed behind me a second before the doors flew open. Because in the jumble of thoughts, one thought—one *name*—was as clear as the sky.

Dani.

Before my brother and our friends had time to process what was happening, I was up and rushing to the doors as they were thrust open.

My ears rang, anger coursing through me. Thoughts tumbled over one another like waves pounding onto the shore, crashing into each other.

Lance, sweaty and breathless, was the first to enter. He opened his mouth, but he didn't get the chance to speak.

I slammed him against the wall, the collar of his uniform twisting inside my palm. "Where is she?"

Lance's pale blue eyes widened. "Your Highness, I—"

I slammed his body against the wall again. The pictures hanging rattled as someone in the room gasped. Fear-filled thoughts filtered into my mind. I tried to block out the extraneous ones—the useless ones, the scared ones—but I struggled to sift through them, to cut their lines.

All my attention was on Dani—on finding the thoughts connecting to her.

I needed answers.

I needed them *now.*

"Where is my—"

A light hand fell on my shoulder, cutting me off.

Fynneares, Terin said down the mental connection, but I cut the connection off before he could say any more. I didn't need his soft words or melodic voice sweeping in and calming the hot fury that buzzed beneath my skin.

It didn't matter if Dani and I were together or not. I had lost too many people I cared about because of the Bullheaded King. I would not lose her, too.

My jaw cracked as I tightened my grip around Lance's shirt. "Tell me where she is," I commanded.

The color drained from Lance's already pale face. "Your Highness, she—she's at home," he stammered.

My knuckles cracked. "*Home*? Has she seen a healer?"

Lance nodded frantically. "Yes, but—"

"Is she *okay*?" I shouted, shaking him.

I tried to focus on his mind. I tried to isolate the thoughts filling my own, but I couldn't distinguish between the various voices filling my mind. I couldn't decipher the nonsense that piled atop each other as people moved around me.

My nails dug into Lance's uniform as I lifted him against the wall, his toes barely grazing the floor.

"Tell me!"

Lance nodded, his fingers scratching against the wall. "She is, but she—she's been unconscious. The healers said—"

"How long?" I growled, my head pounding.

Lance's brows drew together. "Your Highness?"

"How *long* has she been unconscious?" I spat, slamming him into the wall.

"A few weeks, Your Highness," Lance croaked out.

"*Weeks*?" I tugged him toward me, his eyes widening when he was only inches from my face. "When did she arrive?"

"A few hours ago."

"And I am only told of this *now*?"

Lance's mouth parted, his gaze bouncing to the others standing behind me as he stumbled over his words, "The commander said—"

"The *commander*?" A mangled laugh escaped my lips. It was a sound that did not belong to the calm, cocky prince. However, I no longer cared about etiquette or pleasantries or reputations. All I cared about was my best friend. "I am the *heir*."

"No—no one wanted to bother you."

I took a step forward. "*Bother* me? I am her—" I choked on my words.

Her what? I asked myself.

I wasn't her suitor anymore. Not even a fake one.

She was still my best friend; I was sure of that. Yet that title didn't come close to encompassing everything I felt for her at that moment and for the past couple of months.

"Jorian!" I shouted.

"Yes, Your Highness?" Jorian responded.

"Take me to her," I ordered.

"*Fynneares*."

My body went rigid at my mother's voice. I peeled my fingers from the coarse fabric of Lance's uniform—an act that took far more effort than I cared to admit.

When I turned around, my mouth fell open, but I couldn't speak. The anger pumping through me clouded my vision and thickened my tongue.

My mother took a step forward. "We need to talk."

THE FURY, while contained, had not subsided. It vibrated against my bones as the carriage jolted us around. Across from me, my mother sat with her hands folded in her lap, her gaze unwavering as she stared at me with an unspoken question on her lips.

"Mother, whatever it is, I'm sure it can wait. Dani is—"

She lifted a brow. "Danisinia will be *fine*, son."

"How can you say that? She's unconscious!" My voice echoed within the small space, and the horses pulling the carriage neighed as the words poured outside.

"The Royal Seer has said so," she said, her voice calm.

I scoffed, throwing my hands up before digging them into my hair. "Because Yelsania's visions have been so accurate as of late."

"We have an hour ride ahead of us until we arrive at the Ferrios manor. I believe we have the time to chat. But by all means, if you wish to walk there instead of talk to me, feel free to leave." She pointed at the door. "Best to roll, yes? I am sure the guards would love to see you make an even bigger fool of yourself than you already have the past few weeks drinking your way across Pontia."

I tossed my head back and sank into the cushion.

"I thought as much." She shifted in her seat. "Now, I believe there is something you have been keeping from me."

I sat up. "What could I possibly be keeping from you, Mother? It seems you already know everything there is to know."

She sighed. "You have kept the truth about you and Danisinia a secret for far too long, have you not?"

"Dani and I?"

Her brow flicked up, but my mother said nothing else. She stared at me as if her mere gaze could pull the memories from my mind.

I squirmed in my seat.

She couldn't do that. She had to be in contact with her victims to steal their memories.

At least, that's what she had always told us.

My gaze narrowed. Unless. . .

"You lied to me. You do not need to touch someone to pull their memories from them."

My mother rolled her eyes, an act I had never seen her do. "First, I am not the only one who has lied. Second, do not act so shocked. I am your mother, and some things are best kept secret." Her fingers brushed the ring hanging from her necklace. "Contact does help strengthen the memory's potency and allows me to share the memory with another. Long ago, it was the only way I could discover another's memory. But when a connection between soul bonds is realized and unified, our gifts shift and intensify—some in ways we can't even fathom. My soul bond might be gone, but the gift your father gave me all those years ago is not."

Outside, the wheels of the carriage creaked.

I rubbed the back of my neck, a thin layer of sweat forming on my skin. My hand fell to my lap, and my shoulders sagged. Sighing, I asked, "When did you find out?"

My mother reached out, placing a hand atop my knee. "Fynneares, I've known since the beginning."

"Then why didn't you say anything?"

She offered me a sad smile, but I wish she hadn't because there was more emotion within it than I cared to acknowledge.

"It wasn't my truth to tell," she said.

"Are you mad?"

She removed her hand from my knee and folded her hands in her lap, confusion pulling her brows together. "Why would I be mad, son?"

I wiped my hands across my trousers. "Because we have been lying to you for months. Because we tried to trick you into believing something that wasn't real."

When my gaze met my mother's, I was shocked at what I saw. The confusion had disappeared and had since morphed into amusement. Her mouth tipped up, and a quiet laugh rolled off her tongue.

"Why is that funny?" I asked. "We were pretending to court each other. Why *aren't* you mad? You told me I needed to find a wife, yet I lied about my courtship with Dani."

"Oh, you foolish, foolish child," she said, shaking her head. "I do not care about your pretend courtship."

"You don't?"

"Of course not." She tilted her head to the side. "It was real in the end, was it not?"

My gaze dropped to my lap, where I wrung my hands together.

"It does not matter how it began, Fynneares. Neither the status of your courtship nor whether it was pretend or not is the reason I wish to speak to you about Danisinia."

I looked up at her, brows drawn together. "Then what is it?"

My mother sighed, rubbing her temples with two fingers. "Do not tell me that you still do not know?"

"Know what?"

Her hand fell. "Let me ask you this instead: why has your knee been bouncing ever since we entered the carriage? Why are your hands clammy?"

"I—" My tongue grew heavy, and I looked down. Sure enough, my leg was bouncing up and down. I stilled it. Suddenly self-conscious, I also wiped my palms on my trousers for good measure. Clearing my throat, I said, "Dani is my best friend, and she's hurt. Of course, I'm going to be worried about her."

My mother shook her head. "Oh, Fynneares."

"What?"

"You still don't see it, do you?"

"See *what*?"

My mother held out her hand.

I stared at her open palm. She was not simply asking me to hold it to help calm my nerves; instead, she was asking to show me something—something I wasn't sure I was willing to see yet, something I wasn't sure I *deserved* to see.

My mother tipped her head toward her hand. "Your hand, please."

I sighed and gripped the edge of the cushion for extra stability before I reached out.

On contact, the world spun.

Round.

And round.

And round.

Until the world went black.

I WAVERED, *my body simultaneously feeling weightless and heavy.*

Peeling my eyes open, the scene before me slowly came into focus. When the world stopped spinning, the colors slowly separated as the memory unfolded before me.

I recognized the back of Lance's short blond hair immediately. His steps were rushed and haphazard as he raced down the hall in the Wilton manor beside Airos.

The captain glanced back, his graying brows twisting together.

A delicate hand rose in front of my face, and I recognized it as belonging to my mother.

Airos nodded.

Before Lance pushed the door open, a crash sounded on the other side. When Lance and Airos moved, my gaze locked onto the man rushing forward, frazzled and red-faced.

The man was nearly unrecognizable, yet all the same, he was me.

I had never seen myself appear so. . .distraught. So scared.

Others in the room stood, but I couldn't pull my attention away from this version of myself as I slammed Lance against the wall, rage clouding my countenance.

"Where is she?"

Through the small space between Lance and myself, I could see my guard's gaze widen as he stumbled, saying, "Your Highness—"

The pictures rattled on the wall as I slammed his body against it. My knuckles blanched as I gripped Lance's shirt. "Where is my—"

My mother moved forward. She lifted a hand and placed it on my shoulder.

I faintly recalled having believed Terin had reached out as his thoughts tried to break through the rage. But in fact, it was my mother's delicate hand falling upon my shoulder and squeezing.

When her hand fell, the floor dropped beneath me, and the room spun. Flashes of red and black and purple twisted around, melting away the scene and distorting my vision once again.

My BREATHING WAS LABORED as I came to.

I wished I could have blamed my mother's gift, but I couldn't. It wasn't the world spinning around me as she ripped the memory away from me and as the ground shattered beneath my feet.

No, the rapid patter of my heart was not a result of the nauseating effects of her gift.

Not at all.

"You see now. Don't you, Fynneares?" she asked, her voice quiet and careful, as if I was made of glass and would shatter if she spoke too loudly.

My throat seized up as my heart thundered against my ribcage.

For years, I had been looking for that missing piece, waiting for it to fall into place.

I had thought it would feel like floating on a cloud, like the wind on the breeze. Blissful and peaceful.

But what I felt—what I had been feeling since Dani and I had started courting each other—wasn't blissful.

It wasn't sunshine and rainbows or as sweet as strawberries.

Instead, it was earth-shattering.

It was the ground being torn apart.

It was the pressure building inside a volcano.

It was destructive.

Uncontrollable and unpredictable.

I looked up at my mother, and finally, I understood.

I finally understood the chaotic feelings that had been consuming me, the adrenaline that coursed through my veins, and the way everything went silent when I was around Dani—and *only* Dani.

I had almost voiced the truth when yelling at Lance, but the word had gotten stuck in my throat as if my conscience had pulled it back. As if it knew I wasn't ready.

I didn't know if I was ready now either; however, I didn't think I had the choice to deny the inevitable.

Dani was more than my best friend.

She was my *everything*.

The missing piece I had been searching for, waiting for, *hoping* for.

My soul bond.

And the only thing I could think about at that moment was that I might have realized it too late.

CHAPTER 39
FYNN

My knees hit the ground as the tears rolled down my cheek and spilled onto the quilt. With a shaking hand, I reached out and grabbed Dani's hand as she lay in her bed, unconscious.

She was here. She was severely injured, but she was *here*. She was home. And that was all that mattered.

Her curls were flattened and spread across her pillow. Her brown skin was tinted with a sickly hue. Her lips were chapped, and old bruises peppered her skin. A thin blanket lay atop her, covering her legs and stomach. Above it, though, a long cotton bandage wrapped around her entire torso from the stab wound she had suffered. And although I could not see it, there must have been a ghastly scar beneath the wrapping.

I kissed the top of her scarred knuckles. Scooting my stool closer, I leaned over the bed, resting my head upon my other arm.

The Bull King would pay. He would pay for all the pain, suffering, and anguish he caused.

But right now, Dani needed me.

Hours went by as I sat beside her bed. The afternoon turned to dusk, yet I did not move.

At some point, someone called out to me. Someone tried to pull me away.

Someone tried to tell me to leave.

But I wouldn't leave. I couldn't.

I would never choose to leave Dani again. Not while I lived and breathed.

Never again.

"HE'LL BE MAD," someone whispered.

The voice was familiar, yet I couldn't identify it. My mind was too groggy from the exhaustion that plagued my body. I tried to push through the fog, but it was too thick, too heavy.

"It does not matter," another muddled voice said. "The healers need to attend to her."

"But—"

"Do it, Terin."

My eyes sprung open, my hand tightening around Dani's.

But it was too late. My brother already had his claws in me.

Sleep wrapped its shadowed tendrils around my mind and pulled. I tried to fight it—tried to fight the sweet pull of Terin's gift blanketing me. But the more I fought it, the tighter it wrapped around me.

I promised myself I wouldn't leave.

I *promised*.

Yet I fell anyway.

Sleep embraced me, forcing me underneath its heavy pull. And there was nothing I could do to stop it.

CHAPTER 40
DANI

The door to my room flew open.

Helena jumped, screeching in shock, causing me to jolt. I grimaced in pain as the muscles in my body tensed.

"What—" I swallowed my words as I met the intruder's gaze.

Fynn stumbled back, hitting the doorframe. His brown eyes were wild, and the skin beneath them was a deep purple, as if he hadn't slept for days. He gripped the doorknob, his knuckles blanching as he stared, pale-faced.

"You're—you're awake," he said at last. His throat dipped. "When—when did you wake?"

As he scanned me, I shifted, pulling the blanket up. "I woke up this morning."

Standing beside the bed, Helena fell into a curtsy, mumbling, "Your Highness, Miss Ferrios needs rest. You should come back—"

"I'm fine, Helena," I interrupted, my voice steadier this time.

My hand slid across my torso, where a wrapping covered the wound. I had been in and out of sleep for the past several hours. The last thing I remembered was falling. The healers this morning said I had not suffered any permanent damage, but a scar would indeed remain despite the best healers having been assigned to me. Theenah, the head of medicine, personally overseeing my care.

By the request of the Crown Prince.

My throat dipped.

I shifted, trying to sit up. Pain spiked through my torso at the movement, and I fell back onto the bed.

Fynn was in front of me in seconds, his knees smacking into the ground. His hands hovered over me, not quite touching me, as if he were unsure if he could.

I didn't know what was worse: that he no longer felt like he *could* touch me or that I still *wanted* him to.

"You were saying, Miss Ferrios?" Helena retorted.

I rolled my eyes.

"I'll go fetch Theenah," Fynn said, standing. "She can—"

"No," I said before he could finish. "I have already seen Theenah and several other healers. I am *fine*. I am only sore." I tried to move back, but another bout of pain soared through my bones.

Fynn's attention flicked to my ribcage.

The blanket had slipped when I moved, revealing the wrapping. The healers had said the soreness would only last a couple of days. Even Theenah couldn't get rid of all the pain; apparently, there were still limits to the healer's gifts.

Helena leaned forward, hesitant. "Miss Ferrios has only woken up a few hours ago, Your Highness. She needs rest."

"Helena, please." I squeezed my eyes shut.

When I woke up, my mother was knitting at the side of my bed. The moment my eyelashes fluttered across my cheek, she shouted for Helena and the healers. Since then, Helena had barely left my side, and her constant worrying quickly became an annoyance. While the housekeeper might have meant well, her buzzing nerves were doing nothing to help me rest.

"Very well," Helena said before curtsying to Fynn. "Your Highness, please send word if anything—"

"Helena," I grumbled, pressing my head further into my pillow.

Helena hummed dismissively. But as her footsteps exited, I heard Fynn whisper to her, "I will."

When the door shut, Fynn said, quiet and low, "I'm sorry I wasn't here when you awoke."

"I didn't expect you to be. You have your own duties to attend to," I said, but the words were dust on my tongue. While it wasn't a lie, it was hard to say it aloud.

"That's not—" Fynn shook his head, his hair flying in different directions. He dropped his gaze to his hands. "When you returned, I came as soon as I found out. You were unconscious when I arrived. The healers and seer said you would recover, but I couldn't leave. At some point, Terin coaxed me to sleep and dragged me out. He may or may not have received an earful from me when I awoke the next day."

A feeling I did not wish to acknowledge rolled in my stomach. Shoving it down, I asked, "Why didn't you leave? After all, if they said I would be fine, there was no point in staying."

Fynn brushed back his hair, flattening out some of the mess. A flurry of emotions flashed across his countenance, but they were too fleeting to identify. "You are my best friend, Dani. I wanted to be here when you woke."

Not knowing what to make of his words, I said nothing.

According to my father, I had been in and out of unconsciousness for the past two weeks. When I had leaped to save Quint, the assailant who held a blade to Quint's throat had turned and struck me. However, before the enemy's blade could hit a major organ, Moris had dropped his paralysis on another guard and froze the man mid-strike. Quint had then driven his short sword through the attacker's chest. Sylvia had only been knocked out briefly, awakening before the last two enemies had been killed. Once my squad had taken care of the remaining assailants, they ran with Quint carrying me.

Without access to healers, they had made sure to wrap my wound and keep it clean as they traveled through the mountains and the forests. But when I had awoken, I had fought them in a fever-driven haze. My body and mind were still in the fight despite having been miles away from it by then.

After that, Moris had kept me in a semi-frozen state as they traveled back to the ship and then to Pontia.

Eventually, the paralysis mixed with the blood loss had been too much for my body and mind, and I had fallen into a coma soon after.

While the grogginess had since subsided, the pain in my muscles had not due to the mixture of soreness from being immobile and the wounds covering my body.

In the silence, Fynn's gaze remained on me. Part of me wished he would look away. Being under his scrutiny for so long made me want to squirm, but I was also helpless.

And I hated feeling helpless.

I tightened my grip around the blanket.

I had yet to see the gash slicing across my ribcage that the healers had mentioned. However, I had seen a flash of my reflection in the vanity earlier. Old bruises covered my face and skin, my flesh painted with shades of violent purple and green.

I was Danisinia Ember Ferrios.

I was the great-granddaughter of Valor Ferrios, the fiercest warrior in Pontian history, the man who had won the final battle in the Great War. I was supposed to be strong, unshakable, unbreakable. Yet here I was, sitting in my bed, wrapped and wounded after a reconnaissance mission.

This was not the version of myself I ever wanted to show anyone.

"You might be hurt, Dani," Fynn whispered, "but you are neither helpless nor weak."

"Get out of my head, Fynn," I spat, throwing up my walls and staring at the ceiling.

Fynn huffed. "I do not need to be in your head to know your thoughts. I know you better than I know myself."

I scoffed.

The edge of the bed dipped as he leaned his elbows onto it.

"Moris told me what happened," he whispered.

I bit my lip as the back of my eyes burned. "Don't say it," I hissed.

"Say what?"

My nose twitched, my nostrils flaring. I squeezed the blanket. "Don't say I told you so or that I shouldn't have gone. I don't need to hear it, nor do I want to."

"I wasn't going to say that, Dani. I—"

I shook my head. "We were ambushed," I said, ignoring him. "I don't—I don't remember much. We had just made camp. Quint had decided to take the first watch. But I should have been the one to do so." My gaze danced across the room, unable to focus on anything as the memory of the moments before blacking out resurfaced. "I should have searched the surroundings before I went to sleep. But we had been traveling for ten days straight with little rest. We were all tired. I was—"

I peered at Fynn but then looked away immediately.

When I looked at Fynn, I knew what had happened.

I was distracted.

But I couldn't admit that. Not to Fynn.

He reached out, but when his hand was an inch or two above my thigh, he pulled it back. Shaking his head, he stood. "This is all my fault."

"No, it's not. You couldn't have predicted—"

At the end of the bed, he stopped and gripped the railing, his hair cascading down his face as he stared at the foot of the bed. His knuckles blanched as his fingers tightened around the metal rod.

"I should have known, Dani. I should have known, but I was selfish. I was chasing a man who always manages to be one step ahead of us." He pushed himself away from the bed and began to pace, his fingers digging into the brown waves that kissed his chin. "How many times has my mother warned me that the king was not one to be dealt with lightly? That it would take careful, strategic planning if we wanted to beat him?"

"Fynn," I said, but he didn't hear me.

"I didn't listen, though. I never listen, do I?" He dug the heels of his palms across his face. "That's what the entire kingdom says, anyway. I never listen. I'm too rash. I'm too—"

Fynn's mouth opened, but I was done listening to him spit lies.

"Fynn, it doesn't matter. What's done is done!"

When Fynn finally met my gaze, his deep brown eyes were soaked with sadness and regret. However, I didn't want to be another thing he regretted.

"Dani, I'm—"

"You have nothing to apologize for. It was my fault."

"How—"

I pointed at my chest. "*I* was the one who was distracted. I was the one who neglected my duties. I know my role. I should have surveyed the area and made sure we were safe. I should have had the first watch."

"But—"

"No," I said, shaking my head despite the throbbing pain in my side. "No buts and no excuses. If you are going to blame anyone, blame me, but never yourself."

His lips parted, but I gave him one look, and he snapped his mouth shut.

"Never blame yourself, Fynn," I repeated.

After a second, he nodded and sat at the edge of the bed. I tried to move and make more room for him, but Fynn pushed me back down with a gentle hand.

I wanted to fight back, but at his touch, I almost gasped. His palm was cool against my collarbone, a welcome kiss on my scorching skin as the medication worked overtime.

The pit of my stomach twisted, and I squeezed my eyes shut.

He sat back, yet the feeling lingered.

It's the fever, I told myself. *Nothing more.*

"I'm not some fragile princess, Fynn," I said, trying to forget his touch.

Fynn chuckled, reaching forward and brushing a stray curl behind my ear. "I never said you were, nor did I say I wanted you to be."

His tone was light, yet his words were lead in my stomach. Quint's question the night of the attack surfaced, but this was not the time to have that discussion.

Fynn pointed at the discolored bandage. "When was the last time they changed this?"

I shrugged. The wrapping no doubt needed to be changed, and based on the stench of sea and pine on my skin, I also needed a proper bath.

Putting aside my pride, I sighed and asked, "Could you get Helena? Let her know I would like to take a bath?"

"I'll help you," Fynn said, already standing.

My eyes widened. Fynn might have seen my body before, but he hadn't seen the scars. *I* hadn't even seen them. It was one thing for him to *say* I was not weak, but if he saw the truth. . .

"That's a kind offer but not necessary," I mumbled.

Fynn brushed a hand across the bottom of my chin, tipping my face up. "Let me help you, Ferrios. Please."

I had expected to see pity covering Fynn's countenance, but I only found concern, sorrow, and desperation.

Unclenching my jaw, I released the blanket. "All right."

Fynn smiled and nodded before turning around. He slapped the edge of the door frame and disappeared into my bathing chambers.

CHAPTER 41

FYNN

MY MIND WAS A SEA OF THOUGHTS, BUT, FOR ONCE, THEY ONLY belonged to me. Because when Dani hissed as she stood, red rage heated my blood. It soared from my toes to the pit of my stomach to my temples. It was territorial and overbearing. It was absolutely and completely primal.

And it went against *everything* Dani believed in and fought for.

She didn't want someone protecting her.

She didn't want someone controlling her.

She was the fighter, the warrior.

If Dani knew what I was thinking, she would push me away. She would believe I was trying to take everything she was away from her.

So, despite how much it pained me to do it, I pushed everything I was feeling down and kept my mouth shut.

Dani thought asking for help was a sign of weakness. She would rather dig her nails into her bed and swallow the pain down than ask someone to help. She thought that by not *needing* someone's help, she was somehow stronger and more capable. However, I have watched my mother lean on her advisors time and time again. Never once did it make me think any less of her or her ability to rule as queen.

I wanted Dani to know it was all right to lean on someone.

I stepped forward and gingerly wrapped my arm around Dani's waist. When she didn't push me away—when she instead leaned against me—the pit of my stomach heated. As my veins buzzed with an intoxicating energy and set my soul aflame, I wondered how I had never noticed the sensation before. Had this feeling always been there? Had I subconsciously ignored it?

I didn't know how I could have possibly dismissed it, though. It was overwhelming and blatantly obvious.

My mother once told me that soul bonds appear when we least expect them and often when we need them the most.

It should have been a comfort, a relief.

It seemed I had been searching for my soul bond forever. But now that I had found her, I was scared shitless.

Not only because I had almost lost her, but what if Dani decided to ignore the bond? Soul bonds might have been connected by fate, but fate only had so much power over people. Dani already questioned me. She believed I wished her to be someone she wasn't, some idealized version of some obtuse societal expectation, but all I wanted was *her*.

All of her.

Every version I had witnessed—the woman laughing and wiping ale from her lip with the back of her hand at a rundown tavern, the one draped in silk and glowing in the golden hue of the sun, the one who threatened to stab me countless times as a child.

I wanted every single version of her, now and for the rest of our days.

I swore I would protect it with my life if Dani even gave me a sliver of her heart.

She would never question her worth.

She would never question her ability.

She would never question my truth.

She would never question who she was or if she was good enough.

To me, she was already the queen of my heart, and I would gladly bow before her without hesitation.

If she let me.

Dani hissed in pain as she took a step forward. I held her closer, tucking her beneath my arm. While I couldn't erase the pain or make the scars disappear or rewrite the past, I could lessen the pain—at least a little.

And for Dani, I would do anything.

We stopped beside the bathtub, now filled. With a pull of the ribbon, Dani loosened the thin robe. I walked behind her and grabbed the fabric to help her out of it.

"I can manage by myself," she mumbled, spite lacing her voice.

"I know you can," I said, and unable to help myself, I placed a gentle kiss on the back of her head. "But please, let me help. I need. . ."

Dani peered over her shoulder at me. "You need what?"

I bit down on my tongue. I hadn't meant to say anything. This wasn't the time to have this conversation. She was alive. She would heal. And yet. . .

"Fynn, what is it?" Dani asked.

Sighing, I brushed a hand through my hair. "When Lance came storming into the Wilton's manor, I thought—" I swallowed, the words lodging themselves in my throat. But with Dani's eyes locked on me, awaiting an explanation, I forced myself to continue, "I thought I had lost you. His thoughts were wild. I couldn't—I didn't know what happened."

Dani faced me. Then, hesitating momentarily, she pressed her hands lightly against my chest. Her hard exterior softened, her brows smoothing as she said, "You didn't lose me, though, Fynn. You never could."

My gaze flicked across her face, from the freckles on her nose to the faded bruises on her temple. I leaned into her touch, closing my eyes as her warmth surrounded me.

She was here, standing before me, alive and healing, and yet. . .

"Then why does it feel like I already did?" The question left my lips before I could pull it back.

Dani didn't respond, though.

When I opened my eyes, she was looking at me with sorrow clouding her hazel irises, dimming the gold flecks that once sparkled there.

I took a deep, steadying breath and offered her a small smile.

Her lack of an answer was answer enough as she turned away.

So, I turned, too, taking a step toward the door.

"I'll go get—"

"Stay," Dani whispered, her voice as quiet as a light morning breeze. I almost didn't believe I heard her until she added, "Please."

Those two words together. . .they were hope.

They were *everything*.

I returned to her side.

Dani peeled the robe from her shoulders, revealing the bandage wrapped around her torso. Then, the robe pooled onto the floor.

I swallowed, and with some willpower granted to me by the gods, I kept my gaze up. Now was not the time to let my gaze trail down her body despite desperately wanting to after our time apart. I struggled, though. Because at that point, that's who I was: a desperate man.

But Dani deserved better. She didn't deserve desperation.

I offered her my arm. When her fingers wrapped around it as she stepped into the tub, her palm heated the blood in my veins. I wasn't sure if it was because of the soul bond or if it was just *her*. Either way, she was a magnet, and there was nothing I could do but step forward and get closer.

Her face scrunched up as her free hand flew to her side. I shifted, stabilizing her.

"I got you," I whispered.

When Dani narrowed her eyes at me, I cleared my throat and threw on the smirk that could mask everything stirring beneath it.

"Don't want you to fall," I added, punctuating the remark with a wink.

Dani rolled her eyes. But before she could turn all the way around, I saw the flicker of amusement sparkling among the gold and green swirls in her irises and the faintest twitch of her lips.

Once she was standing inside the tub, she reached for the wrapping and grimaced. "Do you mind?" Dani asked, the question almost inaudible.

"Of course," I said.

With shaking hands, I gently peeled the cotton. As I reached around her torso, Dani stood still. Her hands out wide as if she couldn't bear to touch me.

Swatting the thought away, I kept my eyes trained on her back as more and more skin was revealed. I gathered the stained fabric in my hand, balling it up as I breathed through my nose, my chest rising and falling hard. The closer the cotton fabric was to her skin, the more discolored it was.

I tossed the strip of cotton into the bin in the corner of the bathroom. The bundle made a soft thud as it hit the bottom of the trash bin.

Dani looked down at her side, her eyes watering. "Gods, it's hideous, isn't it?"

The scar ran from the back of her hip to the top of her rib cage. The wound had already closed and scarred over, but her russet brown skin was still marked with bruises.

In that jagged line, though, Dani saw her supposed failure. But when I looked at it, all I saw was a warrior who would give her life to save the ones she cared about.

"No, it's not."

Dani snorted. "Very funny, Fynn."

"I'm not joking," I whispered.

Shaking her head, Dani lowered herself into the warm water, her hands gripping the sides of the porcelain tub as her arms trembled.

As she settled in the tub, I hesitated.

Over the years, I had visited many soldiers who were in recovery. One of the hardest things to watch was their view of themselves change, how their confidence faltered and withered away once they were wounded. I didn't know if I could witness Dani experience the same thing.

While she put up a good front, deep down, I knew she was hurting more than she let on. Perhaps what she wanted most was to be alone.

But she asked me to stay, I reminded myself.

Maybe being alone was the last thing she needed.

I grabbed the washcloth and sat on the stool. I placed my free hand softly on Dani's shoulder to avoid scaring her away.

Still, her breath hitched, the muscles in her shoulders straining.

"It's just me, Dani," I whispered.

I didn't move until she exhaled and her shoulders sank. Once she relaxed, I guided Dani back. When her back was against the porcelain, I went to the other end of the tub. Dani's arms were wrapped around her legs. Bubbles covered the water's surface, and the scent of orange filled the air.

Squatting down, I held out a hand.

"What?" She asked, her head snapping up as she squeezed her legs tighter to her torso.

"Give me your leg," I said, wiggling my fingers, hand still extended.

"Why?"

I tilted my head to the side. "Dani, you could barely get into the tub by yourself. Let me take care of you."

"I'm more than capable of washing my feet, Fynn." Her brows bunched together, forcing that stubborn little vein to pulse in the center of her forehead, a perfect little *Y*.

I swallowed the inappropriate chuckle in my throat and held out the washcloth. "Then, by all means, prove it."

Dani looked at the washcloth, then back at me. With a look that could have burned a hole through paper, Dani resigned and leaned back against the tub.

"Fine," she grumbled. She pointed a firm finger at me, the pain that had just covered her features practically extinguished. "But if you dare try to tickle me, there are plenty of knives in my room that I wouldn't mind chucking at you."

"Do you truly think you'll be able to get to them fast enough?" I asked, almost failing to hold back my laughter.

Narrowing her eyes, Dani ran her hand through the water and struck.

Water flew in the air, splashing me in my face.

Wiping a hand over my face and pushing back my damp hair, I winked. "I promise to be a complete gentleman."

Dani rolled her eyes, but a small smile slipped over her lips.

Grinning from the small victory, I lathered the washcloth with one of the essential oils beside the porcelain tub. The scent of cinnamon filled the room as I massaged the oil into the cloth. As I wrung the washcloth, I chuckled and said, "This is just like when I was forced to give my grandmother a bath."

Dani kicked, causing more water to spray out and onto my clothes.

Immediately, she pressed a hand to her side.

Shaking off the water, I sighed, my mouth forming a flat line. "You're only hurting yourself when you do that."

Dani shrugged. "It was worth it. You compared this to bathing your grandmother!" She extended her leg, and I wrapped my fingers around her ankle, stilling it.

"I was only joking. You're much prettier to look at," I said with a wink. Then I leaned in closer, massaging her foot. "Plus, your skin doesn't sag like hers."

Dani's leg jerked in my grasp as she tried to kick me in the face. I tightened my grip around her ankle.

"Grandma Dahlia at least smelled better." I sniffed the air, wrinkling my nose in jest. "Although dirt and sweat are only marginally better than stale roses and an old tin can."

Dani gasped, a red tint blooming across her cheeks. "Fynn!"

"Kidding." A mischievous smirk crept up on my face. "You smell *just* as bad."

Dani's mouth fell open, her hazel eyes widening as she stared at me in horror. Her face flushed an even brighter shade of red, forcing laughter to tumble out of my mouth.

Water smacked my chest immediately, which only caused me to laugh more, and Dani eventually joined in.

When I recovered, I inspected my soaked shirt. Setting the cloth down, I quickly undid the buttons and stripped it off. As I did, I could feel Dani's gaze on me, watching my every move.

I gave Dani an accusatory glance. "If you wanted me out of my shirt, you could have asked, Ferrios."

Dani rolled her eyes again, chuckling. "You are the absolute worst. You do know that, right?"

I arched a brow. "The worst or the best?" I glanced at the leg in my hands and added. "After all, I am washing your feet for you."

"Well, right now, you're not doing much of that. Are you?" Dani retorted. But as she leaned against the tub, her remark lost its bitterness.

Huffing, I shook my head and focused on the task at hand. Using the washcloth, I scrubbed her feet, massaging her calf as I did so. I then ran the washcloth over her shin. At some point in the process, Dani had closed her eyes, the wrinkles in her forehead softening. I smiled to myself as I made quick work of washing her legs.

The jokes were only a distraction. The distraction had worked based on how Dani slunk back against the tub, her head tipping up to the ceiling as her muscles ever-so-slowly relaxed.

Even as I reached out, pulling on the thread connecting her thoughts to mine, I didn't feel the tension swarming the edge of her mental barricade. The dark gloom that had hovered around her mind when I had first entered the room was no longer present.

It may not have been a permanent fix, but it was a start.

Quietly, I moved toward the center of the tub. When I grabbed one of her arms, Dani peered at me through heavy eyes.

Too exhausted to make a snide comment, she shut her eyes again, and I took that as permission to continue.

I massaged the oils first into her arms, then her palms. Her palms were covered with callouses, a testament to the work she put into her training every day for the past decade. Yet, despite the callouses, her skin remained soft and silky. I couldn't help but take a minute while Dani dozed off to appreciate the woman sitting before me. She was tougher than anyone I knew. Fearless, capable, and beautiful.

A thick layer of bubbles covered most of her body. It was hard not to marvel at Dani's beauty—her toned arms, the bow of her knee, her gleaming neck, her flushed face slick with sweat from the steam—

Dani shifted, and I shook myself from my stupor.

Not the time, I reminded myself.

I stood and placed the chair directly behind her. Gently, I brushed a piece of hair from her face, my finger sweeping across the contours of her face as my gaze latched onto the freckles peppering her nose. Carefully, I gathered Dani's curls into my hands.

Dani leaned forward slightly and tilted her head back without saying a word or even opening her eyes.

And I stood there, dumbfounded, as water dripped down her neck and over her collarbone.

After a moment that I wished I could bottle up, I poured water onto her hair with a careful, albeit shaking, hand, using my other to prevent water from spilling into her eyes.

Dani passed me one of the vials along the tub's edge. I took it and popped the top off. Notes of cinnamon wafted out of the clear container, and I smiled because one word came to mind: *home.*

I began massaging the oil into her scalp with meticulous care.

Yet, Dani's shoulders did not relax. They remained close to her ears as she shifted in the tub and wrapped her arms around her legs again. "I'm sorry we failed the mission. I know how much this meant to you."

The blood rushed from my face as I turned to stone.

No mission was more important than her safety.

"Dani," I sighed, my fingers curling into her hair.

"You weren't there, Fynn." Then, Dani relayed every moment of that night.

At first, her words were cold and detached, as if she were trying to remove the emotion from the events. As though she could isolate them from everything else. But as she continued, the muscles in the side of my neck strained as her voice twisted. I didn't need to reach into her mind to know her inner thoughts because they seeped into every word: the disappointment, the anger, the pain.

Dani feared not being strong enough, not being good enough, and not being able to uphold her family's name.

But she was more than enough.

"I should've noticed," she said. "I should've heard them coming."

My hands fell from her hair as I washed away the rest of the suds.

Enough, I thought, pushing myself up and slipping off my shoes.

I stepped into the tub, socks and pants still on.

Dani screeched. "Fynn! What are you—"

I sunk to my knees in front of her, the warm water splashing up from the tub and onto the floor.

I placed my hands on each side of her face and forced her to look at me. "Listen to me, Danisinia."

She blinked, eyes wide, but she didn't interrupt.

"I said it before, and I will say it again: *you* are more important to me than any mission. I thought I lost you, Dani. I thought that you were gone, that I was too late."

"Too late?" Dani asked, brows twisting together. "Too late for what?"

I took a deep breath. We had wasted too much time already, and who knew how much time we had left. Life was too fleeting to be hesitant.

"I should have said this to you before. You, Danisinia Ember Ferrios, are my best friend. I never wanted you to choose between your career and me. I would never ask you to put your dreams to the wayside. And I should have told you that the night of the dinner." My touch softened, caressing her cheek. "I should have said a lot of things before you left, but I was foolish and stupid and stuck in my head. But I'm saying them now."

Her fingers wrapped around my wrist, tugging my hand away from her face. "Fynn, I'm not—your life, your future, it doesn't—"

I shook my head, unwilling to hear the excuses. Because that's what they were—excuses. But we both had been too afraid of the future for too long.

"I do not know what our future will look like, Dani. All I know is I want you in it. I want you beside me for the rest of my life, for as long as that may be."

"Fynn, I—" she swallowed.

"Tell me right now you don't feel what I feel, Dani. Tell me right now that there's something inside of you that you've been trying to make sense of. Something fighting you. A feeling you can't explain," I said, pleading. My fingers curled into her hair, and I inched closer, causing more water to spill over the tub's edge. "Your walls are a mile high. You've never let me in, not completely, not entirely. So please, Dani. I'm begging you. Tell me the truth." I grabbed her hand and held it to my chest, where my heart ricocheted against my ribcage. When her skin met mine, my whole body heated. "Tell me you hear it too."

Her eyes bounced across my face, but in her gaze, I knew I was right. She felt it, too—the song that buzzed between us, where our skin touched. That invisible thread that connected us, that weaved our souls together.

At that moment, it was undeniable.

"If you'll have me, I want you at my side. I want to be the first to say good morning to you and the last one to say goodnight. I want to be the last one to wish you safe travels and the first one to welcome you home."

A tear rolled down her face. With my thumb, I wiped it away. But she shook her head. She was still fighting it. I could see that in the pain that twisted her brows together, that creased her forehead.

"But there's never been a queen who—"

I squeezed her hand. "It doesn't matter what has come before us, Dani. I want you and only you. I will *only* want you for the rest of my life. If you wanted me to abdicate from the throne, I would."

"Fynn, I could never ask for you to do that. You care about this kingdom too much."

"I know you never would ask, for you care about this kingdom, too." I weaved my fingers into the wet curls at the back of her neck and pulled her closer, resting my forehead on hers. "Let me love you the way you deserve to be loved, Dani. I've let you slip through my hands one too many times. I do not want to lose you ever again. It's you or no one for me, Dani."

Her palms caressed my face. Her hands were shaking, her body trembling. I weaved my fingers between hers. When I leaned back and our eyes met, something snapped.

Fire erupted from my core, soaring through my veins and up my chest. It blanketed every limb, muscle, and every other part of me. A sweet, honeyed song rang throughout my body and hummed all around me.

Dani smiled. "It's always been you, Fynn," she whispered, an untamable fire roaring beneath her eyes as the thread connecting our souls wrapped around each other, stringing us together and uniting our hearts.

I leaned back and tipped her chin up. "And it always will be you."

The corners of her mouth flicked up.

"I love you."

Her voice was as solid as iron, yet her lips had not moved.

Shock ripped through me as I reached for the thread connecting her mind to mine.

Her mental shields were down—the fortress she had spent years building completely and utterly obliterated. Everything she had kept hidden from me, locked away in the safety of the farthest parts of her mind, came pouring out.

It had *always* been Dani. I had simply been too blind to see it, but Dani had known.

She had always known.

CHAPTER 42
DANI

FOUR MONTHS LATER

"Sylv, are you sure this isn't too much?" I asked, running my hand over the rough fabric that made my arms itch every time they brushed it.

"Too much of what?" Sylvia asked, fixing their hair in the mirror after the handmaidens had spent the past half hour pinning it up.

Sylvia wore an elegant lavender dress that was simple yet beautiful. Meanwhile, I was covered in layers of tulle, lace, and whatever other fabric and embellishments the royal seamstress, Everly, was forced to add at my mother's request. The dress was beautiful—a true piece of art. It should have been displayed in some marbled hall for people to gawk at and admire—not to be walked or danced in.

However, this was my wedding. A *royal* wedding, my mother had reminded me time and time again. And she insisted that everything be big—including this godsforsaken dress.

Over the past four months, my mother and Esmeray had spent

copious hours planning our wedding. The very moment my mother discovered Fynn and I were soul bonds, she spun into action. Even though I had opposed the extravaganza, my mother insisted. So, when I wasn't training, she forced me to attend meetings about napkins and glassware—long, tedious, tiresome meetings that seemed to have no end.

I didn't care about the minuscule details that only my mother would notice. All I cared about was placing my hand in Fynn's and his in mine as we exchanged the golden rings our parents forged from the isle off the coast.

At one point, I even tried to persuade the mothers to forgo the wedding entirely. The wedding was only a symbolic representation of the bond that connected Fynn and me. We could have exchanged the rings alone in a field of lilacs under the moon and stars. It didn't matter to me.

My mother, however, would hear none of it.

Yet when I did offer my opinion on the cutlery or the flowers, she ignored me. When I would turn to Esmeray for help, the queen looked at me with amusement and sympathy.

The queen was of no help, to say the least.

The dress was the one item on the list I was excited about, but my mother had taken that away from me, too. And now I was stuck in this giant ball of scratchy fabrics that irritated my skin.

I couldn't even see a remnant of who I was in my reflection. I picked up the heavy skirt and swished it as I looked in the mirror. The dress scratched against the hardwood floors, producing a horrendous sound.

"Too much. . .fabric, lace, diamonds?" I asked, my voice raising. "Too much of *everything*!"

Sylvia placed a hand on their hip, cocking their head to the side. "Dani, you are marrying a *prince*. What did you expect?"

"First, I expected to be wearing something—I don't know! Something I liked? But this ball of fluff and organza has my mother written all over it." I tossed the skirts from my hand. When I tried crossing my arms over my chest, a jewel knicked me. I groaned, throwing my hands out wide. "Second, I'm marrying Fynn, Sylv."

"Fynn, the man who is going to be our king one day," Sylvia said, stepping forward and grabbing my shoulders with a firm grip. "Major, *you* are going to be queen one day. It only makes sense that your wedding is extravagant. Did you know that people across the kingdom are celebrating your marriage tonight?"

"You're exaggerating."

"I am not, and you know it. Your marriage is special. Not only because the two of you are soul bonds, but because your unification symbolizes a hope for the generations to come. The rebellions in the southern kingdoms have only increased in the past few months. This wedding is a reminder to everyone that even in the darkness, we need to hold on to the good that comes in our lives. These moments—the moments of happiness and love—are the ones that will get us through the upcoming war. Fynn is a master at charming the hearts of the people, and you are a skilled, selfless leader. Today is a promise not only between you and Fynn, but between you and the people. That you will vow to protect them, lead them, and guide them to a better tomorrow."

Sweat coated my palms. When I tried to wipe them on the dress, the gemstones woven throughout the embroidery did little to help. "No pressure, then, huh?"

"By the gods, you truly are perfect for him." Sylvia shoved me in the shoulder, laughing. "But I'm serious, Dani."

I grabbed Sylvia's hand and squeezed it. "I know, Sylv."

"The title of queen might be a ways away, but it will befall you, nevertheless. This is your wedding day. Nothing is too much. The dress is beautiful, even if it's not. . .you"

I gasped, shoving her. "See! You hate it too!"

Sylvia pursed their lips. "My opinion does not matter."

"But your opinion is the same as mine."

"It's. . ." Sylvia groaned, unable to hold back the lie or the laughter. "It's a lot, all right? Beautiful, but a lot."

I sighed and stared at the ceiling. With a huff, I said, "Everything about today is a lot."

Sylvia held up a hand. "Hold on. Do me a favor and keep your panic at bay."

"I'm not panicking," I argued.

Sylvia started walking backward, heading for the door.

My heart thumped, and my eyes widened. I took a step forward. "Wait, where are you going?"

When they reached the door, Sylvia grabbed the handle and held up a finger. "Give me one minute. I know just the thing that will fix this."

The door cracked open.

"Sylv!" I shouted, but Sylvia was already running out of the room.

The door slammed shut behind them, and I stomped my foot on the pine floors, exhaling a frustrated groan. Did doing so make me appear like a child and the opposite of a queen or a major? Perhaps, but I didn't care.

I was alone, and I was most certainly panicking.

With nothing else to do, I turned back to the mirror and peered at the dress, narrowing my eyes as if, by merely staring at it hard enough, it would burn to ash. When nothing happened, I turned my attention to the dainty tiara sitting atop my head.

The tiara was made of thin, golden arches that twisted together. When Esmeray brought it with her that morning, it took my breath away.

As she set it down on the vanity, she cleared the room of the handmaidens.

The moment the door was shut, she turned to me and grabbed my hands, saying, "The night of the solstice, I didn't tell you this, but I had always hoped it would be you."

"What do you mean?" I asked, my brows drawing together and my heart hammering in my chest.

Esmeray smiled. "That you were the one he had been looking for, his soul bond. When the two of you were growing up, I saw how he protected you, and you him. The way he would help you up when you fell." Esmeray chuckled, her gaze growing distant as if she was reliving a memory. "You, of course, would shove him down whenever he did. You have always been stubborn, but so has he. I knew how much finding his soul bond meant to him, and I had never wanted Fynn to give up that hope. But on the day of the crowning ceremony, I had to make a choice—as queens often must. Soul bonds come to us when we need them the most, when we are not looking." Esmeray cupped my cheek, her touch light and delicate. "Sometimes they are right in front of us, hiding in plain sight. I saw Fynn losing hope. But you never did, did you?"

"Your Majesty?"

The queen quirked a brow. "You have a big heart, Danisinia, but you do not hide it as well as you think. You've known Fynn was your soul bond before the attack, didn't you?"

"I—" My tongue twisted. Esmeray squeezed my hand, and I took a deep breath. "I wasn't sure, but I had a feeling."

Esmeray hummed in understanding. "Your instincts have always been beyond most, my dear. I am simply sorry that my son took so long to realize it himself." Water glistened in her eyes. She blinked, and it was gone.

Releasing my hand, she turned toward the vanity and picked up the tiara. "I wore this when I married Marc. His late father, a great metallurgist, crafted it."

I stared at the golden tiara shimmering in the sunlight. It was magnificent. Despite its age, the metal did not appear worn or tarnished.

"It is beautiful, Your Majesty."

Esmeray pushed the tiara forward. "It is yours."

I took a jilted step back. "I cannot possibly—"

Esmeray shook her head, and I snapped my mouth shut. "It is a tradition in my family that the groom's mother passes on a family heirloom to the bride to welcome them. While I do not feel that I need to welcome you into our family because you have been a part of it since the beginning, some traditions are worth keeping. May I?"

Unable to do or say anything else, I nodded.

Esmeray took a step forward and placed the tiara atop my head.

I held my breath in anticipation, but when it made contact, the tension vanished quickly. I had thought it would hurt, that the metal would feel cold, but it didn't.

Even hours later.

As it sat atop my head, pressing into my perfectly woven curls, I understood Fynn a little more.

A knock on the door pulled my attention away from the mirror. "Sylv—" I began, but I cut myself off as my gift hummed in the pit of my stomach and the soft, sweet song grew louder.

Relief washed away the tension.

"Dani?" Fynn asked from the other side of the door.

My heart thumping in my chest, I pressed my ear against the door. "What are you doing here, Fynn?"

"Sylvia said you were having some sort of"—He coughed, and I could hear the amused lilt in the noise—"meltdown?"

"I am not having a meltdown."

"But. . .?" Fynn prodded.

My shoulders sagged, the dress becoming heavier as the train turned to lead on the floor. "But I don't know what I was thinking when I agreed to wear this dress."

"What's wrong with the dress?" he asked.

"It's too—ugh. It's too much."

"So you keep supposedly saying." He chuckled. I heard him shuffle on the other side of the door, his weight leaning against it. "Dani, would you do me a favor?"

"You want me to do you a favor *now*?" I cried out, my fingers digging into the fabric. "Seriously, Fynn? I'm in the middle of having a breakdown! Do you think now is the appropriate—"

"I thought you *weren't* having a breakdown?" Fynn asked, interrupting.

I groaned.

"Go to the closet."

"What did you forget now?" My eyes rolled back, but I pushed myself away from the door. "Why do I always need to—"

"Ferrios, *please*."

With another groan, I walked to the closet, shouting at the door, "Fine. I don't know what could be so important right now that you need me to—" My words cut off as I pulled the door open.

I blinked, hand frozen in the air.

"Did you find it?" Fynn asked from the other side of the door.

My lips parted, but the words struggled to come out as I stared, mouth agape, at the dress hanging in the closet. "What exactly *did* I find, Fynn?"

"A dress."

"And what am I supposed to do with it?"

"Put it on."

"But. . ." I reached out, running a hand down the satin fabric, which was void of lace, bows, or over-the-top jewels.

"Dani, I know this isn't about the dress, but you should at least feel like yourself today. While you have been around Terin, me, and my mother long enough to understand how royalty changes things, you haven't had to experience it firsthand yet. You never asked for a crown. You never asked for a title outside of the one you have earned in the military. And you most certainly didn't ask for a big wedding—at least not one the entire kingdom was practically invited to. Neither did I, but it was the hand I was dealt. As much as I hate to say it, this wedding is not for us. It's for the people—to give the kingdom hope for better days to come. But that doesn't mean we have to change who *we* are or that you have to change who *you* are. Take off that frilly dress that Sorinia picked out and put on the one on the hanger."

"But it's—"

"Perfect? Exquisite? Everything you wanted in a wedding dress?"

"Sure, but—"

"But what? Don't tell me I actually chose the wrong dress this time."

My hand fell from the fabric of the dress hanging in the closet. Immediately, my arm brushed against the pointed jewels embroidered throughout the skirt of the one I was wearing, scratching my skin.

I sighed. "This isn't the dress of a princess, let alone a queen, Fynn."

Fynn released a heavy sigh that seeped through the door. "A dress does not dictate whether you are a princess or queen. And to be honest? I don't give a damn about what you wear as long as we walk out of the temple hand-in-hand. You are my soul bond, Dani. In less than two hours, you will also be my wife. I told you before, we could have exchanged our rings at The Splintered Oar over piss-poor ale, and I would have been happy."

"I thought you didn't like ale." A quiet hum rose in my core, the blush heating my cheeks.

"I've grown accustomed to it." I could hear his smile through the door.

I looked at the dress again. It was a simple white satin dress with a slit in the long skirt and a corset bodice. It wasn't extravagant, but it was elegant. Based on the light, flowing material, it also allowed for movement and wouldn't weigh me down, unlike the current one. The dress hung from thin, dainty straps.

The dress was perfect.

Somewhere in the castle, a bell tolled, loud and rancorous. Time was ticking.

"Are you going to put the dress on?" Fynn asked after a silent moment passed.

I sighed and lifted the hanger. "Yes, Fynn. I just have to get this one off first."

His fingers tapped along the door. "I could help with that, you know."

I smirked. "Ha. Not a chance, Nadarean. I didn't spend the last three hours getting ready for you to ruin it in five."

"Five?" Fynn asked, humor soaking his voice. "We have at least ten minutes."

"*Fynneares*," I hissed, chuckling.

"It was worth a shot." He knocked on the door, two light taps. Then footsteps sounded on the other side before I could respond.

I love you, I thought as Fynn walked away.

I love you too, Ferrios.

A wide grin split my face as Fynn's voice floated into my mind.

According to Esmeray, the new development resulted from the bond between our souls, the connection enhancing our gifts. As of right now, he could only speak into my mind. But Esmeray believed that once the vows were spoken and the rings forged from the isle were slipped onto our fingers, he would be able to mind-speak to others as well.

At first, it scared me. Having another person's voice in my head made my mind feel too small. However, Fynn had been whispering inside my head for four months now. Over the course of those months, it became a comfort I sought out often.

Sometimes, his voice was faint, little more than a whisper. But whenever he was near, it was there.

I didn't care about why Fynn could now speak into my mind. All I knew was that I never wanted to know what it felt like to be without it.

BONUS SCENE
FYNN

"I, Fynneares Andros Nadarean, offer myself to you, utterly and completely, as your husband and your soul bond," I said, my voice carrying throughout the temple as I locked eyes with Dani. "I promise to be a protector, a friend, a confidant. I promise to be whatever you need me to be. I vow to protect and cherish your heart, mind, and soul. For the rest of my days, I am yours, as you are mine." As I finished my vows, I slipped the thin gold band onto Dani's finger.

We entwined our hands, our gazes locking onto each other. The new gold band, cold only moments ago, heated as our fingers weaved together. Dani's eyes widened as the heat wrapped around our hands, down our arms, and through our bodies—a tether pulling our souls together, unifying them. A honeyed warmth spread over my skin as if the sun was beating down on us. It was a roaring fire inside a hearth on a cold winter's night. But as I looked at Dani, I knew the flame would never extinguish. The heat would never dissipate.

This was the connection between two soul bonds—an eternal flame.

I squeezed her hands. *Forever, Ferrios.*

Forever, she whispered down the invisible thread.

Moonlight poured through the castle's grand ballroom windows as I spun Dani in my arms. Laughter poured from Dani's mouth, a sweet, intoxicating sound I wished I could bottle up and savor forever.

Dani might have been panicking moments before the wedding, but those nerves no longer shone on her face as music swept through the air.

Out of everything that had been decided over the past four months, the date was the one thing I had picked. It was the longest night of the year. The night darkness swept over the lands. But when I was with Dani, I never noticed the darkness. She was my sun, even when the sun was nowhere to be seen.

The celebration was in full swing, and the ballroom was filled with friends and family. Nearby, Terin and Riley danced, whispering secrets back and forth. The usual exhaustion that colored Terin's face was barely visible tonight. Instead, only happiness crinkled the corner of his eyes. Near the musicians, Sylvia was twirling one of the backup singers, who was finally taking a break from performing. I had long since lost sight of Moris as he bounced from one woman to the next.

Past the dozens of guests, I spotted Xander and his wife twirling Dani's niece and nephew around. Earlier, I had seen Sawyer and Ambrosia sneaking away with flushed cheeks and heated gazes.

At the edge of the crowd, Dani's parents held each other, gently swaying to the orchestra. And beyond them, Airos, who had exchanged his uniform for a dark gray, tailored suit, guided my mother toward the dancing crowd.

Although Dani and I had complained nonstop about the wedding for the past four months, there was something to be said about the magic it created. Love floated in the air, wrapping a gentle hand around anyone it touched.

I pulled Dani toward me, spinning her so her back was to my chest. I wrapped my arms around her as we swayed to the sweet ballad. My jaw rubbed against her cheek, and she chuckled as my short beard tickled her.

"Having fun?" I asked, leaning over her shoulder.

"Surprisingly, yes," Dani said, leaning into me. With a hand, she caressed my cheek and then turned toward me slightly. "How long must we stay, though?"

I reached out to the invisible threads surrounding us, opening the floodgates to their minds. Their attention was no longer on Dani and I, though.

I cut off the connection and returned my full attention to Dani.

"Eager for the night to be over, wife?"

She chuckled. "Eager to take off these heels, *husband*."

Tenderly, I kissed her neck, pulling her closer to my chest.

Since the snapping of the soul bond, closing off the connection to the minds of the people around me had become easier. My head no longer ached from the hundreds of voices constantly spinning in my mind. But there was one thread I always kept within reach.

I think that can be arranged, I thought, slipping into Dani's mind with little to no effort.

Spinning on my heel, I tugged her behind me, weaving our way toward the doors.

When we broke through the edge of the budding crowd and escaped through the back doors, Dani tugged me to a stop.

"Wait," Dani said.

"Did you forget something?" I asked.

"Not quite." Dani bent down and hiked up her dress.

"Dani?" I cocked a brow.

Dani peered up at me and smirked. She then slipped off her heels and stood, heels in one hand and a mischievous glint sparkling in her eye.

I narrowed my gaze. But before I could speak, Dani thrust the shoes into my arms and took off, her bare feet slapping on the floor.

"Ferrios!" I shouted, fumbling with the heels.

"Nadarean," Dani shouted over her shoulder, "if you can't keep up, that's your fault!"

Without another word, I was chasing her.

As if we were seven and nine again, we ran through the castle halls with reckless abandonment, our laughter spilling over the music from the ballroom. We ran past guests and staff members. As we passed a pair of guards, they called out, concern flashing across their countenance.

"Carry on, fellows!" I shouted. "I have a wife to catch."

"Ha!" Dani called back from further ahead. "As if you'll catch me."

I faintly heard the guards snicker as we turned the corner.

Dani weaved through the castle halls and headed for the east wing. When she reached the winding staircase, she bounded up the steps.

I took the steps two at a time, quickly catching up to her. Once in reach, I caught her hand and tugged her to a stop.

"Hey!" Dani shouted as I spun her around.

I pressed her back against the railing and smiled down at her.

Her cheeks were flushed red, her eyes bright and wide. Stray curls surrounded her face, free and wild and beautiful.

I curled a strand behind her ear. "Hello, wife."

Suspicion glossed her face, but Dani arched a brow, wrapping her arms around my neck. "Hello, husband."

I cupped the back of her head, my fingers curling into her and pulling her closer. Dani met me halfway, standing on her toes. She tugged me down and kissed me.

I grabbed her waist and deepened the kiss. Her lips were soft; her taste intoxicating. But most importantly, she was mine.

After a moment, though, I detangled my hand from her hair and peeled away from her despite the enchantment.

"Wait, where—" Dani began, reaching for me.

I took my chance. With a wink, I ducked beneath her arms and ran.

"Did you kiss me as a distraction?" Dani shouted after me.

"What can I say?" I asked over my shoulder before turning forward. "I had to catch my breath if I had any chance of beating you." I quickened my pace.

A frustrated noise sounded behind me, and I laughed.

I didn't stop until I stormed through my bedchambers. Inside, I spun around, preparing myself for the oncoming storm as the door slammed shut. My gaze dripped down Dani's body as she stood before me, her back to the door and chest rising fast.

I curled and uncurled my fists at my side and shook my head.

We had all of the time in the world. I would not rush—

"Is there something wrong, husband?" Dani asked, quirking a brow. Her voice was airy and low as she regained her breath.

My gaze flicked up to meet hers. "Yes, in fact, there is."

I walked forward slowly, afraid I would lose control if I moved too fast.

This far from the ballroom, our labored breaths and my heavy steps were the only sound breaking through the silence. Each step I took was like thunder, cracking through the room.

Dani propped her hands on her hips. "And what would that be?"

"This dress," I said.

"I thought you liked this dress," Dani said, her head tilting as I neared.

I nodded. "I do. I love the dress. It's truly divine." I brushed my knuckles over her shoulder, then down her arm. Goosebumps ran across her skin. "But the things I wish to do to you would only ruin it."

In the faint glow of the moonlight, Dani's mouth twisted into a smirk. "Then, by all means, take it off, My King."

My King.

Those two words from her mouth sent a shiver running down my spine while simultaneously sending a wave of heat coursing through my blood.

Over the years, I had given the title of king little thought. Despite being named heir, the title of king had always felt far off, something unattainable. It was as if I knew I would never live up to my mother's rule.

But the way Dani said those two words? In that breathy, heated rasp? She made them mean something entirely different when she whispered them. Something I wanted, something I craved.

She made me want to claim that title.

She made me want to believe in those words just as much as she did.

I lifted her hand, the gold ring on her finger catching the light. I pressed a light kiss against it, and the metal was surprisingly warm against my lips. "Happily, My Queen."

Releasing her hand, I gripped her waist and spun her toward the door. My fingers lightly trailed over her arms as I made my way to her shoulders and the thin, elegant straps of her dress. I flicked the strap down, letting it drape over her shoulder. I brushed a knuckle across her skin, and Dani shivered.

"Do you need help, Nadarean?" Dani asked.

"In a hurry, are we?"

Dani chuckled, and I stepped closer.

I gathered the curls that had fallen from Dani's intricate updo, pushing them over her shoulder. I nibbled the sensitive spot beneath her ear. A small gasp left Dani's lips, causing a satisfied smirk to rise on my face. Pressing light kisses against her neck, I found the ribbons of her corset and took my time unweaving them.

With each kiss and each scrape of my teeth over that sensitive spot on her neck, Dani's chest rose higher and higher.

Once the corset was undone, Dani slipped her arms from the straps. I pushed the dress down and over her hips. The satin fabric pooled at Dani's feet with a soft thud, revealing the true goddess that hid beneath it.

Every inch of Dani was pure perfection. Over the past few months, I had spent many nights devouring and worshiping the woman before me. But tonight was different.

Tonight, the bond tying our souls together was alive and burning with an inextinguishable heat.

Dani was not just my best friend. She was my soul bond, my wife, my everything. When Dani was at my side, everything in the world felt right. When she was near, hope was not some foolish pursuit meant only for dreamers.

I brushed a knuckle down her spine and watched as her back arched. I swept my hand over the muscles, the freckles, and the jagged line that spanned her torso.

My gaze lingered on the scar. Over the past few months, it had healed nicely. However, sometimes, in the early morning hours before the sun came up, I would catch Dani inspecting it and criticizing its existence. During her first few weeks home, sorrow, pain, and regret filled her countenance whenever she looked upon it. Some of those feelings had since dissipated, but we both knew that the pain of the past might never go away.

Some days, all we could do was look to the future and hope for a better tomorrow.

Dani might have feared the responsibility of her new title, but she was the fiercest, strongest woman I knew. I had faith that no matter what she faced in the years to come, she would survive it.

Because that's who she was. She was a fighter.

And she was *mine*, and I would remind her every day just how strong and beautiful she was.

I grabbed her hands, weaving my fingers in between hers. I placed her palms on the surface of the door and brought my lips to her ear. "Now, be a good girl and keep them here."

"Is that an order?" Dani asked, peering over her shoulder with a challenge burning brightly in her heated gaze.

I smirked. "I've never known you to take orders, Ferrios."

Chuckling, Dani bumped her hips back into me. "True, but perhaps I can make an exception."

Releasing her hands, I gripped her hips. Then, without delaying any further, I was exploring her body.

I palmed her breast, the challenge blinking out as Dani leaned into my touch and tilted her head up.

As my other hand ran down her stomach, her hands remained on the door, and her nails clawed at it in anticipation. Her muscles twitched beneath my palm. I brushed a finger across her sex, and a plea slipped from her mouth. I had barely touched her, yet she was already wet.

With my lips pressed against her shoulder, I hummed. "You are a goddess among men."

I continued to work her, teasing her as I slipped a finger inside her. I curled my finger inside her, and she gasped.

Dani slapped her hand against the door, pushing her body against mine. With the other hand, she reached back and dug her nails into my hair. Her chest rose higher; her breaths came faster.

"Fynn," she begged, my name no more than a sigh on her lips.

The moment my finger slipped out, Dani turned, slamming her back against the door and tugging me closer. She clawed at my neck and head, her desire boiling over. Her lips smacked against mine.

It wasn't sweet or careful or timid, unlike many of the kisses we had shared over the past several months. It was so much more. It was everything.

She untangled her fingers from my hair and reached between us. Making quick work of unbuttoning my trousers, she tugged them down. When she released me, I moaned against her lips.

My hands slipped to her thighs. Reaching around her, I grabbed her and lifted her. Dani wrapped her legs around me. Adjusting myself, I pressed my length against her sex, and Dani tugged my hair.

"I need you," Dani said against my lips. "Now."

I answered her by slipping inside her because, at that moment, all I could see was Dani. All I knew was Dani. And hearing her sinful moans shattered my restraint.

I would never not need Dani.

She was my soul, my heart.

So, as the night carried on, I gave in to every single one of Dani's demands. There was nothing I wouldn't do for her, nothing I wouldn't give to make her happy.

Soon, her soft moans turned into screams of pleasure, and Dani and I fell apart against each other, our bodies entwined and our souls wrapped around one another.

HOW TO PLAY
FIFTEEN-HUNDRED

OBJECTIVE: BE THE FIRST TEAM TO 1500 POINTS.

You will need a double deck of cards and 2, 3, 4, or 6 players to play. If there are 2 or 3 players, there are no teams. If there are four people, each team consists of two players. If there are six players, each team consists of three players.

POINT SYSTEM:

- 3-9: 5 points
- 10s & face cards: 10 points
- Aces: 20 points
- 2s: 20 points & are considered "wild"
- Jokers: 50 points
- Queen of Spades: 100 points
- *Bonus points: if the dealer splits the deck perfectly, they earn 100 points for their team.* *

1500 is played in rounds—the round ends when one player on a team goes out (has no more cards). At the end of each round, tally up each team's points. Continue playing rounds until a team reaches 1500.

HOW TO PLAY:

1. Shuffle and split the deck. A perfect split will earn your team 100 points[*].
2. Deal 12 cards to each player. Place one card in the center to start the "discard" pile. The remaining stack of cards sits in the center facedown.
3. Each turn starts with a player either picking up a card from the deck or picking the discard pile. To pick up the discard pile, you must be able to use the top card to make a *spread*[†], using two cards from your hand (either two matching cards or one matching paired with a wild card). If you decide to pick up the card atop the discard pile, you must pick up the entire deck. The player sets down their *spreads* face-up in front of them. The player can place multiple spreads per round. To end the turn, discard a card.
4. Players continue by creating *spreads* until someone goes out. You don't need to discard a card to go out. Once someone goes out, count the points of each card. Unplayed cards are worth negative points.

---

[*] If you're playing with two people, you want to try to pick up exactly 25 cards without counting. If you're playing with three people, 37 cards. If you're playing with four people, 49 cards. If you're playing with six people, 73 cards. If you are successful, you earn 100 points for your team.

[†] A *spread* consists either of three of the same card (ex: three aces) or two of the same card and a wild (ex: two nines and a two). **You can only use one wild per spread.**

OTHER RULES

- You cannot create the same spread as another team. For instance, if the opposite team has played a spread of 3s, you cannot play a spread of three. Instead, use the other team's cards to block them from picking up the discard pile. For example, if the opposite team has a spread of 3s and you do not want them to pick up the discard pile, you can discard your 3 to prevent them from picking it up on the next turn.
- You don't need to discard a card to go out.
- You and your teammate can play additional cards to your spreads on your subsequent turns (example: if you already have a spread of five's, you can add additional five's to the pile throughout the game)
- When a player goes out, the remaining cards in the team member's hands do not count against the winning team. These cards are discarded. The team that loses will deduct the point of the cards still left in their hand from their total score.

Good luck, and remember, no table talk (unless you're playing with Fynneares Nadarean, in which case all bets are off).

Author's Note

Thank you for reading *The Heir's Bargain*! Your support means the world to me, and I hope you enjoyed it as much as I did writing it!

If you enjoyed *The Heir's Bargain*, please consider leaving a review on Amazon or Goodreads. Reviews are so important to authors and help readers find books that are a good fit for them!

When I first started writing *The King's Weapon*, book 1 in the Of Fire and Lies series, in 2022, I did not intend to write a story about Fynn. However, like many of you, I quickly fell in love with the golden retriever prince as the story unfolded. The moment I published *The King's Weapon* (and when my inbox was flooded with messages from readers, most of which revolved around Fynn), I knew his story had to be told.

Once I started writing, this desire quickly became a *need*. I found myself falling in love with Fynn and Dani's characters all over again—and more so. This story reignited something deep within me. Don't get me wrong, I have loved writing Kallie's story in the main series; however, *The Heir's Bargain* was so much fun to write. Part of me is sad that it is finished, but a bigger part is thrilled that it is because now this story is yours.

ACKNOWLEDGMENTS

First and foremost, I want to extend my heartfelt gratitude to those of you who were first introduced to Fynn in *The King's Weapon*. Your love for Fynn, the smug-always-smirking prince, was the driving force behind this book. Whether this is your first introduction to Vaneria and the Of Fire & Lies cast or you have been here since the beginning, thank you for your continued support and willingness to take a chance on me. Without your support, excitement, and enthusiasm, this story might not exist today. I am forever thankful for you.

I also want to thank several people in my life who have helped bring this book to life in one way or another.

To Gabby, who was the first person I told that I wanted to write Fynn's love story. You have listened to me talk about this story nonstop for the past year. Your willingness to be my soundboard has been invaluable.

To Jess, who helped me shape this book to the best it could be. I am forever grateful for your friendship, compassion, and ability to push me to be the best writer I can be.

To Nathan, my husband and best friend, whose undying support and encouragement knows no end. You are the reason friends-to-lovers is a trope I hold close to my heart. If our four-year-old selves could look into the future and see where we are now, I'm sure they wouldn't believe it (although you might have). Soul bonds might be a part of the fictional world of Vaneria, but you continue to prove otherwise.

Thank you to my amazing editor, Emma Jane, for always being a rock.

Thank you to my fantastic proofreader, Kay, for being the best hype woman an author could ask for.

Thank you to my marvelous cover designer, Bianca, for once again creating a masterpiece that perfectly encapsulates this book.

Thank you to the writing community for being a constant source of inspiration. I look up to and admire so many of you, and I am forever thankful for this community.

And lastly, I would like to thank my friends and family for their unwavering support.

With love and gratitude, Neena

About the Author

Neena Laskowski lives in Michigan with her husband and their two pets. She earned her Master's in Secondary Education and Bachelor's in English and Classical Studies from the University of Michigan. When she is not reading or writing about morally grey characters, you can find her camping, wine tasting, painting, or spending time with her family and friends.

For upcoming ARC opportunities and to be among the first to see cover reveals, character art, and more, be sure to join Neena Laskowski's newsletter, found on neenalaskowski.com, or follow Neena on social media.